THE POISONED SERPENT

THE POISONED SERPENT

JOAN WOLF

HarperCollins*Publishers*

HarperCollins books may be purchased for educational, business, or sales promotional use. For information please write: Special Markets Department, HarperCollins Publishers Inc., 10 East 53rd Street, New York, NY 10022-5299.

FIRST EDITION

Printed on acid-free paper.

Designed by Nancy Singer Olaguera

Library of Congress Cataloging-in-Publication Data

Wolf, Joan
    The poisoned serpent / Joan Wolf.—1st ed.
      p. cm.
    ISBN 0-06-019239-9
    1. Great Britain—History—Stephen, 1135–1154—Fiction.
  2. Nobility—England—Fiction.   I. Title.
PS3573.O46 P69 2000
813'.54—dc21   99-051770

00 01 02 03 04 ❖/RRD 10 9 8 7 6 5 4 3 2 1

FOR ALL THOSE WHO KNOW WHAT IT IS
TO LIVE WITH HEADACHES

AUTHOR'S NOTE

The language supposedly spoken by the characters in this book is Norman French. What you are reading is a "translation" into modern English.

A List of Players

STEPHEN, KING OF ENGLAND: Nephew of the previous king, Henry I, who seized the throne upon Henry's death.

THE EMPRESS MATILDA: Daughter and only surviving legitimate child of Henry I, who has challenged Stephen's right to the throne.

ROBERT, EARL OF GLOUCESTER: Oldest illegitimate son of Henry I, who has embraced his half sister's cause.

HUGH DE LEON: Nephew and heir to the Earl of Wiltshire. Foster son of Ralf Corbaille, former Sheriff of Lincoln.

GUY DE LEON: Earl of Wiltshire.

NIGEL HASLIN: Lord of Somerford, vassal of the Earl of Wiltshire.

CRISTEN HASLIN: Daughter of Nigel.

GILBERT DE BEAUTÉ: Earl of Lincoln.

ELIZABETH DE BEAUTÉ: Daughter and heiress of the Earl of Lincoln.

BERNARD RADVERS: Captain of the guard at Lincoln Castle.

GERVASE CANVILLE: Sheriff of Lincoln.

RICHARD CANVILLE: Son of the Sheriff of Lincoln.

ALAN STANHAM: Squire to Richard Canville.

WILLIAM COBBETT: Murdered groom.

WILLIAM OF ROUMARE: Earl of Cambridge and one of the most powerful men in the kingdom. Owns extensive lands in Lincolnshire and wishes to be named its earl.

RANULF, EARL OF CHESTER: Half brother of William of Roumare.

EDGAR HARDING OF DEERHURST: Saxon landowner outside of Lincoln.

CEDRIC HARDING: Edgar's eldest son.

JOHN RYE: Cousin of William of Roumare, holds manor of Linsay in knight's fee from the Bishop of Lincoln.

NICHOLAS RYE: Son of John Rye.

ISEULT RYE: Daughter of John Rye.

LORD RICHARD BASSET: Chief Justiciar of England.

A POYSONED SERPENT COVERED ALL WITH FLOWERS.

—*Sir Walter Raleigh*

THE POISONED SERPENT

1

SOMERFORD CASTLE
December 1139

Cristen was giving haircuts. She had spread a large sheet under a bench in the middle of the great hall, and a procession of her father's household knights submitted themselves to her ministrations during the course of the winter afternoon. As the last of them stood up, blowing the hair off his nose, she turned to the young man sitting in front of the large fireplace playing chess.

"You next, Hugh," she said.

Hugh de Leon ran his fingers through his hair as if to assess its length. "My hair is fine as it is," he said.

"It's too long. It makes you look untidy."

Hugh looked affronted.

Thomas, the young knight who was playing chess with Hugh, grinned. "The rest of us had to get Christmas haircuts, my lord. I think it's only fair that you follow our example."

"I hate to get my hair cut," Hugh complained. "The hair always gets under my shirt and itches."

Cristen flapped the large cloth she had been draping over the knights to keep the hair off of their clothes. "This will stop the hair from going down your neck," she promised.

"Hah," Hugh returned. "I've heard that before."

But he got to his feet and moved toward the chair,

stepping around the tufts of hair that the shorn knights had left behind.

Cristen raised her comb.

Hugh yelped. "You're not going to use the same comb on me that you just used on Lionel!"

"Why not?" Cristen demanded. "His hair was clean."

"I will get you my own comb," Hugh said.

"I'm insulted," Lionel called from the bench where he was repairing a link on his mail shirt.

"Adela always told me never to use any comb but my own," Hugh said firmly.

"Go and get it, then," Cristen said with resignation.

When Hugh invoked the name of his beloved foster mother, she knew that the subject was closed.

He returned with his comb, handed it to Cristen, and took his place on the bench. She ran the comb once through his thick, straight, ink-black hair, and then she began to cut.

"I can feel the hair going down my collar," Hugh informed her after she had been working for a few minutes.

"Be quiet," she replied sternly. "You are worse than Brian." Brian was her father's page.

They were interrupted as the door to the hall opened and the lord of the castle, Sir Nigel Haslin, came in.

"Father," Cristen said with satisfaction. "You are just in time to get your hair cut."

But her father paid no heed. Striding across the room, he was intent on Hugh, still enthroned on the haircut bench. "I've just got word," Nigel said, "that Stephen has named Gilbert de Beauté to be Earl of Lincoln."

Cristen stopped cutting.

"De Beauté?" Hugh said in surprise.

"Aye."

The two men looked at each other soberly.

Resuming her cutting, Cristen asked, "Didn't everyone expect him to name William of Roumare?"

"William of Roumare certainly expected it," Hugh said.

"The king obviously decided it was safer to split the power in Lincolnshire between Roumare and de Beauté," Nigel returned. "We can only hope that this development will not push Roumare and his half brother, the Earl of Chester, into the empress's camp."

The civil war between King Stephen and his cousin, the Empress Matilda, the only legitmate child of England's former king, had been raging since September, when she had landed in England along with her half brother, Robert, Earl of Gloucester. At the moment, the empress's party was securely in control of almost all the western lands. Outside the west, the country was weakly in support of Stephen.

"What do you know about de Beauté?" Nigel asked Hugh, who had been brought up in Lincoln.

Hugh looked thoughtful.

"Ralf thought he was a nuisance. He seemed always to be involved in some lawsuit or other regarding land."

"Hmm," said Nigel through his aristocratic nose. "Well, obviously Stephen thinks he can trust de Beauté's loyalty more than he can trust Roumare's."

"You can get up now," Cristen said to Hugh. "I'm finished." She looked at Nigel. "Come along, Father. Time to get your Christmas haircut."

Nigel sighed. "Oh, all right."

"Once Lady Cristen starts cutting, no one is safe," Brian said mischievously.

"That is right," Cristen agreed. Her large brown eyes regarded her father commandingly.

Nigel took off his cloak and handed it to his squire. "Don't get hair down my back," he warned his daughter.

"I won't," she replied.

"Yes, she will," Hugh said gloomily. "I am going inside to change my shirt."

That evening Nigel retired early to his private solar, leaving the rest of the household singing songs around the fire. He had been brooding in his large, high-backed chair for almost an hour when the door opened and Cristen and Hugh came in.

Nigel took one look at the two young faces and felt a knot form in the pit of his stomach. He knew what was coming.

"May we speak to you for a moment, sir?" Hugh said.

Nigel looked at the young man whom he had known for five months, and whom he had come to love like a son.

"I suppose so," he said heavily.

Side by side, they moved to stand between him and the glowing charcoal brazier.

"I want to marry Cristen," Hugh said.

Nigel shut his eyes. When he opened them again, he fixed them upon his daughter.

Her small, delicate face was pale. Her eyes were shadowed.

Cristen knew what he was going to say.

Wearily, Nigel rubbed his hand up and down his face.

"Hugh, if the decision were up to me, I would tell you that there is no one to whom I would rather give Cristen than you. But my daughter cannot marry without the consent of her overlord. Nor can you marry without the consent of your uncle. And I am very sure that Lord Guy will never agree to such a match."

Hugh's fine-boned face wore a look that Nigel had seen before. When Hugh looked like that, nothing on earth could move him.

He said, "If Guy does give his consent, will you agree?"

Nigel sighed. "Aye, I will give my consent if Lord Guy will give his."

Hugh smiled, suddenly looking as young as his twenty-one years. "Thank you, sir."

Nigel felt impelled to add, "Guy is not going to consent to this match, Hugh. He will want you to make a marriage that will bring more land into the family. The de Leons have nothing to gain from a marriage to Cristen. Somerford already belongs to the Earl of Wiltshire's honor."

The smile disappeared from Hugh's face. His eyes narrowed. "We shall see," he said.

Once more, Nigel looked at his daughter. His heart ached when he saw the expression in her great brown eyes.

I should have kept her away from Hugh, he thought. *I should never have allowed this situation to develop.*

But from the moment Hugh had arrived at Somerford, the two of them had been as close as two people who have known each other forever. Nigel, who was accustomed to the way people responded to his daughter, had taken too long to recognize the nature of the attachment between her and Hugh. Sometimes he thought they could read each other's minds.

"My uncle is attending Stephen's Christmas Court," Hugh said. "I will go to see him when he returns to Chippenham."

"Very well," Nigel said. Once more, he rubbed his hand over his face. "Then you may spend Christmas with us."

It was exactly a week after the Epiphany when Hugh entered the great hall of Chippenham Castle, home to three generations of earls of Wiltshire. A group of men and women were gathered in front of the immense stone fireplace, drinking wine and lounging comfortably in chairs and on benches. Noisy talk and bawdy laughter emanated from the gathering.

One of the three pages sitting on the bench along the wall close to the door jumped up and came over to the new arrival.

"My lord," he said as he recognized Hugh's face.

"Go and tell Lord Guy that I am here, will you?" Hugh said pleasantly.

The page turned and raced across the hall floor. He went up to the man who was sitting in a large carved chair close to the fire, dropped to one knee, and began to speak. Guy turned his head toward the door and waved to Hugh to come ahead.

Hugh was aware that the raucous laughter had died away as soon as he was announced. He crossed the wide, rush-strewn floor, noting fastidiously that as usual the rushes should have been changed at least two days ago. He approached his uncle and bowed his head to the infinitesimally precise degree of respect that was required.

"My lord," he said. "It is good to see you again."

Guy's startling light gray eyes, the eyes that were so amazingly like Hugh's, regarded the slim form of his nephew. "It is a cold day for a ride," he commented.

"Aye," Hugh returned agreeably. "My feet are freezing."

"Come to the fire," Guy said. "Richard, get up and give my nephew your seat."

Sir Richard Evril scowled, but he got to his feet and moved out of the way so that Guy's nephew could sit down. Hugh pushed his mail coif back off his head, baring his tousled black hair to the light of the fire.

"Pour Lord Hugh some wine," Guy said to one of the squires.

The boy came forward with a cup, which he offered to Hugh.

The entire company around the fire was silent, listening to this exchange between Hugh and Guy. Aside from their black hair and gray eyes, the two men bore little resemblance to each other. Guy's face was heavy, with broad cheekbones and a wide jaw. Hugh's bones were narrow and finely sculpted. His cheekbones were high, his jaw firm but finely modeled.

Guy was fifty-six years old and had been the Earl of Wiltshire, one of the most powerful men in the kingdom, since the death of his brother thirteen years before. Hugh had returned to the home of his birth only a few months ago, a young man without memory of his past, the owner of several insignificant manors in Lincolnshire.

Given their histories, the amazing thing was that, of the two of them, it was the younger who appeared the more formidable.

Guy turned to the blond, blue-eyed woman seated on a stool next to him. "When Hugh has finished his wine, my dear, you must show him to his room."

"Yes, my lord," replied Lady Eleanor, Guy's hostess, whom he always introduced as his cousin, but whose real position was far less respectable.

"I'm glad you have come, nephew," Guy said genially. "I have just returned from Stephen's Christmas Court, and I have something I wish to talk to you about."

"I have something I wish to say to you as well," Hugh returned.

Guy grunted. "After you have gotten out of your mail, come to my solar. We can speak there in private."

Hugh nodded, drained his cup of wine, and stood up.

Lady Eleanor leaped immediately to her feet. "I will show you to your room, Lord Hugh."

"Thank you, my lady," Hugh replied courteously. He followed the Lady Eleanor to the wide staircase that led from the great hall up to the next floor, where a group of private bedchambers were located.

Hugh was amused to note that she did not take him to the small room he had been given on his previous visits, but instead showed him to a larger chamber that had a rug on the floor and a fur cover on the bed.

"Thank you, my lady," he said to Guy's mistress.

She smiled at him, displaying a pretty dimple and stained teeth. "I will send a squire to help you disarm," she promised, and left.

Hugh dropped his mantle and gloves on the wooden chest that sat against the wall, and pulled his mail coif off over his head. He was unbuckling his sword belt when someone knocked on the door. "Come," he called, and a boy of about sixteen entered the room.

"I am here to disarm you, my lord," the squire said.

"Thank you," Hugh replied, and stood patiently while the boy undid the laces on his mail hauberk and pulled it over his head. The hauberk was made of leather, with more than two hundred thousand overlapping metal rings sewn on it for protection. Hugh had worn the hauberk as a precaution due to the unsettled times, but he had not worn either the long-sleeved mail shirt or mail leggings that he would have donned had he been dressed in full armor.

He let the squire strip him to his linen shirt and woolen leggings, then washed his face and hands in the water basin the boy had brought him. Once he was clean, he pulled his blue wool surcoat back on over his white shirt, circled it with a soft leather belt, and announced that he was ready to see Lord Guy.

The solar at Chippenham was a much larger room than the one at Somerford. The shutters were closed tightly against the cold January afternoon, and the large charcoal brazier in the middle of the room gave off a warmth that was held within the room by the tapestries that covered the walls. The room contained several handsomely carved chests and two backless benches with beautifully carved arms.

Three chairs with comfortable cushions were placed around the brazier. Seated in one of them was Guy, a fat candle burning on a small table next to him.

"So, Hugh," he said amicably as his nephew came in. "You are looking well."

"Thank you, my lord."

Hugh advanced into the room and took the chair that his uncle pointed to.

For a long moment, two pairs of light gray eyes studied each other.

Then Guy leaned back in his chair and propped his legs on an embroidered footstool. "I had an interesting time at Stephen's Christmas Court."

"Did you, my lord?" Hugh responded politely.

"It caused quite a furor, let me tell you, when I let it be known that Roger's son had been found."

Hugh said nothing.

After waiting a moment, Guy went on, "My brother's reputation as a hero of the Crusade is still cherished by the men of his generation. I was forced to listen far too many times to the tale of how he led the storming of the gates of Jerusalem."

A muscle twitched in the corner of Hugh's jaw, but again he said nothing.

Guy eyed him with a trace of annoyance. "We must make arrangements for you to swear your allegiance formally to Stephen."

At last Hugh spoke. "I am not overly impressed with the way the king has conducted his campaign thus far."

Guy scowled. "What does that have to do with anything? If you wish to receive recognition as my heir, you will have to swear allegiance to Stephen. I agree that we might have been able to accomplish more for the family by remaining neutral, but that is not how things have fallen out." Guy lifted his thick graying eyebrows. "At the moment, it is convenient to show allegiance to Stephen. That does not mean that we cannot change our minds if the times change."

Hugh's expression was unreadable. "My foster father taught me that a feudal oath is sacred and cannot be undone."

"Your foster father was not the Earl of Wiltshire and Count of Linaux," Guy retorted. "Men like us are not bound by the same laws that bind other men. Remember that, nephew."

Hugh did not reply, just regarded his uncle thoughtfully.

Guy said, "Now let me tell you of my greatest coup." He rubbed his hands and smiled with satisfaction. "Gilbert de Beauté, the new Earl of Lincoln, was at Stephen's Christmas Court. As I am sure you know, Stephen named de Beauté over William of Roumare, and with good reason. If Roumare should control Lincoln, then he and his half brother, Ranulf of Chester, would between them command an important triangle right in the heart of the kingdom. The establishment of such a power base would be just as dangerous to Stephen as the threat posed by Gloucester and the empress."

Guy's smile broadened. "But what Stephen has foiled Chester and Roumare from accomplishing, *we* may be able to achieve for the de Leons."

Hugh's eyes narrowed. "What do you mean?"

"Gilbert de Beauté has one child, a daughter. She will bring to her husband vast lands, as well as the earldom of Lincoln."

Guy's smile became sharklike. "Gilbert and I spoke extensively while I was at Salisbury. He knew your foster father and said he was very highly regarded in the shire. The foster son of Ralf Corbaille would be a popular choice for the next earl of Lincoln. The added fact that by birth you are not an insignificant Corbaille, but a de Leon, makes your attraction irresistible."

Hugh's complexion had gone very white. "What are you saying?"

"Gilbert de Beauté has agreed to a match between you and his daughter," Guy said triumphantly. "Just think, Hugh! The de Leons will control all of Lincoln and Wiltshire. And those two lordships will also give us command of a string of manors and castles that form almost a solid line between the two shires. We will accomplish what Chester and Roumare could not. It is the de Leons who will sit astride the kingdom, not Chester and his half brother!"

"And that is precisely the reason why the king will never agree to such a match," Hugh said tersely.

"He has already agreed," Guy said jubilantly. "Now that you and I have reconciled, Stephen knows that he must offer me something else to keep me attached to him. And so he will buy our loyalty with the Lincoln heiress."

A white line formed down the center of Hugh's nose as he said, "The reason I came to see you, my lord, was to ask for your permission to marry Lady Cristen of Somerford."

Guy stared at him in amazement. "You can't be serious. Where is the gain for us in a marriage to Lady Cristen? I already control Somerford!"

Hugh said steadily, "I love her."

"Great men do not marry for love," Guy snapped. "I did not think I would have to tell you that. You were born to one of the highest positions in all of England. You have a chance to make your family even more powerful than it already is. Love does not enter into the marriage of an earl. You will marry where your duty lies, as the rest of us have done."

Slowly Hugh rose to his feet. "I see," he said.

"Don't be a fool, Hugh," Guy said. He, too, got to his feet. "You must consider your own self-interest in the matter of a marriage."

"I will, my lord," Hugh said. There was a white line around his mouth as well. "I promise you that I will make my self-interest a matter of the utmost priority."

Guy looked at him warily.

"And my self-interest dictates that I marry the Lady Cristen," Hugh said.

There was a tense silence.

"Have you gotten her with child?" Guy demanded.

Hugh flushed. "Nay."

Guy took a step toward his nephew. "Then forget her, Hugh. I will never give my permission for such a marriage. It is ludicrous for you even to contemplate it! You will marry Lady Elizabeth and bring honor to your family."

Hugh said, "If Cristen was with child, then would you agree to our marriage?"

"I will never agree to such a marriage," Guy said firmly. "All such an unfortunate situation would mean is that I would be forced to find Lady Cristen a husband quickly."

Hugh said calmly, "I will never marry Elizabeth de Beauté."

Guy set his mouth in a grim line as he regarded his nephew. "I made you my heir; I can just as easily unmake you."

"And I can go to Robert of Gloucester and declare for the empress," Hugh returned. "I am quite certain that he will promise to back my claim to my father's earldom."

There was something strangely compelling about Hugh's slim figure, his glittering gray eyes. Watching him, it was easy to believe that his father had been the greatest soldier of his time.

"Don't be a fool, Hugh," Guy repeated. "You can make Lady Cristen one of your wife's ladies. You won't have to give her up."

Hugh looked at Guy, and involuntarily, Guy took a step back.

Then Hugh turned and strode out of the room.

2

LINCOLN
January 1140

Gilbert de Beauté was coming to visit Lincoln Castle, and the Sheriff of Lincoln exhorted his garrison to do its best to make a good impression on their new earl.

Lincoln was one of the new earldoms that Stephen had created since taking the throne. The king's purpose was to have these additional earls shoulder some of the burden of regional defense. In Lincoln, however, the military readiness of the shire had always been the responsibility of the sheriff. It was the sheriff who collected the royal revenues, who commanded the various fortresses and made certain they were fully garrisoned, who took charge of prisoners, who enforced the law. How the new earl would interact with him was a matter of grave concern to Gervase Canville, who had been Sheriff of Lincoln since the death of Hugh's foster father, Ralf Corbaille.

It was a cold but bright afternoon when young Alan Stanham came quietly into the spartan room on the second floor of the castle that served as the sheriff's office. The sheriff, a worried frown on his face, sat in consultation with his officer. The boy stopped just inside the door, waiting to be acknowledged.

Finally the sheriff noticed his son's squire. "Ah, Alan. What is it that you want?"

"Sir Richard sent me to tell you that the earl's party has been sighted coming down Ermine Street."

"Thank you, my boy," the sheriff replied. He turned to his officer. "Well, Bernard, time to get the welcoming party together."

"Aye, sir," Bernard Radvers said. Neither man looked particularly enthusiastic. "I will see to it."

"You may run along, lad," the sheriff said to Alan, and the youngster gratefully backed out the door and raced across the huge expanses of the enclosed baileys that surrounded Lincoln Castle. He continued along the main town road, through the Newport Arch, arriving on Ermine Street in time to join the collection of townsfolk who had gathered to watch the arrival of their new earl.

Alan was just in time. The earl's procession was coming up the old Roman road, and Alan and the rest of the crowd peered eagerly in the direction of its approach.

It was a lavish entry, led by three fully armed knights. The winter sun glinted off their helmets and mail hauberks and the gleaming coats of their sleek, well-fed horses. Alan gazed admiringly at them as they passed in front of him, their faces mysteriously hidden from the noisy crowd by the nosepieces of their helmets.

A little space behind the knights, riding in splendid isolation, came a tall, slender man on a large black horse. He wore a magnificent hooded scarlet cloak over his riding clothes, and when he saw the people lined up to greet him, he pushed back his hood to reveal a gleaming head of pure white hair. He raised a hand to acknowledge the townsfolk, who began to cheer lustily.

But not everyone was cheering. "The bastard," said a low, intense voice on Alan's right. "May he rot in hell."

Startled, Alan turned to see who had wished the new earl so ill.

The graying yellow hair of his neighbor gave his identity away even before Alan looked into the grim face. It was Edgar Harding of Deerhurst, a landholder whose property lay just to the south of Lincoln.

The Hardings were well known in Lincoln as one of the few Saxon families in the area who had retained their lands and a portion of their preeminence after the Norman conquest.

"Why, whatever is the matter, Master Harding?" said another

man, the town's goldsmith, standing on the far side of the Saxon. "Why such enmity toward our new earl?"

Harding shot an angry look at the man who had asked him the question. "De Beauté has done injury to my family," he replied shortly. "There will never be anything but bad blood between my house and his."

Abruptly the Saxon turned and began to push his way back through the crowd. Alan and the goldsmith watched him for a moment, then turned and looked at each other.

The goldsmith shrugged. "These Saxons," he said. "Do them even the slightest injury and they never forget it."

Alan gave a half smile in response, then turned back to the procession.

The three knights who followed the earl were passing in front of him now. Behind them, two more horses paced sedately abreast. Seated on a fat gray palfrey was a middle-aged woman dressed in an elaborate headdress and wearing a fur-lined blue mantle. But it was not the woman who caught and held Alan's wondering eyes. It was the girl riding next to her.

She was riding an elegant dark gray horse, sitting as light and easy in her saddle as if she had been born there. Even from a distance, Alan could see how beautiful she was. As she drew ever closer, her lovely features and fine white skin became more clearly visible. Spilling out of her fur-lined hood and falling over her shoulder was a great braid of red-gold hair.

"That must be the Lady Elizabeth, Lord Gilbert's daughter," a woman next to Alan said.

"Aye. And she's as pretty as she is rich," agreed another.

The two women on horseback passed by directly in front of Alan, and for a moment he could have sworn that the Lady Elizabeth looked directly into his eyes. He blinkled, utterly dazzled.

Her eyes were a brilliant green.

Behind the ladies came a procession of grooms who were in charge of two deerhounds and two hawks. More servants led eight fully loaded pack ponies. Bringing up the rear of the procession were three more knights.

Alan stared at the deerhounds and the hawks, and thought that it looked as if the new earl had come to Lincoln more to entertain himself than to inspect the shire's defenses.

The earl and his daughter were lodged in the bishop's guest house, while their knights and the rest of the entourage were housed at the castle.

The evening of the earl's arrival, the Bishop of Lincoln hosted a welcoming party for Lord Gilbert and Lady Elizabeth in the comfortable dining hall of the bishop's own residence.

Alan attended with his master, Richard Canville, the sheriff's only son. At a dinner such as this one, a server was required for every plate.

The tables had already been set when Richard's party arrived. Alan cast an awed look at the immaculate cloth that covered the high table. Each of the places had been set with a salt cellar, a trencher, a knife, white rolls, and a spoon resting on a folded napkin. The required basins and ewers for washing the hands were ready on a table along the wall. As most eating was done with the fingers, cleanliness was a rule strictly observed in good company.

The sheriff was to sit at the high table, but Richard was assigned to one of the trestle tables that had been set up on the floor of the hall. Alan followed his master to his seat and took up his place behind him. Shortly afterward the bishop came into the room, followed by the earl and his daughter. Once more, Alan gazed with dazzled eyes at the exquisite figure of Elizabeth de Beauté.

She wore a long-sleeved tunic of shimmering green samite. Her sleeveless surcoat was a deeper green, and lined with a rich dark fur that to Alan looked like sable. Her glorious red-gold hair was covered with a gauzy wisp of a veil.

Alan thought she was the most beautiful creature he had ever seen. The knights seated at his table seemed to agree.

"God's bones," said the man sitting next to Richard. His voice was reverent. "Will you look at that?"

"She's to be betrothed, I hear," the older man on the other side of Richard said.

Richard Canville's head swung around. "Betrothed? To whom?" A sharp surprise could be heard in his deep, mellow baritone.

"To Hugh de Leon," Bernard Radvers answered with perceptible satisfaction.

"Hugh de Leon?" the other knight, William Rotier, said. "Do you mean *our* Hugh? Hugh Corbaille?"

"At one time he was Hugh Corbaille," Bernard agreed. "Now he is Hugh de Leon."

"Jesu," said William, who had known Hugh when he was the foster son of Lincoln's former sheriff. "That boy is one lucky devil. First he turns out to be the son of an earl, and now he is to marry the prettiest girl I have ever seen."

"Not to mention the fact that she is also a great heiress," Richard said dryly. He picked up his wine cup, and Alan hastened to fill it for him. "Are you certain of this, Bernard? I have heard nothing about such a betrothal."

"I heard it just this afternoon, and from the earl's own lips," Bernard said. "He told your father and the bishop, within my hearing, that he and Lord Guy had concluded the arrangements when they met at Stephen's Christmas Court."

"Such a marriage is certainly a great achievement for the de Leons," Richard remarked. "It will give them control of Lincolnshire as well as Wiltshire."

William gave a short snort. "I wonder what William of Roumare will think about such a match."

"He won't like it," Richard replied positively. "He was furious when he wasn't named Earl of Lincoln himself. And now—to see the de Leons attaining the supremacy he and his brother hoped to achieve for themselves!" Richard slowly shook his head. "I wonder at Stephen's consenting to such a marriage. It could be the very thing needed to push Roumare and Chester into the arms of Gloucester and the empress."

"The king needs Wiltshire," Bernard replied. "Wiltshire lies on the boundary of Gloucester's territory, and Stephen cannot afford to lose it. At this point, I should think it would be more important for him to keep Lord Guy loyal than to have the support of Roumare and Chester."

Richard nodded. "That is an astute observation, Bernard."

Bernard looked visibly gratified. There was something about

Richard, young as he was, that made his approval mean something to a man.

"I wonder what Lady Elizabeth thinks of the marriage?" Richard said next.

"Does it matter?" William replied dryly. "She'll do as she's told to do." He grinned, revealing small front teeth with a distinct gap between them. "Besides, once she lays eyes on Hugh, she'll be more than happy to obey her father's wishes."

"True," Richard said with amusement.

Bernard said unexpectedly, "I wonder what *Hugh* thinks of this marriage."

"Once he meets the lady, he'll be singing hallelujahs," Richard said with a laugh.

Bernard, who knew Hugh well, sighed. "Hugh never does what everyone else would do."

"That is true," William Rotier agreed. "It's a strange thought, actually, to think of Hugh married. It's hard to picture him in relation to another person. He always seemed so . . . solitary."

"Perhaps that has changed, now that he has recovered his true identity," Richard said gently.

"I hope so," said Bernard, who had been Hugh's friend as well as Ralf's. "I hope so very much."

The bishop's dinner was a success, but the visit of Gilbert de Beauté to Lincoln went steadily downhill after that. Instead of being pleased and relieved by the obvious preparedness of Lincoln's defenses, the new earl kept calling for changes.

The sheriff struggled mightily to hold his temper as, one after another, his dispositions came under criticism. It was obvious the earl felt that, in order to demonstrate his authority over the sheriff, he had to assert his own ideas.

His own ideas were not good ones.

On the night before the de Beautés were to leave Lincoln to return to their own castle, as the sheriff was drinking a cup of ale with his son in the solar of his town house, Gervase finally exploded.

"Judas!" he said, slamming his hand down upon the table so hard that the ale cups jumped. "I'll be damned if I ruin the defenses of this shire just to placate that . . . that . . . popinjay! The only things he understands are hawking and hunting. He knows nothing at all of military strategy!"

"There is nothing more dangerous than a fool who doesn't know he's a fool," Richard agreed. His intense blue eyes regarded his father sympathetically. "What can you do?"

"I can disregard his orders," Gervase said grimly.

"That might work for a while. But what will happen when he finds out?"

Once more, Gervase smashed his fist upon the table. He shook his head in angry despair. "I cannot understand how Stephen came to appoint such an idiot earl of the shire."

Richard ran his fingers through his short, dark gold hair. "Would William of Roumare have been any better? At least Lord Gilbert will be loyal to Stephen."

"*Hugh* would be better," Gervase said emphatically. "He may be young, but he was raised by Ralf Corbaille. He understands military strategy."

Richard leaned back in his chair, stretching out his long, muscled legs. Alan was sitting by the fire, tossing a set of dice from one hand to the other and listening to the men. He looked at his master with idolatry in his eyes.

Richard was a splendid-looking young man of twenty-two. Over six feet tall, he possessed a magnificent physique, brilliant blue eyes, and strong, even features. He was a superb athlete. In addition to all this, he had never been anything but kind to the young squire who served him. Alan thought he was the perfect example of what a knight should be.

Richard said regretfully, "Unfortunately, Hugh cannot become earl unless Gilbert dies."

Gervase scowled.

Richard changed the subject. "I'm hungry," he announced. "What about you, Father?"

The dark look on the sheriff's face lightened to one of affection. "You're always hungry."

"I missed supper," Richard said with humorous vindication.

The sheriff turned in his chair to look toward the fireplace. "Alan, will you fetch some meat and bread from the kitchen for Sir Richard?"

Alan scrambled to his feet and hurried on his errand. When he returned, he placed the food in front of Richard, along with a napkin, a spoon, and a trencher.

"Thank you, Alan," Richard said with his customary courtesy, and reached for his knife to cut the meat.

He frowned as his hand came away from his belt empty.

"The devil," he said mildly. "I don't have my knife."

"You didn't lose it?" Gervase said in some alarm. He had given Richard that dagger along with his sword when he had been made a knight.

"Nay, I remember now," Richard said. "I took it off this afternoon when I went into the Minster. I put it down on one of the tables in the vestibule, thinking to reclaim it when I left. I must have forgot it, however."

One of the bishop's rules was that visitors must disarm completely before they could enter the church.

"You will be lucky if it is still there," Gervase said sharply.

"Shall I go and look for it?" Alan asked, stepping forward eagerly.

Richard frowned. "It is dark out, Alan."

"That is no matter," returned the enthusiastic squire. "It will take me less than half an hour to get to the Minster and return. I shall be glad to retrieve your knife, sir."

"Let the boy go, Richard," the sheriff said. "He's sixteen years old, not a child. And I do not want you to lose that knife. It belonged to my father before me, and I want you to be able to give it to your own son."

Richard gave Alan a rueful smile. "Very well. I didn't mean to treat you like a child, Alan. Forgive me."

Alan's return smile was radiant. "There is nothing to forgive, my lord."

"I am not a lord," Richard reminded him gently.

"You are to me!" Alan said stoutly, and went to get his heavy wool cloak and a lamp.

It was dark and cold as Alan made his way from the sheriff's town house on the Strait to the Minster, which was situated just within the castle's outer walls. The guard on duty at the castle gate grumbled, but let Alan enter when he explained his errand.

The Minster was always open to the faithful, and Alan used the glow from his dish lamp to light his way up the stairs and into the vestibule of the imposing stone church that served as Lincoln's cathedral.

There, on the small wooden table in the hall, lay Richard's distinctive dagger. Alan lifted the knife, started to slip it into his belt, then decided that first he would say a quick prayer before he returned home.

He laid the dagger back on the table and pushed open the door that led into the center aisle of the church. His attention was instantly caught by the illumination of another lamp halfway down the nave. He stopped dead, then gasped at what he saw caught in the lamplight.

Bernard Radvers, with a bloody knife clutched in his hand, was kneeling over the recumbent figure of a man.

"Who is there?" the knight demanded, squinting up the aisle toward Alan.

Alan's heart was hammering but he managed to reply with respectable steadiness, "It's Alan Stanham, squire to Richard Canville."

In the light of the lantern, Bernard's face was hard as iron. "I've just found Lord Gilbert de Beauté," he said. "He's been stabbed to death. You had better go for the sheriff."

When he was two miles away from Somerford, Hugh sent Cristen a message.

I'm almost home. Meet me in the herb garden.

He had done it once before, cleared his mind of all else and sent her the same message. Neither of them could be sure if she had heard him, but she had most certainly felt an impulse to go down to the herb garden.

A wet snow began to fall as Hugh and his escort approached the high wooden walls that surrounded Somerford Castle.

"Good thing we're almost home," Thomas said, glancing up at the heavy sky.

"Aye," Hugh replied. *Aye* and *nay* were the only two words he had uttered during the entire ride.

The gate to the castle swung open as the men on guard recognized their party. Hugh and his men clattered over the wooden bridge that spanned the moat, and rode between the gate towers into the outer bailey.

Grooms came running to take their horses. Hugh relinquished Rufus, his white stallion, to his customary groom, and without a word to anyone strode across the courtyard toward the fence that marked off the herb garden.

The escort knights he left behind exchanged a look. They had recognized the expression that Hugh had worn ever since his interview with Lord Guy, and they had been as cautious around him as men forced to walk beneath a tottering bucket of boiling oil.

"If anyone can calm Hugh down, it is Lady Cristen," Thomas said as the three knights watched him disappear through the herb garden gate.

"Judas, but he can be a touchy bastard," Lionel said fervently. Lionel had made the mistake of trying to engage Hugh in conversation on the ride home. Hugh had not answered him, but the look he had given the knight had scorched poor Lionel to his soul.

"Something happened between him and Lord Guy," Thomas remarked.

"A brilliant deduction," Reginald returned sarcastically. He scowled. "I wonder if Lord Guy has changed his mind about recognizing Hugh as his heir."

"That would be a most grave injustice!" exclaimed Thomas, who was one of Hugh's most ardent partisans.

"Justice is not often a concern of the great," Lionel commented with resigned realism.

"I wonder what's for supper," said the practical Reginald.

The three knights began to walk toward the bridge that would take them from the outer to the inner bailey, and thus to the castle and their meal.

The door to the herb shed was closed, but Hugh could see smoke from the brazier escaping out the smoke hole in the roof.

She was there.

He covered the last steps at a half run, pushed open the door, and stepped inside. Cristen was just putting down a half-filled jar of some kind of medicinal jelly, and she turned to where he stood in the doorway.

"Did you get my message?" he said shakily.

Her eyes were very large in her small face. "You wanted me to come here," she said. "I felt it." She went to him. "I also felt that things had not gone well."

He reached for her.

"Oh God," he said. "Cristen."

His arms closed around her.

After a moment, she said in an eminently practical voice, "Your hauberk is extremely hard."

His grip loosened instantly. "I'm sorry."

She leaned back in his embrace and looked up into his face. "I gather that he said nay."

"He said nay," Hugh agreed. In the light of the brazier she could see that his eyes were glittering.

"I thought he would," Cristen said.

"I have even worse news," Hugh told her bitterly. "He has made arrangements for me to marry Elizabeth de Beauté, the daughter of the new Earl of Lincoln."

Cristen's slender body went rigid.

A faint smile of satisfaction touched Hugh's mouth.

"Well, you're not going to marry her," she informed him fiercely.

Hugh's smile deepened. "Now you know how I felt about that Fairfax fellow."

After a few beats, her face relaxed and she smiled back. "I always understood how you felt about Henry Fairfax."

Without further speech, the two of them sat down side by side on the bench along the wall next to the shed door. Hugh pulled off his glove, reached out and took Cristen's hand into his bare fingers.

She rested her head against his arm. "What are we going to do?"

"We have two choices," he replied briskly. "I can go to the Earl of Gloucester and offer to join with the empress's party if he will sanction our marriage. Gloucester needs Wiltshire as much as Stephen does. Actually, he needs it more. If he proclaims me the rightful earl, he can march on Wiltshire and hope that those men who still remember my father will rise for me."

I will see the whole world go up in flames before I will lose you.

Those words of Hugh's came into Cristen's mind as she leaned against him in the aromatic closeness of the herb shed.

"And the other choice?" she said quietly.

"We can go to Keal, the manor in Lincolnshire I inherited from my foster father, and be married there by the parish priest. Keal is a nice property, Cristen. We can live there very decently."

Cristen shut her eyes. "I would live with you in a forest hut. You know that. But I do not want you to give up your heritage."

"Then I must go to Gloucester," Hugh said.

She didn't want him to do that, either.

"If you joined with Gloucester, what would happen if he decided to attack Somerford?" she asked.

He rested their entwined hands on his leg and regarded them somberly. "Your father would have to choose between Guy and me."

Cristen opened her eyes and stared straight ahead. "He has already chosen you over Guy. He did that when he brought you to Somerford and told you who you were. What you would be asking him to do would be to choose you over his sworn oath of loyalty to the king."

Hugh ran his thumb up and down the length of her small, tense hand. "Cristen, the easiest way out of this is for us to go to Keal and be married there."

"We would have to run away."

He pointed out practically, "We will have to escape from Somerford no matter where we decide to go."

She removed her head from its resting place against his arm. Her eyes were fixed on the jar she had been filling with medicinal jelly. "I feel as if I am robbing you," she said in a low, troubled voice.

At that, he swung around to face her. "Don't you understand? Nothing means anything to me if I cannot have you! You are . . . you are what ties me to life. If I lose you, I lose my very soul. It would be better for me to be dead than for that to happen."

She gazed up into his passionate face. Her lips trembled. "I know," she whispered. "Oh, Hugh, I know."

He pulled her against him and buried his mouth in her hair.

Hugh's wool cloak was rough and the mail hauberk he wore under it was unforgiving, but this time she made no complaint. Instead, she drew in a long, unsteady breath and said, "All right. We'll go to Keal."

Cristen and Hugh were forced to delay any elopement plans, however, as two days after Hugh's return to Somerford, Nigel came down with a fever. He fussed with his midday dinner, and when Cristen taxed him with his lack of appetite, he confessed to not feeling well. When she put her hand upon his forehead, it was burning hot.

Cristen put her father to bed and made a potion of borage and blackthorn bark to try to reduce his temperature.

For three days and nights, the fever held Nigel in thrall, ebbing and flowing as the herbs did their work and then wore off. As there had not been a resident priest at Somerford since their old chaplain had died six months before, Cristen sent to the abbey at Malmesbury for a priest so that Nigel could confess and be given the Last Rites.

During the days that her father lay ill, Cristen barely ate or slept. She spent all of her time sitting beside her father's bed, her beloved dogs, Cedric and Ralf, keeping vigil with her.

When he was not filling in for Nigel about the castle, Hugh sat with her as well. At times the fever subsided, and Nigel recognized the two of them, but when the fever raged he thought that Cristen was her mother.

Some hours after midnight on a frigid winter morning, the fever finally broke. Hugh, wrapped in his mantle, was dozing in a chair in Nigel's bedroom when he heard Cristen cry, "It's broken. Oh, Hugh, the fever's broken!"

Hugh came instantly awake and went to join her by the bed.

Sweat was pouring off of Nigel, drenching the sheets under him and the blankets over him.

Cristen turned to Hugh and gave him a blinding smile. "Thank God," she said. "I have been so afraid . . ."

He put his arm around her and she leaned against him. It took less than half an hour for the sweating to lessen, and Hugh lifted Nigel so that Cristen could put dry sheets under him. Then they wrapped him warmly in a wool blanket and covered him with a fur rug. They had moved a charcoal brazier into the bedroom, but the January night was very cold and they did not want him to take a chill.

Then Cristen said, "Go to your own bed, Hugh. Father is going to be all right."

Hugh refrained from pressing Cristen about their elopement, realizing that she would never leave until her father was once more hale and hearty and back on his feet.

A week went by, and Nigel was finally out of bed and sitting in front of the fire in the great hall.

Ten days after his fever had broken, the lord of Somerford was well enough to get into the saddle and ride to church in Malmesbury.

Hugh had just about decided that the time had come for him to talk seriously to Cristen about eloping, when a messenger arrived at Somerford with news that upset his plans even more thoroughly than Nigel's illness had done.

It was Sunday afternoon and the Somerford household had finished dinner and were disposed comfortably around the great hall, listening to Reginald's mellow baritone. The hall door opened and one of the knights on gate duty came striding across the floor to where Nigel, bundled in a warm, fur-lined mantle, was ensconced in a chair by the fire.

"There is a man here from Lincoln, Sir Nigel," the knight announced. "He says he is bearing news for Lord Hugh from one Bernard Radvers."

Hugh was sitting on a footstool with his back propped against Cristen's chair. He straightened up, and his black brows snapped together in a formidable frown.

"Send him in," Nigel said.

Hugh recognized the stocky, middle-aged messenger immediately. He was John Melan, a knight who had long served as one of the guards at Lincoln Castle.

John's sword clanked as he strode across the rush-strewn floor. He carried his helmet under his arm, and had pushed back his mail coif to reveal fine brown hair that had begun to recede from his high forehead.

"Hugh!" he said when he saw the object of his search. Then his face, already red from the cold, flushed even redder. "That is . . . *my lord.*"

"I think I had better wait to hear what you have to tell me, John, before I say that I am glad to see you," Hugh replied austerely.

The knight grimaced. Then he glanced around the hall at the listening household.

"I wonder if we might speak somewhere in private," he said to Hugh.

"Go into the solar, lad," Nigel recommended in a voice that had almost fully regained its strength. "You will be undisturbed there."

Hugh hesitated, then rose slowly to his feet. He did not look happy.

"Very well, sir," he said to Nigel. Then to John Melan, "Come with me."

There was utter silence in the hall as the two men began to cross the floor in the direction of the solar. Finally Cristen said gently, "Will you continue with your song, Reginald?"

"Aye, my lady." Reginald cleared his throat and picked up his place in the French love song he had been singing. After a moment, Thomas once more acompanied him on the lute.

In the solar, Hugh looked with narrowed eyes at the knight from Lincoln and, dispensing with pleasantries, said, "So, John, what is it that you have to tell me?"

The stocky knight planted his feet, looked steadily back at Hugh, and said, "I thought you should know that Gilbert de Beauté has been murdered and Bernard Radvers stands accused of doing the deed."

He had the satisfaction of seeing Hugh's eyes widen with shock. "Gilbert de Beauté has been murdered?"

"Aye, my lord. He was found in the Minster, stabbed to death. Unfortunately, Bernard was found there with him, a knife in his hand."

"Bernard would never stab a man to death in a church," Hugh said immediately.

At that response, John's facial muscles relaxed. Obviously he had not been prepared for the seeming hostility with which Hugh had greeted him.

"Of course he wouldn't," the knight agreed. "But there is no denying the fact that he was found in a very suspicious situation. As there are no other suspects, the sheriff was obliged to arrest Bernard."

Hugh looked puzzled. "What motive could Bernard possibly have for wanting to kill Gilbert de Beauté?"

John said, "He was supposed to have done it in order to help you."

The line between Hugh's slim brows sharpened. "That is ridiculous. How could the death of the Earl of Lincoln possibly help me?"

John replied stoically, "You see, my lord, it is known in Lincoln that you are betrothed to Lord Gilbert's daughter. The thinking is that Bernard killed Lord Gilbert so that, when you marry the Lady Elizabeth, you will automatically become the new earl."

There was absolute silence in the room. The afternoon light coming in the partially shuttered window glinted off Hugh's black hair. The brazier in the solar was unlit and the room was cold.

John shifted from one foot to the other, waiting for Hugh to reply.

At last Hugh said in a constricted voice, "That is ridiculous."

"Aye, my lord. It is ridiculous to anyone who knows Bernard. But you see, there are . . . other . . . circumstances."

Hugh looked grim. He gestured the knight toward Nigel's chair. "Sit down, John."

John Melan gratefully subsided into the large, high-backed chair with the lion's paw armrests that belonged to the lord of the castle. Hugh slowly took the smaller chair directly opposite that was Cristen's usual seat. "You had better tell me all," he said.

John was happy to comply. "As you know, my lord, de Beauté was only recently appointed earl, and he had come to Lincoln Castle to meet with the sheriff. However, instead of approving the sheriff's very competent defense dispositions for the shire—which all expected him to do—the earl ordered changes." His eyes flashed with anger. "If I may say so, my lord, the changes were very ill-advised. We all knew it. De Beauté may be good at bringing law-suits, but he knows nothing about military matters."

Hugh nodded, his face expressionless.

"It made us all angry—all of us in the castle guard, that is. Most of us had served under your foster father before we served Gervase Canville, and we know military matters. The new earl's ideas were foolish in the extreme."

Hugh was silent, waiting for the story to continue.

The knight's lips tightened. "The night before Lord Gilbert was murdered, a group of us who were off duty got together at the Nettle." The Nettle was the local inn most favored by the castle knights.

John gave Hugh a somewhat defiant look. "We had a little too much to drink."

Hugh's face didn't change.

John met his eyes. "One or two of the other patrons heard Bernard say that Lord Gilbert would do us a favor by dying so that his prospective son-in-law—*you*—could become the earl."

Hugh's prolonged silence made John shift uncomfortably on his chair.

"It was just the drink talking, my lord!" he said. "Anyone who knows Bernard knows that!"

Hugh finally spoke. "But the very next night, Bernard was

found, knife in hand, next to the murdered body of Gilbert de Beauté." His voice was calm and even.

"Aye, my lord," John said miserably.

"What does Bernard say happened?"

"He says that he received a message from the sheriff to meet him in the Minster, my lord. The message was delivered by one of the castle grooms."

"Does the groom corroborate this?"

"The groom can corroborate nothing, my lord. When the sheriff looked for him to verify Bernard's story, he was found stabbed to death."

An intimidating silence fell.

The knight shifted again on his seat and continued, "The sheriff had no option but to arrest Bernard, my lord. And I'm very much afraid that, unless the true culprit is found, he will hang."

Hugh asked in a neutral tone, "And what is it that you wish me to do?"

John pulled his stocky body into an erect position, lifted his chin, and announced, "I want you to come back to Lincoln with me, my lord, and save Bernard."

Hugh smiled, but it was a smile totally without humor. "That is a rather large commission."

"Your father would want you to try," John said. "Ralf had a great value for Bernard."

"Aye," Hugh returned. "I know he did."

"You should know that I have come here on my own," the knight said. "Bernard is not asking help of you; I am."

After a long moment, Hugh gave a long sigh of resignation and leaned back in his chair.

"I am flattered by your trust, John," he said mildly. "I cannot promise results, but I will go to Lincoln with you and try my best to discover who really killed Gilbert de Beauté."

John Melan grinned. "I knew Bernard could count on you, Hugh!" he said. "I knew it."

Hugh and Nigel and Cristen sat together in the solar after supper. Cristen's faithful dogs had curled up comfortably on the floor by her feet, and she absently stroked their heads.

Hugh had said nothing about John Melan's request. Now that the three of them were alone, he told them about the arrest of Bernard.

Nigel, who knew Bernard Radvers, was outraged. "Of course it is a mistake," he said. "Bernard could have no possible reason to kill the Earl of Lincoln!"

So then Hugh had to tell Cristen's father about the marriage that Guy had arranged between him and Lady Elizabeth de Beauté.

"It is a brilliant match," Nigel said slowly when Hugh had finished speaking. "It will give the de Leons complete control of two shires and partial control of several more. In one stroke, Guy will have accomplished what Ranulf of Chester and William of Roumare have been trying to do for years."

He peered at Hugh intently, trying to read what his intentions might be in regard to this magnificent marriage. Deliberately, he did not look at his daughter.

"Unfortunately," Hugh said, "the match has apparently given Bernard a reason to wish de Beauté dead. It is well known in Lincoln that Bernard was a close friend of my foster father's. In fact, before we marched north to the Battle of the Standard, Ralf made Bernard promise that he would look after me if aught should happen to him."

Hugh's face was bleak as he said these words. As Nigel and Cristen knew, Ralf Corbaille had been killed at the Battle of the Standard. It was in the aftermath of that very battle that Nigel had first laid eyes upon Hugh and marked his resemblance to the lost heir of the de Leons.

Cristen said thoughtfully, "It looks as if someone murdered Lord Gilbert and arranged to throw the blame on Bernard."

"That is certainly what it looks like," Hugh agreed.

"You had better go to Lincoln and look into the matter," she said briskly. "This knight would not have traveled so long a way to fetch you if things did not look bad for Bernard."

Hugh met her eyes, his face very somber.

She looked back, her brown eyes clear and calm. "You have to go, Hugh," she said. "You know that."

Nigel looked from his daughter to Hugh, then back again to his daughter. They were looking at each other as if he were not there.

"Perhaps you can take the opportunity to pay a visit to Keal,"

Cristen suggested. "It wouldn't be a bad idea to check on your chief manor while you are in Lincolnshire. You can make certain that everything is as it should be."

At her words, a faint smile touched Hugh's mouth. "It wouldn't be a bad idea," he agreed.

As too often happened, Nigel had the uneasy feeling that the two young people were communicating in a way that he couldn't comprehend.

He scowled and said crossly, "It's time for bed."

Two pairs of eyes, gray and brown, regarded him with tolerant affection.

"Aye, Father," Cristen said. "It is important for you to get your rest. You have still not regained all of your strength."

Nigel folded his arms and did not move. "I will go to bed when the two of you do."

Hugh got promptly to his feet. "I am going, sir. I need my rest also if I am going to ride for Lincolnshire in the morning."

Cristen came and slipped a hand under her father's elbow. "Come along, Father. I will find William and send him to help you undress."

Nigel didn't know why he felt so grumpy. "Oh, all right," he said, and stumped off to his bedroom.

Cristen and Hugh looked at each other.

Later, they told each other silently.

The dogs, who had got up when Cristen did, came to press against her skirts. She turned to bring them into the great hall, so that Brian could take them for their last outing before sleep.

4

The cold weather lifted the morning that Hugh left Somerford with John Melan. Instead of jarring their legs on iron-hard roads, the horses had to wade through a sea of mud for the several days it took for them to accomplish the journey to Lincoln.

Ever since the days when the Roman legions had ruled Britain, a city had been set on the limestone ridge where the River Witham bent sharply east toward the sea. The old Roman fortifications still formed the walls of twelfth-century Lincoln, although the Roman streets, sewers, and buildings had mostly disappeared.

As Hugh rode along the Fosse Way, his mind turned back to the time he had first come to Lincoln. He had been eight years old and running away from the men who had kidnapped him from his home. Until a few months ago, his first memory of his life had been of Ralf dragging him out of his hiding place on a bitter January night and taking him home to Adela.

On this last day of January when Hugh and John Melan rode their mud-splattered horses toward Lincoln, the weather was humid and warm, not frigid as it had been on that night thirteen years before when Ralf had rescued Hugh. And Hugh was twenty-one now, not eight. But as he stared at the towering heights of Lincoln Castle, perched so intimidatingly on its limestone ridge, he felt once again all the desolation of an abandoned child.

He still missed them. He would always miss them: Ralf and Adela, the parents of his heart.

He shut his eyes, and thought of Cristen, and felt better.

He heard John say, "We had best go to see Sir Gervase first. I didn't tell him where I was going when I asked for leave. I just said I thought I knew someone who could help Bernard."

For the first time, Hugh realized that he didn't want to see Gervase Canville. He had nothing against the man, but he didn't want to see anyone else in Ralf's place. He had not set foot in Lincoln since Ralf was killed.

He drew a deep breath and said, "Aye. It would be best to see Sir Gervase first."

Lincoln was a large city, with a population of more than five thousand people. Most of the houses the two men passed as they rode up the main street belonged to the city burgesses. At one time the majority of the houses in Lincoln had been made of wood, but a fire in 1122 had destroyed a great part of the city, and much of the rebuilding had been done in stone.

A group of boys playing in the street with a leather ball stuffed with straw caught Hugh's eye. They brought back a memory of the time when he had been part of precisely such a noisy, shouting pack of youngsters. Ralf would collect him on his way home from the castle to supper . . .

It was late afternoon and already beginning to grow dark. Hugh was sweaty and itchy and dirty and hungry, and his stallion, Rufus, was the same.

He felt a stab of longing so sharp that it was almost physically painful. If only he could go home! Ralf would see that Rufus was cared for, and Adela would fill the big tub for him, and . . .

He compressed his lips in a hard, straight line.

He had not thought it would be so hard to see Lincoln again.

Lincoln Castle had been built at the order of William the Conqueror himself. The castle was guarded most closely by a shell keep, or inner wall, constructed on top of the steep hill, or motte, upon which the castle keep was perched. Steep stairs led from the keep down to the inner bailey, a large courtyard of about six acres encircled by a second stone wall. In Lincoln this inner bailey was called the Inner bail.

The Inner bail was the heart of Lincoln's garrison. The knights who served on the castle guard lived there, housed in wooden huts. Also inside its walls were a stockade and stables for the knights' horses. All of their food, drink, and weapons were stored in this area as well.

Surrounding this military compound was the outer bailey, an immense space partly enclosed by a section of the old Roman city walls. In Lincoln this outer bailey was called simply the Bail and within its enclosure lay the Minster and the bishop's house.

Dusk was gathering when Hugh and John rode through the old Roman gate into the Bail. Hugh started with surprise at the line of merchant's stalls set up along the east wall.

"This is something new," he remarked to John. There was a faint line between his brows. "Since when have merchants been allowed in here?"

"Since about six months ago," John replied. "The sheriff had the idea to rent some parts of the Bail to local merchants. The rent they pay has been a useful addition to our defense funds."

"I see," Hugh said. But the frown did not lift from his face.

The two rode on, and reached the gate to the Inner bail, where Hugh was recognized by one of the guards on duty.

"Hugh!" the guard boomed in a voice that had to be audible clear to the castle. "By God, it's Hugh Corbaille himself! Welcome back to Lincoln! It's about time you paid us a visit."

"Thank you, Odo," Hugh replied pleasantly.

Odo's greeting acted as a catalyst for the rest of the knights in the courtyard to spin around and come running. Within a minute, Hugh found himself surrounded by a crowd of men who were all talking to him at once. He laughed and held up a hand as if to defend himself.

John Melan barked, "Be quiet and give *Lord* Hugh a chance to hear himself think."

Thus abruptly reminded of the change in Hugh's estate, from

the boy they had all seen grow up to heir to an earldom, the men did indeed fall silent. A few of them mumbled apologies.

"I am very glad to see you all again," Hugh said, and smiled.

At that, the sudden tension in the crowd disappeared. The men grinned back at him.

"Have you come to see Bernard, my lord?" a voice from the back of the group called. "You must know he is falsely accused!"

Hugh's face became grave. "I have come to see Bernard," he agreed.

Before the men could ask more questions, another voice commanded attention.

"I think it would be a good idea for you all to stand back to let Lord Hugh get off his horse."

The speaker began to stride through the crowd, and the men fell away before him, like the Red Sea parting for the Israelites.

Hugh sat on Rufus and watched the tall young man in the blue wool tunic, cross-gartered tan leggings, and soft leather boots approach. He stopped at Hugh's side and looked up. "It is good to see you again, Hugh." He lifted an eyebrow. "Or I must say *my lord*?"

Hugh looked down into eyes that were so blue, they shamed the heavens. "*Hugh* will do," he replied matter-of-factly. "How are you, Richard?"

"I am very well," Richard Canville replied. "Have you come about Bernard?"

"Aye."

Richard looked around at the men surrounding them. "Well, give Rufus into the care of these louts, and I will take you to my father."

None of the castle guards appeared to take offense at being called "louts" by Richard. In fact, a few of them actually grinned at him.

Hugh dismounted and handed Rufus's reins to one of the men, telling him, "He'll need a bath to get the mud off."

"White horses is the worst," the man said mournfully, looking at the filth that matted the hair of the stallion's legs and belly.

"See to it that he is white again the next time Lord Hugh wants him," Richard said. His voice was pleasant but unmistakably authoritative.

"Aye, Sir Richard," the knight replied.

"The rest of you may return to your duties."

"Aye, Sir Richard."

The knights began to trickle back to their stations. John Melan accompanied them, leaving the two young men standing alone in the middle of the courtyard.

Richard was the taller man, and looked down on Hugh from his superior height. "My father is in his office," he said. "I'll take you there."

"That won't be necessary. I know the way," Hugh returned.

Contrition shone in Richard's blue eyes. "I didn't mean that you needed a guide. I just meant that I would keep you company."

There was the briefest of pauses. Then Hugh said, "Thank you."

The two young men crossed the Inner bail side by side, neither of them aware of the girl who watched them from one of the tower windows.

Richard was half a head taller than Hugh, and even in the gathering dusk, his hair looked more gold than brown. The imposing width of his shoulders tapered down to a narrow waist and legs that were long and strong. His teeth flashed white in his strong, clean-cut face as he smiled down at the smaller, slimmer man who walked beside him.

From the height of her tower perch, all the girl could see of Hugh was his tired, dirty face, framed by his mail coif. Her eyes widened and she glanced once more at the splendid young man who was walking beside her prospective husband.

Then, before anyone could notice her in the window, she withdrew.

Lincoln Castle was a military stronghold. An apartment had been set aside in the upper tower for the use of the sheriff and his family, but most of the castle was, quite simply, a fortress. Hugh and Richard passed through the large empty armory hall, which was used for military exercises when the weather was too poor for outdoor practice, went up a flight of stairs, and arrived at the small room that once had been Ralf's office.

Hugh braced himself.

Gervase Canville was talking to one of his knights when the young men entered.

"Look who I've brought you, Father," Richard said cheerfully.

The sheriff's eyes, a paler blue than his son's, rested on Hugh's face. They widened.

"Hugh!" he exclaimed. "Is it really you?"

"Aye." A tense white line formed around Hugh's mouth, and he swallowed. "How are you, sir?" He remained just inside the door as if reluctant to come farther into the room.

The sheriff lifted his arms and stepped forward as if to embrace his visitor, but noting Hugh's hesitation, halted and let his arms drop back to his sides.

After a moment, he said, "I could be better. I suppose you have heard that Gilbert de Beauté was murdered?"

"That is why I am here," Hugh returned.

"That will be all, Martin," the sheriff said to the man with whom he had been talking. Then, as the knight went out, Gervase gestured Hugh and Richard to one of the benches along the wall.

The sheriff's office was as Hugh remembered it, a place of work, not of comfort. The furnishings consisted of a few wooden benches, a table upon which papers were spread, and five wooden chests containing the charters and tax documents of the shire.

Hugh sat down on the hard oak bench, and Richard sat beside him.

Without making a single movement, Hugh seemed to draw away from the man next to him.

Gervase rested his hip against the table, looked at Hugh, and shook his head in sorrow. "It is hard to believe that Bernard would do such a thing, but to all appearances, he did."

"Appearances can be deceiving," Hugh said.

Gervase sighed wearily. "These appearances were damning, I'm afraid."

Hugh didn't answer.

"Do you know the details of what happened that night?" Gervase asked him.

"I know what John Melan told me," Hugh replied. "Is there aught that John doesn't know?"

Gervase's strongly marked brows lifted in sudden enlightenment. "*You* are the man whom John went to fetch!"

"Aye. He came to Wiltshire to seek me out." Hugh shrugged. "I could not refuse to come. Ralf always thought very highly of Bernard."

"As do I," Gervase said crisply. "He is an excellent officer. I do not want to lose him."

"Is it possible for me to see him?" Hugh asked.

"Of course." The sheriff's eyes moved from Hugh's mud-stained boots and leggings to his tired, mud-smeared face. "Where are you staying? At Ralf's town house?"

"*No.*"

Hugh took a deep breath. The word had come out too loudly. "The town house has been closed up since Ralf's death," he went on more quietly. "I thought I might be able to stay at the castle."

"I would be happy to offer you the sheriff's apartment, but I'm afraid it is already occupied," Gervase said regretfully. "Lady Elizabeth de Beauté has insisted upon remaining in Lincoln until we have convicted her father's killer, and I had to take her off the bishop's hands."

An unidentifiable emotion flickered in Hugh's light eyes. "Lady Elizabeth is still here?"

"Aye," said Richard. A hint of admiration colored his voice. "She is here and she is determined to see that justice is done."

"I understand that you are betrothed to the girl," Gervase said.

His voice clipped, Hugh replied, "Your understanding is incorrect. My uncle made the arrangement before he consulted me."

Richard's head turned suddenly, and he looked at Hugh.

Gervase's eyes narrowed. "Gilbert de Beauté told me that the match was settled."

The white line was back around Hugh's mouth. "It was not agreed to by me."

There was a brief silence as father and son continued to look at Hugh.

Then Gervase said, "Well, we in Lincoln were certainly under the impression that the match was a settled thing. I know Bernard thought so, and that, of course, is what gives him a motive for wanting to do away with Lord Gilbert. All do know how close Bernard was to Ralf, and all do know that he would prosper if you became the Earl of Lincoln. It was to his advantage that Lord Gilbert should die."

"If that was indeed his thinking, then surely Bernard would have been wiser to wait until after the wedding," Hugh returned.

"Perhaps," Gervase agreed. "But it would also have been more obvious if de Beauté died after the wedding. As it stands, no one would have suspected Bernard at all had he not been caught leaning over the body, murder weapon in hand."

Hugh turned to Richard. "I understand Bernard was discovered by your squire."

"That is correct," Richard replied.

"I would like to speak to him."

"Of course."

Stone-faced, the two young men eyed each other. Then Hugh returned his gaze to Gervase. "And now, sir, if you don't mind, I should like to speak to Bernard."

"You look exhausted, lad," the sheriff said gently. "Are you sure you wouldn't like to wait until tomorrow?"

Hugh shook his head.

"Very well." The sheriff pushed his hip away from the table and stood upright. "I will have a guard take you to him. He is here in the castle, in one of the cells."

Hugh stood up also, his face somber.

Gervase said kindly, "When you are finished talking to him, return here. Richard and I have a town house on the Strait. You can stay with us while you are in Lincoln."

"You don't have to house me, sir," Hugh said. "I can lodge at an inn."

Gervase said emphatically. "I refuse to send Ralf's son to an inn. You will stay with us."

A second before his silence became so drawn out that it would seem rude, Hugh said, "Thank you."

Gervase escorted Hugh into the hall and signaled to a guard. Within a minute, Hugh found himself descending the stone stairs that led down into the dungeon of the castle, where accused criminals were kept.

5

Bernard Radvers was confined in one of the castle's least noxious cells. It had a high window that allowed a small amount of light and air to enter, and the straw pallet that served as his bed was decently provided with two wool blankets. There was a also a chest and a single stone lamp, which had been lit against the gathering darkness.

No amenities, however, could disguise the fact that this was a small, cold, stinking cell, and that it would be Bernard's last habitation on this earth unless someone else was convicted of the murder of Gilbert de Beauté.

"Hugh!"

Huddled in one of his blankets, Bernard was sitting on the chest, which provided the cell's only seating other than the bed. His broad, middle-aged, weather-beaten face was filled with astonishment as he regarded the young man standing in the cell doorway. "What are you doing here?"

"I've come to see you, of course," Hugh replied.

"Just call out when you want to leave, my lord," the guard said to Hugh before he backed out into the passage. He closed and locked the heavy, partially barred wooden door behind him.

Hugh looked at his father's old friend and said in mock exasperation, "Aren't you growing a little old for this sort of trouble, Bernard?"

At that, Bernard's face lit with a huge smile. He got

up from the chest, shed his blanket, and enveloped Hugh in an enormous hug.

The young man stood patiently, allowing himself to be embraced. When Bernard finally stepped back, Hugh let his eyes run up and down the length of the imprisoned knight.

"You look thin," he said. "Aren't they feeding you in here?"

Bernard grimaced. "Aye, they feed me. But my appetite isn't quite what it used to be. I've a lot on my mind these days."

Hugh continued to regard him appraisingly. "Might one of the things on your mind be an idea of who actually killed Gilbert de Beauté?"

Bernard let out a long, hissing breath. "I have had some thoughts on the subject."

Hugh gestured to the chest. "Do you mind if we sit down?"

Bernard frowned. "Of course not, lad. You look weary." For the first time, he appeared to notice that Hugh was dressed in mail. "Did you just arrive in Lincoln?"

"Aye." Hugh crossed to the chest, removed the lamp that was perched on one side of it, and sat down. He pushed his mail coif off and ran his fingers through his matted-down hair. Then he rubbed his neck as if it ached.

Bernard watched him. "You should have waited before you sought me out," he scolded. "You need a bath and a meal."

A glimmer of amusement showed in Hugh's gray eyes. "You needn't sit next to me if you find my smell offensive."

Bernard wrinkled his nose in disgust. "No smell can be as offensive as the odor of this stinking dungeon."

Hugh's elegant nostrils pinched together. "I have been trying not to inhale too deeply."

Bernard grinned, reminiscing. "Ralf used to say that if ever Adela found her way down here, she would make him have every inch of the dungeon scoured with lye soap."

Hugh smiled faintly. "That would certainly have made your stay more pleasant."

Bernard joined him on the bench, the smile dying away from his face. "Have you heard that they found me clutching the murder weapon?" he asked.

"Aye," Hugh replied grimly. "And I also heard of the very unwise words you apparently let drop at the Nettle."

Bernard groaned.

Hugh said, "I want you to tell me everything you know. I want to hear everything that happened from the time that Gilbert de Beauté first entered Lincoln until the moment you found him dead in the Minster."

The cell was so cold and damp that their breath hung in the air. Bernard coughed and lifted the rough wool blanket to drape once more around his shoulders.

"The visit actually started out well enough," he began, and then went on to tell Hugh about the bishop's dinner to welcome the earl and his daughter, and about the various hunting parties in which both the earl and the sheriff had taken part.

"The trouble began when de Beauté began to criticize Gervase's military preparedness," Bernard continued. He spoke in some detail about the defenses Lord Gilbert had proposed to supersede the ones that the sheriff had put in place.

Hugh listened in silence.

Bernard said disgustedly, "It was clear to all of us at the castle that the earl was trying to show that he had more authority than the sheriff. There is not a single thing wrong with Gervase's military dispositions."

He gave Hugh a sober look.

"He's a good sheriff, Gervase Canville. He's not Ralf—there could never be another Ralf—but he knows his job, and he executes it with judgment and intelligence."

Hugh's eyes were focused on his ungloved hands, which rested loosely on the skirt of his mail hauberk. He didn't reply.

After a moment, Bernard began to recount the story of the night Gilbert de Beauté was killed.

Toward the end of his recitation, Hugh interrupted him with a question. "The message that supposedly came to you from the sheriff was verbal, not written?"

"Aye. It was brought by William Cobbett, one of the castle grooms. He told me that the sheriff wanted me to meet him in the Minster two hours after evening services were done."

"Didn't you think such a request was rather strange?"

"I thought it was very strange," Bernard replied frankly. "But the groom could tell me no more."

"Did you ask the groom if he had received the message from Gervase directly?"

"I didn't think to ask him," Bernard replied. "At the time, I didn't think it was important." He rubbed his forehead. "It's important now, of course, because Gervase claims he sent no such message."

Hugh drummed the fingers of his left hand with slow deliberation on the overlapping metal circles of his hauberk skirt. "So what we can assume, then, is that someone deliberately set out to lure you to the Minster at that particular hour."

"It certainly seems that way," Bernard agreed. He coughed again. "What I don't understand is *why* I was sent there."

Hugh turned to look at him, eyebrows lifted. "Surely that at least is clear. You were meant to take the blame for de Beauté's death."

"I don't know if that is the case," Bernard returned slowly. He shifted a little on the chest, as if trying to get more comfortable. "You must understand, Hugh, that it was a complete accident that Richard's squire should have found me the way he did. Richard had sent the boy to the church to retrieve his dagger, which he had left in the vestibule. The boy had no reason at all to come inside the church. He was supposed to collect the knife and return home."

"Why did he go into the church?"

"Apparently he decided that, since he was there, he would stop and say a quick prayer." Bernard frowned. "I have been thinking about this, and it seems to me that if someone went to such trouble to get me to the Minster at that precise hour, he would have made a more foolproof arrangement to ensure that I was discovered."

Hugh continued to look at Bernard. "Perhaps he did make such an arrangement, and the squire foiled it by appearing when he did. I rather think that if the boy had not turned up, someone else would have come into the church to find you."

Once more, Bernard rubbed his forehead. "Perhaps that is so. On the other hand, perhaps I was only meant to discover de Beauté's body and sound the alarm. Perhaps it was purely an accident that I came to be suspected of the murder myself."

"That is a possibility, I suppose."

Hugh did not sound convinced.

He returned his gaze to his hands and stared at them intently. "Let us assume for the moment that you were meant to be found and blamed for the murder. In order to make you appear a likely culprit, a motive was needed. Do you know who first advanced the notion that you killed de Beauté in order to facilitate my claiming the earldom?"

Bernard shook his head. "I don't know whose idea it first was," he said. "But I can tell you that within hours of the murder, it was going around the castle like wildfire."

There was a long silence. Then Hugh leaned his head back against the stone wall and half closed his eyes. "There is one key question we must ask ourselves in all this. Who profits by the death of Gilbert de Beauté?"

Bernard stared at Hugh's perfectly chiseled profile, and did not reply.

Hugh answered his own question. "The most obvious person, of course, is the sheriff himself. With de Beauté dead, he no longer has to worry about eviscerating the shire's defenses."

From the look on Bernard's face, it was clear that he had thought of this, too. "I can't believe it," he said. "Gervase is not the sort of man who would stoop to such treachery."

"If it was possible to tell what a man was capable of from his outward guise, we could dispatch with all evildoers before they act," Hugh said practically.

Bernard blew through his nose and mumbled a reluctant agreement.

"Gervase had the motive, and he had the opportunity," Hugh said. "He is one of the few people whom de Beauté would go to meet in the Minster. And let us not forget that it was a message from Gervase that put you into the unfortunate position in which you now find yourself."

"I know," Bernard said unhappily.

"So then, we must consider Gervase as a likely suspect." Hugh's eyes were still half-shut. "Who else besides the sheriff might profit from de Beauté's death?"

"I have been thinking and thinking, and I can't come up with anyone else," Bernard admitted.

"I can," Hugh said.

A cold wind blew in the open window, and Bernard coughed and clutched his blanket tighter. "Who?" he demanded.

Hugh opened his eyes and turned his head so that he could look directly at Bernard. "While he was in Lincoln, Gilbert de Beauté raised *two* issues that were sure to upset the political power base of the shire," he said. "The first we have discussed—his challenge to the sheriff's authority."

"And the other?" Bernard demanded when Hugh did not immediately continue.

Hugh's eyes were level and unreadable. "He announced that he was going to marry his daughter to the heir of the de Leons."

For a long moment, Bernard stared at Hugh. Then he said incredulously, "Are you saying that *you* have a motive?"

Hugh smiled. "Not me, Bernard. William of Roumare."

"Roumare!"

"Aye. For years William of Roumare and his half brother, the Earl of Chester, have planned to bring Lincolnshire within the circle of their control. Roumare owns vast estates in the shire and he fully expected to be named Earl of Lincoln. Stephen infuriated him when he named Gilbert de Beauté over him."

"He named Roumare Earl of Cambridge," Bernard pointed out.

"He tried to placate Roumare by giving him Cambridge, but Roumare has no lands in Cambridgeshire. His power is in Lincolnshire, and it is Lincolnshire that he wants. His half brother Ranulf commands all of Chester, as well as controlling a string of estates and castles that run along the line of the Trent right into Lincolnshire." Hugh's eyes narrowed slightly. "The aim of the brothers has always been to seize dominion over this entire part of the kingdom."

Bernard blinked twice, trying to assimilate what Hugh was telling him.

Hugh thrust his fingers through his hair, which had fallen across his dirt-streaked forehead. He went on, "Then my uncle stepped in and won for the de Leons the power that Roumare and Chester had hoped to win for themselves."

"Your marriage to the de Beauté heiress," Bernard said slowly.

"Aye," Hugh agreed. "My marriage to the de Beauté heiress. With that accomplished, Guy would have Wiltshire, and I would be in position to inherit Lincolnshire. The de Leons, not the brothers

Chester and Roumare, would be the ones to control the crucial heart of England." Hugh's voice became very dry. "I doubt that this prospect made either Ranulf or William very happy."

Bernard's brow was deeply furrowed. "Do you think that Roumare and Chester might be involved in de Beauté's death?"

"I think it is extremely likely," Hugh replied. "The time frame certainly fits. Less than two weeks after de Beauté revealed the marriage arrangement, he was murdered. The result of his death is that the earldom is empty, the wardship of the Lady Elizabeth passes to the king, and the de Leons are cut out of Lincolnshire."

"Why shouldn't the marriage go forward?" Bernard protested. "After all, the king approved the match between you and the Lady Elizabeth."

"He approved it when her father was alive and the king wanted to keep him happy. With de Beauté dead and his daughter unmarried, Stephen is free to name anyone he wants to be the new Earl of Lincoln. He can still honor his word to Guy and give me the lady in marriage, but the earldom does not have to go along with her. Stephen might very well decide that it would be wisest to give it to William of Roumare after all."

"Jesu," Bernard said slowly. "I never thought of that."

Hugh nodded. "It would not have been difficult for Roumare to find someone to kill de Beauté for him. As I said before, he has vast estates in Lincolnshire. There are many men who would find it profitable to do him a service."

"It would have to be someone whose presence inside the castle walls would not be questioned," Bernard said. "I have thought about this, and no stranger would have been allowed to remain after the gates were closed. Nor would the guards admit anyone who could not demonstrate legitimate business within."

Hugh nodded.

"I simply cannot believe that it could be one of the castle guards," Bernard said stubbornly. "I have served with all of them for years and I would swear that they are honest."

"Perhaps that is true of the regular garrison," Hugh said. "But what about the men who are serving out their knight's fee?"

Hugh was referring to the fact that the Bishop of Lincoln owed knight service to the king, and to fulfill this duty, he awarded the

use of lands he owned to certain chosen knights. The knights paid
for these lands by performing a month of guard service at Lincoln
Castle.

Bernard's breath wheezed audibly and he said, with a trace of
excitement in his voice, "John Rye has been with the garrison this
month. He has a manor north of Lincoln Fields, which he holds in
knight's fee from the bishop. I believe I heard somewhere that he is
a cousin of William of Roumare."

The two men looked at each other.

"Is this John Rye still at the castle?" Hugh asked.

Bernard frowned. "This is the last day of January. His term of
service should be up tomorrow."

"I will make sure I speak to him before he leaves," Hugh
promised.

Bernard heaved a huge sigh before saying gruffly, "I thank you
for coming, lad. It is good to know that you believe in me."

Moving slowly, Hugh stiffly got to his feet. "Your men in the
castle guard believe in you, too, Bernard. It was John Melan who
came to fetch me, you know."

Bernard looked pleased. "Did he, now? I have wondered why
John has not been to see me."

Hugh headed toward the door. "Keep on thinking about this,
and if you come up with any other suspects, let me know."

Bernard stood up as well. "I will do that."

At the door, Hugh turned around. He seemed to hesitate, then
made up his mind. Holding himself very erect, he said, "What about
Richard?"

"Richard?" Bernard was clearly startled. "What on earth would
Richard have to gain by the death of Gilbert de Beauté?"

"He has a stake in seeing that his father retains his power as
sheriff. And it was his squire who found you in the Minster."

Bernard looked very grave. "I thought that old childhood
rivalry between you and Richard would be over, now that you both
have grown up."

Hugh replied in a voice that was carefully contained. "This has
nothing to do with any supposed childhood rivalry. The fact of the
matter is, it was Richard's squire who found you. And Richard could

easily have given the groom a message for you saying it was from his father."

Bernard took a few steps forward and held Hugh's eyes with his own steady gaze. "Do you really think that Richard would kill an earl, not to mention that poor groom, because he was afraid Gervase might lose some of his power as sheriff? Richard has a bright future in front of him, Hugh. All do know that. He is far too intelligent to endanger that future in such a clumsy manner."

Hugh didn't reply, but his gray stare was defiant.

Bernard shook his head in bewilderment. "For some reason, you and Richard don't like each other. You have never liked each other. Or perhaps I should say that you don't like Richard. It has always seemed to me as if Richard would like to be friends with you."

"Our personalities do not mesh," Hugh said abruptly.

"That may be so, but do not let your dislike trick you into seeing things that aren't there," Bernard said.

For a moment, Hugh remained perfectly motionless. Then he nodded. "Fair enough."

He turned away to face the barred window in the door and called for the knight on guard.

"Where are you staying?" Bernard asked while they waited for the guard to open the door.

A half-rueful, half-amused look came over Hugh's face.

"With the sheriff," he said.

The key sounded in the lock and the heavy door swung open.

"Ready to leave, my lord?" the guard asked.

"Aye," Hugh said. He looked back at Bernard. "I will be back."

"Good hunting, lad," the prisoner returned. "And thank you."

6

Alan quietly entered the bedroom where his master's guest was soaking in the portable wooden bathtub that had been set up under a canopy to help hold the heat.

"Sir Richard sent me to assist you, my lord," he said.

The wet black head turned toward him.

Alan, like almost every other soul in Lincoln, knew all about the boy who had grown up in town as the foster son of the sheriff and who amazingly had turned out to be the missing son of the Earl of Wiltshire. So now he looked with hidden but intense curiosity at the face that looked back at him.

It was a startlingly beautiful face. Alan stared at the light gray eyes, the thin straight nose, the high cheekbones, and severely beautiful mouth, and felt his eyes widen.

A clear, level voice said, "You can hand me that towel, if you would."

Alan stepped forward hastily and brought the towel to the young man in the tub, who rubbed his wet hair with it and then stood up, wrapping it around himself. Deftly avoiding the canopy, he stepped onto the small rug that had been placed next to the tub.

A charcoal brazier had been lit, but the room was still cold. Lord Hugh looked at Alan. "I should like to get dressed quickly," he said.

"Of course, my lord!" There were two piles of clothes

in the room, a heap of muddy ones on the floor beside the tub, and a clean, folded set on top of the chest. Alan went to the neatly folded pile and picked it up.

He began by holding out a pair of linen drawers, which Hugh stepped into and tied at his waist. Then Hugh donned an exquisitely embroidered long-sleeved white shirt. Long hose came next, attaching to the string that held up the drawers, and then, over the shirt, a long-sleeved green wool tunic, which Hugh fastened at his neck with a plain gold brooch. The tunic came to just below the knees and was embroidered along the hem.

When Alan served his own lord, Richard always talked to him, making the squire feel as if he were a friend, not merely a faceless attendant. But Lord Hugh was silent, appearing to be preoccupied by his own thoughts. He hardly glanced at Alan.

Once the brooch had been fastened, Alan handed Hugh a soft leather belt, which he buckled around his waist. Next came a sleeveless blue surcoat, which was lined with lambskin, not fur.

Alan was a little surprised by Hugh's clothes. They were of good quality, and well made, but they were far from new. Somehow, they were not the kind of garments that Alan expected to see the heir to an earldom wearing.

Of course, Alan thought, Hugh had not held that position for very long. Probably he had not yet had the chance to acquire a new wardrobe.

Still wrapped in silence, Hugh sat on a chest so that Alan could cross-tie his hose. Then he slipped his feet into the pair of soft, low boots that Alan knelt before him to put on. The squire buckled them securely.

In all of this time, the only words Hugh had spoken were to ask for a towel and to express a desire to dress quickly.

Alan, who had been spoiled by Richard's very different treatment, was a little put out. He straightened up from his kneeling posture and said steadily, "Will that be all, my lord?"

Finally Hugh looked at him. Alan thought that he could almost see the preoccupation lift from the dark-fringed gray eyes. It was as if Hugh were seeing the squire for the first time. He smiled and said, "Thank you. You are very efficient."

Pleasure out of all proportion to the measured words flooded through the young squire. He found himself smiling back. "Thank you, my lord."

"Are you the boy who found Bernard Radvers in the Minster with the body of Gilbert de Beauté?" Hugh inquired.

Alan's smile died. "Aye, my lord."

"That must have been quite a shock," Hugh said.

"Aye, my lord, that it was," Alan returned fervently.

Hugh walked over to the room's one small table, picked up his knife, and thrust it into the holder that hung from his belt.

"Did you actually see Bernard in the act of stabbing the earl?" he asked, turning once more to face the squire.

"Nay, my lord," Alan replied. He stood erect, with his arms hanging stiffly at his sides. "I never said I saw that. What I saw was Bernard leaning over the earl. The earl was already dead when I came into the church."

"How do you know that?"

For some indefinable reason, Alan felt he had been put on the defensive. He lifted his chin a little as he answered. "I know it because Bernard told me that Lord Gilbert had been murdered and that I should send for the sheriff. And I came close enough to see Lord Gilbert's body for myself, so I knew that what Bernard said was true, my lord."

Hugh nodded and regarded Alan thoughtfully. "What did you think had happened?"

"I did not know what had happened, my lord, but Bernard was holding a knife in his hand, and the knife had blood on it."

"Did you think that Bernard had killed the earl?"

"I thought he might have, my lord," Alan replied deliberately. "But, as I have already said, I didn't see him do it. I only saw him kneeling there."

Hugh nodded gravely. "I see."

His gray eyes studied Alan for a moment in silence. Alan stared back at him a little defiantly. He felt as if he were being interrogated, and he did not like the feeling. He was also slightly intimidated, which he liked even less.

Hugh said, "I have known Bernard Radvers for almost all my life, and I cannot and will not believe that he has done this thing of which he stands accused. I have come to Lincoln to see if I can discover the real culprit. I would be grateful if you would tell me anything you know that might have a bearing on this business."

Alan said stiffly, "I know nothing except what I have already told you, my lord."

Hugh looked as if he did not believe him. "I see. Well, if you should think of anything, or hear anything, I hope you will come to me."

"Of course, my lord," Alan said, even more stiffly than before.

An oddly bleak look came across Hugh's face. "And now," he said, "I suppose I had better join the others."

"I believe they are waiting supper for you, my lord," Alan said.

"That was kind," said Hugh, but he did not sound as if he meant it.

Gervase Canville's town house was one of the newer stone buildings in Lincoln. It was two-storied, and boasted one attic window in its steeply pitched roof. The street door was on the ground floor, which contained the kitchen and the storerooms. The main living room, the solar, was on the second floor, and featured a fireplace built into the wall immediately over the front door. The smoke from the fireplace escaped through flues fashioned to come out on each side of the outside buttress.

Along with other furniture, the room contained a table with four carved chairs set around it. It was at this table that Alan served supper to the sheriff, his son, and his guest.

Gervase had owned the house for less than a year and he was exceedingly proud of it. Alan suspected that he had invited Hugh to stay in order to show off his house to the prospective earl.

Supper was a simple but ample meal. Alan was surprised by how abstemiously Hugh ate. It was almost rude, the squire thought disapprovingly, to eat so little when so much was provided.

The meal only served to confirm Alan's earlier unfavorable impression of Hugh de Leon. Most particularly, the squire did not care for the way Lord Hugh treated Sir Richard. The sheriff's son spent the entire evening going out of his way to be friendly and courteous, and instead of responding in kind, Lord Hugh was close-mouthed and chilly.

As he was undressing Richard for bed later that night, Alan commented tentatively, "Lord Hugh is not very talkative, is he, my lord?"

Richard gave his squire a charming, rueful look. "He has never talked very much to me, I'm afraid."

"Why is that, my lord?" Alan asked in genuine bewilderment.

Richard smiled and reached out to tousle Alan's flaxen hair. "Not everyone thinks I'm as wonderful as you do," he said with amusement.

"They certainly do, my lord!" Alan replied immediately.

Richard shook his head. "Hugh and I have known each other since we were children together at the Minster school. For some reason, I think he has always seen himself as being in competition with me. *He* was the sheriff's son then, and he thought he should be better in everything than everyone else. He did not like it when anyone bested him."

Alan slid Richard's shirt off his shoulders and looked with pride at the half-naked body of his lord. No one was as splendid as Richard, he thought. Why, Hugh was not much taller than Alan himself. Next to Richard, Hugh looked small.

He nodded wisely. "I see."

"The annoying thing is that I like Hugh," Richard said. "I have always wanted to be friends with him. But he holds me at a distance. He always has."

Alan folded Richard's shirt and put it down on a chest. He picked up a fur-lined bedrobe and said, "He is jealous of you, my lord."

"He has no cause to be," Richard said. "Hugh is extraordinarily competent at everything he does. And he is an earl's son! He certainly has no reason to envy me."

"Anyone would envy you, my lord," Alan said with absolute conviction.

Richard laughed. "Yours is hardly an objective opinion, Alan."

The squire held up the bedrobe for Richard to slip his arms into. "He asked me a lot of questions about that night in the Minster," he said with a troubled frown.

Richard nodded serenely. "He asked me if he might talk to you and I said that he could."

Alan's brow cleared. As the evening had progressed, he had begun to wonder if he should have talked to Hugh at all. Although, to be truthful, there was something about the earl's son that made it difficult for Alan to picture refusing him.

"He told me," said the young squire, "that he doesn't believe Bernard is guilty, my lord. He said that he is going to look for the real murderer."

Richard tied the sash of his deep blue robe. "I hope he does find someone else. I would hate to see Bernard hang."

Alan picked up Richard's boots to take them to the kitchen to clean. "Do you believe Bernard did it, my lord?"

Richard's face was sober. "I don't want to believe it but, unfortunately, I haven't been able to think of anyone else to put in his place."

Alan clutched the boots. "I think he did it, my lord. He was kneeling right over the earl. And he was holding the knife!"

Richard sighed. "I know, Alan. I know."

He looked tired, and Alan thought with sudden contrition that he was keeping Richard up with his chatter. "Is there aught else I can do for you, my lord?"

"No, thank you, Alan. I will wish you good night."

"Good night, my lord," Alan replied, bowed, and withdrew to go and clean Richard's boots before seeking his own bed in the attic.

There was frost on the ground the following morning. The warm spell had snapped during the night, and the ground was once more frozen and hard.

Hugh broke his fast in the room where he had eaten supper the previous night. Once again, the only others at table were Gervase and Richard. As had been the case in Ralf's town house, the rest of the household took their meals in the kitchen.

Gervase's house was much larger than Ralf's town house had been, however. The number of rooms was the same, but the Canville rooms were more than twice the size of those in the house where Hugh had grown up.

In truth, Hugh was a little surprised to see how very well Gervase seemed to live. He had always thought that the Canvilles inhabited the same social and economic level as the Corbailles. Like Ralf, Gervase owned several manors within the shire, which had been given to his father by the old king, Henry I. And like Ralf, Gervase swore his feudal oath directly to the king himself.

When Ralf had died, leaving only one foster son who was just twenty, Gervase had been the most likely candidate to become the new sheriff.

Hugh had always assumed that Ralf and Gervase were as similar in terms of wealth as they were in everything else. But Ralf could never have afforded this house.

"What are you planning to do today, Hugh?" Gervase asked as the men ate their bread and drank their morning ale.

Hugh planned to try to catch John Rye before he left Lincoln, but he did not wish to impart this fact to Gervase. He said instead, "I thought I would talk to the garrison guards."

"I have already questioned them thoroughly," Gervase said. "They don't believe Bernard is guilty, but they have nothing substantial to advance that would advocate in his favor."

"Well," Hugh said mildly, "at least talking to them will give me a chance to renew old acquaintances."

There was a moment of tense silence.

Then Gervase shrugged. "Oh, talk to the guards if you will. Just make certain that you let me know if you unearth some important fact that I might have missed." There was the faintest trace of sarcasm in his voice.

"Of course," Hugh replied gravely.

"When do you plan to meet with the Lady Elizabeth?" Richard said.

Hugh had been reaching for his ale cup, but now stilled his hand. "Why should I wish to meet with the Lady Elizabeth?"

Richard's blue eyes regarded him with a mixture of amusement and exasperation. "Good heavens, Hugh, the girl thinks she is betrothed to you! Surely, under the circumstances, she deserves that you at least meet with her."

A sharp line appeared between Hugh's black brows. "I was never betrothed to her. No marriage settlements were drawn up. Nothing was signed. There was no betrothal."

"That may be so," Richard agreed, "but the intention of a betrothal had certainly been announced. Lady Elizabeth had every expectation that you and she would be wed. Now her father is dead and her world has been thrown into chaos. It would be most unkind of you to ignore her."

Hugh scowled furiously. He knew that Adela would have agreed with Richard, and that thought annoyed him intensely.

"Oh, all right," he snapped. "I shall go to see the girl. But I am going to make it very clear that I never had any intention of marrying her."

Richard's squire, who had been in the process of refilling his master's ale cup, jerked his arm and spilled some liquid on the well-scoured wood.

"I am sorry, my lord," he said to Richard, hastily snatching up a napkin to blot up the spill.

Hugh's eyes, wearing a noticeably ironic expression, moved from Alan to Richard.

"How many times have I told you that I am not a lord, Alan?" Richard said tranquilly.

The look of idolatry in the squire's eyes as he gazed at Richard was unmistakable.

Hugh said, "In his heart, you are always a lord, Richard."

Alan flushed. It was what he felt, but Hugh's tone of voice had made the sentiment sound ridiculous.

For a moment, the two young knights stared at each other. Hostility showed clearly in Hugh's cold eyes, but Richard only looked sad.

Gervase said, "There is no need to humiliate the girl by saying that you were going to refuse her, Hugh. Obviously the whole situation has changed with the death of her father. She will be in the wardship of the king now, and he may very well decide to bestow her elsewhere. Under the circumstances no one will expect your betrothal to go forward."

Hugh removed his gaze from Richard and looked at his host. Then he sighed. "All right, sir. I will go to see the Lady Elizabeth."

"Good lad." Gervase nodded his approval.

"Who is in charge of her household?" Hugh asked.

"The knight in charge is a man called Gaspar Meriot. There are nine knights in all that make up the household, and several ladies to attend the Lady Elizabeth. Not to mention the grooms and the body servants." Gervase made a comical face. "Thank God Meriot had the sense to send home the hounds and the falcons."

"All of these people are housed in the sheriff's apartment?" Hugh asked with amazement.

"The ladies have the apartment," Gervase said. "The knights are living in the guard room of the castle."

Hugh looked curious. "What is she eating? Surely she is not partaking of the same food as the garrison."

Dainty, delicately sauced food was not the main staple served up from the castle kitchen.

"I provided her with my own cook," Gervase said.

Hugh looked at his host's face for a moment, then said with amusement, "She sounds like a perfect nuisance."

All of a sudden, Richard laughed. "I doubt that you'll feel that way, Hugh, once you have seen her."

7

After breaking fast, Hugh rode to the castle with Gervase and Richard. The morning streets of Lincoln were as Hugh remembered them—filled with people. The weather outside might be cold, but the small, dark houses that most of the residents of the town inhabited were almost as chilly as the outdoors and considerably less appealing than the brisk fresh air and sunshine.

The Strait was lined with open-fronted booths, which formed part of the ground floor of many of the shopkeepers' homes. Hugh recognized most of them from the days when he would return home from school and Adela would send him out to make a purchase for her.

Ralf had employed both a man and a woman to help his wife with keeping the house, but when they resided in Lincoln, Adela had always done the cooking herself. With such a small household, she had not deemed it prudent to hire servants they did not need.

Gervase had a cook, however. And Richard had his own squire.

Hugh regarded the tall, muscular black stallion that Richard was riding and rated him as being extremely expensive.

Interesting, Hugh thought.

The three men on horseback crossed the bridge spanning the protective ditch that ran all around the outside of the Roman wall forming the outer boundary of the castle grounds. The men on duty at the gate greeted the sheriff and his party, and the three of them rode through.

The Bail was almost as filled with people as the city streets had been. Groups of townspeople were streaming to the Minster, where mass would begin in a few minutes. The market stalls set up along the far wall were doing a less brisk business than the church.

"Who rents the castle stalls?" Hugh asked Gervase.

"Local craftsmen and farmers," Gervase replied. "It's a good location for those who don't have shops in town."

"May I ask what inspired you to allow merchants in the Bail?" Hugh asked with innocent curiosity.

"I needed the money they bring in," Gervase returned a little grimly. "After the empress landed in England last September, I had to increase the garrison knights' pay from seven to eight pence a day. I needed to find the extra funds somewhere, and renting part of the Bail as market stalls has answered the problem very nicely."

Rufus was looking around curiously, as if he remembered this place, and Hugh patted the stallion's thick, arched neck.

"Why did you need to raise the knights' pay?" he asked.

"You know what has been happening in England since the king's right to the throne has been challenged," the sheriff replied impatiently. "Great lords such as William of Roumare and the Earl of Chester are gathering small armies of men to themselves." Gervase threw Hugh a disgusted look. "Why, just this past month, the Bishop of Ely himself revolted against the king!" He shook his head. "If I want to keep my men, I must pay them."

"That makes sense, I suppose," Hugh agreed.

The men reached the east gate of the inner walls through which they entered the castle's large Inner bail. Inside, a dozen or so horses wandered around the stockade searching for the last wisps of hay from their breakfast. A few men were sitting in front of the wooden huts that housed the castle guard, enjoying the sun and mending harness. In one corner of the yard a group of men practiced their archery, and in another corner a wrestling match was going on.

The sheriff and his companions rode toward the stables, and grooms came running to take their horses. The men proceeded on

foot toward the steep wooden staircase that would take them from
the Inner bail to the shell keep that enclosed the top of the motte.

Before they had reached the steps, however, Gervase was accosted
by a knight who began to talk to him in a low, staccato voice that
bespoke urgency.

When the knight had finished speaking, the sheriff said to
Hugh and his son, "Go along without me. There is something I
must see to first." He turned away to accompany the knight back
toward the east gate, leaving Hugh and Richard alone.

Hugh said to his companion, "Go ahead, Richard, you don't
need to escort me. I am perfectly capable of finding my way around
the castle by myself."

"You want to get rid of me," Richard said resignedly.

"You are, as always, wonderfully perceptive."

Richard thrust his fingers through his hair in a gesture of frustration. "Hugh," he said. "Can't we bury whatever ill will there
might have been between us when we were boys? We're men
now—men who have a great deal in common. I can see no reason
why we cannot be friends."

"Can't you?"

Richard's gaze was steady on Hugh's face. "Nay, I can't."

Hugh shrugged. "Fine," he said. "Let's be friends, then. And
now, if you will excuse me, I should like to renew my acquaintance
with some of my father's old knights."

Richard made as if to reach out and touch Hugh, then quickly
suppressed the gesture. "Certainly," he said, and smiled. "Shall I go
and prepare the Lady Elizabeth for your visit?"

"Why don't you do that?" Hugh said. And he turned away, leaving Richard to climb the stairs alone.

Hugh went directly to the area where the butts were set up,
where he had spied William Rotier conducting archery practice.

As soon as William saw who was approaching, his face split
into its gap-toothed grin. "Hugh! It's grand to see you, lad. I heard
you had come to Lincoln. Is it about this business of Bernard?"

"Aye," said Hugh as he walked up to the stocky, wide-shouldered
man. Hugh was not tall, but William was even shorter than he.

At that moment, the man whose turn it was to shoot let fly his arrow. It missed the circle drawn in the middle of the butt by a good foot. Derisive cries came from the rest of the participating knights.

"Do you know if John Rye is still in Lincoln, William?" Hugh asked.

William looked at him with surprise. "John Rye? What do you want with him?"

"I want to talk to him."

"Well, I'm afraid you're out of luck, lad. He's already left."

Hugh frowned. "Knight's fee duty is for a full month. His obligation shouldn't have ended until last night."

"He actually left three days ago," William said. "He got a message from home that his wife was ill, and he asked the sheriff if he might shorten his duty by a few days so he could be with her. Gervase agreed."

"I see," Hugh said quietly.

As he stood for a moment, a slight frown between his brows, a flaxen-haired boy stepped up to the shooting line, his bow in hand.

"Isn't that Richard Canville's squire?" Hugh asked William.

"Aye. Richard has him take archery practice with the knights of the guard. He's a good lad, is Alan Stanham. Everyone likes him."

The two men fell quiet as the boy lifted his bow. It was shorter than the six-foot-long bows of the men, but even so, it was not an easy draw. Alan pulled back his string and let his arrow fly. It buried itself in the butt two inches outside the circle.

"Well done," William called. "You're improving, lad."

For the first time, the competing knights noticed Hugh.

"Come and try a few rounds with us, my lord!" someone called good-naturedly. "Robert here wants to shoot against you!"

Robert was acknowledged to be the best archer in the castle guard. He had joined the guard after Ralf's death and did not know the sheriff's foster son. He looked at Hugh's slender frame and tried unsuccessfully to disguise a contemptuous sneer.

The rest of the men laughed delightedly.

The boy, Alan, stood quietly, listening with a grave face.

Hugh said, "I don't want to interrupt your practice."

"You won't be interrupting us, we're almost finished," William Rotier said heartily.

The rest of the men yelled noisy encouragement.

Hugh sighed. "All right, then." He walked toward the shooting line.

Robert once more regarded Hugh's slim figure. "If you wish to use the boy's bow, you are welcome to do so, my lord," he said with condescending generosity.

Hugh glanced at Alan, then shook his head. "No, thank you. I will borrow Henry's."

With a huge grin, one of the knights came forward and handed his bow to Hugh. It was a good one, made from a single stave of mountain yew, with a string of beeswax-impregnated flax.

The draw weight of Henry's bow, as everyone knew, was close to a hundred and fifty pounds. It was made for a very strong man.

"Would you like to go first, my lord?" Robert asked.

"If you like," Hugh replied carelessly, and stepped up to toe the line. He stood for a moment, his arms lowered, and then he began to raise the bow, all the while pushing the stave and pulling the string to bring the bow into a position of full draw. For the briefest of moments, he stood in the classic position of the archer, string near his ear, his head framed by the bow and the string. Then he let the arrow fly.

It buried itself in the dead center of the target circle.

The men who knew Hugh cheered with delight. Robert and Alan and a few others who did not know him stared in astonishment.

Hugh lowered the bow and turned to Robert. "Your turn," he said pleasantly.

Robert scowled and stepped to the line. He waited while Alan removed Hugh's arrow; then, slowly and deliberately, he raised his own bow, drew it, and shot.

His arrow landed in the exact same place Hugh's had hit. Robert grinned with relief.

"We'll just keep on doing it until one of us misses, shall we?" Hugh asked.

Once more, he stepped to the line and shot. Once more, the arrow hit the center of the circle.

Once more, Robert scowled and followed him. Once more, Robert hit dead center and grinned in relief.

Hugh went again, then Robert. Then Hugh again. And then Robert missed the center by an inch.

The knights of the guard, who did not appear to be overly fond of Robert, cheered Hugh vociferously.

Hugh smiled at his opponent. "You are very good," he said.

Robert looked at Hugh as if he couldn't believe what he was seeing. "You're stronger than you look, my lord," he muttered at last.

"Try wrestling with him and you'll find out just how strong he is!" one of the men boasted.

Hugh looked amused, and beckoned to Henry to retrieve his bow. Then he cast his gaze upward toward the castle keep, and suddenly his face lost all expression. Raising his hand in a gesture of farewell, he turned away and began to cross the Inner bail toward the stairs.

Elizabeth de Beauté was sewing in the solar of the sheriff's austere apartment when her prospective husband was announced. Lady Sybil, her nursemaid-companion-chaperone, put down the shirt she was embroidering and said, "So. At last we are to meet this young man whom your father chose for you."

Elizabeth took another dainty stitch in the tapestry spread on her lap. She was very much aware of the ramifications of her father's death. She knew that this marriage was not likely to happen now, and she did not regret that.

The girl had never wanted to marry Hugh de Leon. Still, she looked at the solar door with curiosity, interested to see up close the man who might have been her husband.

The slender young man she had watched yesterday walking beside Richard came quietly into the room. He wore a simple blue wool tunic with a plain red mantle swinging from his shoulders. His hair was uncovered, and she noted how black it was.

"My lord," Elizabeth said steadily. "How good of you to come to see me."

Hugh crossed the room until he was standing in front of her chair. He bowed his head. "My lady. I am so very sorry for your loss."

The expression on his face was reserved, and his gray eyes held none of the astonished delight that Elizabeth was accustomed to seeing in the eyes of men when they first beheld her.

She felt a flash of annoyance. She was every bit as beautiful as he, and she expected tribute.

"Thank you, my lord," she said graciously. "It has been a difficult time."

He nodded, and looked politely toward Lady Sybil. Elizabeth introduced her companion.

Hugh greeted the lady-in-waiting courteously, and Sybil invited him to sit with them.

Moving warily, rather as if he found himself trapped in a cage with two wild animals, Hugh took the armed, backless bench that Sybil had offered.

The three of them gazed at one another. The winter sun pouring in the open window fell on Elizabeth's hair, turning its red-gold beauty into a glorious flame. She tossed her head a little, to call attention to it.

Hugh said to her, "My lady, do you think it is wise for you to remain in Lincoln? Would it not be better for you to return home, where you will be safe?" He glanced around the room, which lacked tapestries for the walls and was sparsely furnished. "Not to mention more comfortable," he added.

"A very sensible comment, my lord," Lady Sybil said heartily, "and one that has been made by others besides yourself."

Elizabeth's long green eyes flashed. "I am not leaving Lincoln until I am certain that my father's murderer has been convicted and punished," she stated firmly.

Hugh did not look as if he admired her filial loyalty. He just kept regarding her with that reserved look on his face, and asked, "Why?"

Her back stiffened. "It seems perfectly natural to me, my lord, that I should be interested in seeing my father's murderer brought to justice."

Her voice was heavy with sarcasm.

"Of course you desire to see justice done," Hugh said agreeably. "What I actually meant was, what do you think you can achieve by remaining in Lincoln?"

Elizabeth glared at the man who had been her father's choice for her husband. He was looking at her with a detachment Elizabeth found odd and bewildering.

And this man had almost been betrothed to her!

She lifted her chin and said, "I wish to be there watching when Bernard Radvers hangs."

No emotion showed in those cool gray eyes. Not shock. Not respect. Not admiration. Not distaste.

"I see," he said.

The short, uncomfortable silence that followed this remark was broken by Lady Sybil.

"You must realize, my lord, that the death of Lord Gilbert will necessarily mean a halt to any wedding plans between you and the Lady Elizabeth."

For the first time, Elizabeth detected the flicker of an emotion in Hugh de Leon's eyes. The emotion was relief.

Suddenly Elizabeth was furious. While it was true that she had never wished to marry Hugh de Leon, it was quite another thing for him not to wish to marry her. Ever since she was a child, Elizabeth had had men worshiping at her feet. Hugh's obvious indifference piqued her vanity.

Perhaps she wouldn't have minded so much if he hadn't been so good-looking himself.

He was saying to Lady Sybil, "I fear you are right, my lady. The king will have the wardship of the Lady Elizabeth, and I doubt that he will bestow her upon me."

He didn't even have the decency to sound regretful.

Elizabeth's eyes narrowed. *You won't have a chance to marry me, Lord Hugh, but let us see if I can't make you sorry about that,* she thought. She drew a long breath to compose herself, and then she smiled.

Elizabeth de Beauté's smile was dazzling, but the reserve in Hugh de Leon's expression never changed.

"I will be remaining in Lincoln for the present, my lady," he said to her. "We may not be betrothed, but I will be glad to serve you in any way that I can."

"Thank you, my lord," Elizabeth replied demurely. She fluttered her long eyelashes. "We may not be destined to be husband and wife, but I hope that we may be friends."

He looked at her, and Elizabeth had the feeling that it was the first time he really saw her.

At last he returned her smile. "I hope so, too, my lady."

Elizabeth did not like the way that smile made her feel.

"I understand that you are staying with Richard Canville and his father," she said.

The reserved look descended once more. "Aye."

"Sir Richard has been very kind to us," Lady Sybil said.

Elizabeth looked at her hands, which held the tapestry in her lap, and said nothing.

"Richard is a wonderful man," Hugh said with a tinge of irony. He stood up. "I do not wish to trespass on your time any further, Lady Elizabeth, Lady Sybil." He bowed slightly. "Please accept my condolences once more and be assured that I, too, am anxious to see the true culprit brought to justice."

"Thank you for coming to visit me, my lord," Elizabeth said gently.

He nodded, turned, and was gone.

8

Dinner at the sheriff's house that night was braised beef with parsley, onions, and raisins. The food in the house on the Strait had definitely been plain since Gervase's cook had gone to work for Lady Elizabeth.

Alan, who had already eaten, placed the platter of beef on the table in front of Gervase and stepped to the end of the table, where he could watch all three men and see to their needs.

The Canvilles politely waited for their guest to fill his trencher first. Hugh took a small amount of beef and an even smaller serving of vegetables.

Gervase frowned. "Is that all you are going to eat? Why, that's not enough food to keep a hound in flesh!"

"I am not very hungry, sir. This will be ample, I assure you," Hugh replied.

Alan regarded him from under lowered lashes. Lord Hugh was paler than usual, he thought, and his eyes looked shadowed.

"Don't pester Hugh, Father," Richard said amiably. "He's old enough to know how much he wants to eat."

"Thank you, Richard," Hugh said.

Alan felt himself tensing. Hugh's words had been perfectly pleasant, but something about his voice when he spoke to Richard set the squire's teeth on edge.

Richard looked troubled.

What is the matter with Lord Hugh? Alan thought.

He remembered what Richard had told him about how Hugh had always felt himself to be in competition with Richard when they were boys.

But they aren't boys any longer, and for certain Lord Hugh no longer has to fear that he will be outshone, Alan thought, remembering the arrow-shooting contest of the morning.

Meanwhile, the conversation at the table had passed to other matters.

"What was the urgent problem that took you away from us this morning?" Richard asked his father.

Gervase sighed wearily. "It was Edgar Harding. Again. The man is a constant bother."

Richard soaked some gravy up with his white roll. "What did he want this time?"

Gervase leaned back in his chair and looked disgruntled. "He wanted to know why he wasn't offered one of the market stalls in the Bail."

Richard finished his well-soaked bread. "Did he bid on a stall?"

"Nay," Gervase said. "And that is his complaint. He claims he was not made aware that they were for rent."

"Are you speaking of Edgar Harding of Deerhurst?" Hugh asked. Alan noticed that he had not touched any of his food.

"Is there any other?" Gervase replied ruefully. "Tell me, Hugh, did he give Ralf as much trouble as he gives me?"

"He was always rather touchy," Hugh said. His fingers were busily shredding a roll into tiny pieces.

"There is nothing worse than a Saxon with a grudge," Richard said. "There is nothing you can say or do to convince him that he is not being discriminated against solely because he is a Saxon. The fact that the law may be in the other person's favor means nothing. You are ruling against him because you are Norman and he is Saxon, and he will not be convinced otherwise."

Richard's eyes flicked to his cup, and Alan hastily stepped forward to pour him more wine.

"Most Saxons do not have the lands or the wealth that Edgar Harding has," Hugh said. "His grandfather was one of the few Saxons to whom King William showed favor after he conquered England."

A memory stirred in Alan's mind, and he frowned.

Richard noticed. "Is something wrong, Alan?"

"Nay, my lord." Alan hesitated, then decided that since he had been asked, it might be best to bring it out. "It is just that Edgar Harding was standing next to me on the day that Lord Gilbert entered Lincoln, and he said something that was . . . well, strange."

Richard's big hands cradled his wine cup. "What was that?"

Alan said in a rush, "He called Lord Gilbert a bad name, my lord, and said that he had done injury to him. He said that there would always be bad blood between the de Beauté family and his own."

"Injury?" Richard said. He glanced at his father. "What injury could Edgar have been speaking of?"

"He must have meant that land dispute," Gervase said.

Hugh, who had been sitting very still, suddenly shifted in his chair.

"What land dispute?" Richard asked.

Gervase pushed his trencher away from him, signifying that he was finished. He picked up his wine cup.

"A number of years ago there was a lawsuit between the de Beautés and the Hardings over a piece of land that both claimed they owned," he told his son. "The land in question wasn't all that prosperous, but the point was that both families were convinced that it belonged to them. The suit went on forever, and the king himself finally ruled on it three years ago. He gave the land to Lord Gilbert."

Hugh said, "The land had been farmed since before the conquest by dependents of the Hardings, and Edgar swore that it was granted to his ancestor by King William. But Lord Gilbert insisted that it was part of his own honor as de Beauté and took it to law. Stephen ruled in his favor."

Alan thought that Hugh's voice sounded strange, as if it were coming from very far away. He looked more closely at the family guest and realized that Hugh was ill.

He had eaten nothing.

Richard did not appear to notice that anything was wrong. "Why rule in de Beauté's favor if the land had been under Harding stewardship for all those years?" he asked.

"Stephen needed Gilbert much more than he needed Edgar Harding," Hugh said briefly.

Richard's lips curled in a rueful smile. "Of course."

Gervase grunted and said, "I received another interesting piece of news this afternoon."

"What was that, Father?"

The sheriff folded his hands on the table in front of him. "The Earl of Chester is in Lincolnshire visiting his half brother, William of Roumare."

The sudden attentiveness of the two young men alerted Alan to the importance of this piece of news.

"That is interesting indeed," Richard said softly.

Both Richard and his father looked at Hugh.

Hugh said nothing.

Gervase said, "Is there aught we can do to help advance your cause with the king, Hugh? I would much rather have you as the new earl than William of Roumare!"

Hugh's mouth twitched. "Thank you, sir, but that would mean my marrying Lady Elizabeth, and I have no intention of doing any such thing."

"Didn't you meet her today?" Gervase asked incredulously.

"Aye." Alan noticed that Hugh scarcely moved his head when he looked at Gervase. He seemed to be trying to hold it still.

The sheriff's tone was a mixture of amazement and exasperation. "Great heavens, lad, is she not the most beautiful girl you have ever laid eyes on?"

"She is beautiful," Hugh agreed. "I also suspect that she is badly spoiled."

At that, Richard laughed. "You may be right."

Gervase said impatiently, "What the devil does that have to do with anything?"

"I didn't like her," Hugh said. His words were clipped and his voice still had that faraway quality.

"You don't have to like her," the sheriff snapped. "You just have to marry her!"

"Leave Hugh alone, Father," Richard said softly. "He is looking exhausted."

Hugh gave his champion a look of icy dislike.

Richard's eyes crinkled with distress.

Gervase said, "Alan, you may serve the sweet."

* * *

After supper, Hugh surprised the Canvilles by announcing that he
was going to spend the night in Ralf's old town house.

Gervase scowled. "Are you mad, Hugh? It is freezing out and that
house has been uninhabited for over a year. Go in the morning if you
want to see it, but spend the night here, where you will be warm."

But Hugh refused to change his mind. He went to his bedroom
to collect his sword, and was coming back into the solar when he
heard Richard's squire say, "I will accompany Lord Hugh if you
like, my lord. He does not look well."

Richard's reply was impatient. "I don't see why you should have to
suffer just because Hugh has taken this ridiculous notion into his
head. If he wants to spend the night freezing, let him spend it alone."

Hugh shut his eyes for a moment. Then, moving with extreme
care, he walked into the room and bid his hosts good-night.

Gervase looked annoyed.

Richard looked curious.

Alan looked worried.

It was still early evening when Hugh let himself out of the
Canville house and began to make his way through the mostly
deserted streets of Lincoln. Carrying an oil lamp that Gervase had
provided, he went on foot, leaving Rufus to spend the night in the
comfort of the sheriff's stable.

It was not a long walk, but to Hugh it seemed endless. The
headache had intensified all through supper, and now it stabbed with
white-hot pain behind his left eye and up into his forehead. His
stomach was unsteady, and even though he had eaten virtually no
supper, he knew he was going to be sick.

He had not had a headache in over two months and was beginning to hope that he was finished with them.

He clenched his teeth and shut his left eye, and kept on
through the cold, dark streets, trying not to move his head. Finally
he arrived in front of a familiar door.

He had never intended to return to this house, but he simply
could not bear the thought of exposing his vulnerability to Richard.
And there was no other place he could go.

The town house was locked, but Hugh had brought Ralf's keys
with him. He removed the big key ring from his belt and fumbled

around with his distorted vision, trying to determine which key was the right one. At last one of the keys slid into the lock and he was able to turn it and open the door.

He stepped into the hall, noting that the cold felt even more bitter indoors than it had outside. The rooms smelled the way they used to when the family returned from a visit to Keal and the house had been closed up for some months.

It was pitch dark inside, the oil lamp casting just enough light for him to make his way through the house.

The pain in Hugh's head was agonizing. He had had headaches like this before, and he knew there was nothing to be done but to wait it out.

Walking unsteadily, he reached the narrow stairs and went up to the second floor. Blindly, instinctively, he stumbled toward his old bedroom and pushed open the door.

Hugh went immediately toward the washbasin, which was still in the same place where it had always been. He put his lamp down on the table, bent over the basin, thick with dust, and began to retch.

The violence of his nausea made the headache even more excruciating. When finally he was finished, Hugh left the basin where it was and shuffled toward the bed.

His old wool blankets were still on it. Hugh crawled in between the icy sheets and pulled the blankets up over him. The pain stabbed on, and he began to shiver with cold.

He gritted his teeth and prepared to endure.

Towards dawn the pain let up, and Hugh fell into an exhausted sleep. He awoke hours later, shivering and stiff with cold, but his head was clear. The window shutters were closed and locked, and his bedroom was dark. The room smelled of vomit.

Hugh got out of bed and went to the window to open the shutters. It was sunny outside, midmorning, and the breeze that streamed in through the open window was warmer and cleaner than the reeking frigid air in the bedroom.

Hugh stood for a moment, inhaling deeply. Then, slowly, he turned and looked at the small room revealed by the streaming sunlight.

His old bedroom. His one-time refuge.

He remembered the first night he had spent in this house. He remembered how Adela had tucked him into this very bed and bent to kiss him good-night.

Never fret, my lamb. I won't let any more harm befall you.

He could almost hear her voice echoing in the emptiness of the room.

Moving stiffly from the cold, Hugh went out onto the landing. For a long moment, he stood in front of the closed door that was next to his. Then, with a movement that was almost violent, he shoved it open.

The shutters were closed in here, too, the only light being that which seeped in between the shutters and the window.

For a long moment, Hugh looked at the big bed that Ralf and Adela had shared and in which Adela had died.

Then he shut the door and almost ran down the stairs.

The solar was much smaller than the one in Gervase's house. There was no fireplace, only a central hearth with smoke holes along the top of the wall.

Three chairs were arranged around the hearth. After Adela had died, Hugh and Ralf had left her chair in its usual place.

Slowly Hugh walked to the hearth and sat in the chair that once had belonged to Ralf. He ran his hands up and down the wooden arms. He shut his eyes, as if trying to feel his foster father's presence.

He heard Ralf's voice inside his head, heard him saying the words he had so often tried to impress upon Hugh.

Patience, son. That is your one great flaw—you have no patience. Not everyone is as clever as you are. You must give people time to find their own way to the conclusion you have already reached.

The room was bitterly cold and chillingly empty. Adela and Ralf were gone.

Hugh bent his head and cried.

That same morning, Lady Elizabeth de Beauté went, as usual, to the ten o'clock mass in the Minster. As she was returning to the castle to break her fast, she and Lady Sybil were intercepted by Richard Canville.

"Lady Elizabeth," the young knight said with a courteous bow. "Lady Sybil. Have you been to mass? May I escort you back to the castle?"

"Thank you, Sir Richard," Lady Sybil said. "That is kind of you."

Richard fell into step with the two women as they continued to walk across the Bail. Several men of the castle guard rode past them. They saluted Richard and looked surreptitiously at Elizabeth, who appeared not to notice.

"So, my lady," Richard said to Elizabeth after the men had ridden by, "did you finally get to meet Lincoln's most famous foundling?" There was a trace of amusement in his voice.

Elizabeth glanced up at Richard, who topped her by a full head. "That I did, Sir Richard," she replied demurely. "He came to call upon me yesterday afternoon."

"He is certainly a good-looking young man," Lady Sybil said.

"Hugh is magnificent," Richard agreed amiably. "And he is smart as well."

"My," said Elizabeth sweetly. "You are making me sorry that I am not going to marry him after all."

Richard replied with good humor. "You and Hugh would not deal well, my lady. For all his gifts, Hugh has an icicle where his heart should be."

"Do you think I need a man who is . . . ah . . . warmer?" Elizabeth asked innocently.

Lady Sybil frowned.

"I'm quite sure you do," Richard replied softly.

A small smile curled the corners of Elizabeth's mouth.

"Lady Elizabeth will marry whomever the king tells her to," Lady Sybil said sternly.

Elizabeth patted her companion's arm. But her eyes lifted once again to Richard.

9

Cristen was in the pantry at Somerford making sure that the shelves had been scoured according to her standards when she felt Hugh's distress. Without a word to the servants, who were anxiously watching her as she inspected their work, she turned and left, heading for the privacy of her bedroom.

Once she reached the solar she changed her mind, however, and instead of going into her own room she went into the one that belonged to Hugh. She crossed the floor, sat on the edge of his bed, and closed her eyes.

No words formed in her mind. She sensed no attempt on his part to communicate with her. She felt only this utter desolation. It filled her mind and her heart, and she knew that it was Hugh.

He could not be left alone.

She sat there on his bed, in his room, and tried to let him know that she was there. She tried to fill the pain and loneliness within her with comfort and love. After a while she felt she might have succeeded. The bleakness lightened. The sharp edge of pain dulled. She felt calm.

At last she was free to turn to the difficult task that lay ahead. However was she going to convince her father that she must go to Lincoln?

Cristen was still mulling over this problem when she joined Nigel for midday dinner in the great hall. They were halfway through the meat course when the door opened and a strange man dressed in a mail hauberk strode into the room. In the fist of his gloved right hand he carried a rolled parchment.

He wore no helmet, and Cristen recognized him as one of Earl Guy's household knights.

The man advanced to stand before the head table, where he bowed to Nigel and announced, "Sir Nigel, I come from Lord Guy bearing a message for you. I am sorry to interrupt your dinner, but it is urgent."

Nigel frowned and reached out his hand for the parchment. The knight stepped closer to the table and passed it up to the lord of Somerford.

Thanks to the proliferation of church and public schools, much of the English population could both read and write. There were exceptions, of course. The lowest of the low did not have the opportunity to learn, and the highest of the high did not feel the necessity. Nigel, who belonged to neither of these classes, unrolled the parchment that contained the message from his overlord, and read it through.

The friendly chatter that had filled the hall before the entrance of the knight from Chippenham had long since died away. The hall was silent. Every eye was on Nigel as he read.

He looked somber as he rerolled the parchment and turned his attention to Guy's messenger.

"Do you know aught of this Cornish rebellion?" he asked. "I thought that Stephen's man in Cornwall, William fitzRichard, was a loyal follower of the king. Stephen has certainly gifted him handsomely with land and castles."

"Aye. Well, apparently fitzRichard has changed his allegiance. What happened was that the Earl of Gloucester proposed a marriage between his half brother, Reginald, and fitzRichard's daughter. The prospect of being related through marriage to both the empress and Gloucester proved more attractive to fitzRichard than his loyalty to the king. So the marriage was accomplished, and fitzRichard turned all his lands over to his new son-in-law, who promptly declared for the empress."

Nigel frowned. "Reginald is another one of the old king's bastard sons, is he not?"

"Aye. And the empress has named him Earl of Cornwall."

Nigel's frown turned into a scowl. "Judas," he said. "Was ever a king so beset with treachery as Stephen is?"

Cristen said to the Chippenham knight, "Will you not have a seat at one of the tables and take some refreshment?"

The knight glanced at Nigel, who waved his hand and said, "Go along, go along. You must be hungry after riding through the cold."

"Thank you, Sir Nigel, Lady Cristen." The knight bowed and turned gratefully to take an empty place at one of the trestle tables set up in the hall.

Cristen turned grave eyes upon her father. "What does this mean? What will the king do now?"

Nigel gestured to the parchment, which lay on the table next to his trencher. "Stephen is gathering a force to take against Reginald, who has apparently fortified all of fitzWilliam's castles against the king."

Cristen continued to gaze steadily at her father.

Nigel sighed. "Stephen has called upon Lord Guy for his feudal levy and Guy wants me to lead it."

Cristen blinked as if she had taken a blow. "You? Why you?" she demanded. "Why does not Guy lead his men himself?"

"I imagine that Guy does not want to bury himself in Cornwall at this particular moment," Nigel said wryly. "I heard yesterday that the Earl of Chester has gone into Lincolnshire to meet with his half brother. Now that the earldom of Lincoln is empty, the two of them will be plotting ways to earn it for William of Roumare. And, as we both know, Guy has his eye upon that particular earldom for Hugh."

Cristen's small, capable hands were clenched in her lap. "But why ask you to lead his feudal force? You and Guy are certainly not the best of friends."

Nigel looked as if he were debating what his answer should be.

Cristen swept on. "Is it because of Hugh? Guy wants you out of the way so that if he puts pressure on Hugh, you will not be at Somerford to offer him refuge?"

"I don't know why you ask me questions when you have worked the answers out perfectly well for yourself," Nigel said a little grumpily.

Cristen, who was usually so quick to smooth over her father's ruffled feelings, did not appear even to notice that he was put out. Instead, she said decisively, "This is not the time for Stephen to be depleting Wiltshire of its fighting men. Once the king has taken our men into Cornwall, what is to stop the Earl of Gloucester from coming against us with his own forces?"

"Guy is only calling up a portion of the muster owed to him from each of his vassals," Nigel replied. "He is not depleting his forces. We, for example, are only being asked for six men and forty men at arms. I can assure you, my dear, you will be well supplied with defenders here should Gloucester come calling in my absence."

"You are leaving me in charge then, Father?" Cristen asked in a faintly troubled voice.

Nigel looked at her in surprise. "Who else would I leave in charge?"

It was a common custom to leave the lady of the castle in command when the lord was called away.

Cristen was frowning thoughtfully. "Who will command the knights?"

"I will leave you Lionel," Nigel said.

The worried look cleared a little from Cristen's face. Lionel was about forty years of age and had been at Somerford since Cristen was a child. He was very competent and very well respected by the other knights.

"Guy's force is to meet at Chippenham in three days' time," Nigel said. "He wants me there earlier, however, in case some of the men arrive early."

Cristen raised her delicate brows. "Guy can't even be bothered to greet his own feudal levy himself?"

"Guy is not going to be at Chippenham, Cristen," Nigel said soberly. "He writes that he is leaving tomorrow for Lincoln."

After the table had been cleared, Nigel wrote a return message to Lord Guy, then sent Guy's knight back to Chippenham to deliver it. Once the messenger had left the hall, Nigel turned to Cristen, who had kept her seat at his side, and said cheerfully, "Well, if you will excuse me, my dear, I must send for the knights who are to accompany me to Cornwall. We have a great deal to do before we set out."

"Who are you planning to take with you, Father?"

Nigel listed six names, and Cristen immediately objected to one of them.

"I wish you would leave Thomas here with me," she said. "He is one of the few knights capable of thinking for himself. If aught should happen here in your absence, I should feel much more comfortable knowing that I had Thomas to rely upon."

Nigel frowned. "He is one of my best knights, Cristen. He will expect to be chosen to accompany me."

"You have other knights who are perfectly capable of fighting brilliantly, Father. Thomas is one of the few who has imagination. I need him here."

Finally Nigel gave in. "Thomas won't thank you for this," he warned his daughter. "He will be furious when he learns that you subverted his chance to go to war."

"Then we won't tell him that he was originally one of your choices, will we?" Cristen returned serenely.

After a moment, Nigel sighed. "Well, he's young. He'll have other chances."

At this comment, Cristen leaned back in her chair, folded her arms across her breast, narrowed her enormous brown eyes, and regarded her father, who was still sitting beside her.

"You are simply thrilled that you were given this command, aren't you, Father?" Her words sounded more like an accusation than a question.

Nigel looked a little guilty.

"Men," Cristen said. Her small, straight nose quivered in a way that managed to convey utter disgust. "You complain all the time about how terrible war is, and then, when you get a chance to fight, you love it."

"There is not going to be a battle, Cristen," Nigel said defensively. "The kind of combat we saw at the Battle of the Standard happens very rarely. War is usually a matter of besieging and taking castles. You know that."

Cristen's eyes were somber. "And in the process of besieging those castles, men get killed."

"Knights are worth far too much in ransom money to be killed," Nigel reassured her. "It's only the poor wretches who have no armor and no value, the archers and the men at arms, who actually get killed."

"Maybe if the knights did get killed, there wouldn't be so much fighting," Cristen muttered.

Nigel regarded his daughter with exasperated humor. "What are you complaining about? The fact that I might get killed, or the fact that I won't?"

After a moment, her lips curled in a rueful smile. "I'm just annoyed that you are looking forward to leaving me, I suppose."

"Actually, I'm scared to death to leave you," Nigel said. "You will do so much better a job running the castle than I do that when I return no one will want me back."

Nigel, his six chosen knights, and the forty men he had called up from his lands departed from Somerford the following morning under gray skies that promised either rain or snow, depending upon how warm the day grew.

Cristen stood beside the fishpond in the outer bailey and watched the knights ride out, dressed in full armor, their horses gleaming even in the dull light of the overcast morning. The men wore the nosepieces on their helmets up, but otherwise they were fully prepared for war.

Each Somerford knight carried the distinctive Norman kite-shaped shield, which covered a man from shoulder to shin. The skirts of their hauberks of interlinking rings reached to their knees, and were slit at front and rear from hem to crotch to enable the wearer to ride. Under their hauberks the men wore mail sleeves that reached to the wrist, and mail leggings that went down to their boots. Each knight had hung his sword from the sword belt at his side, and in his free hand he carried a lance.

Their faces were grim as they rode past Cristen, but she knew that in their hearts they were supremely happy.

Thomas was not happy. He was young, but he was one of the best of all the knights when it came to swordplay and horsemanship. He could not understand why he had not been chosen to accompany his lord.

He was standing in the bailey, looking forlornly after the dashing party that had just ridden out, when Cristen approached him.

"Don't feel bad, Thomas. I think Father felt he had to take the older knights," she said comfortingly.

"Perhaps. But they had a chance to fight at the Battle of the Standard," Thomas said mournfully. "We younger men have seen no action at all."

Cristen patted him on the arm, rather in the way she patted her dogs. "Your day will come," she promised.

At that moment, Brian came up to her, returning the dogs from their morning exercise. He, too, had been watching the departure of Nigel's chosen few.

"Did they not look splendid, my lady?" His hazel eyes were shining.

"They certainly did," Cristen agreed.

"How grand the whole company will look when all of Lord Guy's vassals join together! I wish I could go with them! How lucky William is to have this chance!"

Nigel's squire had accompanied the knights, along with several grooms to care for the horses.

"I never got to go to war when I was a squire," Thomas said gloomily.

With difficulty, Cristen refrained from comment.

Ralf rolled over on his back and proceeded to rub himself industriously into the dirt of the courtyard. His black legs waved in the air as he scratched.

Cedric watched him with intense interest.

"Come along," Cristen said to her dogs. "I have things to do even if these men do not."

Thomas looked guilty. "Don't worry, my lady. Sir Nigel gave me a long list of tasks to perform."

"How nice," Cristen said pleasantly. "Then why don't you start to do them?"

"Yes, my lady," Thomas said, and hurried off in the direction of the archery butts.

Cristen waited until she was certain that Guy's feudal force must have left Chippenham for Cornwall. Then she sent for Thomas to come to see her in the herb garden shed. She wanted to be sure that she would have complete privacy, and during the day privacy was at a premium within the castle itself.

"My lady," the young knight said when he presented himself. "May I be of some service to you?"

Cristen regarded the round, freckled face gazing at her with such gallantly concealed perplexity.

She removed a small pot of bubbling liquid from the charcoal brazier and placed it carefully on a tile to cool. Then she turned her full attention to Thomas.

"Hugh is in trouble," she said gravely.

Thomas was instantly concerned. "Why? What has happened, my lady?"

Cristen was bareheaded in the warmth of the shed, and now she pushed one of her long brown braids back across her shoulder, where it swung down to her waist.

"I don't know precisely what has happened, but I know that he needs me." She paused, then corrected herself. "He needs *us.*"

The young knight frowned in confusion. "I'm sorry, my lady, but I don't understand."

"It is very simple," Cristen said matter-of-factly. "I am going to Lincoln and you are going to escort me."

Thomas's mouth dropped open.

"We can leave this afternoon," Cristen said.

Thomas shut his mouth with an audible click of teeth.

"We cannot do that, my lady," he said. "I have not got Sir Nigel's permission."

Cristen said, with extreme pleasantness, "Perhaps you have forgotten that in the absence of Sir Nigel, I am the one in charge here at Somerford."

Thomas gazed at her unhappily. "I have not forgot that, my lady. But . . ."

"It will all be perfectly proper," Cristen assured him. "I will take one of my ladies with me . . ." She tilted her head a fraction, as if thinking. "I believe Mabel Eliot will be best. She is not prone to complain."

Thomas's light green eyes sparked with sudden interest. As Cristen well knew, the young knight had a partiality for Mabel. But he shook his head regretfully. "Sir Nigel will have my head if I take you away from Somerford without his permission, my lady. And at such a perilous time! The roads are filled with masterless men these days, looking to prey upon anyone who might easily fall victim to them."

"We won't easily fall victim," Cristen said. "We will have you."

"I am only one man, my lady," Thomas said with exasperation. "You cannot expect me to combat a whole band of outlaws!"

Cristen shrugged. "Then we shall have to avoid the outlaws."

"Nay, my lady," Thomas said, even more decisively than before. "I will not do it. It is too dangerous."

Cristen regarded him thoughtfully. Thomas looked warily back. Then he had another thought.

"Besides, as you yourself just pointed out to me, you are the one Sir Nigel left in charge of Somerford. You can't desert your post, my lady. We are all looking to you for leadership."

"Lionel is perfectly capable of seeing to the knights, and my women will see to the household. I won't be missed."

Thomas looked stubborn. "In normal times, that might be so. But what if we are attacked?"

"We won't be attacked," Cristen said.

"How can you be sure?" Thomas demanded.

A long moment passed in silence. Then Cristen said in a very gentle voice, "I don't think you quite understand, Thomas. If you refuse to escort me to Lincoln, then I shall have to go by myself."

Thomas looked horrified.

"I plan to ride out immediately after dinner," Cristen went on. "Either I go alone, or I go with you and Mabel. The choice is yours."

Thomas ran nervous fingers through his wheat-colored hair, which needed to be cut again. "You are not being fair, my lady!"

"No, I'm not," Cristen agreed. "I am putting you in a horrible position. I know it, and I apologize. But you see, Thomas, I am desperate. I must and I will go to Lord Hugh. I will feel safer if you go with me, but if you won't, I will be compelled to go alone."

Thomas looked miserable.

"I will tell Sir Nigel that I gave you no choice," Cristen said sympathetically. "I promise that you will not be held accountable for my actions."

Thomas ran distracted fingers through his hair once more.

"I really think Sir Nigel will be angrier with you if you let me go alone than he will be if you go with me," Cristen pointed out.

There was a brief silence. Then Thomas said sulkily, "All right, my lady. I will take you to Lincoln."

Cristen gave him a brilliant smile. "Thank you, Thomas."

The young knight did not smile back. "You show no mercy, my lady," he complained.

"I can't afford to," Cristen replied. Her smile died away and her face looked suddenly grim.

Thomas scowled. "How the devil am I to explain our departure to Lionel?"

"I will say that someone is ill in Malmesbury and I have been sent for," Cristen said. "You will be my escort."

"And what will they think when we don't return?"

"At first they will think that we have stayed the night in Malmesbury. I have done that often enough. And we will stop in the town long enough to leave a note at the abbey explaining things. I shall ask that the note be delivered to Lionel tomorrow afternoon. We will have enough of a start by then to prevent him from trying to catch up with us."

"You have thought of everything, my lady," Thomas said with heavy irony.

Cristen stared intently at the pot that she had placed on the tile to cool. "I hope I have," she replied. "I'm sorry I must coerce you like this, Thomas. And I am sorry that I must desert the trust my father left me with here at Somerford."

She drew in a long, uneven breath and concluded starkly, "But nothing is as important as Hugh."

10

The Manor of Linsay

Having regained his composure and feeling somewhat rested, Hugh left the town house where he had lived with his foster parents and returned to the sheriff's. There he washed, changed his clothes, and reclaimed his horse to ride to Linsay, the manor that John Rye held in knight's fee from the bishop.

Patches of lighter sky showed here and there where the cloud cover momentarily thinned, but overall the early sunshine had turned to gray. Hugh followed Ermine Street through the city and out into Lincoln Fields, the meadows and farmlands on the north side of the city walls that belonged to the town.

The winter fields that stretched before Hugh were bare and brown, but he remembered how green and gold they looked under the summer sun. Each freeman of the town held and farmed four to six acres of this open land, and in the warm months the fields were ripe with wheat, barley, rye, oats, vetches, peas, and beans.

The town's hay fields were bare as well. Hugh recalled how Ralf had been forced to restrict the number of livestock a freeman could graze on the common pasture because the town possessed only one hundred acres of meadow on which to grow hay, the only forage available to Lincoln's animals through the winter.

Hugh might not have been reared to manage the great

estates and vast lands he had been born to, but he had learned very young what it meant to administer a large city. Ralf had been more than a mere law enforcer when he had been Sheriff of Lincoln. His competence, his honesty, and his sense of justice had made people turn to him to solve all of the town's problems. In everything but name, Ralf Corbaille had been Lord of Lincoln. Hugh had learned more than just the knightly arts from his foster father. He had learned the skill of governing.

He passed beyond Lincoln Fields into the bare, frozen countryside. He had been told that John Rye's manor lay seven miles to the northwest of Lincoln, near to the hamlet of Kestven. Hugh took the path to the village, planning to ask directions to Linsay once he arrived in Kestven.

The hamlet lay in a valley that in summer would be a vista of green fields and ploughed farmland but which today looked bare and cold under the gray February sky. Hugh stopped Rufus at the first cottage he came to, where an elderly woman was feeding chickens in her front yard.

He dismounted and stood at the log fence that separated the yard from the road. "Good afternoon, mistress," he said. "I wonder if you could tell me the way to Linsay."

The woman straightened up and automatically rubbed the small of her back as if it ached. She turned where she was standing and regarded Hugh at the fence.

"If you bear right at the end of the village, there is a road that will take you straight there," she said at last. At her feet, the chickens pecked industriously in the dirt, searching for their food.

Hugh smiled. "Thank you, mistress."

She smiled back, showing toothless gums, and went back to her chores.

Hugh put his toe in his stirrup, swung up into his saddle, and continued on the single road that went through the hamlet, which consisted of a few modest huts and livestock pens. At the end of the village, the road forked and he turned right.

He had ridden for less than a quarter of an hour when he reached a stockade fence surrounding a manor, which he took to be Linsay. It looked to be about as large as his own manor of Hendly, the third-largest of the properties that Ralf had bequeathed to his foster son.

The gate that led into the courtyard was shut and appeared to be unattended. When no one answered his shout, Hugh dismounted, walked to the tall timber door, and banged on it. He received no reply, but thought he heard scuffling noises within. Holding Rufus's reins, he gave the gate a slight push.

To his surprise, it swung open.

What is going on here? he thought. Cautiously he pushed the door wider so he could have a view of the yard inside.

In the middle of the deserted courtyard stood a girl and a boy. The girl was holding a large stick, which she evidently had been using to play with a light brown mastiff by her side. Upon seeing the stranger, the huge dog flattened his ears and lunged toward him.

Hugh didn't move.

The girl screamed, *"Benjamin. Stop!"*

The dog halted two feet away from Hugh and growled low in his throat.

"Hello there, fellow," Hugh said mildly, and very slowly stretched out his hand.

The children came running up, their feet pounding on the dirt of the courtyard.

Suspiciously, Benjamin sniffed Hugh's proferred hand. His head was enormous. After a moment, the dog's tail wagged back and forth. Once.

"Good boy," Hugh said.

The boy took a firm hold on the thick hair of the dog's ruff.

Rufus, who liked dogs, pricked his ears and bent his head to sniff the mastiff.

The dog flattened his ears and growled.

Rufus lifted his head and blew through his nose.

The boy, who looked to be about eight, took a stronger hold on the dog. "Who are you and what do you want?" he demanded of Hugh.

"My name is Hugh de Leon and I am in search of John Rye," Hugh replied easily. "Can you tell me if he is here?"

The little girl answered in a high, clear voice, "Papa isn't at home right now."

"Iseult!" the boy hissed warningly.

The girl's eyes, which were the exact same blue as the boy's, sparked with anger. Mud was caked on her boots and on the hem of her cloak. Her untidy black hair was spilling out of its braids. She looked about five.

"You are always scolding me, Nicholas," she complained. "I didn't say anything wrong."

"Your brother thinks that you don't know me and that perhaps it isn't wise to let me know that your father isn't here to protect you," Hugh replied. He looked gravely into the suspicious blue glare of the boy. "I mean you no harm," he said. "I only came to have a word with your father. I am alone."

He turned his head to glance around the deserted courtyard, then he looked back at the children. "Shouldn't there be someone at the gate?"

Iseult said sadly, "Everyone ran away when Mama got sick."

Hugh glanced toward the stone hall that was the manor house. "Your mother is sick?"

The boy looked at his feet. "Aye," he muttered.

Benjamin lay down, evidently deciding that the children were safe, and the boy released his hold on the dog's neck.

"Who is looking after her?" Hugh asked.

"Edith is," Iseult said helpfully.

Hugh frowned. "Perhaps I had better talk to this Edith. It sounds as if she might need some help."

The two children could not disguise their relief.

"I think perhaps you are right," the boy admitted.

"May I put my horse in your stable?"

"Aye. There is no one to look after him, though. All the grooms ran away."

"I will look after him myself once I have seen Edith," Hugh said.

The two children and the dog accompanied Hugh to the empty stable, where he unsaddled Rufus and put him in a bare stall with a bucket of water. They left the dog in the stable and went toward the house, which was of a type prevalent among the Normans. In this popular design, the stone hall was raised on a storage cellar, which could be entered by a doorway in one of the side walls. The door to the main part of the house was reached by an external staircase made of wood.

"You have pretty eyes," Iseult said to Hugh as they climbed the stairs to the front door.

"Thank you," Hugh replied gravely.

"Iseult!" her brother commanded. "Don't be rude."

Hugh regarded the boy, whose hair was as black as his own. "It was a compliment," he said.

The boy flushed, pushed open the big front door, and gestured for Hugh to precede him inside.

They entered a long narrow lobby, which was enclosed by the timber partitions that separated the stone hall into two rooms. The children led Hugh through the door on their left, into the room that was the manor's great hall.

A niggardly fire was burning in the fireplace, otherwise the room showed no sign of occupation. The rushes on the floor looked dirty and gave off an odor that made Hugh's nostrils pinch together.

"Iseult," Nicholas said, "go and tell Edith that someone is here who wishes to talk to her."

Hugh realized with a mixture of amusement and approval that the boy had no intention of leaving him alone.

Without answering, the little girl ran back toward the lobby. Hugh was familiar with this type of house and knew there would be a solar on the other side of the lobby, and over the solar, a loft with private bedrooms.

It was some minutes before Iseult returned, accompanied by a heavyset middle-aged woman with gray-blond hair and pale blue eyes. She was dressed in brown homespun and looked exceedingly weary.

"This is the man I told you about," Iseult said in English.

Hugh smiled reassuringly at Edith and spoke to her in the same language. "My name is Hugh de Leon and I have come from Lincoln in search of John Rye. The children tell me he is not here, but you appear to have trouble, and if there is anything I can do to help you, I will gladly try."

Edith said, "Run along, children, and let me talk to the gentleman."

The boy scowled. "I'm not a child! I know Mama is very sick. You don't have to keep trying to hide things from me, Edith!"

Hugh looked at Edith's weary face and said quietly, "Take your sister outside, Nicholas. I will talk to you later."

Nicholas's eyes searched Hugh's. Then he nodded curtly and held out his hand. "Come along, Iseult. We had better go and let Benjamin out of the stable."

The children went out, and Hugh turned to the serving woman. "Shall we sit down?" he said kindly. "You look worn out."

She nodded and moved to one of the benches that was pulled up in front of the meager fire. Hugh sat on a bench opposite her.

"So," he said, still in that gentle tone. "What is going on here?"

The woman spoke English with a thick Lincolnshire accent, but Hugh had grown up hearing such speech and understood it effortlessly.

"Three days after Sir John left Linsay, Lady Berta got sick," Edith said. "I thought she had the smallpox. She had a high fever and her face broke all out in spots."

Hugh had rather suspected something like this. The threat of smallpox was more than enough to scare away a household.

"Have there been other cases of smallpox in the area?" he asked.

"None that I know of," Edith replied. "At any rate, news of Lady Berta's illness soon spread around the manor, and one by one, every-one ran away—the men Sir John had left to protect us, the serving maids, the grooms. Everyone."

Hugh looked grim. "Why did you remain?"

Edith looked down at her lap and did not reply.

"Edith?" Hugh said.

The woman shrugged her broad shoulders. "I took care of Lady Berta when she first come down with the fever, so by the time the spots come out, I reckoned I was sure to catch it. I could not bring such a terrible sickness back to my family, so I stayed."

Hugh regarded her gravely and did not reply.

Edith looked up from her lap. "The strange thing is, my lord, now I am not sure if Lady Berta has the smallpox after all."

Hugh lifted his brows. "Why do you think that?"

"She is getting better, my lord, and the spots seem to be fading. They never turned into pustules, the way the smallpox do."

The fire was almost out, Hugh noticed. He would have to do something about it. "That is unusual," he agreed.

"I don't know what it is, but I do not think it is the smallpox," the woman repeated.

Hugh stretched his legs in front of him and regarded his boots. "You said that Lady Berta became ill *after* her husband left?" he asked casually.

"Aye, my lord."

He glanced up at her. "She was not ill when he returned from his duty at Lincoln Castle?"

Edith looked surprised. "Nay, my lord. She were fine then. She did not get ill till three days after he left to go to Roumare."

Hugh's expression never changed.

"Oh, did he go to see his cousin, then?"

"Aye, my lord. He went the very next day after he returned from Lincoln, and my lady did not get ill till later. He would never have left his son here if he knew of Lady Berta's illness."

Hugh forebore to comment upon the implication that Rye would not have shown the same concern for his small daughter.

Instead, he smiled into the woman's worn face. "You have been magnificent, Edith, but I rather think you could use some assistance. If you like, I will remain here at Linsay and do what I can to be of help."

The woman looked almost pathetically grateful. "I confess I would feel safer if there was a man around. As things stand now, we are completely unprotected. And God knows these times are dangerous."

"That is settled, then," Hugh said. He stood up. "You must let me know what you need: wood, water, meat . . ."

"I didn't mean for you to work for us, my lord," the woman protested, clearly horrified by the thought. "Just your presence will be a comfort."

"Nonsense," Hugh returned briskly. "I was brought up by a very careful housewife and I can assure you, Edith, I know my way about a house and a kitchen." He sniffed and looked around the hall. "The first thing I am going to do is get rid of these disgusting rushes."

Edith's pale blue eyes regarded him with fascination. "You are?"

"Aye. The children can help me."

For the first time since she had come into the room, Edith smiled. "It will be good for them to have something to do. I have kept them away from their mother and I know they have been fretting."

"I can think of a number of things we can do around here," Hugh said, recalling the unkept state of the stable.

"How . . . how long do you think to stay, my lord?" Edith asked timidly.

"I won't desert you until your master returns," Hugh promised.

The woman heaved a great sigh of relief. "Thank you, my lord! You are very kind."

"Not at all," Hugh replied a little grimly. "Now, let me go and find those children."

Three days later John Rye finally returned home. Lady Berta was sitting up, much recovered, and Hugh and Edith had stripped all the rugs off the walls of her bedroom and taken the blankets off her bed.

It had been Hugh's idea to air out the rugs and blankets. Adela had been a great believer in the cleansing benefit of fresh air and sunshine.

He and the children were in the process of hanging these articles out in the cold sunshine when the master of Linsay came riding up to his manor and found the gate locked against him. He yelled to be let in.

Nicholas recognized his father's angry shout. "It's Papa," he said to Hugh. He dropped the rug he had been holding and ran to unbar the gate.

As soon as the wooden door swung open, a brown horse, shaggy with winter hair, came trotting into the courtyard. John Rye scowled down at his son. "What the devil is going on here?" he demanded loudly. "Why was the gate locked?" He looked around. "And where is everyone?"

Hugh left the rugs and began to walk toward the horseman in the courtyard. Iseult stayed close beside him.

"Papa always yells," the little girl confided in a worried voice.

Nicholas was trying to explain things to an angry Rye, who was not listening. Instead, he was glaring suspiciously at the approaching Hugh.

"Who the devil are you?" the manor's owner demanded as soon as Hugh was within twenty feet of him.

Hugh moved a little closer to the horseman, then stopped. He looked into the man's angry blue eyes and said softly, "My name is Hugh de Leon."

The effect of these simple words was galvanic. Rye's eyes bulged and his mouth dropped open.

"Hugh de Leon?" he echoed in utter astonishment.

"That is what I said," Hugh returned composedly.

Nicholas shifted uneasily from one foot to the other. "Hugh has been helping us, Papa," he said. "Mama got sick and everyone ran away. Then Hugh came."

John Rye ignored his son, nor did he ask after his wife's health. Instead, he said to Hugh in a hard voice, "What the devil are you doing here?"

Iseult slipped her small hand into Hugh's. He gave it a quick, reassuring squeeze.

"I came to see you, Rye," he answered, "but when I arrived I found that, except for a single serving maid, your wife and children had been abandoned. I thought it would be best for me to remain with them until you returned."

Rye gave a bark of scornful laughter. Then he swung down from his horse. Holding his reins in his hands, he looked around. "Where are the grooms?"

"They ran away when they thought Mama had smallpox," Nicholas replied steadily.

His father went rigid. "*Smallpox?* Jesus wept, why didn't you tell me? Is there smallpox in the manor?"

Rye looked over his shoulder at the gate, as if he would like to ride right out.

Hugh said ironically, "You can relax, Rye, you are perfectly safe. It seems that it wasn't smallpox after all." He lifted a mocking eyebrow. "I'm sure you will be relieved to know that your wife is almost completely recovered."

John Rye grunted. Then he handed his horse's reins to his son. "Take care of Jake," he commanded. "I want to have a few words with Lord Hugh."

Nicholas shot Hugh a troubled glance. "All right, Papa."

Hugh looked down at the little girl standing so close beside him and said gently, "Go along with your brother, Iseult. Your father and I want to talk."

She nodded, and the sleek braids that Hugh had plaited that morning bounced on her shoulders. "All right, Hugh."

"Shall we go inside?" Hugh said to Linsay's owner.

Without answering, Rye headed purposefully in the direction of the stone hall.

The two men walked into a sweet-smelling room that was strewn with fresh rushes and herbs. A fire was roaring in the fireplace and the shutters had been opened to let in the sun.

John Rye looked around in bewilderment as if he did not recognize his own hall. Then he strode toward the fireplace and the chairs and benches that were set in front of it. He did not sit down, however, but stood holding his hands out to the welcome heat of the flames.

Hugh crossed the floor more slowly and sat in one of the two armchairs.

John Rye turned around and scowled at his guest.

"Make yourself comfortable," he said sarcastically.

Hugh did not reply.

The other man spread his legs and crossed his arms over his broad chest. "All right," he said with belligerence. "You had better tell me what you are doing here."

"I thought I already told you," Hugh replied softly. "I came to see you."

Rye's scowl deepened. "What about?"

Hugh's eyes were steady before Rye's truculent stare. "I am inquiring into the death of Gilbert de Beauté. In order to make a thorough investigation, it is vital that I speak with all the knights who were serving in the castle guard at the time that he was killed. I tried to see you in Lincoln, but I was told that you had taken early leave of your duty."

At that, John Rye's eyes slid away from Hugh's.

Hugh continued, "I was told that you had to go home because your wife was sick."

"Well," Rye blustered, "so she was!"

He was still refusing to look at Hugh.

"Aye," Hugh said, "but she did not become ill until after you left Linsay to pay a visit to William of Roumare."

"She was sick before that." Rye's eyes suddenly swung back to confront Hugh's as he recognized the trap he had just fallen into. "Who said I went to see Roumare?" he demanded.

Hugh ignored the question and continued to pursue his own line of thought. "That is not what I have heard. According to her serving maid and your children, Lady Berta enjoyed perfect health until she became ill with a fever three days *after* your departure from Linsay."

Rye set his jaw. "Didn't anyone ever tell you that it is despicable to question a man's children behind his back?"

Hugh regarded him with detached curiosity. "What made you so anxious to leave Lincoln that you cut your guard duty short, Rye? Your wife wasn't ill. What was it?"

John Rye moved away from the front of the fireplace and flung himself into the chair that faced Hugh's. For a long moment, he stared at Hugh broodingly. "Oh, all right," he finally admitted. "I went to see Roumare. I knew he would want to know what had happened to de Beauté and I thought he might look kindly upon the person who brought him such welcome news."

A log fell off the fire onto the hearth and Hugh got up to push it back.

"You did not leave Lincoln until several days after de Beauté's death," he said as he gave the log an expert kick. "Surely Roumare had heard the news before you reached him."

Dark red flushed into Rye's face. "I thought I would take a chance on being first."

With the log safely back where it belonged, Hugh returned to his chair. "I don't believe you," he said.

Rye's face grew even redder. "You tell me, then," he demanded. "Why do you think I went to see Roumare?"

"What do I think?" Hugh repeated thoughtfully. "I think you went to see him about the death of the Earl of Lincoln, all right, but it was not to take him the news."

Rye's lips tightened. His eyes looked suddenly guarded. "What was it for, then?"

"I think you know who killed Gilbert de Beauté, and it was not Bernard Radvers," Hugh replied.

The only sound in the hall was the roaring of the fire.

The wary look in Rye's eyes did not change. Finally he said, "And what if I do know something? What would such information be worth to you?"

Hugh dropped his gaze to hide the surprise he did not want to betray. This was not the answer he had expected. "What do you think it is worth?" he said slowly.

"A lot of money," Rye returned. He showed his teeth in a shark-like smile. "More money than you have access to, *Lord* Hugh."

"The kind of money that a man like William of Roumare can pay?" Hugh said.

Rye's smile died.

"If you have information pertinent to the earl's murder, you had better tell it to me," Hugh said briskly.

"I know who killed Lord Gilbert all right," Rye retorted stubbornly. "It was Bernard Radvers. And I'll tell you something else, my lord. He killed the earl for you." He pointed an accusing finger at Hugh. "Bernard wanted Hugh de Leon to be the next Earl of Lincoln and that is the reason he killed the man who was standing in your way."

Hugh said wearily, "If Bernard wanted me to be the next earl, he would have waited until after I was wed."

"Bernard miscalculated," Rye said.

Hugh stood up. "I think rather it is *you* who have miscalculated, John Rye," he said. "William of Roumare is not the only one with money to spend for information. Think on that, and if you want to talk to me, you can find me in Lincoln." He turned and strode across the sweet-smelling rushes to the doorway. "Please make my farewells to your lady wife."

Nicholas and Iseult were waiting for him in the courtyard. As soon as he came out the main door of the hall, they ran to meet him.

"You aren't leaving, are you?" Iseult asked anxiously.

"I am afraid that I must," Hugh replied, fastening his cloak.

The little girl's lower lip trembled. "I don't want you to leave. I *like* you, Hugh. Please, won't you stay with us for a while?"

Hugh paused and looked into the child's blue eyes, then said with quiet patience, "Your mother is well now, Iseult, and your father is home. They will look after you better than I ever could."

"No they won't," she replied tearfully. "They never talk to me like you do. All they ever do is tell me to do things."

Hugh squatted on his heels so he was on the same level as the child. "I'm sorry, little one, but I can't stay. I don't belong here."

Her lip trembled again.

"Don't be a baby, Iseult," Nicholas said.

Still on his heels in front of Iseult, Hugh turned his eyes to the boy, who said manfully, "I am sorry you must go, Hugh, but I understand. Thank you for helping us these last few days." Nicholas's back was straight as a lance. His eyes were perfectly steady.

Hugh turned back to Iseult. "Nicholas will look after you, little one," he said.

She sniffled. "He doesn't know how to braid my hair."

"You will soon have serving maids to do that for you." Hugh rose to his full height.

"Will we see you again?" Nicholas asked, not quite able to hide his hopefulness.

"Someday perhaps," Hugh returned.

"When I grow up, Hugh, I am going to marry you," Iseult announced.

At that, Hugh smiled and flicked a gentle finger along her round, apple-blossom cheek.

"Don't be an idiot," Nicholas reprimanded his sister.

"A knight never calls a lady an idiot," Hugh said gravely.

Nicholas sighed and took his little sister by the hand. "Thank you, my lord," he said formally. "I hope we will see you again one day."

"I hope so, too," Hugh returned. And he headed for the stable to collect Rufus.

11

Cristen's party arrived at the gates of Lincoln as dark was beginning to fall. It had not been a pleasant journey; Cristen had pushed the pace without mercy. Mabel Eliot, the young attendant she had brought along for propriety's sake, was sagging with exhaustion. And while Thomas had faithfully seen to the safety of his charges, he had adopted a silent, distant manner to convey his disapproval of this outrageous venture he had been forced to join.

To Thomas's intense annoyance, Cristen hadn't appeared even to notice his displeasure. Her attention was totally concentrated upon getting to Lincoln as quickly as possible.

One of Thomas's greatest worries had been that Hugh would not be in Lincoln when Cristen got there. If that should come to pass, where was Thomas going to lodge his lord's headstrong daughter? He tried to soothe himself with the thought that surely the bishop would have a guest house.

He shuddered at what Nigel would say to him if he allowed his daughter to lodge at a common inn.

As they entered the town through the city gate, Thomas turned to Cristen. "We have arrived, my lady," he said with grim courtesy. "What do you desire to do next?"

"Find Hugh," Cristen returned tersely.

"And how do you suggest we go about that?" Thomas inquired, his voice coldly and relentlessly civil. "You don't know where he is staying."

"We'll try the castle first," Cristen said. "If he's not there, it's likely that someone will know where we can find him."

There was a moment of silence as Thomas regarded the delicate and lovely profile of his liege lady. She looks so fragile, he thought with a mixture of frustration and reluctant admiration. But underneath she's adamant.

"As you wish, my lady," he replied at last.

Mabel, who was usually a sunny-natured girl, almost whimpered. "Will we be able to get off our horses soon, my lady?"

"Very soon," Cristen said.

Thomas bestowed a sympathetic look upon the woebegone Mabel, and she managed a weak smile in return.

The threesome rode on through the town. On either side of the main street, shopkeepers were closing up their stalls, and children home from school were playing games in the side streets. When they entered the Bail, they found it just as busy. It was almost time for the evening service, and various groups of townspeople and castle folk were on their way to the Minster.

Thomas tipped his head and looked up approvingly at the heights of Lincoln Castle towering above them. He nodded in appreciation of the seemingly impregnable defenses posed by the mighty fortress. When at last he returned his gaze to his surroundings, he saw a small party of well-dressed women passing through the gate from the Inner bail. Thomas's eye was immediately caught by the knight who was escorting the women. He was tall, his uncovered hair was darkly gold, and his mantle was lined with fur.

Thomas turned to Cristen, "Shall I ask that knight yonder if he knows aught of Hugh, my lady?"

"Aye, do that," she returned crisply.

Thomas dismounted, and leading his tired stallion, went to intercept the knight and his group of ladies.

When he saw that he was being approached, the knight halted and waited for Thomas to reach his side. The woman dressed in a green mantle who had been walking beside him halted also.

Thomas was tall, but the knight was taller, and Thomas had to look up to meet his eyes. They were very blue.

"Excuse me, sir," Thomas said, "but I wonder if you could tell me where I might find Hugh de Leon."

"Who wants to know?" the tall, broad-shouldered young man replied. His eyes flicked over Thomas's horse, a well-built roan.

Thomas made a small gesture in the direction of Cristen and Mabel. "My name is Thomas Mannyng and I am escorting Lady Cristen Haslin of Somerford," he said. "I am one of Sir Nigel's household knights."

"You are from Somerford?" the young knight said with sudden interest. He looked down at the woman in green standing at his side. "Do you mind if I speak to Lady Cristen for a moment, my lady?"

"Of course not," she replied. "In fact, I will accompany you." She made a shooing gesture toward the four other ladies in her party, who were waiting at a little distance. "The rest of you can go along to church. Sir Richard and I will join you shortly."

Thomas spared a glance for the woman in the green hooded mantle, and his mouth dropped open as he beheld her face. He stood for a moment like one who has been poleaxed, and had to hurry to catch up with the two, who were heading toward Cristen and Mabel.

"Lady Cristen," the tall knight said as he stopped unerringly beside her horse. "I am Richard Canville, son to the sheriff. Hugh has been staying with me and my father in our town house."

Thomas was overcome by a rush of relief so strong that his knees sagged. *What luck that we ran into this fellow,* he thought. He could scarcely wait to relinquish the responsibility for Cristen to Hugh.

The girl next to Richard Canville pushed back her hood, revealing a mass of glorious red-gold hair. "And I am Elizabeth de Beauté," she said.

Good God, Thomas thought in shock. *This is the girl Hugh is supposed to marry?*

His eyes went to Cristen as she took in the incredibly beautiful face of Elizabeth de Beauté. Her large brown eyes never flickered as she responded calmly, "How do you do, Lady Elizabeth. I am so sorry about your father."

Thomas felt a flicker of pride. Nothing ever discomposed Lady Cristen.

"Thank you," Elizabeth replied.

Richard said in a faintly bewildered voice, "Was Hugh expecting you, my lady?"

Cristen transferred her gaze to the knight. "He didn't know when I was arriving."

She might have been discussing the weather, she sounded so unruffled. One was almost tempted to believe that it was perfectly normal for an unmarried young woman, an unmarried *noble* young woman, to arrive in a strange town, accompanied only by a single escort, in search of a young man to whom she was not related.

"I am afraid he is not in town at the moment," Richard said, clearly at a loss.

"Isn't he?" Cristen returned. Not a flicker of dismay showed in her demeanor. "Well then, I shall just have to wait for him."

Thomas glanced at the shadows quickly lengthening across the ground, and stepped forward. "I wonder if you could recommend a lodging for my lady and her companion, Sir Richard," he said. "It is growing late and if Lord Hugh is not available to advise us . . ." He let his voice trail away.

"Good heavens," Richard said in deep surprise. "Have you no place to stay?"

Cristen shot Thomas a warning look. "I thought to ask for shelter at the bishop's guest house, Thomas," she said steadily.

Richard said, "I am afraid that you are not the only one who has come to Lincoln in search of Hugh, my lady. The Earl of Wiltshire arrived here two days ago, and he and his entourage have already taken up residence in the bishop's guest house."

Judas, Thomas thought in barely suppressed panic. *Now what am I to do? Lord Guy will be enraged if he finds that Cristen has come here without her father.*

Cristen continued to look perfectly unruffled.

Thomas said hopefully, "Perhaps you might be able to recommend some other place to us, Sir Richard."

Elizabeth de Beauté said, "Of course Lady Cristen will stay with me."

Everyone stared at the slender figure standing next to Richard.

"The sheriff has very graciously given me his apartment in the castle," Elizabeth informed Cristen. Her voice was clear and bell-like. "There is plenty of room for you and your lady. I should be happy to have your company, Lady Cristen."

For the first time since they had left Somerford, Thomas saw a trace of unsureness in Cristen.

"I do not wish to discommode you, my lady," she said. "We will do perfectly well at an inn."

At this point, Richard earned Thomas's everlasting gratitude by saying firmly, "An inn is no place for the daughter of Nigel Haslin. I strongly suggest that you accept Lady Elizabeth's gracious offer. It is already growing dark."

Thomas stared hard at Cristen, willing her to accept this very generous invitation. She glanced at him and read his thought. He saw her mouth set. She turned back to the young woman who was standing on the ground beside her.

"Thank you, my lady. You are very kind." Her voice sounded grim rather than relieved.

"Not at all," Elizabeth said. She, on the other hand, sounded positively gay. "It will be most enjoyable to have a companion of my own age."

Cristen's small straight nose quivered.

"I think we can forget evening service for tonight, Sir Richard," Elizabeth said. "It is more important at the moment to get our guests into shelter before dark."

As the couple turned to retrace their way back to the Inner bail, Thomas looked at Cristen's straight back and wondered how she was going to like lodging with Hugh's betrothed.

Cristen was not pleased with her lodging arrangements, but there didn't seem to be any alternative. She certainly couldn't go to the bishop. If Lord Guy found out that she was in Lincoln, he would order her home before she had a chance to see Hugh. And Hugh would be absolutely livid if he found her residing at an inn.

Elizabeth de Beauté, who was so aptly named, was both friendly and efficient as she introduced Cristen to her companion, Lady Sybil, and arranged for Cristen and Mabel to share a bedroom.

After Cristen had washed and changed from her travel-stained riding clothes, she returned to the austere main hall of the sheriff's apartment to be reunited with her hostess.

Elizabeth gave her a delighted smile.

She could not look more pleased to see me than if I was her long-lost sister, Cristen thought sourly as she returned her hostess's smile with restraint.

She noted with interest that Richard Canville had remained. He had risen in courtesy as she entered the room and now he informed her, "I must tell you that we expected Hugh back before now, my lady. He went to visit one John Rye, a knight who was serving with the castle guard when Sir Gilbert was killed."

Cristen took the seat between Lady Elizabeth and Lady Sybil, and Richard returned to his.

"Did you know that Hugh is attempting to prove that Bernard Radvers is innocent of murdering Gilbert de Beauté?" he asked her.

Cristen accepted a cup of wine from a servant and regarded Richard over its rim. "Aye," she said. "I know."

"He is wasting his time," Elizabeth said, and for the first time a hard note sounded in her musical voice. "Bernard Radvers murdered my father. He was found standing over his body with the murder weapon clutched in his hand."

"So I have heard," Cristen said mildly.

"Considering all that, I don't understand why Lord Hugh won't simply let justice take its course," Lady Elizabeth complained.

"Hugh has always been loyal to his friends," Cristen returned. "Bernard is a friend of his and Bernard says he did not murder your father. Hugh believes him."

Elizabeth's green eyes shot sparks. "Then Lord Hugh must be very gullible indeed."

"Hugh is not gullible, my lady," Richard said. "I have known him since we were children and I can assure you that he is not gullible at all."

Cristen looked at Richard with more interest than she had shown heretofore. "You knew Hugh when he lived in Lincoln?"

"Hugh and I have known each other since we were ten years old," Richard replied.

Cristen looked at him thoughtfully and sipped her wine.

"I wonder what urgent matter can have brought you to Lincoln so precipitously?" Elizabeth asked guilelessly.

Cristen ignored her comment and said to Richard, "How long has Hugh been gone?"

Richard's blue eyes narrowed with thought. "It must be four days now. John Rye's manor of Linsay is only a few miles to the north of here, so I assume that either he wasn't there and Hugh is waiting for him, or he has gone in search of him." He gave her a charmingly rueful smile. "Hugh has not seen fit to communicate with us, so I cannot tell you for certain."

Cristen knew that Hugh was all right even though she didn't know where he was. She nodded calmly.

A tiny silence fell, broken by Lady Sybil. "Wasn't your father the one who first discovered that Hugh Corbaille was in reality the lost heir of the de Leons?" she asked Cristen eagerly.

"He was," Cristen replied.

"What an exciting story that is!" Elizabeth's companion gushed. "A *jongleur* could make a wonderful *chanson de geste* from it."

Cristen thought of all the anguish Hugh had gone through when he had finally accepted his true identity, and found that she could not reply.

Elizabeth decided on direct tactics to get the information she wanted. "But why have you come to Lincoln in search of Hugh, Lady Cristen? Surely your father should have accompanied you!"

Cristen's eyebrows were fine aloof arches over her astonished eyes. "I beg your pardon?" she said.

Color stained Elizabeth's cheeks and her green eyes glittered. "I was merely wondering what you are doing in Lincoln," she snapped.

"I have come to see Hugh," Cristen replied.

Elizabeth stared at her. Cristen gazed steadily back.

"Does Lord Guy know that you are here?" Elizabeth asked shrewdly. "He is your overlord, is he not?"

"I did not have time to communicate with Lord Guy before I left Somerford," Cristen said. She took another sip of her wine.

Richard said with faint amusement, "If you like, my lady, I will send someone to Linsay tomorrow to tell Hugh that you have arrived."

For the first time since she had entered Lincoln, Cristen gave a genuine smile. "Thank you, Sir Richard. I should appreciate that."

His return smile was utterly beguiling. "Not at all, Lady Cristen," he replied. "It makes me happy to be able to serve you."

Late the following morning, Alan Stanham rode out of Lincoln, his destination the manor of Linsay. Richard had entrusted his squire with a horse and the mission of delivering a message to Hugh de Leon if Hugh was at Linsay.

Alan was thrilled. This was the first time he had been given such an important task, and he felt it was a sign of Richard's faith in him.

To trust him with a horse!

To let him go by himself!

Alan was wrapped in pleasant fantasies of his future as a knight for almost the entire ride. It wasn't until he reached the village of Kestven that he actually awoke from his daydreams and took stock of his surroundings. He got directions to the manor of Linsay and started on the last lap of his journey.

A half a mile outside of Kestven, he ran into Hugh. Alan halted his horse on the pathway and waited for Rufus to come up to him.

"Lord Hugh," he said a little breathlessly. "I am so glad that I have found you!"

Hugh's straight black brows were drawn together as he regarded Richard's squire. "Why are you looking for me?"

"Sir Richard sent me, my lord. I am to tell you that Lady Cristen Haslin has arrived in Lincoln and she desires to see you."

A light flared in Hugh's eyes. "Cristen is in Lincoln?"

"Aye, my lord. She arrived late yesterday. And Lord Guy of Wiltshire is in Lincoln as well. He arrived in Lincoln two days before Lady Cristen."

Hugh began to laugh.

Alan regarded him in amazement. There was a flush of color across his high cheekbones and his gray eyes glittered between their black lashes. "Is Guy looking for me as well?" he asked the squire with genuine amusement.

"Aye, my lord, I believe he is."

Hugh gestured that they should move forward, and Alan turned his horse to accompany Hugh.

"Where are Sir Nigel and his daughter staying?" Hugh asked. "In the bishop's guest house?"

"Er . . . Sir Nigel did not accompany Lady Cristen, my lord," Alan replied a little nervously.

Silence.

"She came alone?" Hugh asked. His voice sounded ominous.

"She was escorted by one knight, my lord. And she brought a lady companion."

Hugh swore.

"She is perfectly all right, my lord," Alan hastened to assure him. "She is staying in the castle with Lady Elizabeth de Beauté."

The face Hugh turned to Alan registered complete disbelief.

"She couldn't stay at the bishop's guest house, my lord," Alan babbled on. "Lord Guy is there, you see."

Hugh's incredulous look did not fade. "Guy is in the bishop's guest house and Cristen is in the castle," he repeated.

"Aye, my lord."

Hugh shook his head.

"I can't wait to get back to Lincoln," he said.

Alan did not know if he was being ironic or not.

12

Cristen was sitting in the castle solar with Elizabeth de Beauté and Lady Sybil when Hugh came into the room. Later he would notice that there were other people present, but in that first moment he saw only her.

Happiness filled his heart.

"You didn't bring the dogs?" he said from the doorway.

She had sensed his presence even before he spoke and was already looking at him.

"I came in rather a hurry," she said. "It seemed best to leave them home."

No one else had eyes like Cristen, he thought. They saw right into your very soul.

He lifted a slim black eyebrow. "Which hapless knight did you coerce into escorting you?"

The hint of a dimple dented her cheek. "Thomas."

He walked toward her. "I don't quite understand what has happened. Where is your father?"

Her eyes were steady on his. "Guy put him in charge of the feudal army he called up to go with Stephen to Cornwall."

Hugh's stride checked briefly and his own eyes widened.

"Precisely," Cristen agreed.

Hugh reached her chair, and for a moment he stood there, struggling with his desire to catch her up into his arms.

She read his thought and smiled.

He laughed softly.

"How nice to see you again, Lord Hugh," a feminine voice said frostily.

With enormous effort, Hugh dragged his eyes away from Cristen and focused them on Lady Elizabeth's annoyed-looking face.

"It was most kind of you to offer Lady Cristen shelter, my lady," he said formally.

"Considering that she arrived here as night was falling and had no place to stay, it was the least I could do." Elizabeth's long green eyes were as cold as her voice. "She said she was looking for you." There was a definite note of accusation in her comment.

"Well, now she has found me and we shall burden you no longer," Hugh said with perfect pleasantness. He turned back to the only person in the room who had any reality for him. "Have your maid pack up your things," he told Cristen. "I'll take you to Ralf's town house. You can stay there."

An outraged voice announced, *"She will do no such thing."*

It was Lady Sybil. "Lady Cristen will remain right here, under my chaperonage," Elizabeth's companion continued. She glared at Hugh. "It is impossible for her to reside in your house in the absence of her father or a suitable female companion."

"I am not staying in the house, my lady," Hugh explained impatiently. "I am staying with the sheriff. There is no reason why Lady Cristen cannot have the use of my foster father's house while she is here."

A masculine voice interrupted from the direction of the doorway. "Hugh! Thank heavens you have returned."

Everyone turned to look at Richard Canville as he came into the room.

"As you see, Richard," Hugh replied in a flat, expressionless voice. "I have indeed returned."

Sybil appealed to Richard to champion her cause. "Sir Richard, will you please tell Lord Hugh that he cannot take Lady Cristen to live in his town house. She doesn't have a chaperone. It isn't proper."

Hugh and Richard looked at each other. Hugh's gray eyes were perfectly shuttered. After a moment, Richard shrugged, leaned casually against the door frame, and looked at Lady Sybil. "I don't see the difficulty, my lady, as long as Hugh continues to reside with my father and me."

"It isn't proper," Lady Sybil repeated firmly.

"I have one of my ladies with me," Cristen said, "but if you feel I need another chaperone, Lady Sybil, perhaps one of your own ladies would not mind bearing my company for a few days."

"I am so glad that you feel comfortable enough with me to make arrangements for my ladies," Elizabeth said to Cristen in an arctic voice.

Hugh's eyes narrowed.

Cristen gave him a warning look.

"I beg your pardon, Lady Elizabeth," she said gently. "I wasn't thinking. Of course I cannot deprive you of the comfort of one of your ladies."

Everyone looked at Elizabeth, whose eyes glittered like twin emeralds. She was obviously furious.

"I don't see why you just can't remain here," she said to Cristen.

"Well, I can if you don't mind taking in my dogs as well," Cristen replied. "They will be coming shortly, and I must have them with me."

"Dogs!" said Lady Sybil in a tone of horror.

"They are perfectly safe as long as you don't show that you are afraid of them," Cristen said guilelessly.

Hugh thought of Cedric and Ralf, and smothered a grin.

Cristen's face was beautifully innocent. "They should be here sometime this afternoon, along with my page and two more of my father's knights."

"Well," Lady Sybil huffed. "If you are to be surrounded by all those people, and if Lord Hugh is indeed staying with the sheriff, then perhaps it would be all right for you to reside in his town house."

Hugh steadfastly refused to look at Cristen. He knew if he did, he would start to laugh.

"Is the house fit for Lady Cristen?" Richard said to Hugh. "It has been closed up for over a year."

"It just needs a little airing out," Hugh said.

"I'm sure I shall manage," Cristen said. "I shall have Mabel and Thomas and Lord Hugh to help me."

Lady Sybil still looked upset. Obviously she did not approve of this transfer of residence, but just as obviously she did not want to live with Cristen's dogs.

"Do not worry, the dogs will make excellent guards, my lady," Cristen said ruthlessly. "They are very protective of me."

Hugh began to cough.

"Why don't you come along with me now, Lady Cristen," he said when he had recovered his breath. "I will show you the house and you can decide what needs to be done."

"An excellent idea," Cristen said briskly.

She got to her feet and looked down at Elizabeth. "You have been most kind, my lady. I appreciate your hospitality more than I can say."

"You're welcome," Elizabeth snapped.

Hugh held out his arm. Cristen took it and they walked together out of the room.

"Well," Elizabeth said ominously once the door had closed behind Hugh and Cristen, "they certainly seem to be a friendly pair."

Richard came into the room and seated himself in a chair near Elizabeth's. "Hugh has been living at Somerford these last six months, I believe," he said. "He and Lady Cristen have clearly become friends."

His words were reassuring, but there was a troubled look in his blue eyes.

"He couldn't wait to get her to himself," Elizabeth said. "I hope the girl knows what she is about. He'll never marry her. He's her overlord, for heaven's sake."

"A fine way to thank the man who discovered him and made him the heir to an earldom," Lady Sybil said severely. "By seducing his daughter!"

"You don't know that that has happened," Richard said fairly.

Elizabeth shook out the embroidery work that had been lying neglected in her lap. "I wonder if Lord Guy knows that Lady Cristen is in Lincoln," she said innocently. She lifted her needle and seemed intent on the pattern she had been embroidering.

"I doubt it," Richard replied.

She raised her eyes and looked at him. "Perhaps someone ought to tell him. I should hate to see the girl ruin herself without making a push to help."

"You are always so kind, my lady," Richard said with a hint of amusement in his voice.

Elizabeth took a stitch in her embroidery. "I try to be," she replied.

"Sir Richard," Lady Sybil said imperiously. "What is this I hear about a town fair? Surely there is not going to be any kind of festivity so soon after Lord Gilbert's murder?"

"It is a very small fair, my lady," Richard replied. "The town holds it every year at this time, before the beginning of Lent."

"Under the circumstances, I do not think it would be proper to hold a fair of any kind, no matter its size," Lady Sybil pronounced.

"My father will not allow it to go on at the same time as the trial," Richard assured her.

Once more, Elizabeth put down her embroidery. "And just when is this trial going to happen?" she demanded. "We have known for weeks who the murderer is."

"As I believe my father has explained to you, my lady, your father's eminence demands that the case be heard in a royal court, not the shire court. Lord Richard Basset, the Chief Justiciar of England, has written to inform my father that he will hear the case himself. He is extremely busy and will get here as soon as he can. We can do nothing but wait for him."

Elizabeth tipped her head back against her chair and shut her eyes. After a moment, she opened them again and looked appealingly at Richard. "I do not mean to sound like a shrew, Sir Richard, but this has been a very trying time for me."

She was breathtakingly lovely.

"I can appreciate that, my lady," Richard returned. "Why don't you let me take you for a ride? It can only benefit you to get some fresh air and exercise."

Elizabeth's lips curled into an entrancing smile. "I believe you are right."

Lady Sybil frowned warningly. "It must be a short ride, Elizabeth."

"Do not worry, my lady," Elizabeth returned. "*I* know what is due to my honor." She sighed. "It is a thousand pities that the same cannot be said of Lady Cristen."

*   *   *

"What made you come?" Hugh asked Cristen as they crossed the Inner bail side by side. Her small hand rested lightly on his sleeve, and he could feel her presence with every fiber of his being.

She didn't reply.

He turned and looked down at the top of her head. He said in a low voice, "Did you know?"

The shining brown head nodded.

"I had a headache," he offered.

She shot him a slanting look. "It wasn't just that."

"No," he replied slowly. "It wasn't." He looked around the familiar environs of the Inner bail. "I didn't think it would be this hard to come back to Lincoln."

Her head nodded once more.

"Does Guy know you are here?" he asked.

"Not yet," she replied ruefully.

As they walked past the stockade that held the knights' horses, several equine heads lifted to watch them go by. The brisk breeze lifted the horses' manes from their necks.

"I wonder what Guy is doing in Lincoln," Hugh said in a puzzled voice.

"He came to find you," Cristen informed him. "First he got Father out of the way by sending him to Cornwall, and then he came here to find you. I have a feeling that Guy has not yet given up on the de Beauté marriage."

"He has wasted a trip then," Hugh said grimly. "I will never marry Elizabeth de Beauté."

"She is very beautiful," Cristen pointed out.

"She's a brat."

Cristen smiled. "Well . . . perhaps just a little spoiled."

Hugh snorted. "More than a little."

"Did you know," Cristen said, "that Ranulf of Chester is in Lincolnshire as well? Father heard that he had gone to visit his half brother."

"Aye, I had heard that." Hugh inhaled deeply. "Cristen, there is a possibility that Roumare himself might have been involved in de Beauté's murder. He is the one most likely to profit from the death of the earl, after all. And John Rye, who was one of the castle guard during January, turns out to be a cousin of Roumare's."

He told her what he had discovered during his trip to Linsay.

She immediately put her finger on the one thing that Hugh could not explain. "But if, as you suspect, this John Rye did indeed murder the earl at Roumare's behest, why would he have offered to sell you evidence?"

"I don't know," Hugh admitted. "Unless he was just trying to put me off the scent."

By this time they had reached the market stalls in the Bail, and someone nearby shouted Hugh's name.

Hugh and Cristen stopped and turned. Edgar Harding of Deerhurst was approaching, his blue mantle blowing in the wind.

"Master Harding," Hugh said as the man came up to them. "How nice to see you again."

The Saxon's gray-blond eyebrows were drawn together in a scowl. "I have a request to make of you, Lord Hugh," he said abruptly.

Hugh looked resigned.

"It is a complaint against the sheriff," Harding said.

"Master Harding," Hugh said gently, "I am not the person to whom you should make such a complaint. I have no authority here in Lincoln."

"You are Ralf Corbaille's foster son," Harding replied fiercely. "Ralf gave his life's work to Lincoln. His son cannot let all of the good he did be trampled underfoot by a greedy successor."

Hugh's brows drew together. "What do you mean?"

Harding took a step closer to Hugh. "I mean that Gervase Canville is robbing from the town." He gestured to the busy market-place behind them. "Did you know that he rented these stalls out?"

"He himself told me about it," Hugh replied. "He also told me that he used the money from the rentals to increase the pay of the castle guards."

The Saxon snorted. "Hah! Perhaps he did increase the guards' pay, but I'll wager all I possess that the increase in pay does not begin to account for the amount of money he is collecting from renting those stalls."

Hugh looked into the angry pale-blue eyes of the Master of Deerhurst. "How do you know that?" he asked.

"He never offered me a stall," Harding said. He wrapped his cloak tightly around him to keep it from blowing. "He should have offered me a stall. I have the largest farm in the area. But he didn't. Do you know why he didn't?"

Hugh shook his head.

"Because he knew that I'd discover his scheme," the Saxon replied vigorously. "*I* know how much money goes to the castle guard because I make it my business to know such things. And I have found out how much money these fellows"—he gestured to the stalls behind him—"are paying Canville. The two figures don't add up."

The wind blew Hugh's hair across his forehead and he pushed it back out of his eyes. When he spoke, his voice was patient. "Master Harding, the sheriff of Lincoln, like all other sheriffs in the kingdom, must account for his financial dealings to the king. Twice a year Sir Gervase must justify all his accounts at the Exchequer board. If there was some discrepancy, I can assure you that the king's officers would have found it out by now."

"Don't be a fool," Harding said contemptuously. "Canville doesn't report half the income from these stalls. It goes straight into his own pocket."

One of Cristen's braids blew across Hugh's arm. He glanced down at her, then turned his attention back to the Saxon. "And what would you like me to do, Master Harding?" There was no anger in his voice. It was perfectly neutral.

"I want you to expose him," the Saxon returned passionately. "I want the rents on these stalls lowered to a reasonable sum. And I want the opportunity to open one myself!"

Hugh surveyed the line of market stalls in silence. Without turning his head, he said to Harding, "How do you know what these merchants are paying the sheriff?"

"I asked them," came the contemptuous reply.

The wind sent a stray glove blowing past them.

"All right," Hugh said. "I shall look into the matter."

"Good," the Saxon replied with the first sign of satisfaction he had shown since the interview began. "Your father was the only honest leader this shire has ever had. De Beauté was a thief and so is Canville."

"De Beauté was a thief?" Hugh said in surprise.

"Aye, a thief," Harding returned emphatically. "Let me tell you, he richly deserved that deadly stab he got in the heart. We shall probably end up with Roumare as our next earl. He's a thief, too, but at least he doesn't covet *my* lands."

On that note, Edgar Harding of Deerhurst spun on his heels and stalked away.

Hugh remained looking after him, brow furrowed. At last Cristen broke the silence. "Do you think he is speaking the truth?"

"He might be," Hugh said. "God knows, Gervase would not be the first sheriff to skim money off the top of the shire's revenues for himself."

"Master Harding was certainly upset that he had not been given a market stall in the Bail."

"Aye," Hugh returned absently, staring down at a long brown hair that had become attached to his red wool sleeve.

Cristen pulled her hood up against the wind. "Do you know what enmity lay between Harding and Gilbert de Beauté?"

Hugh tucked her braids securely into her hood. Then he told her about the land feud between Harding and de Beauté and about how the king had ruled in favor of de Beauté.

"It happened five years ago, but evidently it still rankles," he concluded. "Ralf always said that if there was one thing Edgar Harding knew how to do well, it was nurse a grudge."

They began to walk in the direction of the gate.

"Did Harding perhaps hate de Beauté well enough to kill him?" Cristen asked.

"I don't know," Hugh replied soberly. "But I will tell you this, Cristen. I can't help but wonder how Edgar Harding came to learn that Gilbert de Beauté was stabbed in the heart."

13

Lady Elizabeth had been right about Hugh wanting Cristen to himself. He would send for Thomas and Mabel shortly, he told himself as he guided Cristen through the side streets of Lincoln toward Ralf's house.

"I am trying to picture you growing up here," Cristen said as Hugh turned into the Patchmingate. She looked around at the mix of stone and wooden houses that lined the street. "How did you spend your days when you were a child?"

"I went to school until I was sixteen," he replied. "After that, Ralf took me with him to the castle."

Cristen looked at him curiously. "What school did you attend?"

"I went to the Minster school here in Lincoln."

She nodded thoughtfully.

"The education was quite rigorous," Hugh said. "We studied the usual *trivium*, Latin, rhetoric, and dialectic, but we had the *quadrivium* as well: arithmetic, geometry, astronomy, and music."

"It sounds more like an education for a clerk than a knight," Cristen commented.

"Ralf was a great believer in education," Hugh explained. "He was not born into the baronial class, you see, but he was fortunate enough to go to school at Saint

Mary-le-Bow in London. He did so well that he caught the eye of the old king, who took him into his household. Henry appreciated Ralf's ability and his loyalty, and eventually gifted him with three manors and appointed him Sheriff of Lincoln. Ralf always said that his brain was as important in gaining him his success in life as were his military skills."

It was less chilly here in the town, with the houses to buffer the wind from the street, and Cristen pushed her hood off her head. "What kind of boys went to school with you?" she asked.

"All kinds," he replied. "There were boys who were studying to be clerks, naturally, but a number of the sons of the town's freemen also attended."

Two small boys chasing a stuffed leather ball dashed out in front of them from between two houses. Their high-pitched shrieks filled the air.

Hugh said, "There were also a few younger sons of the local barons."

The ball rolled in front of Hugh's feet and he picked it up and threw it back to the children. He shot a quick, sideways look down at Cristen. "Richard Canville was one of them."

"Richard Canville?" Cristen glanced up at Hugh's contained profile. "Richard Canville is not a younger son."

"He was once. His elder brother died."

"Oh."

A faint frown puckered her delicate brows. She glanced once more at Hugh's unrevealing face.

"It was Richard Canville who rescued us yesterday afternoon," she said. "We arrived at the castle very late in the day with no lodgings reserved. Thomas was furious with me for refusing to spend another night on the road. When we saw Sir Richard and Lady Elizabeth on their way to evening service, Thomas stopped him and asked if he knew where we might find you."

Hugh said, "Richard has the happy facility of always being in the right place at the right time."

Cristen's frown deepened. "You don't like him," she said.

Silence from Hugh.

Finally he replied. "No, I don't."

They had reached the street where Ralf's town house was located and Hugh turned onto it. Cristen followed.

"Why don't you like him?" she asked.

He didn't answer.

They walked halfway down the block without talking. They were almost at Ralf's town house when he stopped and looked at her. "What did you think of him?"

"I have only met him briefly," she returned. "I haven't really had a chance to form an opinion."

"Everyone likes Richard," Hugh said.

"Then why don't you?" she repeated.

His face wore its most shuttered expression. It was not a look he often showed to Cristen.

"He tells people it's because I'm jealous of him," Hugh said.

"Ah." The soft syllable was long and drawn-out.

Hugh stared straight ahead. "He tells people a lot of things about me. All very regretfully, you know. It saddens him unbearably that I won't be his friend."

"I see," said Cristen quietly.

At last she said, "I imagine you must have been competitive when you were boys."

"Richard would compete with me for the air that I breathe," Hugh said.

"He's bigger than you are," she said.

Hugh's eyes narrowed. "Eventually I learned to compensate for that."

"Men," said Cristen, and shook her head.

A woman came out of the house they were standing in front of, carrying a market basket over her arm. She glanced at Cristen and then at Hugh, and a broad smile broke like a sunrise across her face.

"Hugh!" she cried in a deep, hearty voice. "How wonderful to see you again!"

Hugh turned when he heard his name. "How are you, Mistress Romage," he said.

"I am the same as ever I was," the woman replied with a laugh, coming up to them. "But you! By all that's wonderful, I hear that you're a lord."

Hugh said to Cristen. "This is Mistress Romage, Lady Cristen. She and her family have lived next door to Ralf's house for as long as I can remember."

Cristen bestowed a friendly smile upon the woman, and the three of them stood chatting in the street, Mistress Romage informing Hugh in detail about what had happened during the last year to every single member of her large family. Finally the talkative neighbor went off to do her marketing, and Hugh and Cristen walked up to Ralf's doorway and went inside.

They stood in the main hall, which had seemed so desolate to him only days before. He held her hand and looked around the achingly familiar room.

"It's freezing in here, Hugh," she said briskly. "You need to start a fire."

"All right," he said slowly. "There should be wood out back."

She freed her hand. "Go and get some. In the meanwhile, I am going to open these shutters. It's warmer outside than it is in this room."

He nodded and obediently headed for the kitchen and the back door. When he came back into the solar, his arms laden with wood, it was bright with sunlight pouring in through the newly opened windows. Cristen was dusting a table with her scarf.

Hugh looked at her, at her bent head, her long brown braids, her competent hand whisking away the accumulated dust of a year, and all of a sudden the tight fist that had formed in his stomach when they walked inside relaxed.

It is going to be all right, he thought with relief. *Cristen is here.*

He went to the fireplace and started the fire. Then he took her upstairs and showed her his old bedroom, and Ralf's and Adela's, and the extra room that had been kept for guests. She had him open all the shutters so that the sunlight could come inside. They went back downstairs to the kitchen, which looked out upon the small backyard.

Hugh stared at the big kitchen fireplace where Adela had so often stood, stirring one of the pots hanging over the fire. If he closed his eyes, he thought he might smell the aroma of lamb stew. It had been his favorite meal, and she had frequently made it for him.

For the first time since her death, the memory of Adela did not stab him to the heart. Instead, a faint nostalgic smile touched his mouth. Cristen was peering up at the smoke hole in the roof, trying to see if it was still open. He walked over to her and put his arm around her shoulders.

She leaned against him.

"That night," he said, knowing she would know which night he was referring to. "I spent it here. I felt so . . . alone. And I had a headache."

"I felt it," she said softly. "That is why I came."

His arm tightened. "I'm glad you did."

She chuckled. "I don't know if Thomas will ever forgive me. He hardly spoke to me the whole time we were traveling."

"He'll get over it," Hugh said. And he bent and lifted her into his arms.

She looked up into his face, her brown eyes smiling. "Where are we going?"

"Not upstairs," he said. "It's too cold. We'll go into the solar in front of the fire."

She rested her head against his shoulder. "That is an excellent idea."

He took off his cloak and spread it on the rug that Adela had made. Then he took one of the chair cushions and put it down to use as a pillow for her head. The fire was roaring by now and waves of heat wafted into the room. He went to the windows and fastened the shutters halfway so that no one could look in. Then he came back to Cristen.

She had taken off her mantle and dropped it on a chest. At his touch, she lifted her arms and put them around his neck. She raised her face for his kiss.

Passion roared through Hugh. He didn't think it would ever stop, this all-consuming need he had for her. The feel of her soft mouth under his, of her baby-fine skin under his fingers, the silki-ness of her long hair, the way her eyelashes lay against her cheeks. Never would he be able to get enough of her.

They collapsed together onto his outspread mantle and stretched out, young body pressed against young body. She rained small kisses all along the length of his jaw. He shivered.

"Cristen," he whispered. His hands fumbled feverishly with her clothes. "Oh God. I have missed you so much."

"And I have missed you."

Somehow they managed to get their clothes out of their way. And then he was inside her, where he belonged.

They clung together as passion beat through them in great waves, rising like the tide in a hurricane toward a final deluge that flooded them both and left them breathless and shuddering and complete.

And afterward, as she lay quietly against him, Hugh's soul was filled with the enormous peace of being with her, of just holding her and kissing her gently, of feeling her there with him.

Heaven, he thought drowsily, *could not be better than this.*

"Hugh," Cristen said gently. "It is getting late."

"I don't want to let you go."

"I don't want you to. But we can't take the chance of someone walking in and finding us."

His hold on her tightened. "We have to be married, Cristen."

She kissed his shoulder. "We will be," she said.

Reluctantly he loosened his grip. "Now that you are here in Lincoln, it should be easy for us to get away to Keal."

"I thought of that," she said.

He separated himself from her and sat up, pushing his fingers through his disordered hair. "Perhaps we ought to leave straightaway, before Guy learns that you are here and tries to send you home."

She didn't move from where she was lying as she asked, "Have you had a chance to speak to the priest at Keal to find out if he will marry us?"

He looked away from her, his mouth tightening. He shook his head.

"Perhaps you should do that, Hugh, before we go there together." Her voice was very soft. "If Guy catches us before we are wed, he will separate us for sure."

"The priest will marry us," Hugh said grimly. "He will have to. If he tries to refuse, I will kill him." He sounded deadly serious.

"Well, that will certainly solve our problem," she said.

At last he looked at her. After a moment, his mouth relaxed into a crooked grin. "All right, I won't kill him."

"Thank you."

His grin faded. "I would leave for Keal right now and make certain all is in order, but I'm afraid to leave you here. What if Guy sends you home while I'm gone? We need to take advantage of your being in Lincoln. It will be much harder to get you to Keal from Somerford."

He picked up the belt he had discarded earlier and began to put it on.

Cristen still didn't move from where she lay. "I'm quite certain there must be some poor sick soul here in Lincoln who will benefit from my skills," she said serenely. "Even if Guy orders me home, I shall be forced to remain out of pure Christian charity."

He looked up from buckling his belt. Her head was still resting on Adela's pillow and her loose hair, which Hugh had unbraided, was streaming over her shoulders, a mantle of silken fawn.

"Didn't I ever tell you that I have taken a holy oath never to turn my back upon someone who needs my healing arts?" she asked.

He shook his head slowly. "I don't believe you ever have told me that."

"Well, I shall certainly tell Guy," she said.

A log in the fireplace fell with a hissing shower of sparks.

"Cristen," Hugh said with reverence. "You are a dangerous woman."

She smiled with satisfaction.

"I'll leave for Keal right away," he promised, and reached for his boots.

A single strand of brown hair drifted across her mouth, and she blew it away. "You can't do that, Hugh," she said. "What about Bernard? When is his trial going to take place?"

Hugh dropped the boots, his fascinated eyes focused on her mouth. "As soon as the chief justiciar arrives."

"And when will that be?"

"Soon, I should think."

The lips he was watching with such close attention set into a firm line. "Then you don't have time to go to Keal right now. Not if you are going to save Bernard."

He shook his head. "Nothing is more important than our getting married."

At that, she sat up. "Right now, Bernard is more important." She held out her hand to him. "I promise I will stay right here, Hugh. You don't have to worry that I will leave you."

He regarded her hand as it lay in his. *Everything about her is so fine, so delicate, except for these sturdy, capable hands,* he thought.

He said, "I don't trust Guy."

Her reply was absolutely calm. "He cannot make me leave here against my will."

At that, he looked up into her eyes. A faint smile touched his mouth. "In all your life, I don't believe anyone has ever been able to make you do something you didn't want to do."

Her brown eyes were luminous. "It's a gift," she said.

He kissed her palm and gave her back her hand.

"All right. I'll delay going to Keal until after Bernard's trial." He shook his tousled hair back off his brow and added bitterly, "Not that my presence is going to help him very much. All I have are suspicions. I have no proof of anything."

"You'll find out the truth," she said. "I don't doubt that for a minute."

Again he picked up his boots. "Why do you think that?"

"Because I know you." She pushed her hair behind her small, perfect ears and frowned. "You had better help me rebraid this, Hugh. If Thomas and Mabel arrive and find me looking like this, they will know exactly what we have been doing."

Distracted, he dropped the boots once more. "I'll get a comb," he said. "There should still be one in my room upstairs." He got to his feet. "It's a good thing I learned how to braid rope," he told her. "It's a skill I have had to call upon these last few days."

She gave him a puzzled look.

"I'll tell you about it after I get the comb," he said, and went on stocking feet out of the room.

14

The following day, Hugh paid a visit to Bernard Radvers in Lincoln Castle. Once again, he and Bernard sat side by side upon the chest. Outside the day was overcast, and little light came in the one high window. Bernard's cell looked even bleaker than it had on Hugh's previous visit.

Bernard himself was not looking well either. His blue eyes were glazed and he had a dry, hacking cough.

I have to get him out of here, Hugh thought.

"Are you ill?" he demanded of Ralf's old friend.

Bernard shrugged indifferently. "I'm well enough, Hugh. It's just this cursed cough."

"I know someone who has a talent for curing coughs. I'll get her to mix you up some of her special elixir."

Bernard rested his head against the cold stone wall. "To say true, Hugh, some promising news about this murder will do me more good than any elixir. Have you found out anything that may lead us to the real killer?"

"I have a few clues, nothing definite," Hugh said.

"I see." Bernard did not try to hide his disappointment.

Hugh stretched his legs in front of him and contemplated his spurred boots with bemused attention. "Bernard, have you ever noticed anything that might make you suspect that Gervase is stealing money from the shire's taxes?"

Bernard stared at Hugh's profile in astonishment. "What are you talking about?"

Hugh glanced at him. "Edgar Harding of Deerhurst confronted me yesterday and accused Gervase of not reporting to the Exchequer all the money he was earning from the market stall rentals in the Bail."

Bernard scowled. "I don't believe it. Gervase may be a bit hasty in his judgments, and he lacks Ralf's sense of mercy, but I would swear that he is honest."

"He owns a very expensive town house, which is staffed by an impressive array of servants," Hugh commented in a voice that was carefully neutral.

Bernard shook his head in dismissal of Hugh's implied accusation. "Gervase is not a poor man. He owns a number of very profitable manors. He can well afford that town house."

"The Canville manors are not any greater than Ralf's were, and Ralf did not live like that," Hugh countered.

They heard a rustling sound in the far corner of the cell as one of the resident rats scurried into its nest. Ignoring it, Bernard said, "Ralf's tastes were simple, as were Adela's. Gervase likes things a little grander."

"Perhaps." Hugh did not sound convinced.

At that moment, a particularly nasty coughing fit caused Bernard to double over. Hugh said with a frown, "Have you a fever?"

"I don't know." Bernard gave one more cough, then cleared his throat loudly and drew in a deep breath.

"In regard to this accusation of Edgar Harding's," he said. "Did you know that the Saxon hates Gervase and would probably do anything he could to discredit him?"

"Nay," Hugh replied slowly. "I did not know that."

"Well, it's true. I would examine anything Harding says against the sheriff very carefully if I were you."

"What does Harding have against Gervase? I know he hated de Beauté because he won their land dispute, but surely that doesn't have anything to do with the sheriff."

Bernard gave a single cough before replying, "He dislikes Gervase because last year William of Roumare's steward complained that he had caught one of Edgar's men poaching on Roumare land, and Gervase had the man arrested and hung. Harding was convinced that the man had been treated so harshly because he was a Saxon. He has borne a grudge against Gervase ever since."

Someone walked by the high barred window that was the only outlet to fresh air in the cell. The window was at the level of the man's feet, and the sound of spurs jingling sounded like bells of freedom ringing through the dark, dank room.

Hugh lifted his eyebrows. "Is there anyone Edgar Harding does not have a grudge against?"

Bernard was looking wistfully at the window. "Not that I know of. He is a most contentious man."

"Contentious enough to kill in order to obtain revenge?"

Bernard's eyes jerked away from the window and back to Hugh. "Kill? Kill who? De Beauté?"

Hugh said soberly, "He knew that the earl was stabbed in the heart, Bernard. I did not think that was common knowledge."

"Everyone knows it was a knife."

"Aye, but do they know the precise location of the stab wound? Or that it was but a single blow? John Melan didn't know those things when he came to fetch me. I discovered those facts from Gervase."

Bernard stared at Hugh, his brows knit.

"Who else knew the details about the knife wound?" Hugh asked.

"Those who saw the body before it was covered," Bernard replied. "Myself, Richard Canville's squire, and Gervase himself."

"Who washed it and laid it out for burial?"

"One of the lay brothers at the Minster."

"I had better have a talk with him," Hugh said. "What about de Beauté's daughter?"

"I shouldn't think they would have let her see her father until he was decently laid out, but I can't say for sure."

The rats in the corner began to make scratching noises on the hard dirt floor.

Hugh said, "Well, Edgar Harding certainly knew about the wound. I think I had better find out just where the Saxon was on the night that Gilbert de Beauté was murdered."

"It won't hurt to do that," Bernard agreed soberly.

A little silence fell as each man pursued his own thoughts. It was Hugh who spoke first. "Just who is this boy who has become Richard's squire?"

Bernard roused himself from whatever it was he had been contemplating. "There is no mystery about Alan Stanham. His father holds a property outside Lincoln in knight's fee from the bishop. Richard met the boy on some occasion or other and was impressed by him. He invited Alan to be his squire, and Alan's father was delighted to accept. The boy is a younger son in a large family. Richard's patronage will be very useful to him."

"Alan's father doesn't sound like an overly careful parent," Hugh said.

Bernard made a noise indicating exasperation. "I know this is hard for you to believe, Hugh, but most people think that Richard Canville is the perfect knightly model for a young boy to emulate."

Hugh's face was completely expressionless.

"At any rate," Bernard said firmly, "there is nothing at all suspicious about Alan Stanham. He is a very nice lad."

"He is a very nice lad who conveniently discovered you leaning over de Beauté's body," Hugh pointed out. "He is also one of the few people who know about the single stab wound to the heart. And he thinks Richard walks on water. I have no doubt that we can assume that anything Alan knows, Richard knows also."

Bernard said patiently, "If Richard did not learn the details from Alan, he was certain to learn them from Gervase. Gervase trusts his son implicitly. And he has reason to do so."

Hugh's nostrils pinched together.

"I have never understood your dislike of Richard," Bernard said.

Hugh made a dismissive gesture.

Bernard changed the subject. "What about your theory that William of Roumare is involved in de Beauté's death? Have you discovered anything that would bear that out?"

Hugh said, "I have not been to see you because I rode to Linsay to talk to John Rye, the only member of the castle guard I wasn't able to interview here in Lincoln." He proceeded to inform Bernard of everything he had learned at Linsay.

"So we know that Rye left Lincoln early for reasons other than his wife's illness," he concluded, "and we know that those reasons had something to do with William of Roumare. As I see it, there are two possibilities for this behavior. One possibility is that Rye murdered de Beauté at Roumare's behest, and then went to see Roumare in order to collect his payment."

Hugh steepled his fingers on his knee and regarded them with frowning intensity. "The other possiblity is that Rye is not the killer himself, but knows who the killer is and went to Roumare to try to extort money from him in exchange for keeping quiet."

"The first possibility makes better sense," Bernard said. He, too, was looking at Hugh's steepled fingers.

"Perhaps. But if it is true that Rye himself is the killer, then why did he offer to sell me information?"

"Such information is probably false. He is trying to make even more money out of de Beauté's death than he already has."

"That could be so," Hugh agreed. "But it may also be true that Rye actually does have some information about the murder, which he tried and failed to sell to Roumare, and now he is in the market for another buyer."

Bernard said very slowly, "That is so."

Hugh tapped his two forefingers together.

Bernard said, "How much money does he want?"

"We didn't get that far."

Bernard reached out and closed his hand around Hugh's hard forearm. "I'm desperate enough to be willing to pay a bribe if I have to. Can you find out? If we don't get some concrete evidence soon, I don't have a chance."

"Of course you have a chance," Hugh said emphatically. "When you think about it, Bernard, you have absolutely no motive for killing Gilbert de Beauté."

Bernard began to cough. "My motive is supposedly you," he finally got out.

"That justification is tenuous, to say the least. Anyone with a functioning mind must know that my chance to become Earl of Lincoln depended upon my marriage being accomplished during de Beauté's lifetime. With Elizabeth still unwed, her guardianship passes to the king and everything is changed. I lose instead of win."

"Well, apparently the sheriff does not credit me with a functioning mind," Bernard said sarcastically.

"You are nothing more than a scapegoat," Hugh said. "The sheriff has no other suspect. Gervase doesn't really want to accuse you, Bernard. If we can find him a more likely candidate, he will be grateful."

"Well then, find him another candidate!" Bernard commanded.

Hugh got to his feet. "I intend to do just that. I will look into the whereabouts of Edgar Harding on the night of the murder, and I will find out what information John Rye may be concealing."

Bernard remained sitting on the bench. "You don't have much time, Hugh," he said. "Lord Richard Basset is already overdue."

"Have you forgot Saint Agatha's Fair? It is due to start the day after tomorrow and the townsfolk are busy getting ready for it. Even if the chief justiciar arrives, the trial won't start until after it is over."

"I hadn't thought the fair would be held this year," Bernard said with surprise.

"A delegation of the town's freemen asked Gervase to let it go forward. People come into Lincoln from the surrounding country-side for the fair, and it is business the local merchants count upon. Gervase decided a week ago to allow the event to procede. So we have a bit of a respite, Bernard."

Bernard was seized by another coughing fit.

Hugh stood looking down at his father's old friend, a frown upon his face. "I will be back later today with some medicine for that cough," he promised.

Bernard nodded and continued to cough.

Hugh hesitated, then patted him upon the shoulder before he strode to the door and knocked peremptorily upon the heavy wood. A guard appeared to let him out, and Hugh exited without a backward look.

He ran lightly up the stairs and out to the gray light of the court-yard. It had begun to rain. He passed through the keep gate and went down the stairs to the Inner bail, where he collected Rufus. He swung into the saddle and headed the stallion in the direction of the town.

Cristen would know what to do about Bernard's cough, he thought. It was clearly his duty to see her as soon as he possibly could.

When Hugh walked into the hall of Ralf's town house, the first person he saw was his uncle, sitting in Ralf's old chair.

"My lord," he said in a level voice.

Next he looked at Cristen, seated in the chair that had always been Adela's. The perfect serenity of her face told him that she was under siege.

"I have just told Lady Cristen that she is to return to Somerford immediately," Guy informed him. "If you have any sense at all, Hugh, you will tell her the same thing. With her father away in Cornwall, she has no reason to be here. Her reputation will be ruined if she remains."

"I am the one who sent for Lady Cristen," Hugh replied promptly. "Bernard Radvers is very ill and I wanted her to look after him."

Cristen regarded him with grave eyes and knew immediately that he was telling the truth about Bernard.

"I was just getting ready to go and visit poor Bernard when Lord Guy arrived," she said.

Hugh walked over to the fireplace, then turned to face the two of them. "His cough has become much worse," he said with a worried frown.

"There are doctors aplenty in Lincoln!" Guy roared. "Lady Cristen is the daughter of one of my vassals. She is not a traveling herb woman."

"She is a very gifted healer," Hugh said coldly.

Guy narrowed his eyes. "This is not something I intend to discuss. I have made my wishes very plain. Lady Cristen is to go home. Immediately."

Hugh looked back at his uncle, his face very still. "The de Beauté marriage is finished," he said. "It was finished even before Lord Gilbert died. I will never marry that girl."

Guy surged to his feet. "You will marry whom I tell you to marry!"

"Do you really believe that?" Hugh asked. He actually sounded amused.

Guy drew himself up to his full height, which was the same as Hugh's. "Tread carefully, Hugh. I am the one with the upper hand here. I am the one who holds the earldom from the king."

"I believe we have had this conversation before, Uncle," Hugh said wearily. "You may have the earldom from the king, but I have other options."

"If you think that Gloucester will sanction a marriage with Cristen Haslin, you are wrong," Guy said brutally. "He, too, will want an alliance that brings him greater political advantage. It is insane for you to think of marrying the daughter of one of your own vassals."

Cristen said, "I did not come here to marry Hugh, my lord. I came to see if I could help Bernard Radvers. And I believe I have delayed long enough."

Guy swung around to regard her with astonishment. "The only place you are going, my lady, is home!"

Cristen looked genuinely regretful. "I am sorry to disobey you, my lord, but I took a sacred oath never to deny my healing to anyone who asks for it."

"Your father took a sacred oath to me," Guy roared.

"I took my oath to God," Cristen replied. "I believe He has the precedence."

Guy's face slowly turned purple. He took a step toward Cristen and raised his hand.

He was stopped by steel-hard fingers grasping him by the shoulder.

"Don't," Hugh said. He had moved from the fireplace with incredible swiftness.

Guy turned, looked into his nephew's face, and froze.

Cristen looked at Hugh as well.

Don't. She sent him the command silently. *Let me handle this. Please.*

Hugh met her eyes. After a moment, with palpable reluctance, he let his hand drop away from his uncle's shoulder.

Guy's hurried breathing was audible in the suddenly silent room.

Cristen said meekly, "I am very sorry to disobey you, Lord Guy, but I must try to heal Bernard Radvers. I can assure you, however, that once he is on his way to recovery, I shall go home."

"If you disobey me in this, girl, then I wash my hands of you," Guy said. "You will never win my permission to marry anyone, and when your father dies, Somerford will be mine to give where I wish."

Cristen's brown gaze never wavered. "I am sorry you feel that way, my lord."

Guy's mouth set into a grim line, and without looking again at Hugh, he stormed out of the house.

Neither Cristen nor Hugh moved until they heard the door slam behind Guy. Then Hugh went over to Cristen's chair and lifted her out of it into his arms.

"I did take that oath to God," she said into his shoulder. "I swore it last night."

He nodded gravely.

The front door opened again and someone came in. Hugh and Cristen barely had time to separate before Thomas entered the room.

"My lady! I just saw Lord Guy riding away from here . . ." Thomas's voice trailed away as his eyes came to rest on Hugh.

"My lord! I didn't know you were here." His voice was distinctly apprehensive.

Hugh, annoyed at being interrupted, frowned and said shortly, "Well, as you can see, I am."

Thomas regarded Hugh as a deer might watch a circling wolf, and did not reply.

The irritation faded from Hugh's face. "Don't worry, Thomas," he said sympathetically, "I don't hold you responsible. I just watched Lady Cristen vanquish Lord Guy. I'm quite sure you never stood a chance against her."

"She threatened to go alone if I wouldn't escort her, my lord," Thomas said indignantly.

Hugh glanced at Cristen and grinned.

"It wasn't funny, my lord," Thomas said sulkily. "You know Lady Cristen. She doesn't make idle threats."

"If you had let her go alone I would have murdered you with my bare hands."

Thomas looked gloomy. "That's what I thought."

Cristen stood up. "You two obviously don't need me in order to continue this fascinating conversation. I am going into the kitchen to prepare a cough mixture for Bernard. When I am finished, Hugh, you can escort me to the castle. I want to see him for myself."

"Your wish is my command," Hugh said. Amusement still lingered around his mouth.

She shot him a look, then went through the door that led to the back of the house. They heard her calling for Mabel.

Thomas said to Hugh, "Jesu, my lord, but she had me terrified. I found her a convent to stay in on the road, but I didn't know what we were going to do once we got to Lincoln. When we found out that you were out of town and that the bishop's guest house was filled, I nearly cried."

"I understand that Richard Canville came to your rescue," Hugh said blandly.

"Well, it was more Lady Elizabeth," Thomas said. "I was that glad when she said she would take charge of Lady Cristen. God's blood, we had discovered that it was Lord Guy who was staying at the bishop's guest house!"

"Your own blood must have run cold when you heard that piece of news."

"It certainly did, my lord."

Hugh regarded Thomas with commanding gray eyes. "Lady Cristen insisted upon coming to Lincoln because I asked her to look after Bernard Radvers, who is ill."

Thomas looked back at Hugh. "Oh," he said after a moment. "I see."

"Good," said Hugh. He leaned his shoulders against the wall and crossed his arms. "Tell me, who is in charge of Somerford at the moment?"

"Lionel, my lord. Sir Nigel actually left Lady Cristen in charge, but she insisted on coming to Lincoln."

They both knew that if there was a siege of the castle, Cristen would be a far better commander than Lionel.

"I don't think you have to worry about Somerford at the moment," Hugh said. "It will be safe while Sir Nigel is in Cornwall."

"I devoutly hope so, my lord."

"How many troops did Guy call up?" Hugh asked.

Thomas was still telling him about the levy that Nigel was leading when Cristen came back into the room carrying a bottle.

"I'm ready to visit Bernard," she announced cheerfully.

"Excellent," Hugh said. "I brought your horse with me from the castle, so you can ride. You should be able to keep him in the stable out back. I'll get in a supply of hay."

"I can do that, my lord," Thomas said.

"Very well."

After Hugh and Cristen had left, Thomas stood staring into the fire for a long time.

Cristen had never said a word to him about Bernard Radvers being ill.

15

At the castle, Hugh introduced Cristen to the sheriff, who gave his permission for her to visit Bernard. It took Cristen less than half an hour to demand that the sheriff remove Bernard from his chill damp cell and put him into one of the castle's tower rooms, with a charcoal brazier to keep him warm.

"This man is very ill," she told Gervase severely. "If you want to have a living man to put on trial and not a corpse, you had better do as I tell you."

Hugh watched with concealed delight as his small, fragile-looking beloved threatened the sheriff with all sorts of dire consequences if he did not move Bernard.

And she did it so nicely, he thought. Cristen was never hostile or aggressive. She just backed you into a corner, and before you knew what was happening, the only way out was her way.

That was how Bernard Radvers came to be tucked into a warm bed in one of the corner towers, his cough soothed by an elixir of horehound and his fever responding to a draught of wine mulled with borage and assorted other herbs.

The only part of Cristen's assault on Gervase that Hugh did not enjoy was her requirement that the sheriff give her the room next door to Bernard for the duration of his illness.

"I am afraid that his lungs might have been affected," she told Gervase worriedly. "He must be watched closely."

Hugh, who had quite other ideas for Cristen during her stay in Lincoln, listened to these words glumly.

She was right, he told himself as he stood with Cristen and Richard in the tower room where she would be staying. If Bernard was as ill as she said he was, his need was greater than Hugh's. And there was another benefit to her staying in the castle to minister to Bernard. Her vigil would help to convince Guy that she had been telling the truth about her reason for coming to Lincoln.

Hell and the devil, Hugh thought, trying not to scowl too openly. *It would be easier to scale a castle wall without a rope than it is to get Cristen to myself.*

"I will put my squire at your disposal for the duration of your stay, Lady Cristen," Richard was saying. "He will be able to procure for you anything you might need." As he spoke, two of Gervase's men arrived with another brazier for Cristen's bedroom and a pallet for Mabel to sleep upon.

Cristen pointed out to the men where she wanted them to place Mabel's mattress. "You are very kind, Sir Richard," she said distractedly.

He made a little bow. "I am happy to be of service, my lady. It will not reflect well upon us should we allow a prisoner in our hands to die."

A mistake, Richard, Hugh thought acidly. *You just said that to the wrong person.*

Cristen's fine brows lifted. "I will do my best to keep him breathing for you."

The sheriff's men departed, leaving the three of them alone in the room.

Richard said, "It is a shame that Hugh did not inform us sooner about Bernard's condition. Had we known, he might not have become so very ill."

Careful! Hugh sent the silent message to Cristen, afraid she might not see the trap.

"Hugh did what he thought was best," Cristen replied, calmly evading it. "He sent for me."

"That was wise of him," Richard agreed. He turned to look at Hugh. "My real regret is that you have so little trust in us that you felt we would do nothing for Bernard on our own."

"You think I don't trust you and your father?" Hugh said in astonishment.

Richard looked ineffably sad. "You don't trust me, at any rate. And I don't think you like my father because he succeeded Ralf."

Hugh said, "It always amazes me, Richard, how well you are able to read my heart."

Faint color stole into Richard's cheeks. "I had better go."

"Good idea," Hugh said.

Richard turned back to Cristen. "Thank you again, Lady Cristen. My father and I appreciate your generosity."

"She is doing it for Bernard, Richard, not for you and your father."

Cristen said, "Thank you for your assistance, Sir Richard. I should very much appreciate the service of your squire."

Richard bowed once more. His cheeks were still a little flushed as he went out of the room.

Left alone, Hugh and Cristen looked at each other.

"I was touched by his concern for Bernard," she said.

Hugh snorted. "The only person who exists in Richard's world is Richard."

He walked over to her and put his arms around her. She leaned against him.

"Try not to let him disturb you so much," she said softly.

His arms tightened. "Christ, but I wish you didn't have to stay here."

"Bernard really is ill, Hugh. I wasn't exaggerating."

He sighed. "I know."

The sound of leather soles scraping against the floor came from the passage, and Hugh dropped his arms and stepped back.

Mabel came into the room. "Thomas told me that you needed me, my lady."

Hugh felt Cristen's attention shift away from him. "Aye, Mabel. We have a sick man to look after."

"I had better go and leave you to your work," he said resignedly.

Cristen sent him a quick smile, then turned back to Mabel.

Hugh walked out of the room. As he ran lightly down the tower stairs, he decided that he would spend the afternoon paying a visit to Edgar Harding of Deerhurst.

The manor of Deerhurst lay to the south of Lincoln, east of the River Witham. The Harding who had dwelt there during the time of King William had been one of the few Saxons who managed to save his property from the greedy hands of the Norman conqueror. The Hardings had kept their holdings under the rule of William's sons as well, but now, under the conqueror's grandson Stephen, land that had belonged to the Hardings for generations had been given away to a Norman earl.

The property that remained to Edgar Harding, however, was extensive and well cultivated. For generations, the city of Lincoln had depended upon produce and fodder from Deerhurst to feed its people and animals during the long winter months.

Hugh had been to Deerhurst several times with Ralf, and so he knew what to expect once he rode in through the palisaded wooden fence that surrounded the enclave. The Hardings had never adopted the Norman style of building, but had maintained instead the old Saxon timber construction and architecture. Instead of a single castle keep, Deerhurst consisted of a series of separate rectangular buildings: the halls, bowers, sleeping chambers, kitchen, and stable of the manor.

Hugh stopped Rufus just inside the open gate and gave his name to the burly man who had stepped in front of him. He asked to speak to Edgar Harding.

The Saxon stared at him suspiciously, then told him to wait. Hugh remained exactly where he was, giving Rufus a loose rein so he could drop his head and stretch his neck.

About a dozen people were scattered around the courtyard, all looking at Hugh. Their expressions were not friendly.

After almost a quarter of an hour, a slender, fair-haired young man came out of one of the buildings and approached Hugh and Rufus. He stopped next to the stallion's head and said in French, "I am Cedric Harding. I regret that my father is not at Deerhurst at present. May I be of some assistance to you?"

The young man looked to be about Hugh's age and had a similar build. His words were irreproachably courteous, but there was a wary look in his blue eyes.

Hugh made a quick decision. "Perhaps you can. Do you mind if I ask you a few questions?"

Cedric Harding's face was perfectly expressionless as he replied, "Of course not. Come inside with me." He looked at the burly man who had resumed his post at the gate and said in English, "Alfred, take Lord Hugh's horse and see that he is attended to." Then, switching back to French to speak to Hugh, "Come with me."

As Rufus was led away toward the stable, Hugh fell into step with the younger Harding.

"I am my father's eldest son," Cedric informed him.

"I am surprised that we have not met before this," Hugh said. "I grew up in Lincoln as the foster son of Ralf Corbaille."

Cedric Harding's blue eyes flashed toward him. "I know."

Hugh was silent, waiting for an answer to his comment.

Cedric shrugged and said, "My father does not like his household to mingle too closely with Normans."

Hugh, who thought this attitude was supremely shortsighted, forebore to comment. Instead, he followed Cedric into the largest of the wooden buildings, which he knew from previous visits was Deerhurst's main hall.

This Saxon edifice was very different from the Norman-built castles to which Hugh was accustomed. The front door of the large timber structure led into a small porch, which served as an anteroom to the main room. This was a large rectangular hall with a long hearth laid in its center. Smoke holes in the cross-beamed roof let out the fumes that drifted up from the roaring fire. A bench ran along the two long walls of the hall, and above the bench was hung an impressive display of weapons: round Saxon shields, throwing spears, thrusting spears, swords, and battle axes. Directly facing Hugh on the opposite short wall of the hall, several carved chairs with arms were placed on a dais. The wooden floor of the hall was swept and bare of rushes.

A handful of men were seated on the side benches. A low stool in front of them held food and ale, and they paused in their meal to look curiously toward Hugh and Cedric as they came in.

Cedric led the way across the floor to the dais. He sat down in one of the chairs and gestured for Hugh to do the same.

"Witgar," he called toward the group of men, "have one of the women fetch us some ale."

A man got up and went out the door, and Cedric turned back to his uninvited guest.

Hugh said, "I am investigating the murder of the Earl of Lincoln."

Cedric's blue eyes were cold. "My understanding is that the murderer has been caught."

"The sheriff has arrested someone, but I think he has the wrong man."

A long minute ticked by as the two young men regarded each other, rather in the manner of two wrestlers assessing each other's strength. Finally Cedric said, "And what does the murder of the Earl of Lincoln have to do with us here at Deerhurst?"

Hugh spoke blunt words in his softest voice. "It is well known that your father had reason to hate de Beauté. I am simply trying to eliminate as many possible suspects as I can in the hopes of eventually isolating the real killer. If your father can demonstrate he was elsewhere on the night of the murder, he will make my task that much easier."

"Why don't you think the man they have is the real killer?" Cedric asked.

Hugh's relaxed hands were lying palm-down on the carved wooden arms of his chair. "He swears he is innocent and, as he happens to be a friend of mine, I believe him. I am trying to discover the truth before they hang the wrong man."

Cedric leaned back in his chair and regarded Hugh with palpable irony. "It would be so much nicer if you could hang a Saxon, wouldn't it?"

"It would be so much nicer if we could hang a murderer," Hugh retorted. "I have no interest in convicting an innocent man, be he my friend or your father."

Cedric said flatly, "There is nothing that ties my father to the death of the earl."

Hugh gazed at one of the spears hanging on the wall to his right. It was a heavy thrusting spear, its head richly inlaid with copper and bronze.

It must be a ceremonial weapon, he thought. *You wouldn't use such a spear in battle.*

Slowly Hugh returned his eyes to Edgar Harding's son. "There might be," he said. "Your father knew exactly how the earl was killed, and that information has not been made public. I would be interested to learn how he acquired that particular knowledge. I would also like to know where he was on the night Lord Gilbert was murdered. Neither question should pose a problem to an innocent man."

A woman carrying a goblet in each hand came in from the porch and began to cross the floor in the direction of the dais.

"You requested ale, master," she said to Cedric in English as she came up to him.

"Thank you, Hilda," Cedric said. He took both goblets from her and handed one to Hugh. The woman turned and recrossed the floor toward the door.

Hugh took a sip of his ale and waited.

Cedric didn't drink, but instead looked intently at the liquid in his cup. At last, still staring into his goblet, he said, "I can tell you where my father was on the night the earl was murdered. He was here at Deerhurst."

"I see," Hugh said neutrally. "And you remember that clearly?"

Finally Cedric lifted his eyes from his cup and looked at Hugh. "I remember it very clearly. It was the night of my sister's betrothal and we held a feast right here in the hall. My father presided."

Hugh held Cedric's steady blue stare.

"Your father was here all night?"

"He was here all night."

Hugh said gently, "Well then, that resolves that particular problem, doesn't it?" He put his unfinished ale on the floor next to his chair and stood up. "Thank you for your assistance, Harding. I will be on my way."

"I'll have them bring you your horse," Cedric returned.

In silence the two young men, so similar in build, one fair and one dark, walked across the hall and went out the door.

Some minutes later, as he was riding back toward Lincoln, Hugh reflected upon what he had learned at Deerhurst.

Cedric Harding had to have been telling the truth about the

betrothal feast. He would not dare to alter the date of such an event; too many people were involved in such an affair to make for a successful lie.

On the other hand, Hugh thought, the feast probably started well before dark. He had little doubt that by the time evening fell, most of the men in the hall would have been drunk. It would not have been that difficult for Harding to slip out unnoticed and ride into Lincoln. Everyone would have thought he had gone to his bed to sleep off the excess wine.

How did he know about the stab wound to the heart?

Hugh scowled in frustration. His visit to Deerhurst had left him in the same position he had been in before he went. He had no proof that Edgar Harding had killed the earl, but neither did he have proof that he had not.

In fact, he thought, he may very well have added another suspect to his list. Harding's son seemed fully as inimical to Normans as was his father.

In his mind's eye Hugh saw again the cold blue eyes of the young Saxon. Cedric Harding did not appear to be the sort of young man who would flinch from murder if he thought he had provocation enough.

Hugh stared bleakly at the heights of Lincoln Castle in the distance. *I am getting nowhere with this investigation,* he thought in frustration. *If I don't come up with something solid soon, Bernard is going to hang.*

16

Alan had not been happy when first Richard told him that he was to run errands for Cristen while she was caring for Bernard. There were plenty of others who could have been given such a menial task, he thought. Alan's job was to serve as a knight's squire, not as a sickroom servant.

He felt much better, however, when Richard took him aside later in the armory hall and made his assignment clearer.

"I don't trust Hugh," Richard said. "He obviously has Lady Cristen under his thumb, and I fear that he might persuade her to enter into a scheme to help Bernard escape." Richard's blue eyes were somber. "If that should happen, it would not look good for my father."

"That is so, my lord," Alan agreed.

As he and Richard were speaking, a few of the de Beauté knights came into the hall. They were carrying bows and talking and laughing among themselves. As they passed by, several of them nodded a greeting to Richard.

When they had gone, Richard put an affectionate hand upon his squire's shoulder. "That is your real job, Alan: making sure that there is no embarrassing escape. You are to keep an eye on Lady Cristen at all times. You are to let me know when Lord Hugh comes to visit her and, if possible, what they talk about."

Color rose under the boy's fair, beardless skin. "Aye, my lord," he said earnestly. "I understand. I promise I will not fail you."

Richard's hand tightened slightly. "I know you won't."

At the note of approval in Richard's voice, Alan's color rose even higher.

So it was that on Saturday afternoon, when Alan began his service with Cristen, he felt as if he were on a holy mission. It did not take him long to realize, however, that Bernard Radvers was seriously ill. He was so ill, in fact, that Alan strongly doubted he was in any condition to attempt an escape.

Lady Cristen was tireless in her attendance upon the sick man. During the periods when Bernard slept, she remained in her own room, which had a door that opened directly into Bernard's, and she and her attendant lady sewed shirts for the household at Somerford.

Alan sat on a chair by the door and waited to run errands, which consisted mainly of arranging for water and food. It was very dull.

Cristen evidently understood the tedium of her companions, for she sent Mabel to take her supper with Lady Elizabeth's household, and after she and Alan had eaten, she asked him if he would like to challenge her to a game of chess.

Alan was delighted, and volunteered to procure a set so they could play.

Dark had fallen, but indoors the castle was lit by flambeaux affixed to the stone walls. All of the staircases and halls Alan passed through were shadowy and empty. The de Beauté knights were gathered into the guardroom and Lady Elizabeth's household was at supper in the sheriff's apartment. The only people Alan saw as he passed through the silent, high-ceilinged stone chambers were a few servants carrying buckets of water up the stairs to the sheriff's apartment.

Alan knew that Gervase kept a chess set in one of the chests in his office, and he decided to see if by some chance the office was unlocked before he went on downstairs to the guardroom.

To Alan's surprise, a light showed under the office door. The sheriff must be working late, he thought. He knocked briskly on the door and said in a loud voice, "I'm sorry to interrupt you, sir, but it's Alan Stanham. I was wondering if I could borrow your chess set."

No answer was returned. Instead, the door opened abruptly and Alan found himself looking not at the sheriff but at the sheriff's son.

Richard did not appear pleased to see him. "What are you doing here?" he asked irritably.

"I came to borrow the chess set, my lord," Alan repeated. "Lady Cristen expressed a desire to play."

"Couldn't you have gone to the guardroom?" Richard sounded almost angry.

Alan replied steadily, "I am sorry, my lord, to have disturbed you. I will go to the guardroom."

Richard drew a deep breath, as if he were trying to get control of himself. Then he said, "Now that you have already disturbed me, you may as well take the bloody set."

"I will go to the guardroom if you prefer, my lord," Alan said. He had never seen Richard so out of sorts before.

Richard gave him a scathing look. "Stay there and I'll get it for you." He turned back into the room.

Alan remained at the door, knowing that he had blundered, but not knowing why. His eyes flicked around the room, taking in the rolls of parchment heaped upon the desk.

Richard turned from the chest that he had opened, the chess set in his hands. "Come in, Alan," he said in his normal voice. "I have been going over some tax figures for my father and it has given me a headache. I'm sorry I sounded so churlish."

Alan felt as if a weight had been lifted from his chest. He smiled and came a little way into the room. "That is all right, my lord."

Richard rubbed his forehead as if it ached. "How are you faring with Lady Cristen?"

"It's boring, my lord," Alan said frankly. "Nobody has come to see her except the servants. Bernard truly is very ill. I don't think you need to worry about him trying to escape. He has a high fever and most of the time he just sleeps."

Richard dropped his hand from his forehead. His blue eyes regarded Alan shrewdly. "Have you seen Bernard for yourself?"

"Only from the door," Alan returned. "Lady Cristen does not want me to get too close to him, lest I take the infection."

Richard offered Alan the chess set. "Isn't that thoughtful of her?" he said. Irony sounded clearly in his voice.

Alan blinked as Richard's meaning became clear.

"Do you think she is just pretending that Bernard is ill? That she does not wish me to get too close to him in case I see through the mummery?"

"It is a thought," Richard said softly.

Alan flushed. "You must think me a fool."

"Of course I don't think you a fool." Richard put a hand on Alan's shoulder and walked with him to the door. "I'm sure Lady Cristen has been very kind to you and you don't like to think ill of her. It is always hard for a man to think a lovely lady may be deceiving him. It is always wise to keep the possibility alive in one's mind, however."

"Aye, my lord," Alan said in a subdued voice.

"Hugh hasn't been to see her?"

"Nay, my lord."

"All right." Richard patted his squire's shoulder. "I have faith in your good sense and your loyalty, Alan. I know you won't fail me."

"Never, my lord," Alan promised fervently.

Richard gave him a gentle push, and Alan stepped out into the passage. "Good night, then, Alan. God go with you."

"And with you, my lord," Alan replied. Clutching the chess set against his green tunic, Alan returned upstairs to Bernard's sickroom watch.

Cristen's kindness to Alan did not extend as far as allowing him to beat her at chess. They played as equals the first game, with Cristen checkmating him after only a few moves. The second game she gave up a knight, and the game went on a little longer before she won handily. The third game she gave up her queen, and it took her over half an hour to beat him.

"Judas!" Alan exclaimed as he stared in frustration at the board. "I didn't think ladies could play chess like that."

"My father is an excellent chess player," Cristen said. "He taught me when I was very young."

A voice from the doorway said, "Aren't you going to mention the advanced tutelage you received from me?"

Alan had thought that Cristen was very pretty, but the way her face lit when she heard Hugh's voice made her look positively breathtaking.

"You?" she said. "You never tutored me. All you ever did was beat me."

Hugh walked across the room to the stool that held the chessboard. He regarded it with interest.

Alan said glumly, "She even gave me a queen and I still lost."

Hugh grinned. "She's a ruthless woman, Alan."

Alan stared at Hugh in astonishment. There was real warmth in that smile, and genuine gaiety. The look was contagious, and Alan felt his mouth curl in response.

Cristen said austerely, "Alan is not the kind of person who would want his opponent to throw him the game."

Alan said, "Well . . . not if I *knew* she was throwing me the game."

At that, both Hugh and Cristen laughed.

Treacherous delight shot through Alan that he had been able to elicit such a response.

Hugh's face sobered. "How is Bernard?" he asked Cristen.

"His fever has come down a little with my medication, but it is still too high. He has been sleeping for most of the afternoon and evening," she replied.

Alan rose from his stool on one side of the chess board. "If you don't mind, my lady, I think I should return the chess set to the sheriff's office."

Hugh looked at him in surprise. "Won't it be locked at this hour?"

"Sir Richard was there when I went to fetch it, my lord," Alan said. "He may be there still."

Something that Alan couldn't decipher flickered in Hugh's gray eyes. "Richard is certainly working late," he said lightly.

"Aye, my lord. He is helping his father with the tax rolls."

"Oh, then the sheriff was there as well?"

Alan hesitated. The question had been posed carelessly, but he had a feeling that his answer was important. He bit his lip. "Nay," he said reluctantly. "Only Sir Richard was working tonight."

"Such a dutiful, thoughtful son," Hugh said, and the uncomfortable, mocking edge that Alan so resented was back in his voice.

"Take back the chess set if that will make you more comfortable, Alan," Cristen said serenely. "If Sir Richard is gone, you will just have to return it tomorrow."

"Thank you, my lady," Alan said.

As he fitted the ivory chess pieces into the carved oak box that had been made for them, he listened to Hugh and Cristen talking about Bernard. It was clear to him that they knew each other well and were entirely comfortable in each other's company. Finally the last pawn had been put away. Alan picked up board and box and went to the door.

"Would you like me to fetch you anything while I am downstairs, my lady?" he asked.

"I don't think so," Cristen replied with her lovely smile. "But thank you, Alan."

Neither Cristen nor Hugh had given him the slightest overt indication that they wished him gone. Why then, Alan wondered, did he feel their desire so urgently?

He walked out the door, closed it behind him, and walked firmly across the landing to the spiral staircase that led down to the third level of the castle. When he reached the staircase, however, he halted, then retraced his steps on silent feet.

Bernard's room had a door that opened onto the landing as well as one that opened onto Cristen's room. Moving cautiously, Alan opened the landing door and slipped into Bernard's room.

The sick man was asleep, breathing heavily through congested lungs. Alan stood quietly, listening to that stertorous breathing, and thought that Hugh and Cristen had not been misleading the sheriff and Richard about the seriousness of Bernard's illness. He certainly was not breathing like a man who could manage an escape.

The door that opened into Cristen's room was always kept ajar, so that she could hear Bernard. If Alan remained by the landing door, however, he knew he would be invisible from the other room.

Sir Richard had told him to try to listen to what was said between Hugh and Cristen, so even though Alan did not expect to hear anything about a projected escape plan, he remained. He was determined to carry out his mission as thoroughly as he could.

He heard Hugh, perfectly audible through the open door, "Where is Mabel?"

"I sent her to spend the evening with Lady Elizabeth's household," Cristen replied. "I thought it would be more cheerful for her than spending her evening in a sickroom."

Hugh's voice brimmed with amusement. "And Alan has gone to return the chess set. How convenient."

"Isn't it?" Cristen replied softly.

There was a rustling, which Alan interpreted as Cristen getting up from her stool, and then there was no sound.

After a while, as the silence continued, Alan realized with scandalized shock that they must be kissing.

More silent minutes went by. Finally Hugh said in a desperate voice, "Cristen . . ."

"We can't, Hugh." Her voice was breathless. "Alan could come back at any moment."

He groaned. "Damn Richard anyway," he said.

"Richard?" Cristen asked. "What has Richard got to do with this?"

Hugh's voice sounded slightly more under control as he replied, "Richard sent the boy to spy on you. He suspects that I love you and he wants to find out about you."

Alan's eyes widened with shock at this shrewd assessment of his mission.

"But why?" Cristen asked in bewilderment.

Hugh's voice sounded louder, as if he had come closer to Bernard's door. "Richard wants to know everything about me. He wants to know when I go to garderobe and when I cut myself shaving. God knows why. I certainly don't have the same interest in him."

"What do you think he was doing in the sheriff's office tonight?" Cristen asked.

"He was probably altering the books," Hugh replied.

At these words, Alan's mouth dropped open in outrage.

There was silence from next door.

Then Cristen said in a troubled voice, "Hugh, don't let Richard know that Alan told you he was there tonight. He's a nice boy. I don't want him caught in the middle of this power struggle that is going on between you and Richard."

"I don't know that I would call it a power struggle, Cristen," Hugh protested.

"Well, whatever you want to call it, that is what it is," she returned. "And it worries me."

"Never fear, my love." The tenderness in Hugh's voice caught Alan by the throat. "Richard may be clever and ruthless, but he's not as clever and ruthless as I am."

"What a comforting thought," Cristen said.

Hugh chuckled.

In a brisker tone, she went on, "Have you made any progress in your investigation?"

"I'm not sure," Hugh replied. "I went out to Deerhurst this afternoon and talked to Edgar Harding's eldest son. He told me that they were holding his sister's betrothal feast on the night of de Beauté's murder and that his father was there all the time."

"Well then," Cristen said, "that is that."

"Aye. It is the kind of defense that is almost impossible to break. But if Saxon betrothal feasts are anything like Norman betrothal feasts, everyone in that hall was stinking drunk by the time dark fell. It would have been easy for either Harding or his son to slip away and ride into Lincoln without anyone knowing they had gone."

"His son?" Cristen repeated in surprise.

"Aye. Cedric Harding appears to be a formidable young man, and he hated de Beauté fully as much as his father did."

Cristen said curiously, "Do you really suspect the Hardings of this murder, Hugh?"

Hugh was silent. At last he said slowly, "I don't know. In truth, I think the Roumare connection is more likely. This was not a murder done in the anger of the moment. This was a murder that was planned." Hugh's voice became fainter as he turned away from the door, but his diction was so clear that Alan had no trouble hearing him. "The question that keeps coming back to me is, who benefits the most from de Beauté's death? The Hardings don't benefit. Stephen is not likely to return their land to them because de Beauté is dead. I can see either Edgar or Cedric Harding killing de Beauté in a fit of anger, but to plan it out in such cold blood . . . I don't know if revenge could be that important, even to a Saxon."

"You think Roumare benefits the most from Lord Gilbert's death?" Cristen asked.

"Aye. It is almost certain that he will be made the next earl, and that is an honor he covets."

"I think you may be right," Cristen said, "but what I don't see, Hugh, is how you are going to prove it."

"I have to prove it," Hugh said. "If I don't, Bernard will hang. And neither Ralf nor Adela would like that."

Alan jumped as the man in the bed made a sudden, restless movement.

I'd better get out of here, he thought. Silently he melted through the door back out onto the landing. Then he walked to the second door on the landing and knocked. It was opened by Hugh.

"The sheriff's office was locked," Alan said, avoiding Hugh's eyes. "I shall have to return the chess set in the morning."

He went to put the game back upon the stool where it had sat earlier. Cristen was not visible and the door to Bernard's room was open wider than it had been before. Alan glanced in and saw her standing by the bed. She held a cup of something in her hand.

"Hugh," she called. "Come and help me, please."

Hugh went immediately to join her by the bed. As Alan watched from the door, he supported Bernard's head as Cristen got him to drink whatever it was in her cup.

After Hugh had lowered Bernard back to his pillow, they stood together over the sick man and Hugh slipped his arm around Cristen. She leaned her head against his shoulder and for a brief moment, his dark head bent so that his cheek rested against her hair.

Alan turned away from the door and went to stare out the tower window into the blackness below.

Hugh sounded like a completely different person when he talked to Lady Cristen. He actually sounded like someone Alan could like.

That is a pointless conclusion, Alan scolded himself. Hugh was clearly Richard's enemy, and in any contest between the two men, Alan knew whose side he would be on.

17

From the lowest to the highest, the citizens of Lincoln were preoccupied with the upcoming Saint Agatha's Fair, a town event that always took place the week before the start of Lent. With the specter of a murder trial hanging over the city, however, the townsfolk had worried that this year their fair would be canceled.

In fact, if the king's chief justiciar had arrived in time to convene the trial before the fair was scheduled to open, Gervase would have called it off. But Lord Richard Basset appeared to be dragging his feet getting to Lincoln, and under such circumstances the sheriff decided that the fair could go forward.

Saint Agatha's was a purely local gathering, in no way resembling the great international fairs of England and France. No Italian goldsmiths or Flemish clothmakers would make an appearance in Lincoln. The event was actually nothing more than a glorified market day, with games and competitions attached to it.

Ralf had always supported the fair wholeheartedly. Besides bringing good business for the local merchants, it had been a way to bring city and castle together. The knights of the castle guard threw quoits and bowls along with the merchants from the town, and the competition was good-humored and friendly. If a few lads drank too much and ended up spending the night in a castle cell, well, no lasting harm ever came of it.

Gervase had the same outlook on the fair as had his predecessor, which is why he allowed it to be held even though he knew he was outraging the de Beauté party, who remained ensconced in the castle.

"Why doesn't that girl go home?" the sheriff complained as he sat over midday dinner with his son and Hugh on the day before the fair was scheduled to open. "She was in my office again today, with that long-faced companion of hers, protesting the fair and demanding that I get the justiciar here tomorrow." He took a long drink of wine. "God's blood, she can do nothing useful here in Lincoln. All she is is a thorn in my side."

Hugh carefully broke his bread in half. "With the king in Cornwall," he said, "there is no one to assume control over her. Unfortunately."

Gervase glared at Hugh. "You are supposed to be betrothed to her. Can't you get her to leave? It isn't decent for a young girl to want to see a hanging."

"I was never betrothed to Elizabeth de Beauté and the less I see of her the happier I will be," Hugh returned calmly. He broke the bread again and glanced at Richard. "You appear to be good friends with her, Richard. Why don't you try to convince her to go home?"

Richard said ruefully, "My friendship is not as influential as that, I'm afraid."

"Well, all I can say is, she is a cursed nuisance," Gervase said. "All of my knights fall over themselves every time she shows her face. I had to break up a fight today between two of them."

Hugh raised his brows. "A fight, sir?"

"Aye. Apparently the girl smiled at one of them. Guyton thought he was the favored one and Walter thought it was him. They got into a fight about it." Gervase finished the wine in his cup. "I wish the bothersome girl would keep her smiles to herself."

"I don't think you're being quite fair, Father," Richard said mildly. "Her father's death has plunged Lady Elizabeth's life into chaos, and she is frightened. This obsession of hers to see her father's murderer brought to justice gives her a purpose to hold on to. She is only a young girl, after all. I think she deserves some pity."

"Which you appear to be supplying, Richard," Hugh remarked blandly. "From what I can see, you live in Lady Elizabeth's pocket."

"She is alone and I feel sorry for her," Richard replied. "Is the idea of simple kindness so foreign to you, Hugh?" His blue eyes narrowed. "Or perhaps you are jealous?"

Hugh's face lit with amusement. "You are very welcome to Lady Elizabeth, Richard. I have no claim on her, nor do I want one."

Gervase said, in the manner of one settling an argument, "Well, considering all her objections about its propriety, at least she won't attend the fair. That is something, I suppose."

Silence fell as the men continued to eat.

Then, as he soaked up some gravy with his bread, Richard said to Hugh, "Are you entering Rufus in the horse race?"

Hugh shook his head.

Richard seemed disappointed. "That is too bad. I will be riding Durand, and I was hoping to have some competition."

Hugh looked at Richard, his face expressionless, and did not reply.

"I don't think you should ride Durand in the horse race, Richard," Gervase said. "His quality is too far above the other horses that will be entered. It wouldn't be a fair competition, and the townsfolk would resent it."

Richard's face darkened, and for a moment he was not handsome at all. Then the moment passed and his face assumed its usual good-humored expression.

"All right, Father," he said. "If you don't think it's a good idea, I won't enter the race."

Gervase gave his son an approving smile.

"What other events will be held?" Hugh asked.

"The same as always," Gervase replied. "Wrestling, archery—and the horse race will be held on the the first day. The camp-ball game will be played the second day."

"Who are the camp-ball captains this year?" Hugh asked idly.

Gervase's eyes glinted with amusement. "Didn't you know? They are you and Richard."

Hugh paused in the act of lifting his cup and stared at the sheriff in surprise. Then, slowly, he put his cup back on the table. "I don't think that is a good idea, sir."

"Nonsense," Gervase said briskly. "When I suggested it to Master Faren he was delighted."

Master Faren was Lincoln's master goldsmith and head of the group of townsfolk in charge of the fair.

Hugh glanced at Richard's serene face. "Was this your idea?" he demanded.

Richard smiled. "I thought it would be fun."

Hugh picked up his wine cup and drained it.

Fun? he thought morosely. *It will be mayhem.*

Hugh spent the afternoon in the Bail, talking with the various merchants who rented stalls there.

Daniel Merton sold cauldrons, kettles, cups, sickles, billhooks, saws, and fasteners. He told Hugh he was paying three pence a day to rent his stall. Walter Newton, who sold fleeces and sheepskin for making parchment, had told Hugh he paid the same, as did the rest of the merchants who did business all year round.

"That is a lot of money," Hugh said to Daniel as he stood inside the merchant's stall, which was warmed by a charcoal brazier.

"Aye, it is. But those of us who rent here don't have a shop in town. And the farmers who rent seasonally say that they get good business from the castle and the bishop's residence, so it is worth it."

"How many farmers rent during the good weather?" Hugh asked.

Daniel told him.

Hugh figured the sums in his mind, and came to the same conclusion as had Edgar Harding. The sheriff was collecting more in rent than he was expending in additional pay to the castle guard.

Daniel was not the only merchant burning charcoal, and the smell and the smoke from many braziers filled the air. Hugh's eyes were tearing slightly from the fumes, and he blinked to clear them.

"How did the sheriff decide which merchants to rent to?" he asked idly as he lifted a plain wooden cup to examine it.

Daniel shrugged. "For myself, I heard that stalls in the Bail were becoming available and I applied."

Hugh ran his finger over the cup to test its smoothness. "I only ask because Edgar Harding was complaining to me the other day that he had not been offered a stall." He returned the cup to the table.

"No one was 'offered' a stall, Lord Hugh," Daniel said. "We all just heard one way or another that the sheriff was renting market stalls and we applied to get one."

"Who did you apply to?"

If Daniel was puzzled by Hugh's interest, his thin, pointy face did not show it. "We applied to the same person who collects the rents, Theobold Elton. He is the man who supervises the market operation."

Hugh frowned thoughtfully. "I do not believe I know him."

"He came to Lincoln after you left, Lord Hugh. He's one of the castle knights."

"I see."

Hugh reached for his purse. "I believe I will purchase this cup, Daniel. What are you asking for it?"

The man's smile showed two missing front teeth. "Three pence," he said.

Hugh, who knew full well that Daniel had more than tripled the price of the cup, nodded gravely and handed over the money.

"You have made your day's rent," he said.

The man cackled with delight. "Aye," he returned, "that I have." His eyes sparkled as he presented Hugh with his purchase.

As Hugh was crossing the Bail on his way back to the castle, a man came riding in through the main gate. John Rye's hood was down, and his black hair and dark face were clearly distinguishable in the late afternoon sun.

Hugh immediately changed his direction in order to intercept the newcomer. Rye pulled up abruptly when he saw who was approaching him.

"Good afternoon, Rye," Hugh said. "I'm surprised to see you in Lincoln. Don't you ever spend any time at home?"

"I'm here for the fair," Rye said. "I need to replace some of the livestock I lost at home."

"Has your household returned?" Hugh asked. "Who is guarding your wife and children in your absence?"

"My wife and children are none of your business," Rye growled, and abruptly jerked his horse's head sideways to get around Hugh. The animal's mouth opened in protest against the cruel jab and it jumped sideways.

There is someone who will bear watching, Hugh thought as he observed John Rye ride through the gate and pass into the Inner bail.

The first person Rye saw when he entered the Inner bail was William Rotier, standing by the stockade watching as a groom trotted a black gelding back and forth for him.

Rye dismounted and went over to the stockade. He stood in silence for a minute, watching the trotting horse along with Rotier.

"That's enough, Will," Rotier called to the groom.

"Off on the near front, eh?" Rye grunted.

"Aye." The groom came up to them leading Rotier's horse. "Have the blacksmith pull the shoe and then soak the foot in a bucket of cold water," Rotier instructed.

"Aye, sir," the groom answered, and began to lead the lame horse back toward the stables.

Rotier watched his horse being led off and said to Rye, "He just got shoes and I think the smith might have caught him with a nail."

"That's not so bad, then," Rye said.

"I suppose not, but it annoys me. The fellow should take more time and he wouldn't make mistakes like that."

Rye grunted sympathetically.

Rotier finally removed his eyes from his horse and turned to the man beside him. "What are you doing in Lincoln, Rye?" he asked amiably. "Come for the fair?"

"Aye. I thought I'd bed down in the guardroom for the next few days."

This was Rye's usual habit when he came into Lincoln. It was a good way to save the price of an inn, and Gervase always extended the courtesy of the castle guardroom to all the men who did castle duty for their knight's fee.

"I'm afraid that the de Beauté knights have taken over the guardroom," Rotier returned regretfully.

"They're still here?" Rye said in surprise.

"Aye. Lady Elizabeth has refused to go home until someone is convicted of the murder of her father."

Rye scowled. "She didn't have that many knights with her. They can't be taking up all the space in the guardroom."

"The sheriff has been doing all he can to keep the de Beauté party separated from the rest of us," Rotier explained. "Don't worry, though. I'll find you a place somewhere in our own quarters."

"Thanks," returned Rye.

"Your wife is better, I take it?"

"Aye. She is better."

"Good. Well, take your horse to the stable and I'll see what I can do about finding you a bedplace."

Rye nodded and led his horse away.

As soon as he had left his saddlebags in the wooden hut where Rotier had found him a place with a group of other knights, the first thing Rye did was to go in search of the man he had come to Lincoln to see. When it became clear that the man wasn't anywhere in the castle environs, he shrugged and went off to the local tavern for drinks with a group of off-duty guards.

A short while after the midday meal with his father and Hugh, Richard returned to the castle in order to take Elizabeth de Beauté for a ride into the countryside. This outing had become a regular part of his day whenever the weather was fine. Lady Sybil permitted it because he and Elizabeth were never gone too long and because, like most other people, Lady Sybil had fallen under Richard's spell.

The two young people rode north, as usual, into Lincoln Fields. Ploughing and harrowing would not begin for another few weeks, and the fields lay desolate under the chill February sun. In the distance, the sheep and cows that belonged to the townspeople wandered about the bare communal pasture, searching for grass.

Halfway across the fields, Richard and Elizabeth veered east off the main road and followed a track that led into the woods. After half a mile they came upon a small glade, and there they stopped their horses and dismounted.

Richard tied their reins to a fallen branch, turned to Elizabeth, and held out his arms. She glided into them.

The sun shone into the small glade, reflecting off the mingled fire of the girl's hair and the more muted gold of the man's. Richard looked down into the beautiful face uplifted to him. He traced his finger over the girl's cheek and jawbones, then down the front of her throat until he reached the tie on her mantle.

Elizabeth gazed up at him, her green eyes hazy and sensuous.

"What are we going to do, my love?" she murmured. "What if the king refuses to let us marry? What will we do then?"

Richard touched the tip of her nose with his finger. "Stephen prides himself on his chivalry. He will dance to your command the way the rest of us do, my pet."

Elizabeth did not look convinced. "I might have been able to get my father to change his mind, but the king . . ." She frowned. "Besides, you don't dance to my command. Why should you expect the king to?"

Richard's blue eyes glinted. "Of course I dance to your command," he said.

Elizabeth shook her head. "Nay. Half of the time I think you are laughing at me. That is why I noticed you when first I met you last year. You looked at me as if I amused you." She sounded a little indignant.

"You do amuse me," Richard murmured. He smiled and his voice deepened. "And you fascinate me, and arouse me, and . . ."

He bent his head and kissed her again. It was an expert and erotic kiss, and Elizabeth's lips opened and she pressed her body against his.

"I have been thinking, Richard," she whispered when at last he lifted his mouth from hers. "We don't have to wait for the king to approve our marriage. We can run away."

Richard looked at her as if she were mad. "That is impossible. If you do that, the king will be within his rights to strip you of all your property. You do not want that to happen, do you?"

"I thought you said Stephen was chivalrous," Elizabeth retorted. "It would hardly be chivalrous of him to take from me what is rightfully mine."

Richard frowned.

She reached up and ran her finger teasingly across his lips. "Richard, do you want me or not?" she asked huskily.

His eyes were very blue. "Of course I want you."

"Then, once this trial is over, let us elope."

He shook his head decisively. "An elopement would besmirch your honor, my pet."

"I don't care about my honor," Elizabeth said with all the arrogance of the spoiled child that she was.

"Well, I do," he returned firmly.

Her beautiful mouth looked sulky. "I thought you said that you danced to my command."

A reluctant smile tugged at the corners of his mouth. "So I did. But I love you too much to allow you to do anything that might bring harm to you. We will wait for the king's permission." He bent his head and took her mouth in a brief, thorough, possessive kiss. Then he looked commandingly into her eyes. "I know Stephen. Make us sound like lovers out of one of those new French romances, and he will give in to you." He smiled. "He is a man with hot blood in his veins. How could he not?"

A short time later they were back in the saddle and riding toward Lincoln. As they entered the Bail, Richard glanced toward the market stalls and saw Hugh in conversation with one of the merchants.

He frowned.

"What is the matter?" Elizabeth asked. She turned her head and saw Hugh as well. "Are you angry with Lord Hugh?"

Richard's eyes swung back to her curious face and his own expression relaxed. He smiled. "I must confess that of late Hugh has been getting on my nerves. We were never meant to share a house, we two."

"He doesn't like me," Elizabeth said. She sounded amazed, as if such a thing had never happened to her before.

"I don't think Hugh likes anyone," Richard responded sadly. "It might sound like a foolish thing to say about someone who is the heir to an earldom, but I feel sorry for him. He is a bitter man."

"Sir Richard!" One of the knights of the castle guard was running toward them from the direction of the Minster. "The sheriff is looking for you, sir," he said when he arrived beside Richard's big black horse.

"Thank you, Walter," Richard returned pleasantly. "Is my father at the Minster?"

"Nay, my lord. He is at the castle."

"I will seek him out directly, then." He turned back to his riding companion. "Shall we continue on, Lady Elizabeth?"

"By all means, Sir Richard," she replied demurely.

The guard stood his ground and watched admiringly as the beautiful woman and the tall, splendid knight made their way toward the Inner bail.

18

On Sunday evening Bernard's fever dropped, and by Monday his cough had loosened, his chest was less painful, and his fever was almost gone. When Hugh came into the sickroom on Monday morning and wanted to take Cristen to the fair for a few hours, Mabel insisted that she go.

"I will remain with Bernard, my lady," the girl said earnestly. "Go with Lord Hugh. You need to get outdoors for a while."

"But what about you, Mabel?" Cristen said. "Don't you want to see the fair?"

Mabel's round kittenish face took on an expression that was almost comically prim. "Thomas said he would escort me to the fair later this afternoon, my lady. I will go when you get back."

Eventually Cristen allowed herself to be persuaded, and she and Hugh exited the dark, damp castle into one of the fairest, warmest days Lincoln had seen in quite some while.

"Saint Agatha is providing good weather, I see," Cristen commented. She tipped her face up toward the sky as she and Hugh crossed the courtyard of the keep to the stairs that would take them to the Inner bail.

Hugh smiled down at her. "You look like a flower drinking up the sunshine."

She laughed.

"I have some news that will make the day seem even finer," he said. "Guy and his household left Lincoln early this morning. We won't have to worry about running into his friendly face in town today."

They reached the top of the steep stone steps and began to descend them. As soon as they were once more on level ground, she turned to Hugh with a faint frown between her delicate brows. "Do you know where Guy has gone?"

Hugh gave her an ironic look. "He did not leave me a message, but I think I can make a good guess. The sheriff received word late yesterday that the king's Cornish campaign was successful. Apparently, Stephen retook all of the castles that the rebels were holding. He put the Earl of Richmond in charge of them, and should be returning north himself very shortly."

Two knights walked passed them, and Hugh nodded in return to their greeting.

"What of Father?" Cristen asked tensely.

"He's fine," Hugh assured her, "and so apparently are all the Somerford muster. There were no reported deaths or serious injuries."

She shut her eyes. "Thank God."

They walked for a few more steps, then she said, "Do you think Guy has gone to meet the king?"

"Aye," Hugh said. "He still wants the marriage with Elizabeth de Beauté for me, and he wants the earldom of Lincoln along with it."

As they neared the stockade, Hugh looked for Rufus. The white stallion had been turned out in the stockade with several other horses and was now stretched out on his side in the sun, his legs sticking straight out in front of him. He was so deeply asleep that Hugh walked a little closer to the stockade fence to make certain he was breathing. Then he turned back to Cristen.

"Guy provided de Leon knights and men at arms for Stephen's army," he said. "You can be certain that he will remind the king of the value of his loyalty."

Two grooms carrying brimming buckets of water passed them on their way to the stockade. On such a warm day, the horses would be drinking more than usual.

Hugh went on, "I don't know if Guy will tell the king about your visit to Lincoln, but you can be certain that he will tell your father."

Silently Cristen nodded.

Hugh put a hand on the red wool of her sleeve to halt her and turn her to face him. "We can't wait much longer, Cristen," he said intensely. "Once your father hears about us, he will come directly to Lincoln to take you home."

"You can't leave Bernard to hang," she protested.

"If I have to, I'll break him out of the castle and hide him until I can find out who the real murderer is."

Cristen searched his face to see if he meant what he had said.

He did.

She bit her lip and looked worried.

"Damn Guy," Hugh said with suddenly explosive anger. "I should be the earl, not he. He has no legitimate authority over me. I should be able to marry whomever I choose to marry!"

Cristen glanced around and saw that several of the foot soldiers were looking at them curiously. She put her hand on his arm and walked him forward.

"I have been thinking, Hugh." She gave a shadowy smile. "One has a lot of time to think when one is watching by a sickbed."

He nodded tensely.

"I thought, what if you went to Stephen and promised him your support if he would allow you to marry me?"

Hugh looked puzzled. "Guy has promised Stephen his support in payment for the de Beauté marriage," he pointed out. "Why should my offer be more attractive to the king than Guy's? He has the power. He is the earl, not me."

"Stephen must know that Guy's allegiance is only good for as long as it is useful to Guy," Cristen returned. "You are not like that. Once you swear an oath of loyalty, you will not break it."

Hugh slowly shook his head. "You may know that, Cristen, because you know me. But the king does not know me like you do."

"He knows whose son you are," Cristen said.

Hugh's face went very still.

They had almost reached the east gate, where the knights on duty watched them as they approached.

Cristen said, "Your father was the greatest crusader of his time. Considering the conduct of his own father, it is a fact that Stephen is not likely to forget."

"When I proposed going to Robert of Gloucester and making him this very offer, you opposed it!" Hugh flared. "Why send me to Stephen?"

They silenced their conversation while they passed through the east gate, not resuming it until they were outside the hearing of the knights.

Then Cristen said, "I am not sending you to Stephen. I am simply asking you to think about it."

"Why Stephen and not Gloucester?" Hugh repeated.

"The answer to that is very simple," Cristen returned. "I do not think that Gloucester can win this war."

Hugh said nothing.

Cristen went on, "You are right when you say that Stephen is not the most clever of kings. But you must admit that he is facing an almost impossible situation, Hugh. Not only is he fighting Matilda and Gloucester here in England, but he is fighting Matilda's husband, Geoffrey Plantagenet, in Normandy. Then there are the Scots, who are just biding their time before they strike again. Add to all this the fact that he cannot count on the loyalty of most of his nobles."

A sharp line formed between Hugh's straight black brows. "If the situation is, as you say, impossible," he said, "then why do you think Stephen will win?"

"Because Gloucester has no support outside the west."

Hugh was silent.

"You know all of this," Cristen said. "What I think you may not realize is how valuable you could be to Stephen."

"I know it," Hugh said grimly. "But does Stephen?"

The Bail was busy with fairgoers shopping at the market stalls. Hugh and Cristen stopped once more, before they were swallowed up by the crowd, to finish their conversation.

"What I think is this," Cristen said. "Stephen would be very happy to see you make a marriage that does not increase the power of the de Leons."

"That is certainly true, but if he approved our marriage, he would alienate Guy."

"If Stephen has you, he has a lever against Guy. Guy would know that if he went over to Gloucester, Stephen would name you earl in his place."

Screams of delight came from two small boys chasing each other through the crowd, to the obvious annoyance of the people around them.

"We would be taking a chance," Hugh said slowly. "If Stephen does not approve our marriage, we might find ourselves irrevocably separated, whereas if we take matters into our own hands and run away, there will be nothing anyone can do about it."

One of the boys exploded out of the crowd and came careening into Hugh. Hugh lifted him off the ground so he could look him in the face. "No more running," he said. "Go and find your mothers, the both of you."

His voice was perfectly pleasant. He put the child back on his feet and the boy stared up at him out of wide dark eyes before he gulped, "Yes, sir."

Cristen was not at all surprised when the boy began to walk quietly back toward the market stalls.

"If we run away, Guy will disown you," she said. "And, since we will have married in defiance of Stephen as well, the king will denounce you also."

Some people were making their way to the Bail gate, their arms filled with purchases, while others pressed forward to have their turn.

Hugh said, "I will still have my manors from Ralf. The king won't bother to take those away from me."

"I don't want you to rust away on three little manors in Lincolnshire!" Cristen cried passionately. "You were made for greater things than that."

He said stubbornly, "I was made to be with you."

She touched his sleeve. "I know, Hugh," she said. "But I want you to have both."

Once more, his brows drew together.

"Will you at least think about it?"

Silence.

Then, "I will think about it."

"Good."

They began to walk toward the crowd.

"It would be a way of securing your reputation, too," he said. "If we run away, there will be a scandal."

"I don't care about that."

"Perhaps you don't," Hugh said. "But I do."

Richard had invited his squire to accompany him to the fair Monday morning, and Alan was having a wonderful time. They went by the livestock market first, which was filled with the animals that farmers had brought into Lincoln to sell. Most of the beasts were end-of-winter thin, but it was a good time to purchase livestock because the grass would be coming in shortly and the new owner would have the benefit of a whole spring and summer of free grazing.

The streets around the livestock market were filled with stalls, some permanent structures in the front of people's homes and some temporary for the two days of the fair. As they walked along the Strait, Alan and Richard passed by enticing displays of fresh fish, butcher's meat, honey, salt, oil, butter, and cheese. The two men passed next into the Drapery, where the cloth merchants had their displays. There were also stalls offering woad and other dyes for sale.

They cut through one of the small streets that connected the Drapery to the Patchmingate and passed by stalls surrounded by peasants poring over knives for pruning vines, sickles for cutting corn, and spades for digging.

As Alan and his lord moved about the streets of Lincoln, the townspeople acknowledged Richard with such respectful admiration that Alan felt himself honored simply to be seen in the company of such a man.

After walking down the Patchmingate, they returned to the Strait and stopped at the silversmith's. Even inside the shop, Richard attracted admirers, and while Alan waited for him to free himself from the man who had engaged him in conversation, he admired the wares on display. To his delight, once Richard had finished his conversation, he bought Alan a small, elegant silver-hilted dagger.

They left the silversmith's and continued up the Strait, then turned down the Danesgate until they reached the area between the Danesgate and the Bail wall where most of the games had been set up.

They stood for a while watching the stoolball with enjoyment.

This was a sport where women perched on milking stools and tried to avoid being struck by balls which were bowled by men. A particularly pretty girl with long golden braids took her place on one of the stools, and Richard stepped forward and bowled a ball that caught her neatly on the foot. Accompanied by cheers from the onlookers, Richard claimed his prize of a kiss from the blushing maiden.

"I don't think she even tried to get out of the way of that ball," Alan said accusingly as they walked through the laughing crowd toward the next game.

"Now, why would you think that?" Richard returned, with a wicked glint in his eyes.

The next game they came to was the quoits, where men threw horseshoes at a stake in the ground. Points counted only if you landed your horseshoe with the stake in the middle. Records were kept of the scores throughout the day, and winners would be announced at the end of the fair.

"How are you at quoits, Alan?" Richard asked amiably. "Want to try a set?"

Alan agreed eagerly. He had often played quoits at home with his brothers and he knew he was good at them.

He took a set of horseshoes from William Henry, Lincoln's master carpenter, and stood at the marked-off distance, concentrating on the stake some fifteen feet away from him. He wanted very badly to impress Richard with his skill.

He inhaled deeply, then let fly the first horseshoe, which sailed through the air and came to rest with its top leaning against the stake.

Alan tried not to let his disappointment show.

"Very close," Richard said admiringly. "Try again."

The second time the shoe hooked the stake and settled around it with a satisfying thud. Alan couldn't control his grin. A group of young girls had stopped to watch, and their cheers made his fair skin flush.

Two of the next three horseshoes hit their mark as well.

"Very good, Alan," William Henry said. "As of now, you are tied for the lead."

"I'll come back later and try again," Alan said, and he and Richard walked on.

At a little distance from the rest of the games, several archery butts had been set up along the city walls. A group of men, knights from the castle and men from the town, were waiting in line to compete. A crowd had gathered to watch, and Richard and Alan joined them.

One of the younger knights, a man Alan knew to be one of Richard's group of friends, called, "Hallo, Sir Richard. Come and have a go at the butts."

Richard flashed his most beguiling smile. "Nay, Theobold, not today."

"Come on, Sir Richard," Theobold Elton urged. "Just shoot a few arrows for us."

Still smiling, Richard shook his head.

He doesn't want to show the men up, Alan thought admiringly.

At that moment, two more people joined the crowd around the archery butts.

"Hugh!" one of the men in line called happily. "You'll shoot for us, won't you?"

Beside him, Alan felt Richard stiffen.

Alan looked in the direction of Richard's stare and saw Hugh standing at the edge of the crowd. Lady Cristen was with him.

"What's the matter, Matt?" Hugh called back. "Can't you draw your own bow?"

The crowd and the men in line hooted with laughter.

Richard said, "I'll shoot if you will, Hugh." Something in Richard's voice made Alan stare at him.

"A friendly match?" Hugh said mockingly. But he began to walk forward, and the crowd parted to let him through.

"Why not?" Richard said with a brilliant smile.

At Hugh's side, Lady Cristen looked worried.

"Why not indeed?" Hugh said. "You go first."

Richard walked calmly to the line of men, who had fallen strangely silent, and put out his hand for the bow the archers were using. He turned to face the butt, put his foot on the mark, raised the bow, and pulled effortlessly on stave and string until it was in a position of full draw. He paused a moment, sighting the target, then he let the arrow fly.

It landed exactly in the center of the small painted circle in the middle of the butt.

Relief surged through Alan. He could not have borne it if Richard had lost to Hugh.

A murmur of appreciation came from the watchers.

"Very good," Hugh said admiringly. "You shoot eight first, then I'll shoot eight."

"Very well," Richard agreed, and put his hand out for another arrow. "You had better take that arrow out so there is a space for my next one," he said.

To Alan's profound satisfaction, all of Richard's shots landed inside the center circle, and six of them were dead in the middle.

Then it was Hugh's turn.

He took the bow from Richard with careless grace. Richard was half a head taller, and a casual onlooker would not have thought that the slender Hugh stood a chance against the other man's obvious strength and skill. Alan, who had seen Hugh shoot before, was not fooled.

At least it will be a tie, he thought.

He knew, without thinking how he knew, that Richard would hate it if Hugh beat him.

Hugh raised the bow and, without pausing at all, let the arrow fly. It buried itself in the thin line that formed the outside circle of the butt.

A sigh of disappointment ran through the crowd.

Richard said gently, "Your hand must have slipped. We won't count that one. Try again."

He is so honorable, Alan thought. Richard wanted to win this contest, yet he would not take advantage of his opponent's bad luck.

Hugh didn't reply. He just raised the bow again and fitted another arrow. This one buried itself in the thin line directly opposite to the first.

The crowd stirred with interest.

Hugh shot his third arrow, which quartered the circle. Then the next and the next and the next, until the entire circle was pinned with arrows.

The painted line into which Hugh had shot was an eighth of an inch wide.

"This is a nice bow, Edwin," Hugh said as he handed it back. "Whom does it belong to?"

"It is one of the castle bows, my lord," Edwin replied. "The sheriff loaned us a few of them for the day."

Hugh said, "I'll buy a drink for anyone who can hit that line."

The men whooped with delight.

It had been deliberately done, Alan realized. Richard, who had shot brilliantly, was quite forgotten as the men concentrated on Hugh's challenge.

Across the crowd, Alan's eyes met Lady Cristen's gaze. She looked resigned.

Beside him, Richard stood in silence. Alan did not know what to say.

"Shall we move along to watch the wrestling?" Richard suggested at last.

"Aye, my lord," Alan responded eagerly, relieved that Richard's voice sounded so normal. The look on Richard's face was pinched and sallow, however, as Alan glanced up at him.

Richard was clearly furious, and Alan did not blame him one little bit.

"Was it necessary to shoot against Richard?" Cristen asked in an astringent tone as she and Hugh walked down the Danesgate in the direction of the Strait.

Hugh had not had to take any of the men for a drink, as none of them had managed to pin the line with an arrow.

"Perhaps it wasn't necessary," Hugh admitted. He grinned. "But it was fun."

Cristen started to say something, then stopped in surprise as Hugh's hand came up to cover her mouth.

"Don't say it," he said.

Say what? she asked him with her eyes.

"Men," he returned in a disgusted tone, and rolled his eyes.

Behind his hand she smiled.

They continued on until they reached the Strait, where they turned north and began to walk in the direction of the Patchmingate.

"Do you know what I have been thinking?" Hugh asked.

"I always know what you are thinking."

He stared down at her. "Always?"

She replied imperturbably, "Well, I always know what you are thinking when you are thinking what you are thinking right now."

Hugh grinned.

That is two smiles in two minutes, Cristen thought with satisfaction.

They passed a family of parents and five children, all dressed in their fair-going best. The children were so excited, they looked as if they might explode.

Hugh said, "Well, what am I thinking then, Madam Mindreader?"

The elusive dimple in her cheek flickered. "You are thinking that we are so close to Ralf's house that it would be a shame not to stop in."

He shouted with laughter.

Cristen continued, "And *I* am thinking that you are right."

He sobered instantly, and the line of his mouth grew grim.

"God, Cristen. I hate having to sneak around with you like this."

"I know you do, Hugh," she said gently.

They turned into the Patchmingate and walked in silence past the shoemaker's shop.

Then Hugh said slowly, "I think I know who killed de Beauté. I just don't know if I can prove it."

She bent her head, exposing to him the delicate nape of her neck.

"Do you know the reason for the murder?" she asked.

He didn't answer, and she lifted her head. Their eyes met.

"I think so," he said.

Very briefly, she rested her head against his arm.

19

The first day of the fair was marred by only a few minor incidents. In one of them a few of the town youngsters stole several jugs of wine and proceeded to get noisily and obnoxiously drunk. The sheriff returned them to their parents and collected money to reimburse the irate vintner whose stall had been plundered.

Aside from the wine incident, five people were arrested for attempted theft, and a husband and wife became so enraged with each other over a purchase that one of the sheriff's men had to be called in to separate them.

Late in the evening, after the streets were quiet, Alan was sitting in the family hall with Gervase and Richard when Hugh came in.

Alan was shocked to see him. After the way he had humiliated Richard, the squire wondered how he had the nerve to show his face in the sheriff's house.

Gervase, who knew nothing about the archery contest, greeted Hugh amiably and invited him to have a cup of wine.

Hugh accepted, and sat down on a stool beside the fire. Alan, a look of disapproval upon his young face, poured some wine and brought it to him. Hugh took the cup and sipped the wine.

"Did you enjoy the fair, Hugh?" Gervase asked.

"It was very pleasant," Hugh returned. "Did you make many arrests?"

"A few," the sheriff admitted. "No blood was shed, however, and that is the main thing."

"Aye." Hugh took another sip from his wine cup, then rested it on his knee.

Alan looked at him. Both the sheriff and Richard were seated in chairs, and their elevated height and dignified posture should have made them the dominant figures in the room. Hugh was folded upon a low stool, balancing a wine glass on his knee, yet he managed effortlessly to be the center of attention.

It was odd, Alan mused, how one always felt compelled to look at Hugh to gauge his reaction to whatever was happening.

Of course, Richard had the same kind of ability to command attention, Alan thought with immediate loyalty. But Richard was so physically magnificent that one expected him to have a dominating presence. Next to Richard, Hugh looked like a boy. Yet he had this magnetic quality about him.

"Did you hear that Lord Guy left Lincoln early this morning?" Gervase said to Hugh.

"Aye." The fire flamed up behind Hugh's head. His hair was purely black, Alan noticed. There was no brown in it at all.

"Do you know where he was going?" Gervase asked.

Hugh quirked an ironic eyebrow. "He didn't confide his plans to me. However, it doesn't take a great deal of imagination to surmise that he is going to meet the king. I doubt that Guy has given up hope on either the de Beauté marriage or the earldom."

Alan thought he sounded supremely indifferent to this enticing prospect.

Richard spoke for the first time. "What if Guy is successful and wins both of those things from Stephen? Will you take the earldom?"

"I'd take the earldom if I didn't have to take the girl," Hugh replied instantly. "As it is, I already know who I am going to marry, and it is not Elizabeth de Beauté."

Alan remembered the scene he had eavesdropped upon, and blurted out before he could stop himself, "Is it Lady Cristen?"

Hugh shot him a quick smile. "Aye. It is Lady Cristen."

Unexpectedly warmed by that friendly look, Alan met Hugh's eyes. "She is nice," he said a little shyly.

Hugh regarded him with approval. "Aye. She is very nice."

A flood of pleasure rushed through Alan.

Hugh looked at Richard. "Did you know that John Rye was in Lincoln?" he asked.

Richard gave him a thoughtful look. "I believe I might have glimpsed him in the castle courtyard this morning. Why do you ask?"

Hugh shrugged.

Richard regarded him steadily.

Alan frowned, opened his mouth to say something, changed his mind, and closed it again.

"Why should Richard care whether or not John Rye is in town?" Gervase asked Hugh gruffly.

"No reason," Hugh responded lightly.

Gervase looked puzzled.

Richard continued to look thoughtful.

Hugh looked bland.

Alan's worried frown deepened.

Then Hugh said, "Let us hope that we get through the camp-ball game tomorrow as smoothly as we have gotten through this first day."

"Aye," Richard agreed. He gave his father a sympathetic smile. "But it's not likely."

Gervase sighed. "I know."

"Is it dangerous?" asked Alan, who had never attended the camp-ball game before.

"It can get a little rough," Hugh said with amusement.

"This year we've limited the boundaries of the camping close," Gervase said. "I hope that will help eliminate some of the fighting in alleys that always tends to go on."

"What are the new boundaries?" Hugh asked.

"The length of the close will be the same as always, from the city wall to the Bail wall, but this year we are going to confine the game to the Mickelgate and the Strait."

"*What?*" The identical exclamation, made in identically out-raged voices, burst from Richard and Hugh simultaneously.

"That is what the town committee and I have decided," Gervase said sternly. "I don't want a mob of overstimulated players running through the streets of Lincoln. There was a great deal of damage done to private property last year and I won't allow that to happen again."

"The street is too narrow for all the players," Richard objected.

"Aye," said Hugh, for once in agreement with Richard. "I can see the value of limiting the playing field, but one narrow street is not enough space for two hundred players. There will be a constant pileup of men, and no one will be able to move the ball at all."

"The committee and I have discussed that possibility," the sheriff said in a measured tone. "If there is a pileup of players and no one can move, the game will be stopped, the pile will be separated, and the side that has possession of the ball will get to throw it."

Both Richard and Hugh scowled.

"And who is going to have the pleasure of trying to separate the pileup?" Richard asked grimly.

"I am," Gervase replied.

Silence prevailed while Richard and Hugh digested this information.

"It will make it a different game," said Hugh.

"The idea is to make it a less destructive game," the sheriff returned. "At least as far as private property is concerned."

Hugh took a swallow of his wine. "There goes my idea of letting loose Mistress Chapman's pigs." His voice held real regret.

Richard laughed with genuine amusement. "I was going to use that huge swine that belongs to the shoemaker."

Hugh grinned.

"Well, you boys will just have to think of something that does not involve other people's livestock," Gervase said firmly. "If you try to do something like that on the Strait, the whole game will stop."

Hugh lifted one black eyebrow. "A challenge, Richard," he said softly.

Richard's blue eyes glinted. "So it is," he replied. "So it is."

The second day of the fair was not as warm or as clear as the first day had been. Clouds had moved in from the east overnight, and there was a dampness in the air that foretold rain.

The weather did not dampen the spirits of the men of Lincoln as they prepared for the camp-ball game, however. The sport itself was very simple. It was played by two teams, each of which had to try to get the leather camp-ball to the opposing side's goal. The chief rule was that the ball had to be run or thrown, not kicked. The game started when the ball was tossed up between the two sides. Whichever side gained control of it immediately took off for the opposing side's goal, and went as far as it possibly could.

There were no rules beyond getting the ball to the goal. How you ran the ball, how you stopped the ball, how you stole the ball, all of these things were left to the imagination and invention of the players.

There were always a large number of injuries, ranging from bruises to sprained ankles to broken bones. All the young men of Lincoln adored the game and looked forward to it throughout the whole of the long dark winter.

As soon as ten o'clock mass was finished on Wednesday morning the players gathered in the yard of Saint Peter ad Placita near the city wall in order to choose up sides. This was done quite simply by having each captain call men from among the packed crowd of waiting players.

Hugh, as befitted his superior status, went first.

"Hubert Dunning," he called, to Alan's surprise. Hubert was the son of the town's silversmith. Alan had expected that the men of the castle guard would be taken before the men from town.

A slender, fair-haired young man separated himself from the crowd and went to stand behind Hugh. He was grinning.

Richard chose as Alan had expected. He took one of the largest of the knights from the castle.

Alan tried not to feel disappointed that Richard had not chosen him first.

It was more difficult to restrain his emotions, however, as the choosing of sides went on. Hugh took a variety of men, some from the town and some from the castle. Richard continued to go for the knights first.

He took John Rye, who was not even a permanent member of the castle guard.

Richard did not look once at Alan.

Don't be a fool, Alan castigated himself. *You are not half as strong as these men. You can't even pull a full-size longbow! Richard wants to win and he is choosing accordingly. He can't be concerned about your puny feelings.*

Then, to Alan's surprise and intense relief, he heard his name being called.

"Alan Stanham."

But the voice that had called his name belonged to Hugh.

Alan walked forward, his cheeks flaming, to join the team that opposed his lord.

At last the sides were chosen, and each captain gathered his men on opposite sides of the courtyard for an encouraging talk.

There were slightly more than a hundred men on each side.

The two meetings went very differently. From Richard's side of the courtyard, Alan could hear uproarious cheers and shouts. Richard knew exactly how to get his men in the right frame of mind for a battle.

Hugh, on the other hand, was all business.

"This is how we are going to play," he said briskly. He was standing with his back to the church wall, with his team gathered before him. His voice, which was pitched normally, was perfectly audible to the men in the last row. "As you know, the field this year has been confined to the main street, so our tactics must be a little different from in the past. The primary ball carriers today will be Hubert Dunning, Rob Walker, Thomas Mannyng, Michael Baxter, and Alan Stanham."

Alan's eyes widened in shock as he heard his name.

"They all throw with accuracy," Hugh said. He grinned. "I was not wasting my time at the games yesterday, as you can see."

Everyone laughed.

"Each of the ball carriers is to have a circle of men to protect him. I am going to name the men for this job and who it is they are to protect."

He reeled off a list of one hundred names, twenty for each of the ball carriers. He did it without notes. He had all of the men's names in his memory.

The men stood in perfect silence under the overcast sky and listened intently.

Hugh continued, "You are to form up as if the ball carrier was a castle and you are the walls that protect him. There must be a space like a courtyard between the wall and the castle so that the thrower will have room to throw the ball without interference and to receive the ball without it being intercepted by the other team. Is that understood?"

The answers came back: "Aye, my lord," and "Aye, Hugh," according to how well the speakers knew their captain.

"Good," Hugh said. "Once we have formed up, we will spread our five castles along the length of the street. The idea is to pass the ball from one castle to the next. Each castle will run the ball as far as it can and, when the pressure becomes too intense for the walls to hold it back, the thrower will pass the ball to the next castle."

"What happens if the ball is intercepted?" someone called. "The other team will have an open run to our goal."

Hugh raised his brows. "Oh, are you planning to let the other team intercept the ball?"

Laughter.

"Seriously, that is a good question," Hugh said. "Two of our castles will be placed defensively, behind the ball. Their job will be to recover the ball and once more pass it forward."

The men all nodded intently.

"What about those of us who have no assignment, Hugh?" someone called.

"We are the rovers," Hugh said. "There will be twelve of us, and our job is to watch what is happening and help out where we are needed."

Hugh looked over his team in front of him. "Does everyone understand what they are to do?"

The men responded with determination:

"Aye."

"Aye."

"We do."

"Excellent," said Hugh. He grinned, his face bright with anticipation. "Then let's go out there and have some fun."

For as long as he lived, Alan would remember that camp-ball game. The starting place was by the shoemaker's on the Strait, halfway between the two goals. As he had explained to his team, Hugh posted three offensive castle formations between the start and Richard's goal, which was at the Bail wall at the end of the Strait, and two defensive formations between the start and his own goal, which was at the city wall at the end of the Mickelgate.

Alan's group was the middle castle between the start and the Bail. He stood in the center of his protective wall of men and tried to quiet the pounding of his heart.

Ralf Haywood, one of the chief freemen of the town, stepped forward to start the game, the leather camp-ball in his hands. The line of men protecting Hubert Dunning, the thrower for the first castle, jostled for position. The men whom Hugh had designated as rovers were at the fore as well.

Alan looked at the mass of men lined up on the other side of the ball.

Richard had objected at first to Hugh's placing men on his side of the line, but the sheriff had ruled that there was nothing in the rules against it. So then Richard had dispatched a group of his own men to hold position behind Hugh's lines. He retained most of his team in an offensive position, however, clearly intending to catch the ball first and make a strong aggressive run.

Ralf Haywood stepped into the space that had been left empty between the two sides. He did not come all the way into the center of the street, however, but stood near the shoemaker's stall and tossed the ball high in the air into the middle of the street.

The two teams surged forward to catch it.

As the mass of men stood on the ground, shoving for position, their eyes and hands uplifted toward the descending ball, a figure sailed into the air over the men and swatted it toward the first of Hugh's offensive formations.

As Alan watched in fascination, Hugh came down horizontally, landed on three men, and disappeared from sight.

A roar went up as the men defending Hubert got the ball to him and began to move up the Strait, easily bulling their way through the line that Richard had posted for defense.

They had progressed a full eighty yards before the rest of Richard's team caught up and began to slam into them in deadly earnest.

Over the noise of the crowd, Alan heard Hugh's voice calling calmly, "Throw it."

Hubert threw, but his throw was short, and the ball was batted away by one of Richard's knights. With a roar, the rest of his team-mates came running to protect him. The direction of the ball reversed as Richard's team began to push its way south. All that stood between the opposing team and the goal were the two castles Hugh had posted for defense.

They won't be able to hold, Alan thought as he tried to see what was happening over the heads of the men surrounding him.

A roar went up from the men around the ball.

"What's happening?" Alan screamed frantically to the men in front of him.

"It's a pileup," one of his teammates shouted back. "One of our men got to the carrier and knocked him down. Everyone else has piled on."

Minutes passed while the sheriff tried to peel off the kicking and pounding men on the pile to see who on the bottom had the ball in his hands.

Finally another roar went up.

"We have it!" the men in front yelled back to Alan. *"One of our knights recovered the ball!"*

"Get ready," someone else warned. "It will be coming back our way."

"Hugh is going to throw it," someone else said. "Get ready."

A roar went up from the crowd along the sides of the street.

"He's got it to Hubert!" one of Alan's wall knights shrieked. "Get ready to move back if Hubert's castle can run the ball up the street."

The thud of players running sounded like a herd of horses, Alan thought. Richard's men must be racing forward to get in front of the ball.

"Back!" Alan's defenders began to shout. "Back up to give them room to move."

Alan followed the movement of his men as they advanced up the street.

"Stop!" one of the knights shouted.

Alan looked up and saw the ball arching in toward him. He stepped to his left, leaped into the air, and caught it.

A roar of approval went up from the surrounding men. Alan grinned and hugged the ball to his chest, and prepared to follow his defenders as far as they could take him.

They made good progress for almost a hundred yards. Then his protective walls began to crumble. Men went down under the onslaught of Richard's team. Alan lifted the camp-ball and cocked his arm. Just before he threw, he saw Richard coming at him in a diving lunge.

The look on his face was murderous.

Alan released the ball and went down under a bone-crunching tackle.

He lay still, groaning and fighting for breath. Richard's weight lifted off him almost instantly and Richard was gone, leaving Alan facedown in the dirt of the road, trying to breathe.

A voice said, "Are you all right?"

Alan groaned again and managed to roll over. He looked up into Hugh's filthy face.

"I . . . I think I just had the breath knocked out of me," Alan managed to croak.

"You had better get over to safety on the side of the street," Hugh said. "I'll get someone to take your place."

"Nay," Alan said grimly. "I'll be all right."

Hugh held out a hand and pulled the squire to his feet. Alan was relieved to find that nothing felt broken. He stood still for a moment, still fighting for breath. Then he said to Hugh, "Let's go."

Hugh gave him a blazing smile, turned and ran down the street in the direction of the game. Alan, absurdly buoyed by that brilliant look, followed at his heels.

The camp-ball game went on for another hour. Richard's team recovered the ball three more times, but each time there was a greater distance between the players and their goal. And no matter how far they managed to advance, they never seemed to make back the ground that they had lost on Hugh's team's previous drive.

Slowly but relentlessly, Hugh's castles advanced toward the Bail wall.

Alan had the ball in his hands twice more during the course of the game, and both times he managed to throw it successfully to Thomas Mannyng, the thrower in the last castle. It was Thomas who was the one who finally got the ball to Richard's goal and claimed the victory.

Jubilation roared through the winning side. Alan found himself showered with compliments about how he had handled himself and about how accurately he had thrown the ball. The wild celebration culminated with the team lifting the five ball carriers on their shoulders and marching with them down the Strait, accompanied by cheers from the onlookers.

It was the best day of Alan's life.

He was still perched high above the crowd on the shoulders of his defenders when he saw Hugh break away from the mass of men and begin to race on ahead of the victory parade. He was followed by a tall, thin man whom Alan recognized as one of the sheriff's constables.

It was a good half hour before the party in the street began to break up. Its dispersal was hastened by the grim news that one of the players, John Rye, had been found stabbed to death.

20

The body of John Rye lay beneath a linen cerecloth in the mortuary chapel of the Minster. The light from the candles set at his head and feet flickered on the faces of the Bishop of Lincoln, the Sheriff of Lincoln, and Hugh de Leon as they stood talking together in low voices.

"It had to be an accident," the sheriff said. He rubbed his forehead as if it ached. "Someone must have been wearing a knife at his belt and, in the rough and tumble of the pileup, it cut through its sheath and stabbed Rye."

"The fellow with the knife might not even have realized what happened," the bishop said.

"Have you been able to discover who among the players was wearing a knife?" Hugh asked.

"Not surprisingly, no one will admit to wearing a knife," Gervase said wearily. "And no one remembers seeing anyone else wearing one, either. I shall continue to ask questions, of course, but to be honest, I have little hope of finding the man responsible for this tragic accident."

Hugh stood staring down at the covered body in front of him. "I take it, then," he said, "that neither of you thinks there is any possibility that this was done deliberately?"

Both older men looked surprised by the question. It was Gervase who finally answered Hugh by posing another question.

"Why should anyone want to kill John Rye?"

The candles at the foot of the coffin flickered over Hugh's expressionless face. "He may have had an enemy we don't know about."

The sheriff made an impatient gesture. "Perhaps. But even if someone did want him dead, this is surely a very chancy way to go about accomplishing a murder. To kill a man in front of dozens of people! Really, Hugh, it makes no sense."

"I should think it a very clever way to kill a man," Hugh returned. "In the crush and confusion of the camp-ball game, no one would think it was unusual for Rye to fall down. The murderer could do the deed and be away before anyone realized that something was wrong."

The bishop's long, noble fingers adjusted the white stole he wore around his graceful, aristocratic neck. "That may be so," he said in his sonorous voice, "but why should anyone want to kill a man like John Rye?"

"I can't help but wonder if this stabbing might be related in some way to the stabbing of Gilbert de Beauté," Hugh replied.

The sheriff and the bishop stared at him in annoyance.

"That's ridiculous," the bishop snapped. "What connection can possibly exist between the Earl of Lincoln and a mere knight like John Rye?"

Hugh returned steadily, "Once we find the answer to that question, my lord, we will have caught a murderer."

The bishop haughtily lifted his nose and looked dismissively at Hugh. "You are being absurd."

Gervase agreed. "I know you will do anything to save Bernard, Hugh, but this is a bird that will not fly. There is simply no way to connect de Beauté with a man like Rye."

Hugh's mouth set into a hard, strict line. He did not reply.

Silence fell as the three men stood side by side, contemplating the outline of John Rye's body under his cerecloth.

Finally the bishop said, "I suppose I shall have to find someone else to hold Linsay Manor. Perhaps you might be able to suggest a few names to me, Sheriff."

Hugh frowned. "Linsay will not go to Rye's son?"

The bishop's nose elevated once more. "Linsay belongs to the Bishopric of Lincoln, Lord Hugh. John Rye's son is much too young to serve out the feudal duty required as a fee to hold the land, so naturally I will have to give the manor elsewhere."

Gervase said, in the manner of a man concluding a discussion, "Certainly I can suggest some names to you, my lord." He turned to Hugh. "I will continue to make inquiries among the players and spectators as to who might have been wearing a knife, but I doubt I will learn anything more."

"It was a tragic accident, nothing more," the bishop pronounced. He stepped away from the candlelit body as if to leave, then stopped and looked at the sheriff. "Have you sent anyone to bring the sad news to Rye's wife? She will have to decide where she wants him buried."

"I am sending a man first thing in the morning," the sheriff replied.

"I will ride to Linsay for you," Hugh volunteered.

The bishop looked at him with suspicion.

The sheriff said, "You don't have to do that, Hugh."

"Rye's wife and children know me," Hugh explained briefly. "It will be better if I am the one to go."

The bishop and the sheriff exchanged a glance, then Gervase shrugged. "Very well. If that is what you want."

"It is what I want," Hugh said.

"Just be sure you don't further upset the lady with talk of murder," the bishop said sharply.

Hugh did not reply.

"Did you hear me, young man?" The bishop's voice grew louder. "I do not want to hear any more talk of murder."

"I hear you quite clearly, my lord," Hugh returned. "I will not speak of murder again." He paused. "Until I have proof."

The bishop grunted. "Well, that is something you will never have." He was a tall man, and when he drew himself up to his full height he was very impressive—a fact of which he was well aware. "Good night, Sheriff," he said to Gervase.

"Good night, my lord."

Without speaking again to Hugh, the bishop walked regally out of the chapel.

"You put his back up," Gervase said to Hugh.

"I don't think it was the suggestion of murder that offended him as much as it was the suggestion that the murder of a mere knight could in some way be connected with the murder of an earl," Hugh returned cynically.

The sheriff sighed. "You may be right. The bishop comes from a very noble family, something he never forgets." He touched Hugh's arm lightly. "Come, you and I had better be going as well."

Hugh nodded, and the two men left the chapel, closing the door behind them on John Rye and his eternal sleep.

The streets of Lincoln were quiet as Hugh made his way alone toward the sheriff's house. The only activity in town seemed to be at the Nettle, where a number of the camp-ball champions were getting noisily and rambunctiously drunk.

Gervase had excused himself from accompanying Hugh, saying that he had a few things to see to at the castle before he returned home.

Hugh walked past the uproarious waves of sound cascading out of the Nettle and continued on down the Strait. He checked his stride slightly as he perceived someone coming out of the Danesgate and turning in his direction. The sky had cleared and the full moon glimmered off hair so fair, it looked like silver in the pale moonlight. It was Cedric Harding.

"Harding," Hugh said as the young man came abreast of him. "I did not know you were in Lincoln."

The young Saxon stopped, showing no surprise at being addressed. He must have recognized Hugh before Hugh spoke.

"I did not know that I had to apprise you of my every move," Cedric replied. His words were sarcastic, but his voice was surprisingly mild.

Hugh ignored the comment and regarded the moon-bleached face of the man standing beside him. "Did you come for the fair?"

"Aye. My father wished to sell off some of his sheep, and so we took a stall at the livestock market."

"I saw the stall," Hugh said. "I did not see you, however."

"I was not standing about hawking the sheep, if that is what you mean," Cedric said. "I came in early this morning to make sure that our men got home all right."

A roar of laughter came from a group of men who had just exited the Nettle.

"Come and have a drink with me," Hugh said. "The Nettle is still open for business."

To Hugh's surprise, Cedric accepted, and the two young men made their way back up the Strait to the door of Lincoln's most popular inn.

The noise hit them first, then the smell. Apparently more than one reveler had not made it to the door before becoming sick.

As they walked in, a jubilant shout went up from the men standing packed shoulder to shoulder in front of them.

"Hugh! It's Hugh himself, lads. Let's hear it for our captain!"

"Good God," Hugh muttered under his breath.

"Apparently you are the hero of the hour," Cedric said into his ear. There was amusement in his voice.

Hugh did not advance any farther, but shot a few quick, sharply funny comments at several of the revelers crammed into the inn's main room. Then, as the room roared with laughter, he said to Cedric, "Let's get out of here."

"Gladly," Cedric said. "It stinks."

Before the men could even realize that he was leaving them, Hugh was out the door.

"Whew!" he said, waving his hand in front of his face as if to waft away the smell.

"That was pretty disgusting," Cedric agreed. "My father's house is not far from here and it's a lot quieter."

"Lead the way," Hugh said.

The Harding town house was of the old-fashioned wooden style with a straw thatched roof. Cedric and Hugh entered directly into a large main hall, which had a log fire burning on the central hearthstone. Three men were asleep on the wooden bench that lined the wall.

Cedric led Hugh to the fire and invited him to sit in one of the two high-backed chairs that were placed before it. Then he said he would fetch some wine and disappeared through a door in the far wall of the hall.

Hugh sat in silence, listening to the snoring of the sleeping men, the crackling of the fire, and wondering why Cedric Harding had agreed to talk to him.

Cedric came back into the room carrying two cups of wine in his hands. He gave one to Hugh, then took the chair next to him.

"So," Cedric said, regarding Hugh with interest. "There has been another death in Lincoln."

"Aye," Hugh returned. "The sheriff has ruled it an accident."

"Do you think it was an accident?"

Hugh shook his head and took a sip of wine, noting that it was very good.

"Why don't you think it's an accident?" Cedric asked.

"I find two deaths by stabbing within two months of each other to be a little strange," Hugh returned.

Cedric tilted his wine cup and thoughtfully regarded the liquid in its depths. Without looking at Hugh, he said, "I think I ought to tell you that my father did not come into Lincoln for the fair, so if you think that this is another murder, you can eliminate him from your list of suspects."

Hugh was silent, digesting the fact that apparently Cedric had wanted to talk to him in order to establish an alibi for his father.

"He didn't come in to oversee the stall?" Hugh asked.

Cedric shook his head. "He is ill, as a matter of fact. My mother has made him keep his bed these last three days."

Hugh watched Cedric's face. "And he can prove that, I suppose?"

"My mother has been taking care of him, along with her serving women." Cedric lifted his eyes from his cup and stared at Hugh a little truculently. "If a Norman will accept the word of Saxon women, that is."

"A Norman always accepts the word of a lady," Hugh replied gravely.

Cedric rested his head against the straight back of his chair. "I watched the camp-ball game today," he said.

Hugh, who had been in the process of lifting his wine cup for another sip, stilled. "Were you by any chance present when John Rye was killed?"

"As a matter of fact," Cedric said, "I was."

Hugh put his cup down. "Will you tell me what you saw?"

"Why not?" Cedric said lightly. He shifted slightly in his seat. "The accident happened when one of the men on your side knocked aside an opposition pass. The ball went flying off, and in a second a whole pile of men were jumping on top of it, trying to gain control. One of the men in the pile was John Rye."

"Who else was in the pile?" Hugh asked sharply.

"At least thirty men from both sides were involved," Cedric said. "It took the sheriff and his men a long time to disentangle them. When they finally got to the bottom of the pile, they found one of your men clutching the ball. He immediately jumped to his feet, threw it, and the game started up again."

"What of Rye?"

"He was left behind, lying on the ground. No one stopped to see how badly he was injured, so after everyone else had run off up the street, I went out to look at him."

"You were the one who discovered he had been stabbed?" Hugh said, clearly startled.

"Aye. He was lying on his back in the dirt, and when I put my hand behind him to lift him a little, it came away covered with blood."

A tense white line formed around the edges of Hugh's nostrils. "Was he dead?"

"He was still breathing, but he was not aware."

"Was there anyone else around?"

"There was no one else in the street. An old woman who had been watching the game from inside her house came out when she saw me kneeling over Rye." Cedric's blue eyes were sober. "We tried to stop the bleeding, but he died before we could get him out of the street. Then I sent for the sheriff."

"Who was the woman who helped you?" Hugh asked. "I should like to talk to her. Perhaps she saw something that will be of use."

Cedric shrugged. "I don't know her name. She lives in the house with the yellow shutters between the Patchmingate and the Danesgate."

Hugh nodded and reached for his wine. He took a long swallow.

"It was most probably an accident," Cedric said. "Men were clawing and kicking, trying to get to the ball. A knife worn at someone's belt could easily have slid into another man's back."

"If you think that, then why did you take such pains to tell me that your father was not in town?" Hugh countered.

Cedric raised silver-blond eyebrows. "Because I had a feeling that you might jump on Rye's death like a hound on a scent. As indeed you have."

Hugh didn't reply.

Cedric took a sip of his own wine and regarded Hugh over the rim of his cup. "The camp-ball game was very interesting," he said. "I almost bet on Canville's team to win. He had all the strongest men on his side."

Along with horse racing and wrestling, the yearly camp-ball game was the biggest betting event in Lincoln.

"Almost?" Hugh said.

Cedric smiled. "I finally decided that brains would prevail, and I bet on you."

"I am flattered," Hugh said.

"How did you find that strategy you used?" Cedric asked with undisguised curiosity. "That is how our Saxon thanes used to fight. We formed a shield wall for defense and advanced behind it."

"I did not know that," Hugh lied.

"Aye," Cedric responded, and launched into an animated discussion of Saxon battle tactics.

Hugh listened with real interest to Cedric's enthusiastic descriptions. As he talked, the young man's face was animated, his blue eyes bright with ardor.

Hugh realized that Cedric had probably come into town just to watch the camp-ball game, and would have very much enjoyed being part of it. He wouldn't dare admit that, however, Hugh thought. The young Saxon was too much under his father's influence to join in any game run by Normans.

"Hastings was probably the last major battle we will see for a long time," Hugh said when Cedric finally finished dissecting the battle that had lost England for the Saxons. "The tactics of war have changed tremendously in the last century. Warfare today consists of the defense and besieging of castles. It is the control of castles that defines power in today's world, not the clash of armies."

Cedric looked disgusted. "There is little glory in siege warfare."

"Possibly," Hugh replied, "but open battle, such as you have been describing, is no longer efficient. For example, there has been constant war in Normandy for the last five years, yet not a single battle has been fought. Battle is risky and most good commanders avoid it as far as possible."

"There was a battle against the Scots not long ago," Cedric pointed out. "Your foster father was killed in it."

A bleak look came across Hugh's face. "It was a rout, not a battle. Ralf's death was an accident."

"It was an accident that you beat us at Hastings," Cedric said passionately.

"The English certainly had bad luck," Hugh agreed. "But winning that battle was only the first step in the Norman conquest of England. We secured England, Cedric, by building castles. William built castles all over the country in order to establish his authority. He built castles to defend against a hostile English population and to give a secure base to Norman troops."

"I know this," Cedric said stubbornly. "I even agree that castles are effective. I just do not think it is an honorable way to wage war."

Hugh lifted an ironic black eyebrow. "Do you really think that any war is honorable, Cedric?"

The young Saxon flushed. "Alfred of Wessex's fight against the Danes was honorable. He was defending his country against a pagan invader. Harold was defending his country against an invader also when he took an army to Hastings."

Hugh regarded Cedric's passionate face in silence. When at last he spoke, his voice was quiet and final. "There can be no doubt that a war in defense of one's home is morally more palatable than a war of conquest. But we live in an age of conquest, Cedric."

"I am well aware of that," Cedric said bitterly. "You Normans talk about the sacredness of your feudal oaths, and then you turn your backs upon honor and pursue your own personal power."

"Oh, there are still a few of us around who honor our feudal oaths," Hugh said. "And I daresay that even Alfred of Wessex had power-hungry men to deal with."

Cedric stared into the fire and didn't reply.

"Your father is living in the past and that is not a wise thing to do," Hugh said bluntly. "The Hardings were a power in Lincoln once. If your father used the resources at his command, he could be a power still."

"My father would never truckle to Normans!" Cedric flared.

"I am not speaking of truckling," Hugh answered patiently. "I am speaking of accepting the realities of the present power structure and working within it, not against it."

Cedric scowled at him and did not reply.

Hugh got to his feet. "Think of this, Cedric," he said. "It is safer by far to be one of the powerful than it is to be one of the powerless."

He put his wine cup down on a low stool and walked out of the room.

Alan was huddled on a stool in the corner of the solar of the sheriff's house when when Hugh came in. Richard was sprawled before the fire, a cup of wine in his hand. He had been drinking for some time, and Alan was worried about him.

"Ah," said Richard thickly when he saw who had entered. "The hero of the day is here at last."

"You should join the crowd at the Nettle," Hugh said. "It's more fun than drinking alone."

"I'm not alone," Richard said, slurring his words. "I have Alan. My squire." He turned to look at Alan. "Isn't that right, Alan?" he demanded.

"Aye, my lord," Alan replied softly.

Richard laughed and took another sip of wine.

Hugh folded his arms and regarded the man critically.

"You cheated," Richard accused him. His blue eyes were too bright and his fair skin was flushed. "They shouldn't have allowed you to put men behind my lines. That's never been allowed before."

"No one ever tried to do it before," Hugh corrected coolly. "There's nothing in the rules that says you can't spread out your team."

Richard slammed his cup down on the small table next to him so hard that the wine sloshed out.

"You made me look like a fool," he said furiously. "You even used my own squire against me."

Alan winced.

"I gave you plenty of chances to pick Alan," Hugh returned. "You didn't."

"I didn't think I had to pick him!" Richard shouted. "He belongs to me. Of course he would be on my side!"

Alan felt Hugh looking at him, but he refused to meet Hugh's eyes.

"Do you know what your problem is, Richard?" Hugh said lightly. "You're a bad loser."

Don't taunt him, Hugh, Alan thought with distress. *It isn't fair. Don't make him say things he doesn't mean. Don't make him look small.*

"Someday you're going to lose, Hugh, and then we'll see how well you take it," Richard said.

Hugh laughed.

Richard's face went dark with a rush of blood.

Alan jumped to his feet. "May I get you some more wine, my lord?" he asked, going to stand at Richard's side. "Your cup is almost empty."

For a moment, Richard stared at his squire as if he did not know who he was. There was a wild, glittering look in Richard's blue eyes that frightened Alan. Then the look cleared away and recognition dawned.

"Thank you, Alan. I would like more wine."

Alan fetched the pitcher from the table where it stood, then paused to stare at Hugh.

"Good night, my lord," he said steadily. "I hope you have a good rest."

Hugh gave him a mocking look. "Are you banishing me to bed, Alan?"

Alan didn't reply, just continued to look at him steadily.

Hugh shot a quick look at Richard that made Alan's blood run cold. Then, without saying anything more, he turned and went through the door to his bedroom.

Alan went to Richard and poured him some more wine.

21

To Alan's great relief, Richard appeared to have returned to his normal self as the members of the sheriff's household gathered the following morning to break their fast.

"I think I owe you an apology," he said to Hugh with charming diffidence. "I drank too much last night and I remember saying some things that were rather objectionable."

Hugh took a drink from his ale cup. "Think nothing of it, Richard," he replied, placing the cup on the table.

Richard went resolutely on. "At any rate, I apologize." His blue eyes were rueful. "I should never drink more than two cups of wine. Whenever I do, I tend to say things that I don't mean."

Alan, who knew how difficult it must be for Richard to apologize to Hugh, was immensely proud of his lord's grace.

"Really?" Hugh returned, somehow managing to make the single word sound like an insult. "Wine has just the opposite effect on most people."

Alan grimly restrained an impulse to smash Hugh across one of his elegant cheekbones.

At this moment, Gervase joined them at the table. He lifted his napkin, shook it out, and looked at his son.

"You were drunk last night, Richard."

His tone was perfectly neutral, but the expression on his face was grave.

"I know, Father. I know." Richard returned regretfully. "I have just finished apololgizing to Hugh and now I will apologize to you. If I said anything to upset you, I didn't mean it."

Alan poured ale into Gervase's cup.

"Well, you certainly weren't alone in your inebriated state," the sheriff remarked as he lifted his cup to take a drink. "We made ten arrests at the Nettle last night."

As they ate, Gervase related the story of the brawl that had finally closed down the Nettle. Alan listened to the tone of the sheriff's voice and tried to figure out what else might be wrong. Surely the brawl had not been bad enough to cause the sheriff to sound so grim.

When he had finished eating, Hugh stood up and announced that he was leaving immediately for Linsay Manor.

"Linsay?" Richard said with a frown. "Why are you going to Linsay?"

Hugh looked at Richard, his face expressionless. "Someone has to tell John Rye's family that he is dead."

For a long moment, Richard didn't reply. Then, "Why don't you take Alan with you?"

Alan had not been expecting any such suggestion. He stared at his lord as if he had gone mad. Last night Richard had been angry that Alan had played the camp-ball game on Hugh's side, yet this morning here he was, throwing his squire into Hugh's company.

Alan didn't understand.

"Why?" Hugh said, the insulting note once more in his voice.

"You will probably have to bring Rye's wife and children back to Lincoln with you," Richard replied calmly. "I think you might very well welcome some assistance with that chore."

To Alan's surprise, Hugh's gray eyes glimmered with sudden amusement.

"How thoughtful of you, Richard," he said gently. "Very well, Alan may come with me."

He turned to the squire. "I am leaving within the quarter-hour."

"Aye, my lord," Alan replied stoically, thinking that he would have to change into boots and spurs and get one of the horses ready in record time.

Minutes later, when Alan arrived at the stable booted and spurred and wearing the warm, green woolen mantle that Richard had given to him, he found Richard holding his already saddled horse.

"Alan," Richard said gravely as the squire came up to him. "I want you to keep a close eye upon Hugh today. Watch who he talks to at Linsay. Will you do that for me?"

Enlightenment struck Alan. *So that is why he wanted me to accompany Hugh.*

He answered Richard in a steady voice. "Aye, my lord. I will keep careful watch on him."

Alan's spirits soared in the radiance of Richard's approving smile.

"I have one quick stop to make before we leave Lincoln," Hugh said as they walked their horses out onto the Strait.

Alan nodded, certain Hugh would be going to see Lady Cristen. He was surprised, therefore, when they stopped only a short way up the Strait and Hugh dismounted, gave Alan his reins to hold, and went up to an old wooden house with yellow shutters. He knocked on the door.

After a long wait, the door was opened by an elderly woman. Hugh said something to her, then he disappeared inside. When he came out again several minutes later, his face was grave but unrevealing. He took Rufus's reins back from Alan, mounted, and turned once more up the street.

The ride to Linsay was silent. Alan knew his place well enough not to initiate conversation, and Hugh appeared to be sunk in his own thoughts. It wasn't until the high wooden fence of Linsay appeared in the distance that he surfaced.

The stockade door was closed. Hugh shouted out his name and asked for entrance, but no one answered.

The cloudy gray sky looked down on a Linsay that was apparently deserted.

Hugh muttered a curse under his breath and dismounted. He led Rufus to the door and tried to open it.

It was locked.

"It seems that Lady Rye and her children are not here, my lord," Alan ventured timidly.

Hugh didn't reply. He just opened his saddlebag and took out a long coil of rope. He told Rufus to stand and then, under Alan's fascinated eyes, he looped the rope around one of the points of the stockade fence. He then proceeded to climb up the wall. Alan watched with interest as he disappeared over the top.

A minute later, the door to the manor was unlocked from the inside and Hugh reappeared. He pushed the door open wide, reclaimed Rufus, and rode into the deserted courtyard of Linsay. Alan followed close behind.

Alan looked at the empty yard, at the apparently uninhabited servants' huts, at the forsaken stables, and felt a shiver run up and down his spine.

Suddenly the sound of a dog barking cut through the eerie silence. It seemed to come from the stable at the far end of the yard.

Hugh rode Rufus to the stable, dismounted, and opened the door. An enormous light brown mastiff rushed out at him, ears pinned back, barking ferociously. Alan quickly unsheathed his dagger, reached to go to Hugh's assistance, but Hugh didn't even flinch.

"Benjamin," Hugh said conversationally. "No need to be so noisy, fellow. I'm a friend."

Alan was enormously surprised to see the dog stop short and prick his ears forward at the sound of Hugh's voice. The barking stopped.

Hugh reached out his hand and the dog sniffed it. Hugh patted the dog's massive head. Benjamin rubbed against his hand.

"Good fellow," Hugh said. "What is happening here, eh? Where are Nicholas and Iseult?"

He walked into the stable, followed by Benjamin, then reappeared almost immediately. "The dog has a full dish of water," he reported. "Someone must be looking after him."

"There is someone now," Alan said, his eyes caught by movement near the manor house.

It was a moment before he realized that it was two dark-haired children he was seeing. They were walking hand in hand, stiff-backed and wary, toward the stable. They must have heard the dog barking, he thought.

Hugh stepped forward from the shadow of the stable doorway into the light.

"Hugh!" A high, piercing child's shriek split the air. *"Nicholas, it's Hugh!"*

At that, both children ran full-tilt across the courtyard. Under Alan's amazed eyes, they hurled themselves against Hugh, who somehow managed not to stagger under the combined assault.

"I knew you would come," the little girl said over and over. "I knew it. I knew it." She clasped her arms around Hugh's legs, pressed her face into his stomach. The boy, a sturdy youngster of about eight, did not cling to Hugh, Alan noted, but stood very close.

"Of course I came," Hugh replied in a brisk, no-nonsense voice. "Now, tell me," he went on. "What is going on here?" He looked at the boy. "Nicholas?"

"Mama is dead," the child said starkly.

Hugh's face went perfectly still. "What happened? I thought she was getting better."

Nicholas swallowed. "She was, but then the fever came back and she died."

Hugh reached an arm around the child's shoulders and drew him closer. "I am so sorry, Nicholas."

Mutely the boy nodded. He turned his face into Hugh's chest.

Hugh looked around the empty courtyard. "The servants did not come back?"

Nicholas's head moved in a negative gesture.

"Is Edith still here?" Hugh asked.

Nicholas stepped away from Hugh. He rubbed his hands against his eyes then shook his head. "Her brother came two days ago and took her away. She said she would send someone, but no one came."

Benjamin nudged Nicholas, asking for attention.

"Do you mean that you and Iseult are alone here?" Hugh asked incredulously.

The boy's lip quivered, and he nodded.

Alan was appalled. *Dear God,* he thought. *What a horrendous situation.*

Very gently, Hugh asked, "Did anyone bury your mother, Nicholas?"

Another shake of the untidy black head. "She is still in her bed," Nicholas said.

Alan felt sick.

"When did she die?" Hugh asked in that same surprisingly gentle voice.

"The day after my father left."

Alan counted in his mind. Rye had come to Lincoln the day before the fair, Monday. That must mean his wife had died on Tuesday. It was now Thursday.

Jesu. The woman had been dead for two days and these children had been left alone with her.

"She smells," the little girl said tearfully.

Alan felt even sicker.

"Do you know where my father is, Hugh?" Nicholas asked. "He was supposed to come home after the fair."

Hugh avoided the question. "This is what we are going to do," he said briskly. "I am going to take the two of you back to Lincoln with me where you will stay at my house. Then I will have some men come out to Linsay with a coffin and bring your mother's body back to Lincoln as well, so we can bury her with proper respect in holy ground."

The children were silent.

Hugh smoothed the loose hair off of Iseult's forehead. The little girl still had her arms around him.

"How does that sound?" he asked Nicholas.

"Is my father in Lincoln?" Nicholas said.

Alan clenched his fists. He felt like crying himself.

Hugh responded gravely, "I am sorry to have to tell you this, Nicholas and Iseult, but your father is dead."

Silence.

Iseult dropped her arms from around Hugh and looked up at him, her eyes dazed. "Papa is dead?"

"I am afraid that he is, little one."

The little girl looked at her brother. "W-what is going to happen to us, Nicholas?" she whispered.

The boy's face was white with shock. He shook his head, unable to reply.

Hugh said, "You will both live with me until we can find one of your aunts or uncles to take care of you."

"We don't have any aunts or uncles," Nicholas said stoically.

It was the stoicism that broke Alan's heart. If the boy had whined or cried it would have been bad enough, but to hear such a tone from so young a child was devastating.

Hugh said, "Well, if no family members can be found to care for you, you will just have to keep on living with me."

The boy's blue eyes searched Hugh's face. He bit his lip. "Do you mean that, Hugh?"

"Of course I do," Hugh replied.

With amazement, Alan realized that the children believed him.

They left Linsay an hour later. Hugh had the children pack some of their clothes, and while they were doing this, he went into Lady Rye's bedroom. He would not allow Alan to come with him.

When he came out, his face was perfectly expressionless. "I hope the children have not gone in there recently," was his only comment to Alan.

Iseult clung to Hugh, so he took her up on Rufus with him and told Nicholas to ride with Alan. Benjamin trotted along at their heels.

Alan had thought that surely Hugh would leave the mastiff behind for the sheriff's men to deal with, but he had included the dog in their party as though it was the most natural thing in the world. Alan supposed that for the moment Benjamin was going to live at Hugh's house as well.

Alan and Nicholas rode mostly in silence. After offering his regrets, Alan could think of nothing else to say to a boy whose life had been so devastated, so he decided it would be best to say nothing.

Halfway across Lincoln Fields, they met up with two riders entering the main road from a side path. With surprise, Alan recognized Richard and Elizabeth de Beauté.

Every time Alan saw Elizabeth, he was astonished anew by her beauty. Today her skin was delicately flushed and there was a shine in her eyes that made her look even more breathtaking than usual.

Both parties pulled up and regarded the other under the lowering gray sky.

Hugh spoke first. "Did you enjoy your ride, Lady Elizabeth?"

There was a note in his voice that Alan did not understand, but Elizabeth's rosy flush deepened.

"Aye, my lord," she returned a little defiantly. Her green eyes flashed from Iseult to Nicholas. "Who are these children?"

Iseult was asleep in Hugh's arms, but in front of Alan, Nicholas was awake and alert.

Benjamin had been off investigating a scent, and now he trotted up and immediately began to bark at the two new riders.

"Benjamin, stop," Nicholas ordered.

The dog barked twice more, sharply, then went to stand protectively between Nicholas and the strangers.

"These are John Rye's children, my lady," Hugh said.

"But where is Lady Rye?" Richard asked in a puzzled voice.

"Lady Rye is dead," Hugh returned.

"God Almighty." Richard looked with compassion upon the sleeping child in Hugh's arms. "The poor mites. Where are you taking them, Hugh? To the convent in Wigford?"

"They are coming home with me," Hugh returned. "Bernard is well enough now to allow Lady Cristen to return to my town house. I am sure she will look after them until we can settle their future."

Richard bestowed a look of warm approval on Hugh. "That is kind of you."

"Isn't it?" Hugh replied woodenly.

"These poor children," Lady Elizabeth said. "Why, they are orphans!"

Alan felt Nicholas's small, sturdy body stiffen.

"Fortunately, they have friends," Hugh returned coolly. "Now, if you don't mind, we had better be on our way."

Iseult stirred in Hugh's arms and opened sleepy blue eyes. She made a sound of alarm when she saw the strangers.

"It's all right, sweetheart," Hugh said to her gently. "You're with me."

"Oh," she said. "Hugh." She nestled against him again and closed her eyes.

"Lady Elizabeth and I will ride on ahead of you," Richard said. "Shall I alert Lady Cristen that you are coming?"

"Do that," Hugh returned. "Tell her that I'll meet her at Ralf's house."

"Very well." Richard said something to Elizabeth, who nodded, and then they both cantered off.

Hugh put Rufus into a walk so as not to disturb the sleeping Iseult, and the two horses and one dog traveled slowly on.

22

Cristen was waiting at Ralf's house when Hugh and Alan and the children rode up. After a flurry of introductions, Hugh left Nicholas and Iseult to her competent care and rode back to the castle to make arrangements to have Lady Rye's body brought into Lincoln. She would be buried from the Minster along with her husband.

Cristen took one look at the shocked, exhausted children Hugh had turned over to her and immediately sat them down for a meal of hot soup and bread. Alan wondered how long it had been since last they ate. He joined them at the table, and approved of the way Cristen allowed the children to eat in silence while she and Alan talked together of ordinary things.

She even put a bowl of food on the floor so that Benjamin could join in the repast. The huge mastiff slurped noisily right behind Nicholas and Iseult, and Alan sensed that the presence of their dog was a comfort to the bereaved children.

"What would you like to do next?" Cristen said to the children after they had hungrily finished second helpings of the soup.

Two pairs of blue eyes gazed at her with dazed bewilderment.

"Where is Hugh?" Iseult whispered at last.

"He has gone to the castle to see about having your mother's body brought to Lincoln," Cristen said practically.

Both children continued to gaze at her. Neither said a word.

Cristen leaned comfortably back in her chair and said conversationally, "Did you know that Hugh's foster father used to be the Sheriff of Lincoln? Hugh grew up in this very house we are sitting in now."

"I didn't know he grew up in Lincoln," Nicholas said, showing the first spark of interest Alan had seen in him. "My father said he came from Wiltshire, that he was to be the next earl there."

Iseult sat up more alertly in her chair as well. Alan thought that Hugh seemed to be the one topic capable of rousing the children's attention.

Cristen craftily fed them more information. "Hugh's real father was the Earl of Wiltshire, but when he was very young, about your age, Nicholas, he was stolen away from his home by robbers. He managed to get away from them and make his way to Lincoln, where he was found by Ralf Corbaille, the sheriff. But the shock of being kidnapped caused Hugh to forget his past, and he was unable to tell the sheriff anything about himself. So Ralf adopted Hugh and brought him up right here in Lincoln as his own son."

Both children were gazing at Cristen with their eyes stretched wide and their mouths open.

"Hugh was kidnapped?" Iseult said in a hushed tone.

"Aye." Cristen's own eyes were steady and honest. "It was a terrible thing that happened to him. But he was lucky enough to find a new family who loved him very much. And he loved them—even more than he loved his first family, I think."

The children continued to stare at Cristen, faces grave, eyes solemn. Alan waited cynically for her to tell them that the same happy fate awaited them.

"So you see," she said, "Hugh knows how you must be feeling right now. A terrible thing has happened to you as well. But he will help you. And so will I."

Nicholas blinked. Then he nodded slowly.

Benjamin belched loudly.

Iseult giggled.

"I am so glad you brought your dog," Cristen said. "I have been missing my own dogs very much. A house without a dog is such an empty place."

"What kind of dogs do you have, Lady Cristen?" Iseult asked curiously.

"I'm afraid that neither one of them is as handsome as Benjamin," Cristen said, "but I love them dearly." And she launched into a detailed description of her dogs and how she had rescued each of them from abandonment. The children listened with rapt attention.

"Now then," Cristen said when she had finished the saga of her beloved animals, "we must decide what to do next. You can have a bath and put on clean clothes and then, if you are tired, you can have a nap and wait for Hugh to come home. Or, if you like, we can go up to the castle ourselves and find him."

"Find Hugh," both children replied in unison.

"Right away," Nicholas added.

"All right," Cristen said briskly. "Then that is what we will do."

Alan looked at the bedraggled children. Nicholas had smudges of ash on his face, probably from rubbing it after trying to fix the fire. And Iseult's long hair was more a tangle than a braid.

"Perhaps a bath would be in order first?" he suggested.

Nicholas frowned.

"Nay," Iseult said stubbornly. "Find Hugh first."

"Baths can come later," Cristen agreed. "If you have finished eating, we will go up to the castle and look for Hugh."

Cristen made sure the children were warmly dressed, and they left the house on foot to walk to the castle through the streets of Lincoln, where just yesterday their father had been killed.

Until now, John Rye's death had seemed an unfortunate but insignificant event to Alan—an unlucky accident that had marred the otherwise splendid camp-ball game. But now, as he looked down at the tangle of black hair on Iseult's small round head, he saw it for what it really was: a tragedy.

Every human life touches someone else's, he thought. *John Rye might have been unimportant in the worldly scheme of things, but his death has changed his children's lives irreparably.*

What were these children going to do? Alan worried. Surely,

there had to be some surviving relative somewhere who would take them in. Even if they had no aunts or uncles, their parents must have had cousins who would care for them.

Unfortunately, Nicholas and Iseult were that most expendible of commodities: well-born children who had no fortune. The only feasible future for Nicholas was to earn his living as a knight in some lord's household. And Iseult, if no one could be found to marry her, would end up in a convent, if one could be found to accept a girl with no dowry.

To Alan, the idea of having no relatives was utterly terrifying. He had always known that as a younger son he would have to support himself by his sword. He had known when he left his father's home to serve as squire to Richard Canville that he probably wouldn't be going back there to live ever again.

But still, his mother and father and eldest brother were *there*. If the worse ever came to the worst, and he had nowhere to go, they would take him in.

Nicholas and Iseult did not have that security. Until a relative could be found, Nicholas and Iseult had only Hugh.

Alan had to acknowledge that it had been kind of Hugh to take the children in. He had understood that it was important for them to be in a home with someone they knew and trusted. They would have panicked if they had been thrust into a convent.

As their small party entered into the Bail, Nicholas's gaze was fixed on the towering heights of the castle rising above them. Alan smiled, remembering his own awe the first time he beheld Lincoln Castle.

"It's bigger than I thought it would be," Nicholas said in a low voice.

"It is one of the biggest castles in the kingdom," Alan responded.

"My father served his knight's fee here every January," Nicholas said, a note of pride in his voice.

Iseult whimpered. "I'm tired. When are we going to find Hugh?"

Cristen glanced at Alan, who immediately bent and scooped the little girl up in his arms. "We'll find him very soon," he said bracingly. "I'll carry you for a little, shall I?"

She put one small arm around his neck. "Thank you, Alan."

Her little body rested against him so trustingly. Alan smiled into the small face so close to his. "You're a very brave little girl, Iseult. Do you know that?"

A dimple flashed in her cheek. "I am?"

"Aye. You are."

"I like you, Alan," Iseult said. "You're nice."

Alan felt absurdly pleased by the compliment.

When finally they reached the castle, it was to discover that Hugh was with Bernard. Even though Bernard was much better, Cristen refused to allow the children to go into the sickroom. Instead, she took them upstairs to Lady Elizabeth's apartment and sent Alan to inform Hugh where they were.

"John Rye was killed by the same man who killed de Beauté. I'm sure of it."

Alan heard Hugh's voice as soon as he opened the door to Cristen's bedchamber. Hugh was speaking softly, but with such clarity that Alan couldn't mistake his words.

Next there came the rumble of Bernard's deeper, less-clear baritone.

Alan stopped as if he had walked into glass. After a moment, he quietly closed the door behind him. Moving on silent feet to the partially open door that led into Bernard's room, he took up a position that was out of view and prepared to listen.

Hugh's voice was even clearer this close-up. Alan listened as he told Bernard, "I think that John Rye had dangerous information about the earl's murder and he tried to use it to extort money from someone. Instead of paying up, however, the man killed Rye. If it was the same man who killed de Beauté—and I think it was—he wouldn't hesitate at another murder. He got rid of the man he sent to deliver his message to the earl fast enough."

"You may very well be right," Bernard replied. From this closer vantage point, Alan could hear the man's deep voice more clearly. "John Rye tried to get William of Roumare to pay for his information and was unsuccessful. It would only be natural for him to turn next to the actual man who did the deed."

"So I think," said Hugh tersely.

Bernard began to cough. Alan heard movement in the room and

the sound of water being poured. *Hugh must be offering Bernard a drink,* he thought. Finally, when Bernard had recovered his breath, he said, "Well, your first suspicion appears to have been the right one. William of Roumare was behind the death of de Beauté all along."

This comment was met by silence. Alan's brain was in a whirl as he tried to understand this sudden introduction of William of Roumare into the picture. He frowned in concentration as he tried to sort out what he was hearing, so that he could relay it correctly to Richard.

Finally Hugh said, "If Roumare was involved, Bernard, then why didn't he buy off Rye?"

"Exactly what information do you think Rye offered him?" Bernard countered.

"John Rye was in the castle serving out his knight's fee at the time of the murder. I am guessing that he saw who gave the groom the message that summoned you to the Minster. After the groom turned up murdered as well, Rye must have realized that he had a valuable piece of information. That is when he left Lincoln with the excuse that his wife was ill and went to visit his cousin, Roumare."

Alan was concentrating so intently on the conversation in Bernard's room that he scarcely remembered to breathe. *But why would William of Roumare want to kill the Earl of Lincoln?* he thought in confusion.

"It seems to me that if Roumare was indeed involved in the earl's murder," Hugh went on, "he would have bought off John Rye. Instead, he turned him away."

Bernard replied matter-of-factly, "He turned him away because he knew there was nothing concrete that could connect the murderer to him. There can be little doubt that Roumare was the one who paid the assassin, but I will wager you that he did it in such a way that he would not be implicated. That is why he would not bribe Rye to keep quiet."

"That could be what happened," Hugh conceded, but he did not sound convinced.

"It must be what happened," Bernard said firmly. "Roumare is the only man with sufficient motive to want de Beauté dead. The whole kingdom knows he wants to be the Earl of Lincoln, and now that de Beauté is dead, he probably will be."

So that is it, Alan thought, enlightened. It made sense, he thought, mulling this new information over in his mind. Roumare was a much more likely culprit in the earl's death than was Bernard Radvers, who had gained nothing by the death of de Beauté.

"Unfortunately, I have no proof of any of this," Hugh was saying grimly.

"It doesn't matter," Bernard replied. "We have only to bring forth before the chief justiciar the information you learned from Rye, and establish the possibility that Rye may have been murdered by the same man who killed the earl. That information will save me, Hugh. I was under arrest when John Rye was killed."

"I suppose," Hugh said discontentedly.

Bernard grunted as he shifted in the bed. "Don't look so gloomy, lad! You've done what you promised. You've saved my life. I should think you would be rejoicing."

"I will rejoice when you are declared innocent," Hugh returned.

Suddenly his voice sounded much closer. Alan flattened himself against the wall, afraid that Hugh had moved nearer to the doorway. "I would feel happier if I could be certain that these murders really were connected to Roumare," Hugh confessed. "As it is . . . I simply am not convinced."

"*If?* What do you mean, if?" Bernard sounded oddly angry. "Who else besides Roumare could possibly have benefited from the death of the earl?"

Hugh didn't reply.

"Hugh." Bernard's voice was sharp and worried. "Please don't tell me you are still trying to fix the blame on Richard Canville!"

Alan felt as if someone had punched him hard in the stomach. His fists clenched at his sides, and his nostrils widened as he sucked in air.

Richard? he thought. *How could anyone, even Hugh, possibly suspect Richard?*

"I haven't eliminated him," Hugh said. His voice seemed to come from right next to the door.

Bernard raised his voice as if talking to someone across the room from him. "If you try to cast suspicion on Richard, you will make yourself a laughingstock. I know you don't like Richard. Perhaps you even have cause for not liking Richard. Perhaps Richard is not quite as perfect as everyone thinks he is. But he is not a murderer, Hugh! For God's sake, what reason would he have to murder the Earl of Lincoln?"

"Do you remember that I told you Edgar Harding came to me and accused the sheriff of embezzling from the market stall rents?"

"Aye, I remember." Bernard sounded cautious.

"Well, I have proof that Harding was right."

A heavy silence was Bernard's only reply.

Alan's teeth bit into his lower lip until they drew blood.

Hugh went on relentlessly. "The sheriff is collecting more money from the market stalls than he declares on the tax rolls. I talked to the shopkeepers and found out that they are in fact paying considerably more than what Gervase told me."

More silence from Bernard.

Alan felt sick to his stomach.

At last Bernard said heavily, "If that is so, he will not be the first sheriff to do such a thing. But I am surprised. And disappointed. I thought better of Gervase."

"Think of this," Hugh said. "Perhaps it is not Gervase who is behind the scheme. Perhaps it is Richard."

Alan didn't know if he wanted to run into Bernard's room and scream denials at Hugh, or just run away.

"Why do you say that?" Bernard asked.

"The man who collects the stall rent is Theobold Elton, and he seems to be a good friend of Richard's. Richard also appears to have a good deal more money than I would expect him to have. He keeps a squire. He has a very expensive horse. And Alan told me he found Richard in the sheriff's office late one night, going over the tax books."

Alan remembered that meeting. He remembered how upset Richard had seemed at the unexpected appearance of his squire. He shut his eyes and shook his head in vigorous denial.

"What are you suggesting, then?" Bernard said grimly. "That the earl discovered the cheat and threatened to expose it and so Richard killed him?"

"Aye." Hugh's voice seemed to come from Bernard's bedside once again.

"And just how would the earl discover the cheat?" Bernard

demanded. "I am quite sure he didn't go around asking the merchants how much rent they paid for their stalls!"

"I don't know how he discovered it," Hugh replied steadily. "But it is entirely possible that he did. The word was that he and Gervase were not on good terms. Perhaps this was one of the reasons for their falling-out."

There was silence in Bernard's room. Alan looked longingly at the door leading from Cristen's room into the passageway. He should leave while there was still a chance he would not be discovered eavesdropping.

But he couldn't seem to tear himself away.

Bernard broke the silence. "What of Edgar Harding, Hugh? He certainly hated de Beauté. And he had that piece of information about the single stab wound to the heart that killed the earl. Perhaps Harding himself was the murderer and then he told you this information about the market stall cheat just to throw suspicion on someone else."

Alan remembered that he had unexpectedly met Edgar Harding the morning after the murder, and his heart jumped.

"I suppose it is possible," Hugh said, "but Edgar Harding has people who will swear that he was at Deerhurst on the night the earl was killed."

"Are these people to be believed?"

"I don't know," Hugh replied frankly. "But Harding also appears to have a defense for the day that John Rye was killed. His son told me that his father was at home, ill, in bed, and being attended to by his wife and daughters."

"Hmm."

There came the sound of a stool being pulled across the wood floor. Hugh must be sitting down, Alan thought.

"On the other hand," Hugh said, "Cedric Harding was here in Lincoln on Wednesday. In fact, he was the man who discovered that Rye had been murdered."

There was a little silence as Bernard digested this piece of information. Then he replied, "Why would Harding's *son* want to kill the earl?"

Hugh sighed. "Edgar appears to have passed all of his extreme prejudices down to his offspring. Cedric hates all Normans, and in particular, he hates the Norman who robbed the Hardings of their land. Perhaps he was the man whom Rye saw talking to the groom that night."

"That's pretty far-fetched," Bernard said.

"Aye," Hugh agreed readily. "It is."

"The fact of the matter is, all of this is speculation. You have no proof of anything," Bernard said.

"I know that, Bernard," Hugh replied irritably.

"Then our best hope is to cast doubt upon the sheriff's case against me. I think your testimony about what John Rye told you will do that quite satisfactorily."

Hugh didn't reply.

Alan, realizing that he had heard all that was going to be said, decided that it was time to leave. He had actually taken a step when Hugh came into the room through the connecting door. He looked Alan up and down and said pleasantly, "What an interesting time you must have had, Alan. Do you have any comments you would care to add to the conversation?"

Alan's cheeks and ears were scarlet as he made his way down the tower steps, Hugh's last contemptuous words ringing in his ears. *Now, run away like a good little spy and report everything you heard back to Richard.*

Of course, it had been Alan's intention to do just that, but something in the way Hugh had regarded him made him feel uncomfortable.

He called me a spy and he was right, Alan thought shamefacedly. *I am someone who listens to other people's private conversations and reports them back to someone else.*

It was the first time it had occurred to Alan that what he was doing might not be considered honorable. He had never looked at it that way before. Why?

Because Richard asked me to do it.

The answer was immediate. If Richard, his idol, his perfect model of a knight, had told him to do it, then it must be all right.

But Hugh had made Alan feel besmirched. Dirty. Like a spy. What would Hugh think of him if he knew that Alan had listened to his conversation with Cristen? Alan shuddered at the thought.

He tried to work up some anger against Hugh for treating him so contemptuously, but it was difficult. It was too easy for Alan to see the situation from Hugh's point of view. He couldn't find it in himself to blame Hugh for being angry.

Richard shouldn't have asked me to spy for him, Alan thought soberly. *It wasn't right.*

It was the first time in his life that he had ever had a critical thought about his lord.

As the sound of Alan's footsteps died away, Bernard looked from where he was lying propped against his pillows toward the young man standing by the single small window in the tower bedroom. "For how long did you know that he was there?" he asked.

"I heard him come in," Hugh replied. He turned toward Bernard, one of his hands resting, fingers spread out, on the stone windowsill.

"How did you know that it was Alan?"

"I knew it was Alan when he stopped to listen. Richard has been using him to spy on me."

Bernard frowned in bewilderment. "Then why didn't you accost him immediately?"

"Because I have a feeling that Alan knows things that could be very helpful to us," Hugh replied. "I wanted to see if I could shake his faith in Richard a little."

Bernard shook his head in a decisive negative. "You can't. Alan worships Richard."

"I know he does. But Alan is a bright youngster. Even more important, he has a sense of honor. Once his eyes have been opened, I think he will begin to see things as they really are, not as Richard has made them seem."

Bernard pushed himself until he was sitting upright in the bed. "For God's sake, Hugh, *why* do you dislike Richard so intensely? It is not like you to bear such bitter enmity over a childhood rivalry."

Hugh turned his back on Bernard and looked out the tower window. He said nothing.

Behind him, Bernard persisted. "There has to be some reason. I know he used to bully you when you were young, but as you grew, you more than got your own back on him. So *why?*"

Hugh stared down at the small group of men-at-arms who were

walking from the keep walls to the castle. Still facing the window, he said, "I never told this story to anyone but Ralf." He turned to face the man in the bed. "I am only telling you now because it bears on your own situation."

Bernard said, "You know I can keep a quiet tongue in my head, lad."

Speaking in an ordinary, matter-of-fact voice, Hugh said, "I saw Richard murder his brother."

Bernard's mouth dropped open in shock. He stared at Hugh, his bushy eyebrows twin marks of astonishment, and didn't say a word.

"I was there," Hugh repeated. "I saw it happen."

Bernard closed his mouth and found his voice. "*What* happened? And why didn't you ever say anything?"

Hugh's face was bleak as he replied, "Because no one would have believed me."

Bernard leaned back against his pillows, suddenly looking very tired. "Tell me."

Hugh stared down at his linked hands as if they held the answer to Bernard's question. He began to speak in a carefully expressionless voice.

"As you know, Simon was Gervase's eldest son and, as is customary, he remained at home while Richard was sent to the Minster school in Lincoln." Hugh opened his hands and then linked them together again. "About once a month, Simon used to come into Lincoln to visit Richard. He was a nice boy, Simon. A kind boy. He loved his brother."

Hugh fell abruptly silent.

"I remember Simon," Bernard said encouragingly. "He *was* a nice boy. He was only fourteen when he died, I believe. He drowned in the Witham, I remember."

Hugh looked up. "Aye. There had been a lot of rain that spring, and the river was running very high. Simon and Richard took a boat out, the boat capsized, and Simon drowned."

Bernard frowned as he cast his mind back to the past. "Richard tried to *save* his brother, Hugh. I remember that someone told me he himself nearly drowned, diving over and over trying to recover Simon's body."

"That is what most people think," Hugh agreed.

Bernard's pale blue eyes narrowed as he remembered something else. "Didn't you go to Richard's assistance? I seem to remember that you helped him recover the body."

"I was there all right," Hugh replied somberly. "I was there from the beginning."

Once more, Bernard said, "Tell me."

There was a white line around Hugh's mouth but his voice was perfectly steady as he related his story.

"I was by myself, fishing along the shore, when I saw Simon and Richard's boat come around a bend in the river. They didn't see me, however. I was fishing under those big willows that lean into the water about a quarter mile above the mill."

Bernard nodded to indicate that he recognized the place.

"The water was deep out in the middle where the boat was. I was holding my line, watching the boat casually, when I saw Richard suddenly lean over, raise his hand, and strike Simon over the head. Simon crumpled and Richard shoved him so that he went over the side of the boat and into the water. Then Richard threw whatever it was that he had hit Simon with into the water after him."

"My God," Bernard said. The words were barely a breath of sound.

The white line around Hugh's mouth became even more pronounced. "I dropped my pole and ran along the shore to an open place where the willows did not hide me, and I shouted to Richard. *That* was when he began to pretend to look for Simon. He yelled to me to help him, and jumped out of the boat and began to dive. I swam out and dove as well. We both stayed in the water until another boat arrived and made us stop. Richard told everyone that Simon had stood up in the boat, tripped, and hit his head on the edge of the boat as he went into the water."

"You didn't tell Richard that you had seen what happened?"

Hugh shook his head. "I wanted to talk to Ralf first."

"And what did Ralf say?"

Hugh's gray eyes darkened noticably. "I don't think he believed me. He told me to keep what I had seen to myself, that I had no proof and it would be just my word against Richard's. He said . . . he said that I was an unknown quantity, while everyone knew Richard and his family and that it would probably go ill for me if I accused him."

"Ralf didn't say that he didn't believe you!" Bernard interrupted.

Hugh shrugged as if it didn't matter. "Not in so many words, but why else would he tell me to hold my tongue? I knew that if Ralf didn't believe me, no one would, and so I did hold it. But I have always known what Richard is."

"How old were you when this happened?" Bernard demanded.

"I was eleven and Richard was twelve."

"Dear God," Bernard said again.

Hugh's gray eyes regarded him somberly. "Do *you* believe me, Bernard?"

"Aye, I believe you," Bernard replied. "And I'll tell you something else, Hugh. Ralf believed you as well. If he pretended to doubt you, it was to ensure your silence. He was right. If you had accused Richard of such a thing, you would have been crucified."

"And if I accuse Richard of this murder, will the same thing happen?"

"You are not a foundling any longer, Hugh, but everyone in Lincoln knows how much you dislike Richard. You certainly never tried to make any secret of it."

Hugh lifted one straight black brow in a gesture of irony. "Unwise of me, wasn't it?"

"Well, you must admit, it doesn't put you in a very good position to accuse him of anything," Bernard returned. "Especially if you have no proof."

Hugh said gloomily, "That is what Cristen says."

Bernard's chin came up sharply. "I thought the only person you told about this was Ralf."

Hugh looked at him in genuine bewilderment. "But of course I told Cristen."

Bernard stared at Hugh's face, and after a moment his mouth softened. "She is a wonderful girl. You are lucky to have found her."

Matter-of-factly, Hugh nodded. Then, "I think Richard murdered the earl, Bernard. Who better to deliver a supposed message from Gervase than Gervase's own son? No one would doubt Richard."

Bernard coughed a few times. "And you think he did it to protect himself from being found out as an embezzler?"

Hugh began to walk toward the bed. "Aye."

Bernard sighed and leaned his head back against his pillows. "Perhaps you are right, lad. But you will never convince the chief justiciar unless you have some proof."

"I have proof of the embezzlement. All I have to do is call one of the merchants to testify about how much rent he pays."

"But you have no proof that ties Richard to the murder."

"I know that," Hugh replied evenly. "That is why I let Alan overhear our conversation. I have a feeling that Alan is the person who has the proof we need, if only he can be brought to understand."

Bernard did not reply.

"I've exhausted you," Hugh said contritely, looking down into the older man's pale face. "Cristen would be furious with me if she could see you now."

"Nonsense," Bernard said gruffly. "I am perfectly fine. I plan to get out of this bed tomorrow."

"Well, I'll leave you now so you can get some sleep."

As Hugh was turning away, Bernard reached out a hand to catch his sleeve.

"Be careful, lad. If Richard is what you think he is, he won't blink at ridding himself of you if you feels you are a danger to him."

"Don't worry," Hugh replied grimly. "I don't underestimate Richard."

On that note, he walked out of the room, leaving a sleepless Bernard to worry about all that he had heard.

23

After Hugh had dismissed him, Alan bolted down the tower stairs and kept on running until he had reached the armory hall. There he stopped, his heart beating fast, his thoughts in a chaos of humiliation and uncertainty. He was still standing there, alone in the hall, when Richard himself came in.

For the first time in his life, Alan wasn't overjoyed to see his lord. He didn't want to have to face Richard now. He wanted some time to sort out in his mind all the distressing information he had so illicitly overheard. Unfortunately, there was little hope of hiding himself in this empty, cavernous hall.

Richard hailed him genially and crossed the room to his side. Alan watched his lord approach, so tall and strong and handsome, the perfect knight in looks as well as performance.

"Did you get the Rye children safely to Lincoln, then?" Richard asked.

"Aye, my lord," Alan replied. He avoided Richard's gaze, staring instead at the fine blue wool of his tunic's shoulder.

"Good." Richard took a step closer. "Poor little brats. It was extremely kind of Hugh to take them in." He sounded agreeably surprised at finding such kindness in Hugh.

With great effort, Alan brought himself to look into

the blue eyes of his lord. They were regarding him with perfect benevolence.

It isn't true, he thought. *Richard would never do the things that Hugh accused him of.*

But someone was overcharging on the stall rents. Hugh couldn't have made that up. If the culprit wasn't Richard, then it had to be the sheriff. Alan drew a deep breath and decided that it would only be fair to alert Richard to Hugh's knowledge.

"My lord," he said. He could feel his cheeks flaming, but he manfully kept his gaze on Richard's face. "I am very sorry to tell you this, but Lord Hugh has found out that someone is cheating the king out of taxes on the market stall rents."

Richard went perfectly still. "How do you know this?" he asked sharply.

Alan's eyes dropped away. "I overheard Hugh talking to Bernard," he mumbled.

Richard was silent for so long that Alan finally looked at him again. His face was white with fury and there was something in his eyes that Alan had seen once before, when Richard had tackled him in the camp-ball game.

Alan involuntarily backed up a step.

When Richard finally spoke, his voice was perfectly controlled. "Tell me exactly what you heard."

In a low monotone Alan repeated the part of Hugh's conversation that pertained to the sheriff and the market stall rents. He hesitated, looked at Richard's angry face, then decided to refrain from saying that Hugh also suspected that Richard himself might be the thief.

When Alan had finished, Richard looked away from him and toward the sheriff's office.

"How could he be so stupid?" The contempt in his voice was withering.

Alan stared at his feet and said nothing.

Richard turned on his heel and started across the hall. "Come with me," he said. Alan trailed behind him reluctantly. The last thing he wanted to do was accuse the sheriff of cheating the king out of his taxes.

They met Gervase in the hall outside his office door. "Come

inside, Father," Richard said. His words were a command, not a request. "There is something you need to know."

Gervase glanced once at his son. Then, without speaking a word, he turned and went back into his office. Richard and Alan followed.

Richard closed the door and the three of them stood just inside it, Gervase and Richard facing each other, Alan a step behind Richard.

Gervase said calmly, "What is it, Richard? I am late as it is."

"Alan," Richard said. "Tell my father what you overheard."

With his eyes focused on Gervase's chest, Alan said in a color-less monotone, "I overheard Lord Hugh telling Bernard Radvers that he had discovered someone was overcharging for the market stalls in the Bail and not reporting it on the tax roll."

Gervase didn't make a sound. Alan glanced up at his face. The sheriff was gray.

"Is it true?" Richard's voice was harsh. "I looked recently at the tax roll myself and it seemed to be in order, but if Hugh can bring wit-nesses to testify that what the merchants pay in rent is higher than what is being reported to the Exchequer . . ." His mouth set in a hard, grim line.

"Jesus wept," Gervase said heavily. "How in the name of God did Hugh find this out?"

"It is true, then?" Richard demanded.

Moving as if he were eighty years old, Gervase went over to the backless bench that stood in front of one of the room's chests and slowly lowered himself onto it.

"Aye," he replied bleakly. "It is true."

Richard's fists clenched at his side. He cursed.

Gervase winced.

"Christ," Richard said in a low, furious voice. "How could you be so *stupid*, Father?"

"I don't know," Gervase replied. He rubbed his eyes. "It was just so easy, Richard. I didn't plan to do it when first I decided to rent out the Bail for market stalls. But, as I thought about it, I saw how easy it would be to take a piece of the rent for myself. The merchants would never know that what I collected from them was not what I declared on the tax rolls. And the Exchequer office was certainly not going to come to Lincoln to question everyone from whom I collected money for the king." He shrugged wearily and repeated, "It was just so easy."

"I saw Hugh talking to one of the merchants the other day," Richard said grimly.

Gervase buried his face in his hands. Alan looked away. It was not pleasant to see a proud man like the sheriff brought so low.

"Cheating on the taxes is bad enough, but don't you realize that this gives you a motive for killing Gilbert de Beauté?" Richard demanded.

At that, the sheriff lifted his head. "What are you talking about?"

"Suppose de Beauté discovered this cheat. Wouldn't that be a reason for you to want him out of the way?"

"But he didn't discover the cheat, Richard! I swear to you, he knew nothing about the stall rents."

Richard said coldly, "Can you prove that?"

"Oh God." Gervase's eyes were full of despair.

Richard went on relentlessly. "You were the man de Beauté was supposedly going to meet in the Minster the night he was killed. Your stupid cheat has made it very easy for Hugh to maintain that you yourself were the one who gave the messages to be delivered to the earl and Bernard. Given this information about the stall rents, you have more of a motive for wanting de Beauté dead than Bernard does."

Gervase stood up. "I didn't do it," he said. "You must believe me, son. I didn't do it."

"Oh, *I* believe you, Father." Richard's voice held more than a trace of sarcasm. "The question is, will the king's chief justiciar believe you?"

Silence fell as father and son looked at each other.

Alan reluctantly decided that he had better tell Richard that the sheriff was not Hugh's only suspect.

"My lord," he said in a a low voice, "Lord Hugh thinks that you may be the one who is responsible for cheating on the stall rents."

Richard's head whipped around to look at his squire. *"Me?"*

"Aye, my lord. You know . . . you know how Lord Hugh does not like you . . ." Alan's voice trailed away at the look on Richard's face. He stared at his feet.

"How perfectly splendid," Richard said with excoriating bitterness. "And did Hugh offer any reasons, beyond his dislike, for thinking me guilty of such a deed?"

With difficulty, Alan refrained from nervously shuffling his feet. "Well . . . he told Bernard that you appear to have a great deal of money. You keep a squire and have a nice horse and . . ." Alan's voice petered out.

"*I* gave Richard the money for those things," Gervase said strongly. "He is not implicated in this cheat in any way at all."

"*God damn it*, Father," Richard burst out. "What you stole was a pittance! How could you risk so much for so little?"

Alan blinked at this point of view.

For the first time since they had come into the office, Gervase actually looked at Alan. "Is Hugh prepared to bring this matter up before the chief justiciar?"

"I think so," Alan replied unhappily. "He is determined to save Bernard from being convicted, and he thinks that this information will cast doubt upon Bernard's guilt."

"Did Hugh say anything else that might pertain to this case?" Richard demanded.

All Alan wanted to do was get away. He hesitated, looked into Richard's angry eyes, and decided not to tell him what Hugh suspected in regard to John Rye. It could have nothing to do with either Richard or the sheriff, he assured himself.

"No, my lord," he said in a subdued tone.

"Very well, Alan," Richard said. "That will be all for now."

"Aye, my lord," Alan said, and backed up a step.

For the first time since Alan had broken the news about Hugh's information, Richard's face lost its hard, angry look. "I am sorry that you had to be involved in this sordid business, Alan." Briefly he touched his squire's shoulder. "But you were right to come to me."

"Aye, my lord," Alan gulped.

Richard smiled, the old intimate smile that always warmed Alan's heart. "You won't say anything to anyone else about this, will you?"

"Of course not, my lord," Alan replied stiffly.

"Good lad."

Alan nodded, backed up, turned, and thankfully made his escape.

* * *

Cristen accepted a cup of wine from Elizabeth de Beauté while
Nicholas and Iseult sat like statues, side by side on a stool against the
wall. Cristen had chosen to wait for Hugh here because it would be
an easy place for him to find them, but she devoutly hoped he would
not be long. Elizabeth de Beauté's conversation was far too personal
for Cristen's taste.

Elizabeth smoothed her skirt and regarded Cristen with wide,
feline eyes. "You don't mind that Lord Hugh has made you nursemaid
to his orphans?" she asked, glancing once at the two children huddled
together near the door.

"I don't mind at all," Cristen returned, taking a small sip of her
wine.

Elizabeth tapped long, elegant fingers on the arm of her chair.
"I imagine you would do anything he asked of you," she said next.

"Perhaps," Cristen replied evenly.

Elizabeth's green eyes glittered. "You must have been heart-
broken when he promised to marry me."

"I didn't know that he *had* promised to marry you," Cristen
returned calmly.

"Of course he did," Elizabeth snapped, her eyes gleaming all
the more. "All the world knows that we were betrothed."

"I did not realize that papers had been signed," Cristen said
with mild surprise.

Elizabeth's gaze narrowed, becoming more catlike than ever.
"My father died before the papers could be signed. But the marriage
was arranged and well you know it, Lady Cristen."

"I know that Lord Guy arranged it with your father," Cristen
agreed in a perfectly pleasant voice. "However, I do not believe that
Hugh was consulted."

Elizabeth stiffened visibly. "What are you implying?" she
demanded. "Are you implying that Lord Hugh was going to refuse
to marry me?"

Cristen fine brows lifted into two aloof arches over her luminous brown eyes. "Did I say that?"

Elizabeth's beautiful pale skin was flushed with anger. "Well, let
me tell *you*, my lady, that Lord Hugh was not the only one who was
not going to agree to our marriage."

Cristen peered into her wine cup to hide her sudden alertness. "Indeed?" she said softly.

"Aye, indeed! Don't think that you have stolen away from me a prize that I ever wanted. My heart has long been given elsewhere, and where my heart lies, so shall my hand in marriage. I told that to my father and I shall tell it to the king as well!" Elizabeth's voice rang with temper and pride.

Cristen turned her head and gave her companion a look that was simultaneously sympathetic and admiring. "Good for you, Lady Elizabeth. For your sake, I hope the king will approve your choice."

"He will approve my choice or I will refuse to marry at all," Elizabeth said loftily.

Cristen's eyes filled with respect. "That is very brave of you," she said. "It is so difficult to be a woman, don't you think? One has so little power."

Elizabeth raised her chin. "I have power. I am the de Beauté heiress. My lands will go with me when I marry. The king cannot take them away from me without looking like a churl. Nor can he force me to wed someone I do not like. The pope has said so."

Cristen chose not to dispute these remarkable statements. "Would you really go into a convent if the king does not approve your choice?" she asked in wonder.

Elizabeth laughed scornfully. "Can you imagine me in a convent?"

Cristen smiled and shook her head. "But what would be your alternative?"

"There are ways to marry without the approval of one's overlord," Elizabeth announced.

"An elopement?" Cristen said.

"If necessary," Elizabeth said, lifting her chin even higher.

"You must truly be in love, Lady Elizabeth," Cristen said soberly.

Elizabeth looked at her, and Cristen could see the exact moment when she realized what she had just given away.

"I can count on your discretion, can't I, Lady Cristen?"

"Of course you can," Cristen replied in her most soothing tone. "I of all people understand how you must feel. It is a terrible thing to think of losing the man that one loves."

Elizabeth smiled radiantly. "I knew you would understand."

"I do," Cristen replied. "Believe me, I do."

* * *

Later that evening, after Nicholas and Iseult had been put to bed
with Benjamin to keep guard, Hugh and Cristen sat together in the
main hall of Ralf's house and Cristen told him about her conversation with Elizabeth de Beauté. They were alone, as Thomas and
Mabel had made an excuse to busy themselves in the kitchen.

"Why on earth did she tell you all this?" Hugh asked in astonishment. He was sitting in Ralf's old chair by the fire.

Cristen raised one eyebrow. "Because she was insulted when I
implied that you were going to refuse to marry her. She told me so
that I would know that she didn't want you either."

"Good heavens," said Hugh, still astonished.

"She is not accustomed to rejection," Cristen said.

He laughed, stretched out his legs in front of him, and crossed
his booted feet at the ankles.

Cristen, seated in Adela's old chair, looked at him thoughtfully.
"Who do you think the man is?"

"It has to be Richard," Hugh replied. "They appear to be very
close."

Cristen nodded her agreement. "If it is Richard, however, she
must have known him for longer than we thought. Even Richard
could not charm an already betrothed girl into defying her father on
the acquaintance of a few weeks. He must have fixed his interest
with her earlier."

"Mmm. It would be just Richard's style to pick out a wealthy,
high-born girl like Elizabeth and make her fall in love with him.
Undoubtedly he was hoping that she would be able to convince her
father to let him marry her." He raised an ironic eyebrow. "Richard
would love to be the next Earl of Lincoln."

Cristen frowned. "If that theory is correct, Hugh, it means
Richard would want the earl alive rather than dead. I should think
that Elizabeth's doting father would be more likely than the king to
allow her to choose her own husband."

Hugh leaned his head against the back of his chair and rested his
hands on the chair arms. "Perhaps," he agreed. "But what if the earl
had discovered the market stall cheat? If he knew about it, and if
Richard is indeed the man behind it, then it would be imperative for

Richard to get him out of the way. Under those circumstances, the earl would never allow Richard to marry his daughter."

The light from the fire illuminated Hugh's dark head as it lay against the high chair back. Cristen looked at his relaxed figure and nodded thoughtfully.

Comfortable silence reigned as they both pursued their own thoughts.

Finally Cristen said, "What are we going to do if we can't find relatives to care for Nicholas and Iseult?"

"I doubt that there *are* any relatives I would feel comfortable entrusting them to," Hugh replied. "I suppose we could prevail upon a distant cousin to take them in, but can you imagine what their lives would be like under such circumstances?"

"Shall we take them, then?" Cristen asked.

"Would you mind?"

She lifted affronted eyebrows.

"I only asked for form's sake," he assured her.

She smiled.

"So there is another reason that we must be married soon," Hugh said.

"Aye."

"Can you just see us, Richard and me, trotting in one after the other to beg the king to allow us to marry the girl of our choice?" Hugh said with irony.

"Your situations are rather different," she pointed out. "Richard wants to marry above his station and you want to marry below yours."

Hugh held out his hand, and Cristen got up from her chair and went over to join him in his. He put an arm around her shoulders and they sat quietly, their bodies pressed together in the confines of the chair, her head resting on his shoulder.

They stayed that way as the fire slowly died down.

Finally Hugh said, "I should go."

She sighed. "I know."

Neither of them moved.

The room was growing cold when finally Hugh kissed the top of the silky brown head that lay on his shoulder. "Soon I won't have to leave you at all," he said fiercely.

"That will be wonderful," she replied softly. And smiled so that he wouldn't see the fear she harbored in her heart.

Precisely at noon on Friday, the king's Chief Justiciar of England, Lord Richard Basset, entered the city of Lincoln. With him he bore the official seal of his office: the device of a knight in full armor striking with his sword a rampant monster which grasped in its mouth a helpless, naked figure.

Lord Richard was received by the sheriff and the bishop, and was made comfortable in the guest chamber of the bishop's house.

He was a very busy man, the chief justiciar announced, and he had to be back in London within the week. Therefore, the trial of Bernard Radvers would begin promptly on the morrow.

The chief justiciar was given a splendid dinner by the bishop, and attended evening services in the Minster. After these devotions he retired to his room to look through the documents that the sheriff had submitted to him pertaining to the murder case he was to hear on the morrow. After the sand had run out in his hourglass, the chief justiciar went to bed and slept the sleep of the just.

Hugh did not have so tranquil an evening. He spent most of it prowling the perimeter of an imaginary rectangle while Cristen and the children sat close to the fire, along with Mabel and Thomas. Mabel was singing for them in her lovely clear soprano.

Finally Cristen turned to Hugh, pacing at the end of the room, and said with a mixture of sympathy and resignation, "Stalking around like a hungry tiger isn't going to help anything, Hugh."

Across the room their eyes met.

"I know." Slowly he came to join the group by the fire and stood next to Cristen in her chair. "I just keep thinking that there is some important piece of evidence that I have missed."

Nicholas was sitting on a stool with Benjamin's head lying on his lap. He gazed up at Hugh and asked, "What are you worried about, Hugh?"

Hugh looked at the boy's inquiring face and didn't reply.

"You don't have to tell me if you don't want to," Nicholas said with dignity. "I am sorry if I pried."

Hugh said, "I'm worried because a friend of mine goes on trial for murder tomorrow and I need to prove that he is innocent."

"Did he murder my papa?" Iseult asked curiously.

"He didn't murder anyone, sweeting," Hugh returned. "Somebody else did the murder and is trying to lay the blame on my friend."

"Was my father really murdered?" Nicholas asked in an awestruck voice. "I thought it was an accident."

"I think he was murdered, Nicholas. I think he was murdered by the same man who killed the Earl of Lincoln. That is whose death the trial tomorrow is about, you see. Bernard Radvers, my friend, is accused of killing the Earl of Lincoln."

"What about my father?"

"I think your father knew something about the earl's murder and he was killed to keep him quiet."

Nicholas's eyes were huge pools of blue. "My father did go into Lincoln to see someone special," he said. "Do you think that is the man who killed him?"

All the attention in the room converged on Nicholas.

Hugh said carefully, "Do you know who your father was going to see, Nicholas?"

"Well . . . he didn't tell *me*," the boy replied, "but I overheard him telling my mother. He said that this man was sure to pay him good money and then he would be able to buy a manor that would be truly our own."

The room was deadly silent. Nicholas had gone very pale. Seeking reassurance, he played with Benjamin's ears.

Then Cristen said gently, "This is very important, Nicholas. What was the name of the man your father told your mother he was going to see?"

Nicholas bit his lip and answered, "He was going to see the sheriff."

24

As soon as Lord Richard Basset had arrived in the city, the sheriff had sent official summonses to all those who would be required to appear as witnesses in the trial of Bernard Radvers. These witnesses had been notified weeks earlier to hold themselves in readiness, and so were expected to present themselves upon demand.

Since he was the person who had discovered the earl's body, Alan was one of those who received a summons. On the day of the trial, after breaking the morning fast, he and Richard walked together through the damp, foggy streets of Lincoln up to the castle. The Bail was busy as usual with those arriving for mass at the Minster and those who had come to shop at the market stalls, but in the Inner bail the knights of the castle guard went about their business in a silence that was almost eerie. Even the horses seemed to munch their hay with unnatural quiet.

Alan and Richard were silent also as they climbed the stairs to the keep and entered the castle. The trial was to be held in the armory hall, whose vast emptiness had been transformed into a hall of justice for the occasion.

Alan looked around with curiosity as he and Richard came in. A long wooden table with three chairs behind it had been placed in the middle of the hall. The two end chairs were already occupied, one by a tonsured clerk, whose duty it was to take notes of the trial's proceedings, and the other by the sheriff, the king's chief law officer in Lincoln. Alan looked at Gervase's face, which was as expressionless as a mask.

He must know that Hugh intends to reveal his dishonesty, Alan thought, and felt a twinge of pity for the hapless sheriff.

The various witnesses had been provided with five rows of benches, which had been set up to face the chief justiciar's table. Bernard, as the accused, was already in place on the first bench, with Hugh beside him.

The armory walls were punctuated with four small windows, but as the murky day offered little light, the flambeaux affixed to the walls had been lit. There was no source of heat in the hall and nearly everyone present was wearing a warm mantle.

Richard chose a bench in the third row and Alan sat next to him. Cristen was sitting directly in front of them, and Alan was surprised to see that she had Nicholas Rye with her.

Nicholas turned around and gave Alan a quick, shy smile.

Two of the Bail merchants sat at the end of Alan's row. Alan shot a quick look at Richard's grim profile, then looked away. The merchants must be there to testify about the amount of rent they paid to the sheriff, he thought.

Once more, Alan looked at Gervase's masklike face.

A sudden rustle of sound behind him caused Alan to turn his head, and he saw Elizabeth de Beauté, accompanied by Lady Sybil, entering the armory hall.

Elizabeth wore a white wimple over her glorious hair and a green tunic with an embroidered neckline over a pristine white undertunic. Around her graceful shoulders was a gray wool mantle lined with fur. Her lovely face looked infinitely sorrowful.

Gilbert de Beauté's daughter was making good her promise to witness the downfall of her father's murderer.

From the martyred expression on Lady Sybil's face, Alan deduced that Elizabeth's companion was not pleased with her charge's decision.

Head held high, looking at no one, Elizabeth walked to the second row of benches and sat down at a little distance from Cristen.

The next person to enter the room came from the far side of the hall. Walking briskly, carrying a rolled document under his arm, was Lord Richard Basset, Chief Justiciar of England. All of the witnesses rose to their feet.

Richard Basset sat in the empty chair, handed his document to the clerk, and folded his hands. The rest of the room remained standing as the clerk unrolled the parchment and read in a loud voice so that all could hear:

> "Stephen, King of the English, to the earls, barons, bishop, sheriff, and citizens of Lincoln and to all his faithful people in Lincoln and Lincolnshire, Greetings. Know that I have granted to Richard Basset my justice of Lincoln and Lincolnshire. Wherefore I will firmly command that the same Richard Basset shall hold my justice well and in peace and honorably and fully. Witness, Hugh the Bishop of Durham, Richard de Luci, and William of Ypres at Drax."

The clerk carefully rerolled the parchment and informed the assembled courtroom, "You may be seated."

Lord Richard Basset lifted his eyes from his clasped hands. He was tall and rail-thin, with a beak of a nose and eyes so dark, they almost looked black. He was dressed in a long-sleeved brown tunic and a wine-colored cloak lined with ermine. On his dark hair he wore a soft wine-colored cap trimmed with a fur band.

For a long, silent moment, he surveyed the group gathered before him, his eyes lingering for just a second on Elizabeth and Cristen. Everyone sat as still as petrified wood and gazed back. Finally, in a voice that was oddly husky coming from such an emaciated frame, he announced, "I hereby declare open the case concerning the murder of the Earl of Lincoln brought by the Sheriff of Lincoln against Bernard Radvers."

The intense black eyes focused on Bernard. "How do you plead?"

In a clear, steady voice that betrayed none of the weakness of his illness, Bernard replied, "I am innocent of these charges, my lord."

"Do you stand ready to prove your innocence?"

"Aye, my lord, I do."

The chief justiciar's eyes flicked to Hugh, then back again to Bernard. "And have you an advocate to assist in your defense?"

"Aye, my lord, I do," Bernard replied. "Lord Hugh de Leon will act as my advocate."

There was absolutely no expression on the chief justiciar's face as he nodded his acceptance.

All Alan could see of Hugh was the back of his head.

Next the justiciar turned to the sheriff, who was seated on his right. "Are you ready to prove this charge, Sir Gervase?"

"Aye, my lord," Gervase replied. He looked as if he had not slept for a week, but his voice was firm. "I am ready to prove this charge."

"Very well," the justiciar said. "You may call your first witness."

Alan's hands clenched into fists as he heard the sheriff call his name. Richard gave him an encouraging look, and Alan stood up on trembling legs and walked forward to take his place in front of the justiciar.

"My lord," the sheriff informed Richard Basset, "this is Alan Stanham, the boy who found the body of the earl."

Alan looked into the penetrating black eyes of the justiciar and tried not to show his nervousness.

"Tell us, please, how this discovery came about," the justiciar said.

"My lord, I went to the Minster on an errand for Sir Richard Canville, to whom I am squire," Alan replied in a steady voice. "Sir Richard had left his knife in the vestibule earlier in the day and he asked me to retrieve it for him. I found the knife and then I decided that, since I was right there in the Minster, I would go inside and say a quick prayer. So I opened the door to the church."

Here Alan stopped, certain he could feel Hugh's eyes on his back.

After a moment, the justiciar said, "You may continue."

"Aye, my lord." Alan swallowed. "Well, as I came into the church, I noticed a light about halfway down the center aisle. I was surprised, as you can imagine, and I looked to see who could be there at such an hour. That is when I saw Bernard Radvers bending over the body of the Earl of Lincoln." Alan paused with unconscious drama. "In his hand he was holding a knife that was covered in blood."

There was a little stir among those assembled in the hall.

"What happened then?" the justiciar asked in a level voice.

"Bernard saw me standing there and said that the earl was dead and that I should go for the sheriff."

"Let me be clear about this. Did you or did you not see Bernard Radvers in the act of stabbing the earl?"

"I did not, my lord."

The justiciar nodded. "Did you then go for the sheriff?"

"First I ran up the aisle to see for myself what had happened," Alan said.

"And what did you see?"

Alan swallowed again. "I saw that it was indeed the earl lying there, my lord, and I saw that he had been stabbed in the heart, most probably by the knife that Bernard was holding."

Lady Elizabeth buried her face in her hands.

The justiciar looked at Bernard. "Is this information accurate?" he asked.

Bernard stood. "Aye, my lord. But it was not as it seemed to Alan."

"How was it then?" the justiciar asked.

"I found the earl lying there, my lord, and I knelt beside him to ascertain his condition. When I saw that he was dead, I noticed the knife lying by his side. Unthinkingly, I picked it up to look at it. That is the explanation for my position when Alan came in and found me. I did not stab the earl, my lord. I swear it."

"What were you doing in the Minster at such an hour?"

"I had received a message from the sheriff, my lord. At least, I was told it was from the sheriff. It said I was to meet him in the Minster two hours after evening services."

"Didn't you think this message rather odd?"

"I thought it was very odd, my lord, but I obeyed it."

"Who brought you this message?"

"William Cobbett, one of the castle grooms, my lord."

The chief justiciar turned to Gervase. "This is the groom who was killed?"

"Aye, my lord," the sheriff replied grimly. "He was stabbed in the heart."

One of the assembled witnesses exclaimed out loud, and Lord Richard frowned at him before turning back to Bernard. "So you have no proof that you did indeed receive this message?"

"My only proof would be the word of the groom, my lord, and he is dead."

Once again the chief justiciar turned to Gervase. "Is it known what brought the earl to the Minster at such an unlikely time?"

"My lord, we presume that Bernard sent him a message by the dead groom that asked him to come to the Minster at that hour. Our contention is that Bernard killed the groom in order to conceal this information."

"My lord." The quiet yet perfectly audible voice belonged to Hugh.

The chief justiciar's face was unreadable as he regarded Bernard's advocate. "Do you have something to say, Lord Hugh?"

At the sound of Hugh's voice, Alan turned so that he was half facing the justiciar and half facing the witnesses. For the first time that day, he saw more than the back of Hugh's head.

Hugh was soberly dressed in a plain blue wool tunic and darker blue hose. In this chill, unheated hall, he wore no cloak. Alan noticed that his uncovered black hair had been newly cut.

Hugh said mildly, "I just wondered, my lord, if Bernard were so desperate a character that he murdered the earl and this groom, why did he not murder the young squire who found him in such a compromising situation? It would not have been difficult for him to overpower a youngster like Alan Stanham. Instead, however, he sent Alan for the sheriff. Surely that is not the behavior of a guilty man."

"A good point, Lord Hugh," the chief justiciar conceded. He turned his gaze to Alan. "Did Bernard Radvers make any threatening gestures toward you?"

"Nay, my lord," Alan replied.

The chief justiciar nodded.

Hugh said, "My lord, I would be interested to know what brought Alan Stanham to the Minster at the exact time that Bernard was discovering the earl's dead body."

The chief justiciar looked annoyed. "We have already had that question answered, I believe. The boy was on an errand for Sir Richard Canville."

"I realize that, my lord," Hugh replied. "What I do not understand is how such an errand came to be timed so exactly."

The chief justiciar's black eyes hooded themselves. "Just what are you implying, Lord Hugh?"

"I am implying nothing, my lord," Hugh replied. "I am only wondering if the timing of Alan's errand was merely chance."

Alan, who understood exactly what Hugh was trying to do, stood taller. "I can answer that question, my lord," he said in a clear ringing voice. "Sir Richard noticed that he didn't have his knife when he went to cut a piece of meat that I had served him. The timing was pure chance."

"It was rather a late hour to be eating supper," Hugh commented.

"Sir Richard is a large man," Alan said defiantly. "He gets hungry more often than the rest of us."

A light breath of laughter ran through the hall.

"Did Richard himself say he was hungry and ask you for food?" Hugh said.

"Sir Richard is the only one capable of knowing whether or not he is hungry, my lord," Alan retorted.

Once again there came a ripple of laughter.

Careful, lad, Bernard thought worriedly.

Hugh went on, "So Sir Richard asked for food, discovered that his knife was missing, and sent you to the Minster to recover it just in time for you to find Bernard kneeling over the earl's dead body."

The chief justiciar said impatiently, "I fail to see the point of these questions, Lord Hugh."

Hugh's face was grave as he replied, "My lord, Bernard Radvers has been accused of murder on evidence that depends solely upon interpretation. I merely wish to show that there are other people whose actions could also be interpreted to show their guilt if one were so inclined to see them in that light."

"Are you suggesting that one could point the finger of guilt at Sir Richard simply because he sent his squire to the Minster at the time that he did?"

"One could certainly question his actions, my lord," Hugh returned. "It seems to me, however, that the only person whose actions have been questioned is Bernard Radvers."

The black eyes of the justiciar bored into Hugh's steady gray gaze. When at last Lord Richard spoke his voice was crisp. "Very well, you have made your point. Are you now finished with this witness?"

"I have just one more question, my lord," Hugh said.

"Very well."

Alan set his jaw, determined to say nothing that would be harmful to Richard.

Hugh said, "You told us that when you saw Bernard, knife in hand, bending over the recumbent figure of the earl, you ran down the aisle to see for yourself what had happened. Is that correct, Alan?"

"Aye, my lord. That is correct."

"You did not think that Bernard was a dangerous man and it would not be safe for you to approach him?"

Alan hesitated for a moment, looking for a trap. Hugh's gray gaze was cool and impersonal. At last Alan replied, "I never thought of any danger to myself, my lord."

"In other words, you were so convinced of Bernard's harmlessness that you approached him with no fear. Is that correct, Alan?"

"Aye," Alan returned cautiously. "That is correct."

"Another question, Alan. How closely did you look at the body of the earl?"

"Close enough to see the blood around the stab wound in his chest, my lord," Alan replied spiritedly.

"Did you touch him?"

"Nay, my lord. I did not touch him."

"Then you did not notice if he was still warm or if he was already starting to turn cold."

Alan's eyes dilated as he saw where Hugh was heading. "I . . . I could not say, my lord."

Hugh nodded. "Thank you, Alan." He turned back to the justiciar. "That is my last question, my lord."

The justiciar looked thoughtful. "Have you any questions, Sir Gervase?" he asked the sheriff.

"No questions, my lord," the sheriff replied.

"Then you are dismissed," the justiciar informed Alan, who returned to his seat, uncomfortably conscious that everyone in the room was watching him.

As the sheriff called his next witness, Alan leaned toward Richard and whispered anxiously, "Did I do all right?"

Richard smiled and nodded. "You did very well, Alan."

Alan was not completely reassured, however. Richard may have smiled with his mouth, but his eyes had remained cool.

As the next witness gave his testimony, Alan went over in his mind everything that he had said and couldn't find anything that could possibly harm Richard.

The sheriff's next few witnesses testified to the fact that Bernard had made threats against the life of the Earl of Lincoln. When the justiciar questioned Bernard about the truth of these statements, he said stoically that he could not remember making them, that he had been drunk.

"Was there any reason for you to wish the Earl of Lincoln dead?" the justiciar asked.

"None, my lord," Bernard replied.

"If that is so, then why were you making these threats while you were drunk?"

Hugh was on his feet in a flash. "May I say something, my lord?"

The justiciar's mouth pinched at its corners with suppressed annoyance. "Go ahead, Lord Hugh."

"In the testimony of the witnesses, I heard no mention that Bernard ever threatened the life of the earl. The witnesses maintain that he said the earl would 'do us a favor' by dying. The implication of these words is that it would be good if the earl died of natural causes. That can hardly be construed as a threat."

The sheriff leaned forward and said, "There was an implied threat, Lord Richard. Bernard knew of the betrothal of the earl's daughter to Lord Hugh de Leon, and Bernard has long been a friend of Lord Hugh's. He would have benefited greatly if Lord Hugh had become the next Earl of Lincoln. In order to hasten this desirable end, I believe he killed the earl."

"If that was indeed my motivation, Sir Gervase, I would certainly not have been stupid enough to kill the earl before Hugh was married to Lady Elizabeth," Bernard replied. His voice was level but the anger he was suppressing was evident.

"You weren't thinking. You acted in a moment of passion," the sheriff said.

The justiciar's oddly husky voice interrupted. "This is hardly an act of passion, Sir Gervase. This is a premeditated act of murder. The earl was lured to the Minster for one reason only: to kill him."

"That is so, my lord," the sheriff returned. "But in this discussion of motive, one fact must not be forgotten. Bernard Radvers was found, bloody knife in hand, bending over the dead body of the earl. If he is not guilty, then who is?"

"My lord," Hugh said. "I have some further evidence that may shed light on this question."

"You will have your turn to present evidence, Lord Hugh," the justiciar said with a frown. "At the moment, we are hearing the sheriff's side of the case."

Except for a single nervous twitch at the corner of his mouth, Gervase's face had maintained its masklike look. "I have presented my evidence, my lord. Bernard Radvers was found bending over the dead body of the earl, a bloody knife in his hand. He had previously been heard by several men threatening the life of the earl. It seems to me that this is sufficient evidence to convict him of the murder of the Earl of Lincoln."

"Thank you, Sir Gervase," the justiciar said. He looked at Hugh. "Then you may present your evidence, Lord Hugh."

Richard didn't move, but Alan could feel his body stiffen. Alan's own stomach tightened. Was this when Hugh was going to bring up the sheriff's tax cheat?

Much to Alan's relief and astonishment, Hugh said, "I would like to call Brother Martin to testify, my lord."

A short, portly figure garbed in a brown robe and sandals came from the last bench to approach the witness's place in front of Lord Richard.

"My lord, Brother Martin is one of the lay brothers at the Minster," Hugh explained. "He is the one who laid out the earl's body on the night he was killed."

A noise that sounded suspiciously like a sob came from Elizabeth. Lady Sybil put her arm around the girl and patted her shoulder.

"What have you to tell us, Brother Martin?" the justiciar asked.

"My lord, I saw the earl's body but half an hour after he had supposedly been stabbed to death in the Minster. He was cold, my lord. Very cold. Too cold to have been dead for such a short time. He began to stiffen shortly after we moved him to the mortuary chapel. I would say that he had been dead for at least an hour before he was found."

A muted uproar arose among the watching witnesses.

The black eyes of the justiciar bored into the innocent brown eyes of the lay brother. "Why did you not come forward with this information sooner?" he demanded. "You must have known that Bernard Radvers was being held in custody."

"My lord, I did not," Brother Martin replied earnestly. "The day following the death of the earl, I was called to work at the hospital of Saint Mary's in the north of the shire. I only returned to Lincoln yesterday. When I learned about the trial, I tried to see the sheriff. When he was not available, I went to Lord Hugh."

"You are quite certain that the earl had been dead for an hour before Bernard Radvers was discovered bending over his body?" the justiciar asked sternly.

"Quite sure, my lord," the lay brother returned. "I have seen many dead bodies, and the earl was not newly dead when I received him."

The justiciar turned to the sheriff. "Have you anything to say in regard to this evidence, Sir Gervase?"

"Nay, my lord," the sheriff replied. His face was bleak, and he looked older than his years.

"Thank you, Brother," the justiciar said. "You may go back to your seat."

As Brother Martin left the witness area, the justiciar said, "I think we can dispense with further evidence, Lord Hugh. I believe you have cast sufficient doubt upon the sheriff's case for me to declare it inadequate."

Hugh stood. "My lord, I ask your indulgence. I have further evidence that I believe will be helpful in identifying the man who truly did murder the Earl of Lincoln."

The justiciar tapped his long, thin, immaculate fingers on the table. A deep line ran between his brows.

Hugh said, "This evidence has to do with another man who has been killed recently in Lincoln. John Rye is a knight who was serving his yearly knight's fee at Lincoln Castle when the earl was murdered. Several days after the murder, Rye asked for early leave so that he could go home to his sick wife. In fact, his wife was not sick at all. He wanted time to pay a visit to his cousin, William of Roumare, Earl of Cambridge."

There was a rustle throughout the room, as if everyone had just sat up straighter.

Lord Richard Bassett froze.

Hugh went relentlessly on. "I know this because I paid a visit to Rye's home of Linsay in order to talk to him. I sought him out because he was the only one of the castle guard whom I had not been able to question in regard to the murder. He was not at Linsay when I arrived, but he did return several days later. He admitted to me then that he had information that pertained to the murder of the earl and that he had tried to sell this information to William of Roumare."

A number of exclamations of surprise issued from the audience. The clerk called for silence.

In a dangerous-sounding voice, Lord Richard said, "Why would Rye have gone to Lord William?"

"My lord, I am not the man who has benefited from the earl's untimely death," Hugh said. "Lady Elizabeth's husband will no longer automatically become the next Earl of Lincoln. The earldom is once more the king's, to give as he will, and I do not think there is much doubt as to who will get it."

Next to him, Alan could feel some of the tension leave Richard. Apparently, Hugh was not going to reveal the market stall cheat after all.

The justiciar's face was grim. "If I were you, I would be very careful whom I accused, Lord Hugh," he warned.

"I have no intention of accusing William of Roumare of having a hand in the Earl of Lincoln's death, my lord," Hugh assured the justiciar.

Lord Richard's face softened a little.

"William of Roumare did not purchase the information that John Rye offered him, my lord. I know this because Rye offered to sell the information to me."

Once more, Alan felt Richard's tension.

"I should have bought it," Hugh said regretfully. "It was a mistake not to. If I had, John Rye might still be alive. I didn't buy it, however. Instead, I demanded that he tell me what he knew. He refused, and I left Linsay. Soon after, Rye himself came to Lincoln. I believe he planned to use this knowledge of his to extort money from the murderer himself."

The justiciar's eyes narrowed to long black slits. "What information could a man like John Rye possibly have had?"

"My lord, I believe he saw the murderer giving the fatal messages to the groom, who is now dead. I call the messages 'fatal' because one certainly resulted in the death of de Beauté and the other was intended to convict Bernard Radvers of murdering him."

There was not a sound in the armory hall. Everyone was so still that the scene might have been a painting.

The justiciar stirred first. "And you say that this John Rye was killed during his visit to Lincoln?"

"Aye, my lord."

At this, the sheriff interrupted angrily. "My lord, John Rye's death was an accident. It occurred during the camp-ball game that is played every year at our local Saint Agatha's fair. One of the players was wearing a knife at his belt and Rye was stabbed by accident. It was unfortunate, but these things happen. You know that they do."

"Do you have the man whose knife stabbed him?" the justiciar asked.

"We have been unable to discover who was wearing a knife, my lord," Gervase admitted reluctantly. "No one will admit to seeing anyone with a knife at his belt and, needless to say, no one is stepping forward to confess."

The justiciar said, "It seems excessively odd that three people should die of knife wounds in Lincoln within the span of two months. Do you have many such incidents here, Sir Gervase?"

"Nay, my lord," the sheriff admitted.

Hugh made an infinitesimal movement, and in so doing managed to draw the attention of everyone in the room.

How does he do it? Alan wondered with a strange mixture of awe and resentment.

Hugh said, "May I point out to you, my lord, that Bernard Radvers was in custody during the time that John Rye was killed." He took one step toward the justiciar's table. "If indeed it is true, and I think it is, that John Rye was killed by the same man who killed the Earl of Lincoln, then that man cannot possibly be Bernard Radvers."

The audience burst into excited talk while Hugh and the chief justiciar looked at each other.

The clerk called for silence.

The justiciar said, "If the murderer we seek is not Bernard Radvers, Lord Hugh, then who is it?"

"I believe I can answer that question, my lord. I would ask for an opportunity to question several witnesses, and as I do so I believe the truth will be made clear."

Under his warm cloak, Alan felt icy cold. *He is going to accuse Richard. He is going to expose the market stall cheat and accuse Richard.*

"Very well," said Lord Richard Basset. "You may call your witnesses, Lord Hugh."

The sheriff protested angrily. "My lord, I object to this latitude you have afforded Lord Hugh! We are here to try Bernard Radvers, not conduct a general inquisition."

"Lord Hugh has raised a number of interesting points that appear to exonerate Bernard Radvers," the justiciar returned coldly. "It seems to me that in your haste to claim that you had discovered the culprit, you may have been neglectful of inquiring too deeply into this matter, Sir Gervase. I would like to hear what Lord Hugh has to say."

Gervase's face was ghost-white as he replied in a monotone, "If that is your wish, my lord."

"It is my wish," the justiciar replied. "The king desires justice to be done in this matter, and I am here as his deputy to see that justice is indeed carried out."

He looked at Hugh.

"Call your witnesses, Lord Hugh," he said. "Let us see if you can bring a more convincing case than the sheriff has done."

25

Bernard leaned over and whispered urgently, "Don't go any farther, Hugh. You have already done enough to establish my innocence. Don't attack Richard in public. You haven't sufficient evidence."

Hugh just shook his head and continued to regard the justiciar. "My lord, I should like to call Sir Richard Canville as a witness."

Bernard clenched his fists in anguished frustration.

The armory hall buzzed with excitement as Richard walked past the benches and took up his place between the chief justiciar and Hugh. Bernard knew that nearly every person present, with the exception of the justiciar, was aware of the long history of Hugh's dislike of Richard. Hugh would find it almost impossible to convince this audience that his evidence was objective.

Richard looked magnificent as he stood there, his wide shoulders caped with a green, fur-trimmed mantle, his dark gold hair gleaming in the flickering light of a flambeau.

Hugh walked forward until he was standing only a few feet from his witness, making even more obvious the height difference between them.

That isn't smart, Bernard thought despairingly. Hugh's slender, cloakless figure looked almost boyish in comparison to Richard's superior height and breadth.

"Sir Richard," Hugh said in a level, impersonal voice. "I have only a few questions to trouble you with."

Richard looked down at his adversary's composed, unreadable face. "Ask them," he said crisply.

Hugh clasped his hands loosely behind his back. "Were you at home all evening on the night that the Earl of Lincoln was murdered?"

"Certainly," Richard replied. "You have heard the testimony of my squire that I was at home."

"I heard your squire tell us that you were home for a late supper. He said nothing about your whereabouts earlier in the evening."

Richard frowned. "I'm afraid I don't understand you."

"Let me make myself clear, then. We have heard testimony that the earl was probably killed at least an hour before Bernard Radvers found his body. Where were you at that time? Were you at home?"

Richard said, as if addressing a small child who has been rude, "I find your questions impertinent."

"Humor me," Hugh said.

Richard's voice was even as he replied, but the set of his mouth betrayed anger. "I accompanied Lady Elizabeth and Lady Sybil to evening services at the Minster and they invited me to partake of supper with them. I returned home after that."

"I see." Hugh regarded him thoughtfully. "You had supper with Lady Elizabeth, and when you returned home you asked for something more to eat."

"I require somewhat more food than ladies do," Richard retorted.

Laughter came from the benches behind Bernard.

Careful, lad, Bernard thought worriedly. *Don't let him make you look a fool.*

"Did the earl join you and Lady Elizabeth?" Hugh asked.

"He did not," Richard said.

"Did you see the earl at all that night?"

"I did not," Richard said.

"Let us move on to another subject," Hugh said smoothly, not seeming at all discomposed by his witness's able defense. "John Rye was killed when a group of camp-ball players piled up in an effort to retrieve the ball. Were you in that pileup, Sir Richard?"

At this, Richard turned to the chief justiciar. "My lord, there is no reasonable basis for these questions. Lord Hugh is trying to harass me, and I object."

Lord Richard Bassett looked at Hugh. "What is the reason for these questions, Lord Hugh? For I must tell you, it seems to me as if Sir Richard is right."

Hugh's clear, flexible voice reached every corner of the vast hall. "My lord," he said, "I believe that Sir Richard Canville is guilty of the murders of the Earl of Lincoln, the groom William Cobbett, and John Rye. If you will allow me to continue my questions, I will prove that this is true."

A loud babble of voices came from the benches.

The sheriff stared at Hugh as if he were a madman.

Jesu! Bernard thought in despair. *Now he's done it.*

Grim-faced, the chief justiciar glared at Hugh. He said, each word pronounced with great precision, "This is the trial of Bernard Radvers, Lord Hugh, not of Richard Canville."

Hugh stood before the justiciar, straight and slim, his gray gaze level on the justiciar's, his hands resting, open-palmed, at his sides.

Richard stepped forward. "My lord, this is nothing more than the continuation of a grudge that Hugh has held against me since our childhood." He looked at Hugh, and when he spoke it was pity and not anger that resonated in the deep tones of his voice. "I have always wanted to be your friend, Hugh. There is no need for you to feel you must put me down in order to boost your own importance."

Hugh ignored him and said to the justiciar, "My lord, the king has charged you with finding and punishing the man who murdered the Earl of Lincoln. I can give you that man if you will allow me to proceed."

The chief justiciar's narrowed black eyes were trained on Hugh. Bernard turned around to look at the witnesses assembled on the benches behind him, and found that they too were totally focused on Hugh.

It was a thing that Bernard had seen before, but still it amazed him, this ability of Hugh's to dominate a room. It was not his words, it was something in him, some quality in his very existence, intangible yet absolutely commanding.

The chief justiciar said, "Give me a reason why Sir Richard Canville should desire the demise of the Earl of Lincoln." And Bernard knew that he was going to let Hugh continue.

Hugh said, "My lord, I have witnesses present who will testify to the fact that the amount of money the sheriff was charging for the market stalls in the Bail was more than the amount of money he declared to the Exchequer. I believe that the Earl of Lincoln discovered this cheat and was killed in order to keep him from exposing it."

Pandemonium erupted behind Bernard. The chief justiciar shouted angrily for silence, and slowly the noise died away.

The justiciar turned to look at the sheriff, who was sitting beside him. "How do you answer this charge, Sir Gervase?"

The sheriff's face was as bloodless as a corpse. When he spoke, his voice was not quite steady. "Lord Hugh's information is correct, my lord, but my son knew nothing about the cheat. I am the responsible party."

The room was deadly silent.

Hugh said, "Are you speaking the truth, Sir Gervase, or are you lying to protect your son?"

"It is the truth," the sheriff said. "I will swear to it on a relic of the Holy Cross if you wish. Richard only discovered what I was doing two days ago. He was . . . very upset about it."

"Did the Earl of Lincoln discover this cheat?" the chief justiciar asked.

"Nay, my lord, he did not." The sheriff's voice was emphatic. "Lord Gilbert never once asked to look at the tax rolls. His interest was in my military preparations. He knew nothing at all about the tax cheat."

"Can you prove this?" the justiciar asked.

"I believe I can, my lord. The only way the earl could have found out about the cheat was if he asked the Bail merchants what they were paying and then checked that sum against the tax rolls. I believe if you question the merchants you will discover that the earl made no such inquiries."

Lord Richard Basset nodded. Then he turned to Hugh. "The Crown thanks you for calling its attention to this matter, Lord Hugh, but I agree with Sir Gervase that it is highly unlikely that the Earl of

Lincoln would have discovered it. Which means that neither Sir Gervase nor Sir Richard had any reason to wish the Earl of Lincoln dead."

Bernard felt sick to his stomach. The whole of Hugh's case hinged on Richard's motive of wishing to hide the tax cheat. If it was true that the earl had not known of it, then Richard had no reason at all to kill him.

Hugh said, "If you will allow me to continue to present my evidence, my lord, I promise you that I will establish Sir Richard's guilt beyond a reasonable doubt." The soft intensity of his voice echoed through the silent room.

Give it up, lad, Bernard urged Hugh in his mind. *Don't make yourself look any more petty than you already have.*

Leaning back a little in his chair, the chief justiciar yielded before the will of the younger man. "Very well, Lord Hugh. You may proceed."

Hugh turned to Richard and said, "Were you one of the men in the pileup where John Rye was killed?"

"I was, along with thirty other men." Anger and contempt rang clearly in Richard's deep voice.

"But you were there."

"So I have said," Richard returned evenly.

"Did John Rye communicate with you in any way during his last visit to Lincoln?"

"He did not," Richard said. "I scarcely knew John Rye. There would be no possible reason for him to seek me out."

"You are certain of that?"

"Of course I am certain."

Hugh turned to the justiciar. "I would like to ask Alan Stanham a few more questions, my lord."

After a moment of silence, the justiciar said, "Very well."

"My lord," Richard said commandingly. "I object to Lord Hugh's attempting to intimidate my squire."

"He has not yet questioned the boy, Sir Richard," the justiciar returned, "so it is rather beforehand to accuse him of attempted intimidation. If you would like to remain here in the witness area while your squire is questioned, you may do so."

Richard looked grim. "I will remain," he said.

Please God, please God, please God, repeated itself monotonously in Bernard's brain. This calling of Alan was a calculated risk on Hugh's part. He had no idea how the boy was going to answer.

You're a fool to call him, Bernard had said when Hugh had told him what he planned to do. *The boy idolizes Richard. He will never say anything that might hurt him.*

Hugh had disagreed. *Alan's adoration has been shaken a bit these last few days,* he had told Bernard. *I do not think he will lie to protect Richard. I think he will tell the truth.*

The voice of the chief justiciar calling Alan Stanham as a witness broke into Bernard's thoughts.

Richard's eyes were intensely blue as they followed the progress of his squire from his bench to the witness place in front of the justiciar.

Alan looked very young as he stood there, his fair hair shining like silver in the light of the flambeau. He looked at Hugh as if he were a wild boar about to attack.

Hugh said pleasantly, "Alan, I believe you accompanied Sir Richard around the fair on the day before the camp-ball game. Is that so?"

"Aye, my lord." In contrast to his clarity when he earlier gave evidence, Alan's voice was so faint, it could scarcely be heard beyond the first bench.

The chief justiciar frowned. "Speak up," he commanded.

"Aye," Alan said more loudly. "I was with Sir Richard for most of that day."

"Do you know John Rye?" Hugh asked him.

"Aye, my lord."

"You would recognize him without fail if you should meet him?"

"Aye, my lord."

"During the time you spent with Sir Richard that day, did you ever see him in conversation with John Rye?"

Hugh's voice never varied in its pleasantness. He might have been asking if Sir Richard had drunk any water, so matter-of-factly did he pose the question.

Bernard clenched his fists, waiting for Richard's squire to reply.

Alan was so pale, the few light freckles that dusted his nose were clearly visible. He looked at Richard, standing like a splendid statue but a few feet away from him. Richard's blue gaze returned his squire's look steadily.

Alan said shakily, "It was a very busy day and I expect Sir Richard has forgotten, but John Rye did have speech with him that day."

Thank you, God. Bernard's eyes closed in a momentary prayer of gratitude.

Richard said, "You are mistaken, Alan. I never spoke to John Rye."

"Don't you remember, my lord? We were in the silversmith's shop and he asked to speak to you . . ."

Richard's eyes were blue ice. "You are mistaken," he said again.

Hugh said, "Alan, did anyone else witness this encounter between Sir Richard and John Rye?"

Alan's hazel eyes were huge. He looked utterly miserable. Bernard felt a pang of pity for the boy.

"I believe the silversmith saw them, my lord," Alan said in a voice that was close to a whisper. "I was looking at some knives and he was with me while Sir Richard and John Rye spoke."

"Thank you, Alan," Hugh said gently. "You may return to your seat."

Alan did not look at Richard as he took his place in the middle of the benches.

"My lord, next I would like to ask Nicholas Rye to come forward as a witness," Hugh said.

Nicholas looked very small as he came forward to stand in front of the chief justiciar. His brown hair was neatly combed and he wore a serviceable blue cloak around his shoulders. He appeared to be more composed than Alan had been.

"My lord," Hugh said, "this is John Rye's son, Nicholas. He has some information that I believe is important."

In a voice that he unsuccessfully tried to make sound kindly, the justiciar said, "What have you to tell us, Nicholas?"

Nicholas's little-boy voice was clear. "My lord, I overheard a conversation between my father and my mother before my father left to go into Lincoln for the last time. They were talking together in front of the fire in the great hall, and I was sitting nearby pulling burrs out of my dog's coat. They knew I was there. I did not mean to eavesdrop on them . . ."

For the first time, Nicholas looked a little worried.

"I understand," the chief justiciar said crisply. "You may continue."

"Aye, my lord. Well, Papa was talking to Mama about something he wanted to sell. I remember that he said, 'I should have gone to him right away instead of trying my luck with Roumare.'"

Richard made a small movement, which he instantly controlled.

"I remember that, my lord, because my father had just come back from a visit to Lord William of Roumare and we had needed him at home," Nicholas said.

The justiciar shot a piercing look at Hugh.

Nicholas continued, "Well, Mama said that such information could be dangerous and Papa should be cautious. Papa laughed and said he knew how to take care of himself. He said he was not going to be greedy. He would only ask for enough to buy our own manor and not be dependent upon the bishop's knight's fee any longer."

The room was thick with attentive silence.

The justiciar said, his voice sharp, "Did you hear your father mention the name of the man whom he was going to see?"

"My lord, at first I only heard him say 'the sheriff . . .'"

A gust of wind blew through the room, as if dozens of held breaths had been let out simultaneously.

Nicholas went on, "But then he said the name 'Richard.' He said it several times, my lord. I thought the sheriff's name must be Richard, but now I know that Richard is the name of the sheriff's son. Papa must have said 'sheriff's son' and I did not hear the second word."

The benches erupted.

Holy Mother of God, Bernard thought. *Holy Mother of God.*

The justiciar called for quiet. When silence had finally been achieved, he turned to Richard.

"Sir Richard," he said. "What have you to say to these charges?"

Anger filled Richard's intensely blue eyes. "What do you expect me to say, my lord?" he replied. "This *evidence* has been produced by children whom Lord Hugh has insidiously influenced. They would say anything he asked them to say."

"Alan Stanham is *your* squire," the justiciar pointed out.

"He is my squire, but Hugh chose him to be one of the main-stays of his side in the camp-ball game. Then he deliberately humiliated me in front of Alan during an arrow-shooting contest. Poor Alan." Richard's voice took on a note of reluctant compassion.

"He has been suborned away from his true lord by a clever manipulator."

"And what about the testimony of Nicholas Rye?"

"Perhaps you do not know this, my lord, but after the death of both their parents, Hugh took Nicholas and his sister to live with him. Poor little orphans. I imagine Nicholas is so grateful to Hugh that he would say anything Hugh asked him to."

"That's not true!" Nicholas said indignantly.

Richard regarded him with pity.

"I spoke the truth, my lord!" Nicholas said to the justiciar.

"My lord," Richard said reasonably. "Hugh has long held a grudge against me. I do not know what I ever did to him to provoke it, but you may ask anyone who knows us both and you will hear that Hugh has always hated me." He shook his head in sorrow. "But I never thought that he would carry that dislike so far as this."

"So you deny the testimony of Alan Stanham and Nicholas Rye," said the justiciar.

"I do, most emphatically, deny it."

"My lord!" The voice came from behind Bernard, and he turned to see Alan standing in front of his bench.

"My lord, I believe that if you question the silversmith, he will uphold my testimony," Alan said steadily.

Richard regarded his squire with compassion.

"These witnesses have certainly brought forward information that must be further investigated, Lord Hugh," the justiciar said. "But the evidence is strongly suborned by the fact that I can see no reason for Sir Richard to desire the Earl of Lincoln to die."

Hugh began to say, "I think we must—" when he was interrupted by a feminine voice from the benches.

"My Lord Chief Justiciar, I believe I might have something to add to this testimony."

It was Elizabeth de Beauté.

The attention of the entire room riveted on the girl.

Richard stood motionless.

"Would you care to come forward, my lady?" the justiciar said.

Slowly Elizabeth came into Bernard's view. She passed so close to him that he could have reached out and touched her mantle. Then she halted in the open space between the benches and the table where sat the chief justiciar and the sheriff. She kept a distance between herself and Richard.

"My lord," she said in a low voice, "on the night that my father was killed, I went to my bedchamber immediately after Sir Richard Canville had left us. The single window in this room looks directly out on the front courtyard of the bishop's guest house. The shutters were still open and I went to the window to close them. Before I did so, however, I looked out."

She paused, and Bernard could feel the hardening of attention in the room.

"My lord, I saw my father meet Sir Richard in the courtyard and then the two of them walked around the side of the bishop's house and out of my sight."

Bernard began to breathe again.

"Why did you never mention this, my lady?" the justiciar asked sternly.

Elizabeth raised a hand to touch her wimple. "I did not think it had any bearing on my father's murder, my lord. You must realize that this meeting occurred almost a full hour before my father's body was found."

Hugh said matter-of-factly, "And now you know that your father was probably killed very shortly after the time you saw him with Sir Richard."

Elizabeth's eyes were intensely green. She had not once looked at Richard, and she did not do so now. "Aye."

"Did you ever mention to Sir Richard that you had witnessed this meeting?" the justiciar asked.

"I did, my lord."

Bernard found himself physically straining forward, and forced himself to relax. Elizabeth continued, "Sir Richard told me that my father had said he was going to the Minster to pray. Of course, I thought that he had gone to the Minster in response to the false summons of Bernard Radvers."

"You never suspected Sir Richard of complicity in this matter?"

Color flushed into Elizabeth's face and suddenly she seemed very young. "I did not, my lord."

The justiciar's voice softened. "Is there any particular reason for you to have shown so much faith in Sir Richard?"

"I was going to marry him," Elizabeth replied.

A moan came from Lady Sybil. The sheriff, who had been staring at his hands folded on top of the table, jerked his head up and looked at his son.

Richard stood like a statue.

"I thought, my lady," Hugh said delicately, "that you were going to marry *me*."

Elizabeth, still carefully refraining from looking at Richard, spoke to Hugh. "That is what my father wanted me to do, but I was going to refuse the match. I had promised to marry Richard."

"May I ask when this attachment between you and Sir Richard developed, my lady?" Hugh asked.

His voice was quiet, almost intimate, the sort of tone he would have used in the coziness of a family solar. Elizabeth visibly relaxed in reponse and began to talk more easily.

"Richard used to come to Beauté to visit one of our knights who was a friend of his. That is how I got to know him. We were on the brink of asking my father if he would allow us to marry, when he made that agreement with Lord Guy for me to marry you."

"You must have found such news disconcerting," Hugh said sympathetically.

"I did," she replied. "I told my father about my love for Richard and asked if we might marry. He was very angry. He said I would marry the man he chose for me and that man was not Richard Canville, it was Hugh de Leon."

"Did you tell this to Richard?"

"Of course. But I promised him that I would not wed you, that even if my father forced me to the altar, I would not make the vows."

Her chin lifted as she said these words and her voice rang with pride. For a moment, she looked like a woman, not a girl.

"Did Richard believe you?"

"I thought he did. Now I am not so certain. Listening to this evidence today, I feared . . ." Her voice ran out.

"What do you fear, Lady Elizabeth?"

Elizabeth whispered. "I am afraid that Richard killed my father because he stood in the way of our marriage."

Pandemonium erupted in the courtroom.

"That is not true," Richard said, his deep voice clearly audible over the tumult.

At last Elizabeth looked at him. "I don't think you ever loved me. All you wanted was to be the next Earl of Lincoln!"

"Elizabeth," Richard said, his voice like a caress. "That is not so. You know that I love you."

"I don't think I know anything about you at all, Richard," Elizabeth replied bitterly.

A small silence fell while the two erstwhile lovers stared at each other.

The chief justiciar spoke. "We have heard compelling evidence against you today, Sir Richard," he said sternly. "More than I believe can be attributed to Lord Hugh's acting against you out of malice."

"Let us put it to the proof, then," Richard said. Color burned high in his face, and he laughed. "Are you willing to do that, Hugh? Are you willing to face me in a trial by combat?"

Behind him, Bernard heard Cristen give a little cry and then quickly stifle it.

"It would be my pleasure," Hugh replied.

Richard looked at the chief justiciar. "I am weary of listening to these malicious charges against me, my lord." His voice, clear as a bell, resounded throughout the cavernous room. "I demand a Judgment of God."

26

A Judgment of God. Trial by combat. Two men fighting each other until death proved which one heaven found guilty. This was one of the most ancient tests for justice, and its validity was recognized by both Church and State.

Once combat had been called for, and accepted, the chief justiciar decreed that it must be accomplished that very afternoon, as he had business back in London and could not afford to be delayed. He announced the dismissal of the witnesses and requested Richard and Hugh to attend him in the sheriff's office immediately. Then he departed. Gervase and Richard went out behind him.

The discharged witnesses did not leave the armory hall right away, but clustered in small groups, buzzing with excitement and casting speculative looks at Bernard and Hugh, who stood together in front of the justiciar's table, talking intently.

"Let *me* be the one to fight Richard," Bernard was saying to his young advocate. "I am the one who has been accused. I am the logical man to oppose him."

Hugh looked amused. "Bernard, you are only just arisen from your sickbed. You are hardly in condition to oppose Richard."

"Then let someone else fight for me. You don't have to be my champion."

The amusement died, and Hugh's face turned deadly sober. "Bernard, I want Richard dead. He is like a snake who drips his venom on everything good that he touches. He killed his brother. He killed Gilbert de Beauté and William Cobbett and John Rye. He seduced and injured Elizabeth de Beauté. And that is just the damage that we *know* about. I want him dead, and I am the man most likely to accomplish that. So talk to me no more about taking my place."

There was nothing left for Bernard to say.

Forgive me, Ralf, he thought as he stared into Hugh's dedicated face. *I have done an ill job of taking care of your boy.*

A feminine voice tinged with annoyance intruded. "Really, Hugh, do you always have to be so dramatic?" It was Cristen, with Nicholas at her side, come to join them.

"The Judgment of God wasn't my idea," Hugh protested. "It's Richard who wants to be the center of everyone's attention, not me."

Cristen's lips curved into a smile, but Bernard could see that her large brown eyes were somber.

Hugh saw it, too. "Don't worry," he said lightly. "I really do believe that God will be on my side this afternoon."

"Of course He will," she replied instantly.

"Are you really going to *fight* him, Hugh?" Nicholas asked in awe.

"I am," Hugh replied.

Nicholas looked Hugh up and down, his awe turning to worry as he said the words that everyone else was thinking, "But he is so much bigger than you!"

"He may be bigger," Hugh returned with serenity, "but I promise you that I am better."

Nicholas smiled, as Hugh meant him to, but the worry did not leave his eyes.

"Lord Hugh." It was the clerk who had been transcribing the trial. "My lord, the chief justiciar wishes you to come to the sheriff's office so he may settle the terms of combat with you and Sir Richard."

Hugh nodded and looked at Cristen. "Go back to Ralf's house," he told her. "I will meet you there as soon as I can."

She nodded, and Hugh turned away to follow the clerk.

Cristen said to Bernard, "What kind of a swordsman is Richard?"

Bernard hesitated, wondering how he should answer. He looked into Cristen's eyes and realized the impossibility of lying to this girl.

He said, "Richard is one of the finest swordsmen that I have ever seen."

"This is what I was afraid of," she replied gloomily.

"I tried to convince Hugh to let someone else take his place," Bernard said, "but he wouldn't listen."

"He never does," Cristen said. She looked down and encountered Nicholas's frightened blue eyes. She hugged the child and assured him, "Don't worry, Nicholas. With all of us praying for him, he will surely win."

"Aye, my lady," Nicholas responded stoutly. "I know that he will."

Hugh was crossing the Inner bail, on his way home from his meeting with the chief justiciar, when he spied Alan Stanham standing all by himself next to the horse stockade. After a moment's hesitation, Hugh approached the boy.

Alan's eyes were full of blank misery as they focused on Hugh's face.

Hugh said, "I am so very sorry, Alan."

Alan dropped his gaze to the ground and said, his voice stifled, "How did you know that I had seen him in conversation with John Rye?"

"I didn't know," Hugh replied. "I just thought it was a good possibility, and I trusted you to speak the truth."

Still staring at the ground, Alan said achingly, "I betrayed him."

"He was never what you thought him to be, Alan," Hugh said. "He is nothing but a brilliant facade that disguises a seething maw of raw ambition."

Alan looked up, a heartbreakingly haunted look on his boyish face. "He was so good to me." His voice broke, and he quickly looked downward again.

"Of course he was good to you," Hugh replied. "You were his adoring disciple. You reflected back to him the image that he wanted to see of himself."

Rufus was one of the horses turned out in the stockade, and now he spied Hugh and trotted over to the fence to visit.

"So it's true, then?" Alan asked. "He really did kill the earl and John Rye?"

Hugh stroked Rufus's soft nose. "It's true."

Alan's eyes searched Hugh's face. "But how did you know it was Richard?"

"I didn't know right away," Hugh replied. "I suspected him, but I also thought that William of Roumare had a strong reason to want the earl dead. And I wondered about Edgar Harding. You yourself were the one to tell me of Harding's words when he saw de Beauté riding into the city. And then Harding let slip that he knew the earl had been stabbed in the heart. This was not common knowledge and I still don't know how Harding came to discover it."

A flare of color showed in Alan's pale cheeks. He lifted his chin as if bracing himself, and confessed, "He knew because I told him."

Hugh's brows lifted.

As a diversion, Alan reached out to pat the crest of Rufus's neck. "He stopped me in the Bail the morning after the murder. He asked me so many questions and . . . and I fear I was upset and not as discreet as I should have been . . ."

He shot a quick glance at Hugh, who said mildly, "Well, that is another mystery cleared up."

"What I don't understand is why you suspected Richard and not the sheriff," Alan said. "The sheriff was the one most likely to be cheating on the taxes. Did you suspect Richard just because you didn't like him?"

Hugh said gently, "I suspected Richard because I already knew that he was a killer."

Alan's eyes grew so large, they seemed to fill half his face. "What do you mean?"

Hugh said, "When he was twelve years old, I saw him kill his brother."

Alan's lips opened but no words came out. He stared at Hugh as if in a daze.

Rufus nudged Hugh, wanting his attention again, but Hugh ignored him. "Did you know that Richard once had an elder brother?"

Alan nodded once, convulsively. "Aye. I thought that he drowned."

"So he did," Hugh replied grimly. "I saw Richard hit him over the head and push him out of the boat. I was the only witness. To this day even Richard does not know that I was watching. The only person I ever told was Ralf, my foster father, and he commanded me to keep quiet. There was already bad blood between me and Richard and no one was likely to believe such a story coming from me."

"He killed his brother?" Alan said blankly.

"Richard could never bear to take second place to anyone," Hugh said.

Rufus nudged Hugh harder and Hugh once more began to stroke his pink nose.

"So that is why you hate him," Alan said slowly.

"That is why," Hugh agreed.

In an unsteady voice, Alan said, "I have been telling myself that he was driven to these terrible deeds by his love for Elizabeth de Beauté."

A stableboy was leading a mare toward the stable, and Rufus flashed to instant attention, his ears pointed straight ahead.

Hugh said to Alan, "Richard Canville is driven solely by ambition and self-love. You should feel no remorse for having testified as you did, Alan. You have done the world a favor by ridding it of a monster."

Alan swallowed. "We are not rid of him yet."

Hugh said, "I plan to finish the job this afternoon." He began to scratch behind Rufus's right ear, and the stallion lowered his head in bliss.

Alan said steadily, "I shall pray for God to be with you, my lord."

"Thank you," Hugh replied. He took his hand away from the horse and regarded Alan's forlorn face sympathetically. "I fear that neither of us will be overly welcome at the sheriff's house for dinner."

Alan managed a small chuckle. "That is what I was thinking."

"I am meeting Lady Cristen back at my foster father's house," Hugh said briskly. "You had better come with me."

A little brightness came into Alan's eyes. "I have been wondering where I should go," he confided. "Thank you, my lord."

"Benjamin will be glad to see you," Hugh said, and Alan actually laughed.

The whole of the household was gathered in the solar of Ralf's town house when Hugh and Alan walked in.

Thomas was the first to speak, demanding imperatively, "What are the terms of the combat, Hugh? Do you fight on horseback or on foot?"

"On foot," Hugh replied.

Thomas swore. On horseback, Hugh would have the advantage. He and Rufus were so in tune with each other that they functioned as a single unit. No matter how splendid Richard's black mount may be, Thomas knew he would not be the match of Rufus.

"You should have demanded horses," he said grimly.

"The chief justiciar is anxious to get back to London," Hugh said. "He wants this combat ended as quickly as possible."

"And so no horses," Cristen said.

"And so no horses . . . and no armor, either, I'm afraid."

"What! No armor? Is he mad?"

The indignant exclamation came from Thomas.

Cristen merely turned white. "You can't wear your mail coat?" she asked.

Hugh shook his head. "No mail, no helmet, no shield. Just a sword and a dagger."

This was stunning news. A duel such as the one Richard had called for was usually fought by two fully armed men. With the mail protection, it could take the great broadswords almost a full day to so hack and tear and rip at the mail that a man would finally go down with a mortal wound.

Cristen said steadily, "You have God on your side. You will win."

He gave her a brilliant smile.

"Can you wear a leather jerkin?" Thomas asked practically.

"My understanding was that the less protection we have, the happier the chief justiciar will be," Hugh said drily. "In fact, I got the distinct impression that he would be delighted if he somehow managed to rid the world of both of us."

"Well, that is not going to happen," Cristen said. "I won't stand for it."

Hugh looked at her.

"You should eat something," she said.

"All right."

Her brow furrowed in thought. "A bowl of stew, I think. Just enough to give you strength, not enough to weigh you down."

He nodded docilely.

"Come with me to the kitchen," she commanded.

"I will check over your weapons," Thomas said. "And I think you should use my dagger. Its blade is longer than yours, Hugh."

"Very well," Hugh said.

"Mabel, will you take the children upstairs, please?" Cristen said.

Nicholas opened his mouth to protest, and found himself skewered by a pair of level gray eyes. "Do as Lady Cristen asks," Hugh said.

Nicholas responded to that look in the same way everyone else did. He obeyed.

"Alan," Cristen said. "Perhaps you could help Thomas with Hugh's gear."

"Of course, my lady," Alan responded, glad to be given a task that included him in the group.

In less than a minute, Hugh and Cristen were alone in the solar. He held out his arms and she moved into them.

"I have to do this," he said. He pressed his mouth against her hair and she could feel his lips move.

"I know you do," she said. "I hate it, but I know you do."

"I will be all right," he said. "For all his touted brilliance with a sword, Richard has a flaw, and I know how to exploit it."

"What is his flaw?" Her face was pressed into his shoulder and her words sounded muffled.

"The same one that he evinces in every other area of his life. He thinks he is invincible."

She didn't reply.

He put his hands on her shoulders and held her away from him. "Don't worry, my love. Richard has called for a Judgment of God, and that is what he is going to get. I am merely God's chosen instrument."

"I know that you are, Hugh," she replied gravely. "I have always known that you are."

The duel was to be held in the Inner bail, within a rectangular area that William Rotier, acting as marshal in place of the sheriff, decreed should be marked off on three sides by rope. The fourth side was the stone wall that separated the space from the Bail.

Chairs for the chief justiciar and the bishop were placed along one of the short roped-off sides. The presence of the bishop was necessary since a Judgment of God was viewed as an ecclesiastical matter as well as one of civil justice.

A line of knights from the castle guard stood behind the ropes to keep the onlookers from spilling into the dueling area. They were also charged with the duty of keeping the combatants from getting out.

Word had spread through the town like fire in a drought, and it seemed that most of Lincoln had poured into the castle to watch the fight. Most of the citizens were refused entrance to the Inner bail, and had to content themselves with remaining outside the wall, where they could only strain to hear the sound of the broadswords clashing and wait to find out who had won.

Thomas had been horrified when he realized that Cristen meant to view the fight, but nothing he said could persuade her to remain at home. Hugh had left earlier, so it was left to Thomas and Alan to escort her to the castle.

They were admitted to the Inner bail, and Thomas ruthlessly elbowed his way through the crowd, demanding loudly that everyone "make way for Lady Cristen Haslin," while Alan did his best to shield her from being jostled by the eager onlookers.

Thomas managed to secure her a good viewing place between two of the knights who were guarding the arena perimeter, and he and Alan took up a protective stance behind her.

Hugh and Bernard were standing in the corner of the arena nearest the wall, talking quietly. Cristen looked at Hugh's slender figure and felt her chest tighten painfully with fear.

Save him, God, she prayed. *Please, please, God. Save him.*

There was a movement along the wall on the opposite side of the arena, and Richard ducked under the rope and entered the arena alone. As he stood there, looking out over the crowd, the wind blew a hole in the gray sky and the sun shone through, lighting Richard's uncovered hair to gold and glinting off the polished steel of the broadsword he held in his hand. Cristen thought grimly that he looked like an archangel making ready to go into combat for the Lord.

Behind her, Cristen heard Alan's breath catch in what sounded like a sob.

Suddenly the whole of the crowd behind them began to shift, and there came angry exclamations and curses as people were once again shoved aside. Cristen turned her head and saw a wedge of armed knights thrusting their way toward the front. In the midst of the knights walked Lady Elizabeth de Beauté. The girl had removed her wimple, and her red-gold hair shone in the sudden sunlight. She saw Cristen, and indicated to her knights that she wished to join her.

Elizabeth's beautiful face looked tense as she took up her place beside Cristen. Cristen felt sorry for this girl, who had been forced to choose between avenging her father and a lover she adored. Richard's betrayal must have broken her heart.

Cristen said quietly, "I think it was very brave of you to stand up and testify as you did, Lady Elizabeth. It could not have been easy."

Elizabeth's green eyes glittered with what could have been suppressed fury or unshed tears. Or both.

"He killed my father," she said. "I sat there, and I listened to the testimony, and I saw it clear as day. Richard killed my father."

"I am afraid that he did," Cristen said with pity.

"He had dinner with me, and when he met my father in the courtyard after, he lured him into the Minster and he killed him. I saw them walk away together. I saw him lead my father to his death."

"I am so sorry," Cristen said gently.

"He played me for a fool," Elizabeth said, her voice hard. "He lied to me. He told me that he loved me and I believed him. Well, I'll wager he's sorry now."

Cristen stared at her in astonishment.

"I showed him," Elizabeth said.

"Aye," Cristen said faintly, "you certainly did."

"If he had killed my father because he loved me, perhaps I could forgive him. But that wasn't it at all."

Cristen was speechless.

"Do you know how I know that?"

Cristen shook her head.

"I said I would run away with him, but he wouldn't. Do you know what he wanted? He wanted me to beg the king to allow me to marry him. The king was very persuadable, he said. The king would not be able to deny me." She turned to look at Cristen, and now it was quite clear that it was fury and not sorrow that shone in her magnificent eyes. "He wanted my property and he was afraid that if we ran away together, the king would confiscate my lands. It wasn't me he wanted. It was my lands!"

Cristen said to Elizabeth, "I am afraid that the only person Sir Richard is capable of loving is himself."

To herself she thought, *And in you he would have found a perfect match.*

The blast of a horn caught Cristen's attention and she turned to look at the man standing a few steps in front of where the bishop and the chief justiciar were enthroned in high-backed chairs. The herald blew another blast, to make certain he had everyone's attention before he announced into the attentive silence:

"Hear ye, hear ye, hear ye. We are here today to witness trial by combat to prove the guilt or innocence of Sir Richard Canville of the death of Gilbert de Beauté, Earl of Lincoln. Guilt is maintained by Lord Hugh de Leon, who will defend this charge with his body. Guilt is denied by Sir Richard Canville, who will refute the charge with his body. Let God be the Judge."

The herald stepped back, and William Rotier ducked under the ropes and advanced to the middle of the arena. Hugh and Richard walked to join him, their unsheathed swords in their hands.

Rotier stood stoically between the combatants, a red flag raised above his head. At a sign from the bishop, he brought the flag down and stepped away, leaving the opponents facing each other.

The Judgment of God had begun.

The two men raised their swords. They looked to be an ill-matched pair as they stood in the windy sunshine taking each other's measure.

Cristen thought that Hugh looked no more than a boy, with his light, slender frame and his black hair blowing in the stiff afternoon breeze. He moved like a boy, too, lithe and graceful, his weight perfectly balanced on the balls of his feet.

Richard, on the other hand, was every inch a man: tall and powerful and supremely confident as he regarded his opponent. Cristen saw his lips move as he said something to Hugh.

In reply, Hugh struck with his sword.

It happened so fast that Richard was not expecting it, and barely had time to get his own sword up to parry the blow. As it was, Hugh's blade drew blood from Richard's hand.

Anger showed briefly on Richard's face, and then he struck back with the full strength of his powerful body.

Hugh parried the tremendous blow, his own sword scarcely dipping in response to the force of Richard's stroke.

"Jesus," Thomas said behind her. "Hugh must have wrists of steel."

The fight went on for what seemed to Cristen an eternity. Without the protection of a shield, each man had only his sword to keep him safe, forcing the fight into a contest of thrust and parry, thrust and parry. Both men gripped their swords with two hands for maximum power, and the echo of the great blades as they fell upon each other was audible even to those packed into the Bail on the other side of the wall.

Every once in a while the combatants' lips moved as they spoke to each other, gasping out words between the exertion of dealing out and defending against blows.

Surprisingly, the two men appeared to be evenly matched. An astonishing level of strength and power resided in Hugh's slim body, and Richard's superior height and weight did not give him the advantage that everyone, Richard included, had expected it to. On the other hand, Richard seemed to be fully as fast as Hugh, and Hugh's left-handedness caused him no problem.

How could they bear it? Cristen thought. How could their arms take such a pounding and still lift the heavy sword to strike again? How long would it be until one of them was a little too slow to parry and felt the cutting edge of that powerful blade?

She felt sick thinking what such a weapon could do if it fell on unprotected flesh.

The February day had turned cold and windy, but the two men in the arena sweated profusely. For half an hour they had remained in the center of the arena, advancing, retreating, and sidestepping within a relatively small area, neither man able to drive the other one back.

Then, before her horrified eyes, Richard escalated his attack, increasing the rhythm of his strokes, attacking Hugh's guard with a relentless assault of powerful blows.

After a minute, Hugh slowly began to back away.

"Jesus," Thomas said in anguish. "Hugh is tiring."

Richard evidently had come to the same conclusion, for he began to smile. Again and again he struck at Hugh, always attacking, not giving Hugh a chance to launch a blow of his own. Again and again Hugh parried, moving back slowly but inevitably to escape the punishment of the other sword.

Step by step, Richard advanced; and step by step, Hugh retreated. Back and back and back toward the high stone wall, where Hugh would be unable to retreat any farther, where he would be trapped.

Cristen's nails bit into her palms as she watched Hugh being driven to his death.

Help him, God. God, please help him. Do not let him die. Do not let him die.

Next to her, Alan moaned in distress.

Thomas was muttering, "Come on, Hugh! Come on, Hugh! You can do better than this! Come on!"

The angle of the sun bathed the entire arena in a merciless light. Richard's hair was dark with sweat and Hugh's blue tunic was drenched. The breathing of both men was audible in the breathless silence of the packed courtyard.

They were almost at the wall. Hugh had only a few more steps before his retreat would be cut off.

Cristen saw him take a quick look behind, to ascertain just how far he had to go.

That look almost cost him his life as Richard, quick to take advantage of the momentary lapse of attention, struck with all his power. Hugh managed to get his sword up in time to protect his body, but the white sleeve of his sword arm suddenly turned scarlet.

"He's hit!" Thomas cried in anguish.

This can't be happening, Cristen thought. *I can't believe that this is happening.*

Now Hugh was at the wall. His left arm dangled at his side, useless. With his right hand he raised his sword, ready to parry Richard's blow. Blood poured from his left sleeve and dripped on the ground.

How could he possibly withstand Richard with only one arm?

Richard seemed to tower above his victim as he lifted his sword in both hands for the last time and drove it hard, drove it directly at that single, vulnerable sword arm, drove it at tendon and bone and muscle and flesh, drove it with intent to maim and then to kill.

What happened next happened so fast that it took the onlookers a full twenty seconds to realize what had occurred. As Richard drove at him, Hugh dropped his own sword and ducked under Richard's thrust.

An aghast intake of breath came from the onlookers. Why would Hugh give up his sword?

Then, to everyone's astonishment, Richard's sword clattered from his hand, and he fell to the ground.

And Hugh stood up.

"Jesus," Thomas said.

"What happened?" Alan cried. "How did Hugh do that?"

It was Cristen who answered in a shaky voice, "I believe he must have used Thomas's nice long dagger."

27

Richard Canville was dead. God had spoken. The murder of the Earl of Lincoln was requited.

So pronounced Lord Richard Basset, Chief Justiciar of England, as Hugh stood before him, head bowed, black hair hanging in sweat-drenched strands, left arm slowly dripping blood into the packed-dirt footing of the Inner bail.

The Bishop of Lincoln concurred with this judgment, saying in a stern voice to Bernard, who stood beside Hugh, "Bernard Radvers, you are a free man." Then, on a more kindly note, he recommended that Hugh have someone see to his arm.

Hugh nodded and turned and blinked as Thomas put an authoritative hand on his good arm. "Lady Cristen will take care of your arm," he said. "Come with me."

The silent crowd parted to allow Hugh through, Thomas on one side of him and Bernard on the other. Now that the excitement of the combat was over, the townsfolk were just beginning to take in the significance of what had happened.

Richard Canville had murdered the Earl of Lincoln.

It didn't seem possible.

But it had to be true. God had spoken.

Still speechless, groups of people began to filter out

through the east gate to join those clustered on the other side of the wall.

Bernard said to Thomas, "This bleeding must be staunched immediately."

Then they saw Cristen approaching with a roll of bandage in her hands.

"Let me see that arm," she said to Hugh, gesturing to Bernard to step out of her way. She placed the bandage right over Hugh's sleeve. "I'm just going to bind it now. I'll clean it and sew it when the bleeding stops."

"How nice," he said. They were the first words he had spoken since Richard fell.

Cristen began to wrap the roll of linen around his arm. He winced once when she tightened it, but otherwise he stood stoically and did not speak.

"All right," she said when she had finished. She looked into Hugh's pain-darkened eyes. "The castle or Ralf's house?"

"Ralf's," he replied, and she nodded and turned to Thomas.

"He can't walk that long way. Get Rufus."

Thomas turned and ran to the stockade.

"Alan," Cristen said. "Help Thomas."

Alan raced toward the stockade as well, leaving Hugh alone with Bernard, who was bracing him with an arm around his waist, and Cristen, who was regarding him somberly.

"You took a dangerous chance," she said.

He managed a fleeting smile. "There are some advantages to being smaller."

"Did you deliberately let him drive you back to the wall?" Bernard demanded.

"Mmm. In his enthusiasm to crush me with his sword, Richard appeared to have forgotten all about the daggers." Hugh's words were clipped, as if he were expending as little energy as possible to form them. "But I hadn't. And I can use my right hand as well as my left."

He swayed slightly, and Bernard tightened his grip.

"Here comes Rufus," Cristen said briskly.

The white stallion was led up to Hugh and Alan held the bridle while Thomas and Bernard lifted Hugh onto the horse's unsaddled back.

"Lead on," Bernard commanded Alan, who began to gently lead Rufus forward. Thomas and Bernard walked on either side of Hugh to hold him upright.

"I can stay on Rufus by myself," Hugh protested with annoyance.

"We are not in the least interested in your opinion," Cristen informed him in the same brisk tone as before.

"Oh," Hugh said. His voice sounded meek, but there was a brief glint of amusement in his eyes.

At Ralf's house they were greeted by an ecstatic Nicholas and Iseult. Cristen issued a few short, crisp orders, and Hugh found himself being guided upstairs to his old bedroom by Bernard and Thomas. He sat on a chest by the window and impassively awaited his fate.

She arrived shortly, followed by Mabel carrying a tray that held a water jug, a bowl, more linen bandage, a scissors, a needle, thread, and an ointment jar. Hugh eyed these items warily.

Mabel put down the tray on the chest next to him, and Cristen drew up a stool and sat down. "This will hurt," she warned him.

His arm was already on fire with pain and he was feeling sick and dizzy. "Really?" he managed to say.

To his great relief, she dismissed Bernard and Thomas before she went to work, cutting away sleeve and bandage to expose the long ugly gash in his forearm.

"Can you make a fist, Hugh?" she asked.

Resolutely ignoring the pain it caused, he closed his fingers into a fist.

"Good." Relief sounded in her voice. "Nothing vital is severed."

"That is good news."

Cautiously he moved his head from side to side. It had begun to ache shortly after the duel, and now there was a tight band of pain around the base of his skull.

It's just because of the wound, he told himself firmly. *It's not a headache.*

Cristen said, "The first thing I am going to do is clean it."

Hugh stared at the corner of his bed and maintained a resolute silence as she washed his injury with warm water and soap. He made no sound all the time it took her to stitch the edges of the wound together and to anoint it with an ointment of centaury.

As she worked on his arm, the band of pain around his skull kept getting fiercer, and he could no longer ignore the fact that he was getting a headache.

Blood of Christ! he thought, half in anger and half in despair. *Will I never be free of this crippling ailment?*

Cristen was bandaging his arm once more.

He felt the pain begin to move into his forehead.

"Cristen," he said. "Do you have any of your betony elixir with you?"

She looked at him and knew instantly what was the matter. "Aye," she said. "I'll get it."

She stood and instructed her assistant, "Thank you for your help, Mabel. You may take the tray down to the kitchen."

The door closed behind the girl. "Another headache?" Cristen asked.

"So it seems," he said.

"Oh, Hugh." Her voice ached with compassion. Then, more matter-of-factly, "Let me get you out of these filthy clothes and into bed. Then I will get the elixir for you."

"All right."

His lips formed the words but scarcely any sound came out.

Cristen had kept her scissors, and took care of his sweat-stained tunic and shirt by simply cutting them from top to bottom and sliding them off of his shoulders. Then she easily slipped his hose off his legs and feet. Once she had him stripped to his drawers, Hugh got under the blankets, which she had turned down for him.

By now the pain in his head was a furnace of agony.

Cristen pulled his blankets over him. "I'll be right back," she said.

He rested his head against his pillow, shut his eyes, and tried to think of something else beside the agony in his head.

Time passed.

"Hugh."

It was Cristen again, the only person he could bear to have near him at such a time.

"The betony has never relieved you that much," she said. "Let me give you some poppy juice instead. It will help the pain and perhaps put you to sleep."

He squinted up into her large brown eyes. Cristen knew what she was doing, he thought. She would never give him anything that could harm him.

"All right," he said and pushed himself up on his good elbow to drink from the cup she was holding out.

He lay back down and closed his eyes. His stomach began to churn.

He opened his eyes. "I need a basin."

She had one ready, and held it for him as he vomited up the stew he had eaten for dinner.

The pounding in his head was sheer anguish. How could he endure hours more of this?

He felt her take his hand.

Time passed with excruciating slowness.

Then, slowly, the sharp edge of the pain began to dull. His head still throbbed, but it was not as unbearable as it had been.

"It is feeling a little better," he said to her.

"Good."

He was actually feeling sleepy. His stomach heaved again, but he forced it down.

Breathe, he thought. *Think about breathing. In and out, in and out, in and out . . .*

Suddenly he felt a strange humming sensation along all of his nerve endings. Then nothing.

He woke in the middle of the night. His mouth tasted terrible and his brain felt sluggish. His arm still hurt but the pain in his head was gone.

"Hugh?"

A shaded candle was burning and he saw her sitting in a chair next to his bed.

"You shouldn't be here," he said. His tongue felt thick and the words were hard to pronounce.

"Is the headache gone?"

"Aye. But my brain feels soggy."

She smiled. "The aftereffect of the poppy juice, I'm afraid. Would you like some water?"

"Please."

She brought him a cup and he finished it thirstily.

"How much poppy juice did you give me?" he demanded.

"A bit."

"Even my arm doesn't feel too bad."

"Good." She gave him more water and he drained the second cup.

"It's after midnight," she informed him. "Go back to sleep. Your brain will be back to normal in the morning."

If Cristen said it would be so, then it would be so. He closed his eyes and went back to sleep.

When he awoke in the morning he was alone. His mouth still tasted terrible, but his head was clear.

His arm hurt, but the pain was negligible compared to the pain of a headache.

Cristen had left him a pitcher of water and a cup. He got out of bed and drank the entire contents of the pitcher, which made him feel much better.

He was regarding his pile of torn clothes when his bedroom door opened slightly and Alan Stanham peeked in. When he saw that Hugh was up, he opened the door farther and said, "How are you feeling, Lord Hugh? Would you like me to help you dress?"

"I would," Hugh replied, "if I had anything to dress in."

Alan carried Adela's old wooden wash tub into the room. "I went around to the sheriff's house earlier and asked one of the kitchen boys to pack up your clothing for me," he said. "I'll bring it to you after you have bathed."

"Alan," Hugh said appreciatively. "You are a gem of a squire."

Alan looked bleak. "A squire who has lost his lord," he said.

Hugh flicked him a look, but did not reply.

After his bath, Hugh dressed in clean clothes and went downstairs to break his fast.

He was only just beginning to realize that his long conflict with Richard was over. Richard the brilliant athlete, the charming lover, the deadly friend—Richard was dead.

He stopped at the bottom of the stairs and listened.

She was in the kitchen.

Hugh made his way to the back of the house.

She was stirring something in the big pot that hung over the fire, and her head was already turned in his direction when he came in.

Her skin, delicately flushed from the heat of the fire, looked beautiful, set off by the plain gold tunic she wore over her dark green undertunic.

They looked at each other.

Nicholas and Iseult had been sitting on one of the kitchen benches next to Bernard, and as soon as they saw Hugh, both children jumped up and ran over to him.

Iseult regarded the bandage on his arm with huge blue eyes.

"Does it hurt, Hugh?" she asked.

"It's not too bad."

She slipped her hand confidingly into his good one and smiled up at him.

"I won't be able to help you with your braids for a while, I'm afraid," he told her.

Iseult gave him a sunny smile. "That's all right. Cristen helped me. She is good at making braids."

Nicholas snorted to indicate his impatience with this foolish conversation. "I wish I could have seen the fight yesterday," he said. "I wish I could have seen you kill Sir Richard." His tone was indignant. Obviously he felt that he had been deprived of something that was his due.

"He murdered my father," Nicholas went on. "If I were old enough I would have killed him myself."

"I'm sure you would have," Hugh said gravely. "I hope you don't mind too much that I did it for you."

"I don't mind at all," Nicholas said. "What I mind is not being allowed to watch!"

"Iseult could not watch, and she could not be left alone," Hugh said.

Nicholas scowled. "Having a sister is nothing but a nuisance."

"Well, it's just as much of a nuisance having a brother, *I* think," Iseult retorted.

They glared at each other.

Cristen said serenely, "The porridge is ready. Who wants to eat?"

Food proved to be a wondrous diversion. Both children helped to carry bowls of porridge into the solar, and everyone sat down around the table to eat it.

Hugh knew it was for his sake that Cristen had cooked this meal instead of the usual ale and bread, and he ate hungrily. The porridge wiped out the last of the bad taste that the poppy juice had left in his mouth.

"There is one thing I don't understand," Bernard said, his eyes on Hugh. "Why did Richard think it was necessary to kill de Beauté when he had Elizabeth's promise that she would defy her father and refuse to marry you? All along we thought that his motive was to hide the tax cheat, but it seems he knew nothing about that." He shook his head in bewilderment. "It doesn't make sense."

"I wondered the same thing," Hugh said. "We had a little time to chat while we were hacking away at each other yesterday, so I asked him for the answer."

He scraped the last bit of porridge out of his bowl and ate it. Then he looked up, a distinctly sardonic look on his face. "It seems that Richard was afraid I would charm Elizabeth into changing her mind. He was determined to keep me from marrying her, no matter the cost."

Everyone stared at Hugh.

"That makes sense," Bernard said slowly.

At that moment, someone knocked upon the front door. Alan went to see who it was, and returned with William Rotier.

"My lord," Rotier said to Hugh. "We have just received news that I think you will wish to hear."

Hugh waited.

"An hour ago a messenger brought word to the castle that the king is on his way to Lincoln and will be here this very afternoon."

Bernard and Thomas exclaimed in surprise.

"He is accompanied by the Earl of Wiltshire and by William of Roumare, Earl of Cambridge," Rotier went on.

Silence reigned in the solar.

Then Cristen asked, her voice a little breathless, "What of my father? Do you know if he accompanies the king?"

"I believe he does, my lady," William Rotier replied.

More silence. Nicholas and Iseult exchanged anxious glances, not understanding what was happening.

Then, "What a merry gathering we shall be," Hugh said.

"Aye, my lord," Rotier replied impassively.

Hugh frowned. "What is the temper in the town, William?

"The town is in a state of shock, my lord. Richard was very well liked. People are having difficultly realizing that he was a villain."

Hugh nodded soberly, his gaze on his empty porridge bowl.

"However, you are well liked, too, my lord," Rotier continued. "Neither the townsfolk nor the castle guard appear inclined to dispute the result of yesterday's combat."

Bernard said gruffly, "What of the sheriff?"

"He is under house arrest. There can be little doubt that Stephen will replace him once he learns of Gervase's dishonesty." Rotier grimaced. "God knows who he will name as sheriff in his place."

Hugh lifted his eyes from his contemplation of the empty porridge bowl. "What a jolly time we are in for," he said lightly.

"The king won't take us away from you, will he, Hugh?" Iseult asked nervously.

Hugh looked at her in astonishment. "Why ever would he do that?"

She gazed back at him, wide-eyed and apprehensive.

"No one is going to take you away from Hugh, Iseult," Cristen said calmly. She looked at Rotier. "Thank you for bringing us this news. We will prepare ourselves as best we can."

Rotier bowed to her and turned to go.

Bernard stood and said, "I'll go back to the castle with you."

The two men went out together.

Thomas said gloomily, "Sir Nigel is going to murder me."

"Nonsense," Cristen said briskly.

"Why would Sir Nigel want to murder you?" Nicholas asked curiously.

Hugh stood up. "I suppose I really can't return to the sheriff's house, but I wish I weren't staying here."

"It doesn't matter now," Cristen said.

He looked somberly at her small, tense face.

"All that matters now," she said, "is that you convince the king."

28

It was precisely two hours past noon when Stephen, King of England, entered his city of Lincoln. He came as a triumphant war leader, having, by judicious use of his feudal army and his paid mercenaries, put to rout the rebels in Cornwall.

Most of the king's feudal troops had returned home, and he was accompanied to Lincoln by his Flemish mercenaries and their captain, William of Ypres. Also riding in the king's train were the Earl of Wiltshire and the Earl of Cambridge, two powerful men bent on increasing their ascendancy by acquiring the additional honor of Earl of Lincoln.

A worried Sir Nigel Haslin accompanied his outraged overlord, Lord Guy. Nigel was grimly determined to rescue his daughter from her own folly and remove her to the safety of Somerford.

Stephen took up residence in Lincoln Castle while most of his troops quartered themselves outside the city walls. The king had expected to be greeted by the sheriff, but was met instead by Lord Richard Basset. Over a late afternoon dinner, his chief justiciar apprised him of the situation in Lincoln.

The king was not happy with the justiciar's news. Stephen wanted to bask in the glory of his triumph in Cornwall, not listen to tales about more betrayals.

God knows, the king thought irritably, he had had few enough victories to celebrate since his cousin Matilda had landed in England and raised war against him. Now, at last, he had achieved a clear-cut success in Cornwall, and what happened afterward?

The minute he set foot out of Cornwall, he had been met by two of his most powerful and dangerous earls, both of whom demanded the same thing: the lordship of the murdered Earl of Lincoln. Now he had to hear how the Sheriff of Lincoln, whom he had trusted, had been cheating him out of the tax money he needed to pay his troops. Not to mention the fact that the sheriff's son, one of the most promising young men in the kingdom, had been found guilty of murder.

Stephen was weary of situations where, no matter what he did, he could not win. If only he could trust his English nobles, he might be able to rely upon a feudal army to prosecute the English war and so use the money he was expending on the Flemings to fight Matilda's husband in Normandy. But he could not trust his nobles. Most of them were no more than jackals, caring little who sat upon the throne as long as they could expand their own power base and increase their own wealth.

A perfect example of his perpetual quandry was the situation he found himself in at the moment, with two of his most powerful barons pressuring him to award them the lordship of Lincoln. To choose one was to alienate the other. And Stephen could not afford for either man to take his extensive holdings and his immense feudal army over to Gloucester and Matilda.

The king was not in a good mood as he finished his dinner, and he regarded with disfavor the men who sat with him at the table. The chief justiciar and William of Ypres had a place on either side of him. They were flanked by the Earls of Wiltshire and of Cambridge. At one end of the table sat Sir Nigel Haslin, the man who had so ably led Wiltshire's contingent in Cornwall. The king had heard some gossip about Sir Nigel's being in search of a runaway daughter. Finally, at the other end of the table, sat the man who was representing the dis-graced sheriff—the very man, it seemed, who had just been acquitted of murdering Gilbert de Beauté.

With the exception of William of Ypres, it was not a group that the king found overly congenial. Nor was he at all pleased when a servant approached him with a request that he grant an audience to Lord Hugh de Leon when the meal had finished.

The king knew what Lord Hugh wanted—to wed the de Beauté heiress, whose lands would give the de Leons control of the whole middle of the kingdom. Lord Guy had been pestering Stephen on the subject ever since he had joined the king's retinue.

The king was fed up with the lot of them. Suddenly, as he scowled at the knight in front of him, he decided how he would handle this powder keg of a situation. He would give the heiress to the de Leons and the earldom to Roumare. Both hounds would get a piece of the bone. They would neither of them be satisfied, but they should have enough to keep them from selling their allegiance to Gloucester.

Stephen was irritated enough to want to make things as uncomfortable as he could for all these greedy barons. "Tell Lord Hugh he may approach me now," he said.

He would deny this importunate boy the honor of a private audience, would force him to ask for his favor in public, the king thought sourly as he took a drink of ale and leaned back in his chair. He remembered Hugh from their one previous meeting, and thought that it would be pleasant to see that annoyingly self-possessed young man shaken a little.

There was only the single long table set in the dining room this afternoon. Daylight came in through the open window, but the table was lighted by candles as well. Behind each of the seven men who were dining stood a server to present the food and pour the wine and offer finger bowl and napkin as needed.

There had not been a great deal of talk during the meal, but even that died away as the slender, black-haired figure of Lord Hugh de Leon entered the room and approached the king.

Stephen looked into the fine-boned face and startling light eyes of Roger de Leon's son.

"Your Grace," Hugh said, and went down on one knee.

Stephen could see the bulk of a bandage under the sleeve of his left arm. "You wish to have audience with me," the king said. "I grant your request."

It irritated Stephen that nothing on Hugh's grave face indicated any discomfort at being forced to speak in front of an audience. The king had not given him leave to rise, so Hugh remained on one knee as he said, "Your Grace, I have come to offer you my allegiance. I am ready to swear my personal faith to you and, once I am Earl of Wiltshire, I will pledge the loyalty of all that I have power over to your person and your cause."

There was stunned silence in the room.

Then Lord Guy of Wiltshire said in an angry voice, "He already owes you his allegiance, Your Grace! He pledged it when you recognized him as my heir. There is no need for this extravagant show."

Still on his knee, Hugh replied calmly, "*You* pledged my faith for me, Uncle. I never swore an oath myself."

Stephen thought back over the events of the last few months and realized that what Hugh had said was true. *What was the boy trying to do?* the king wondered with a mixture of anger and bewilderment.

The answer came to him almost immediately. Hugh was trying to bribe the king into giving him the de Beauté girl in return for an oath of allegiance.

Stephen, who had just decided that he would indeed give Elizabeth to Hugh, abruptly changed his mind. He did not like having his hand forced, particularly by a cub who was younger than his own son.

Young Hugh had just overplayed his hand and lost himself an heiress, the king thought grimly.

"I believed your uncle's pledge of your loyalty, Lord Hugh," the king said coldly. "That is why I granted you status as his heir. Have you by chance come to ask me for something else?"

Stephen's blue eyes were as cold as his voice. With his splendid physique and leonine head, he looked every inch a king, as he regarded the kneeling young man with palpable displeasure.

"Your Grace," Hugh said soberly, "I have come here on behalf of myself and the Lady Cristen Haslin of Somerford. We wish to wed, Your Grace, but my uncle is Lady Cristen's overlord and he will not give his consent. As you well know, he wishes me to marry Elizabeth de Beauté instead."

A stifled moan came from somewhere to Stephen's left. Sir Nigel, the king thought. He looked at Hugh measuringly. So this was the man Lady Cristen had run off with.

The king's eyes narrowed as he sought ways he might turn this new development to his advantage. To gain time, he asked, "Is Lady Cristen the daughter of Sir Nigel Haslin of Somerford?"

"Aye, Your Grace," came the firm reply.

Stephen stared thoughtfully into the gray eyes that watched him so steadily. Hugh did not look at all foolish, or subservient, kneeling before him in front of a tableful of men. Rather, he looked perfectly composed and in command.

"Your Grace, this is infamous!" Guy burst forth furiously. "The boy has some foolish notion that he is in love with Lady Cristen. As if that had anything to do with marriage!"

"Your Grace," the boy said softly. "You are beleaguered and hampered by barons whom you cannot trust. Two sit here in this room with you."

Outraged denials came from both Guy and William of Roumare. Hugh ignored them.

"I am not such a one," he said. "I was brought up by Ralf Corbaille to believe that a feudal oath is an oath made to God. If I take an oath to you, Your Grace, I will uphold it until I die."

Stephen looked into those compelling gray eyes and saw, with some astonishment, that Hugh was telling him the truth.

"And what if I refuse to allow you to wed Lady Cristen?" the king asked. "What will you do then?"

Hugh smiled. "I did not come here to threaten you, Your Grace."

The kneeling, slim, black-haired young man dominated the room. Everyone present understood perfectly that his pleasant words denying a threat were in fact a threat in themselves.

He must love Lady Cristen very much to have taken this bold step, Stephen thought. The king, an emotional man who dearly loved his own wife, was moved.

He gestured for Hugh to stand. When he had gotten to his feet, the king asked him, "Is Lady Cristen in the castle?"

"I believe she is, Your Grace."

"Go and get her."

The boy didn't move, but gave Stephen a long, wary look.

The king met his eyes steadily. "Go," he said again.

Hugh went.

As soon as he was out of the room, Guy broke out in passionate fury.

"You cannot mean to give in to him, Your Grace! I have told Hugh that if he marries Lady Cristen, I will disown him as my heir."

"If you do that," the justiciar said practically, "you will drive him right into Gloucester's arms."

"Then arrest him," Guy said grimly. "He can't go over to Gloucester if he is in chains."

Stephen looked at the pale, worried-looking man who sat beside Guy. "Sir Nigel," he said. "How say you?"

"Your Grace," Nigel Haslin replied, "If Hugh de Leon pledges you his faith, he will keep his word. And Hugh de Leon would be an enormous asset to Your Grace's cause. He is a brilliant young man whose sword and counsel you could rely upon utterly. He is a man of honor, Your Grace. Do not let him get away."

Guy turned to Nigel in fury. "*You* have plotted this! For all this time, this is what you have been maneuvering for—to marry your daughter to the next earl!"

"That is not true, my lord," Nigel said.

"Do you mean that you knew nothing of this?" the king asked.

"I knew what Hugh wanted," Nigel replied. "But I told him that he could not marry my daughter without the consent of her over-lord."

"Well, she does not have my consent!" Guy shouted.

"Contain yourself, Lord Guy," the king said. He was beginning to enjoy himself. "It seems to me that this is a matter of true love."

"Love has nothing to do with marriage, Your Grace," Guy returned in a voice that was only slightly less than full volume.

"I find it rather touching," said William of Roumare.

Guy glared at his rival with loathing. The Earl of Cambridge, a broad, powerfully built man with auburn hair and brown eyes, looked back imperturbably. He undoubtedly would be delighted to see Hugh marry one of his own vassals and not the heiress to a quarter of Lincolnshire.

Stephen understood this very well. He also understood that Hugh's offer of allegiance might be a boon. Nigel Haslin had said that the boy was brilliant. Something about Hugh made the king think that Nigel might very well be right. And Stephen could hold the threat of recognizing Hugh as earl over Guy as a weapon to keep Guy in line.

I can't lose, Stephen thought with satisfaction. *If Guy betrays me, I will recognize Hugh. At the very least, Wiltshire's forces will be divided against themselves. Internal dissension will render them useless.*

The king gestured for more wine.

I will also keep Elizabeth de Beauté and all her lands in my hands, a gift to smooth my way with some other wavering baron, he thought as he took a pleasurable drink of the newly poured wine.

As Stephen was putting down his cup, Hugh came in the door with a girl at his side. The two young people walked solemnly forward and went down on their knees before Stephen.

"Your Grace," Hugh said. "May I present the Lady Cristen Haslin."

Stephen looked with approval into the delicately lovely face of the young woman who was going to save him so much trouble. Large, luminous brown eyes looked gravely back, and Stephen suddenly remembered that he had met Lady Cristen before.

"Rise, my lady," he said genially, and gestured for Hugh to do the same. "We remember well your generous hospitality to us during the siege of Malmesbury."

She smiled. "I am honored, Your Grace."

"So," he said. "Lord Hugh de Leon has informed us of his desire to wed with you. Are you in agreement with his wish?"

"Aye, Your Grace," she said.

As Hugh and Cristen stood and looked at him, Stephen was struck by the intense feeling he had of their oneness. They were not looking at each other, nor were they touching, but the feeling they gave off was very powerful. Stephen felt it, and he imagined everyone in the room must feel it, too.

It was touching, and it was convenient.

"I will welcome your pledge of loyalty, Lord Hugh," the king said. "And I will be happy to dance at your wedding."

Stephen came around the table and accepted Hugh's oath right there, in the presence of a livid Lord Guy. Then he invited Hugh to attend him in his bedchamber, and the two went off together alone.

As soon as the king had left the room, Guy stalked out as well, walking by Cristen as if she did not exist. Nigel hurried to the side of his daughter and she gave him a sympathetic smile.

"Come with me back to Hugh's house, Father. He will return there once he has finished with the king."

Bernard joined them, and she invited him to accompany them.

They were met at home by the children, Thomas, Mabel, and Alan. Cristen told them her good news and then they all settled down to wait for Hugh.

He did not come for another hour.

"Can he be talking to the king all this time?" Thomas was wondering aloud for the fourth time when the front door opened and Hugh came in.

His eyes went immediately to Cristen and he grinned.

She smiled back.

"So it seems I am to have you for a son-in-law after all," Nigel said, coming forward to embrace Hugh.

Hugh laughed. "You found me, sir. Now you're stuck with me, I'm afraid."

Bernard was next, enveloping Hugh in a bear hug and saying over and over, "Masterly, lad. You were masterly."

Hugh's eyes were brilliant as he returned a joking reply to the compliment. Bernard's heart swelled with joy at the sight of that look on Hugh's face.

He's going to be just fine, Ralf, he thought. *Your boy is going to be just fine.*

"Were you talking to the king for all this time?" Thomas asked.

Hugh shook his head. "I spent about half an hour with the king. It took me another half hour to get away from the barrage of questions I was hit with from the castle knights."

"You were with Stephen for half an hour?" Nigel said. "What did you talk about?"

"We talked about a number of things," Hugh said.

"Are you going to tell us, or are you going to be mysterious?" Cristen inquired pleasantly.

He looked at her. "I am going to tell you."

"How nice. Why don't we sit down and have some wine?"

"I'll get it, my lady," Alan said, and as the rest of the household took up positions on chairs and benches in the solar, Alan went around handing out wine cups and filling them.

Hugh waited for Alan himself to take a seat before he began.

"I talked to the king about the situation of Nicholas and Iseult," he said.

The two children, who were sitting on a stool in front of Cristen's chair, went stiff with nervousness.

Hugh regarded the two young faces. "I asked the king if Lady Cristen and I could become your guardians, and he agreed."

Two pairs of blue eyes widened.

"Wh–what does that mean?" Nicholas asked.

"It means that you and Iseult will live with Lady Cristen and me," Hugh replied matter-of-factly. "It means that we will be your foster parents."

Iseult screamed and ran to throw herself at Hugh. He winced a little as she cannoned into his bandaged arm.

Nicholas remained where he was, but his eyes were very bright. "Thank you, Hugh," he said. "We will be good, I promise."

Iseult, who had established herself in a proprietary position on Hugh's lap, said generously, "*I* was going to marry Hugh, Lady Cristen, but I don't mind if you marry him instead."

"Thank you, Iseult," Cristen said solemnly. "You do me great honor."

Iseult smiled radiantly.

"Is that all you talked to the king about?" Bernard demanded. "The disposition of two children?"

"We discussed a few other things," Hugh returned.

"Did he ask you to become the next Sheriff of Lincoln?" Alan asked with suppressed excitement. It was clear that this was what he had been hoping for.

Thomas gave Alan a look of pity.

Hugh shook his head and said gently, "He needs me in Wiltshire, Alan, to keep Guy in check."

"Oh," Alan said in disappointment.

"I did recommend someone to him for the post of sheriff, however," Hugh said.

"Who did you recommend?" Bernard demanded.

"I recommended that he consider Cedric Harding of Deerhurst."

"What?!" Bernard was incredulous.

Iseult was busy tying and untying the cord that closed Hugh's shirt at the neck, sublimely disinterested in any conversation that did not pertain to her. Hugh spoke over her head, "The sheriff must be a man who has sufficient lands to make him a power in the shire, and Deerhurst is a formidable holding. Cedric is much smarter than his father. I think he would make an excellent sheriff."

"You once told me that he hates all Normans," Bernard protested.

Hugh shrugged. "He thinks Saxons are treated unfairly by the Norman system of justice. However, if the chief law officer of the shire is a Saxon, then that perceived bias doesn't exist anymore."

"Cedric will never accept," Bernard predicted.

"You may be surprised," Hugh returned. "The fact is, whoever is appointed sheriff is going to need your help, Bernard. I believe the king is going to name William of Roumare as earl."

"No surprise there," Bernard said grimly.

Nigel said, "That will give Chester and Roumare together a dangerous amount of power."

A little silence fell as they all contemplated this menacing prospect.

Hugh looked at Cristen. "The king and I also discussed our marriage."

"And what did you and the king decide?" she returned politely.

At the mention of the word *marriage,* Iseult dropped Hugh's shirt tie and became attentive.

"It's to be tomorrow, in the Minster," Hugh said, then grinned at the expression on Cristen's face.

"Tomorrow?" she said in astonishment, and Iseult bounced with excitement on Hugh's lap.

"Apparently," he said, "the king is determined to honor us with his presence, and he must be in London the following day."

Cristen's elusive dimple flickered. "He is determined to outrage Guy, isn't he?"

"I believe Stephen has decided that I would make a more trustworthy ally than Guy," Hugh returned imperturbably.

"Good heavens, my lady," Mabel exclaimed in horror. "What will you wear?"

"Clothes?" Hugh said helpfully.

"Ignore him, Mabel," Cristen advised. "We had better go and find out what I have that might be suitable for a wedding."

She stood up, then invited the little girl who was perched on Hugh's lap, "Would you like to help me, Iseult?"

"Aye, my lady!" Iseult replied with alacrity. She scrambled off Hugh's lap, in the process once more knocking against his arm, and the three females departed to look over Cristen's wardrobe.

After they had gone, Hugh said to Nigel, "Will you mind if we continue to reside at Somerford, sir? I am afraid that Chippenham would be a trifle uncomfortable for Cristen."

"I would be delighted," Nigel replied emphatically.

Hugh refastened his shirt tie, which Iseult had left open, and rose from his chair. "I suppose I had better go to see the bishop about this wedding."

Thomas laughed. "That sounds a good idea, particularly if you expect him to perform it."

Hugh's gaze fell on Alan, sitting forlornly on a low stool, ready to leap up and refill wine cups as needed. "Now that I am to be a married man, I will have need of a squire," he said to the boy. "Do you think you might be interested in the position?"

Alan's face was transformed from disconsolate to radiant. "I should like very much to be your squire, Lord Hugh," he returned a little breathlessly.

"Well then, how about fetching the rest of my clothes from the sheriff's house," Hugh said. "I can't let Lady Cristen outshine me tomorrow."

"Aye, my lord," Alan replied eagerly. He catapulted off his stool and was out the door in a flash.

Nigel laughed. "He seems to be a nice lad."

"He is," Hugh replied briefly.

His future father-in-law regarded him with amusement. "You and Cristen appear to have saddled yourselves with a ready-made family, my boy."

"And you haven't even counted the dogs," Hugh said.

Nigel laughed, but he turned quickly sober. "I don't think you will regret your oath to the king, Hugh. Stephen may have his flaws, but he is a good man."

"Gloucester is a good man, too," Hugh said grimly. "I'm afraid that it will take more than a good man to save England from the horrors of this war, however. It will take a miracle."

"There have been precedents," Nigel reminded him.

Hugh smiled, suddenly looking almost as young as Alan. "True. And I will be getting my miracle tomorrow, sir," he said. "Her name is Cristen."